I0709352

Shifting Tides
Summer Adrift

E V McMillan

Color Your World Press, 2024

ISBN: 978-1-7338788-8-3

Cover design by Rebecacovers

Printed in the United States of America

Color Your World Press, 2024

Letter To The Reader

Dear Reader,

I hope this letter finds you well, and I want to start by expressing my heartfelt gratitude for your support and enthusiasm for my writing journey. You, my readers, are the lifeblood of the stories I create, and I couldn't do it without you.

I'm writing to introduce you to a special edition of a book that is dear to my heart. It's a book that marked the beginning of an incredible adventure – my first foray into storytelling. Since its original release as Summer Adrift, I've had the privilege of crafting more tales in this series, and your feedback has been invaluable in shaping the world and characters within.

In this revised edition, Shifting Tides is the first book in the Summer Adrift series, and you'll find significant changes. I've listened to your comments and embarked on a journey of refinement, revising not only the words on these pages but also the essence of the story itself. Characters have evolved, scenes have been re-imagined, and the narrative has been honed to its truest form. As you delve into these pages, you may notice shifts, both subtle and significant. Perhaps the characters will resonate with you in new ways, or you'll discover fresh layers to the story that have emerged in the process. I believe these changes have elevated the tale to new heights, and I'm excited for you to experience it anew.

I want to extend my appreciation to those who supported the original version and to newcomers who are embarking on this adventure for the first time. Your engagement and feedback are invaluable to me as I continue to craft stories that captivate and entertain. So, whether you're revisiting this world or stepping into it for the first time, I hope you enjoy the journey.

EV McMillan

PART I

CHAPTER ONE

Biarritz Pays Basque Airport, Biarritz, France

Josh

Josh Brenner sat at the table in the airport lounge, looking very GQ in his charcoal gray suit, pale blue shirt, and dark, calf leather moccasins, sipping an espresso and reading the latest copy of the glitzy sports magazine *Waves*.

He'd opened the magazine to Mike Ryder's article, Riding High: Josh Brenner's Epic Surfing Triumph, and was reading it with amusement, making note of the exceptional photos that were sprinkled throughout.

In the world of professional surfing, there were legends, and then there was Josh Brenner, the Aussie sensation who'd been making waves — quite literally. His team had the privilege of witnessing his epic showdown in Biarritz, France, where he'd faced off against none other than the defending champion, Piper Lewis.

As the sun-kissed shores of Biarritz served as the backdrop, the stage was set for a showdown of epic proportions. This wasn't just another surf competition; it was a battle for supremacy, and this final heat had been his best opportunity to take the title from the American, Lewis. The clock was ticking, with only five minutes left on the timer. If Brenner couldn't pull off a 9.33 or better, Lewis would continue his reign. It was down to the wire, and the stakes couldn't be higher.

Brenner had been a force to be reckoned with throughout the competition. His fearless approach to every wave and the jaw-dropping maneuvers he executed left both spectators and judges in awe. It was safe to say that he was the surprise package of the event.

What set this man apart? Was it his willingness to take big risks? He was known for crushing every turn. Was it his aerials, like the big air reverse he pulled off in the previous heat? It was that move that secured his spot in this final showdown. Was it his cool, calm, and ability to remain undistracted? He knew what he needed to do. He did it well, with focus, determination, and a dash of Aussie resilience. Altogether, these things are what made him the new Ultimate Surfer Challenge Champion!

With a big grin on his face, Josh folded the magazine and leaned over to show Sean Hargrove, his best friend, the photo of him standing on the winner's platform, the Ultimate Surfer trophy held high over his head and a huge grin on his face.

"Yeah, I saw it. Did they mention how your face graces the covers of surfing, sports, and gossip magazines and is a favorite on all the major 'The Most Eligible Bachelor' and 'Bachelor of the Year' lists?" Sean asked satirically.

"Yeah, he did. Right here. Wanna read it?"

"Of course, they did. Don't they ever write anything new? Same old stuff over and over."

"Why bother when the old stuff, as you call it, is still so true?"

"Come on, we need to get to the gate. Boarding should start in a few minutes."

Josh closed the magazine and tucked it into a pocket of his duffle bag before standing and shouldering the strap. He followed Sean and Colin from the Air France lounge as they headed to their gate. The three of them were off for a well-deserved vacation in the US after three long years of hustling non-stop on two surfing circuits. Josh had only recently agreed to take a break, but now he was excited. They were flying into Paris tonight and catching the red-eye to Los Angeles. California awaited, and the waves were calling their names.

~

May 12th, San Diego, California, USA
Ten Days Later

The water off the coast of San Diego was warm, yet it had a nice, clean texture that Josh appreciated.

He could always tell the difference, which made him feel like he belonged to two worlds—land and sea. Today, floating on his surfboard, he felt the ocean's embrace as a sweet reminder of why he'd turned pro. Surfing wasn't just a sport for him; it was the sense of communion with nature, a dialogue between him and the vast expanse of the ocean.

He also loved the challenge of maintaining control of his body and his board at lightning speeds while atop a wall of powerful, rushing water. The extreme momentum and unpredictability of the water left no room for doubt or errant thoughts. He needed to stay focused as a wall of water approached and feel the wave as it rushed beneath his board. Instinctively, his awareness and concentration would shrink to a single point of tension between the foaming, churning water and the waxed surface of his board. Like now, he'd paddle hard to match its speed.

Standing up on his board, the world around him brightened, the sunlight almost blinding as it refracted in the spray. The wave curled, forming a monstrous barrel over his head—a tunnel of aquatic power. Josh felt like he was in the belly of some mythical sea creature, and he loved it. Time seemed to stretch, making his ride through the barrel feel both instantaneous and eternal. Finally, he burst into the sunlight, exhaling a breath he didn't realize he'd been holding. He was exhilarated and breathless. That had been the tallest, most powerful wave of the morning and that barrel the most impressive.

He could have almost ridden it standing straight.

For the past nine days, he, Sean, and Colin had free surfed some of the most iconic spots along the California coast: from Ventura to Malibu, Hermosa, and Redondo, Huntington and Newport Beaches, down to the Trestles and San Onofre State Beach. And their last stop was here in San Diego. Ten days of pure relaxation. Tomorrow, they were returning to Los Angeles to fly to vastly different parts of the world. Sean was headed to Hawaii to surf the Pipeline in Oahu. Colin was going home to Australia to check on his family. Josh was flying to Johannesburg to meet with execs at Walther Industries, a top manufacturer of wetsuits, and one of their major sponsors. He would spend the next two weeks doing a promotional tour and magazine shoots.

Josh's stomach growled. They'd been out since early morning, and he was ready to dig into the sandwiches and drinks they'd packed in Igloos in the back of the truck. He was about to call it a day when an annoying buzzing sounded above his head. Turning, he spotted a drone, its camera aimed squarely at him.

"Oh, come on! Really?" he muttered, rolling his eyes. Then he thought better of it and offered his best photogenic smile. Instead of taking his picture and moving away, the drone dipped lower, almost within arm's reach. Amateurs, he thought, shielding his eyes as he looked up into the sun. He sat upright on his board, letting his feet dangle in the water, and faced the horizon. The reflection of the sun on the water was dazzling, making it difficult to immediately identify Sean and Colin among several other groups of surfers. When he saw them, he waved to catch their attention and hooked a thumb towards the shore.

The drone began to fly in a wide circle, flying away from Josh and then returning to hover over his left shoulder. Becoming irritated by the drone, he started swatting at it. Didn't the fool operating the drone know any basic rules of etiquette? It was so annoying— and distracting, to be buzzed, especially while engaging in water sports. It was important to be alert to changing conditions on the water, not a stupid drone trying to take action shots. Besides, shouldn't there be some local ordinance in effect against flying too low and too close to people? Josh felt like he could almost grab the damn thing as it flew past him.

Colin seemed to see and understand that Josh was going back to shore and started paddling towards him. Josh turned around and laid on his board, and with long, powerful strokes, he started to make quick work of the fifty yards or so back to the shore. Suddenly, he heard a loud splash and felt his board jerk violently. A few seconds later, something struck his board so forcefully that it lifted him and his board out of the water.

CHAPTER
TWO

Mia

Dr. Mia Thomas clocked out and left the hospital.

Her shift had been grueling, but that was nothing new. It was always demanding in the ER, especially when the beaches opened and tourists flocked to the city. She gathered her hair into a tight ponytail and began a series of stretches to limber up. Dressed in running shorts, a cropped shirt that bared her midriff, and her favorite, most comfortable running shoes, she was ready to burn off some of the adrenaline she'd accumulated overnight. A run on the beach for a few miles would feel good and help her sleep.

It was a beautiful morning; a cool breeze blew in off the ocean, and the sky was a clear lazuline blue, free of clouds. The ocean was only a ten-minute walk west of the hospital, but she decided to drive the few miles north to her favorite stretch of beach.

Dolphin Beach was a beautiful sweep of white sand and serpentine coastline, a favorite spot of local surfers and paddle-boarders. After a long, hard run, she would often sit on the rocks to catch her breath and watch them take on the powerful, pounding waves. Swinging into the parking lot, she noticed it was unusually empty — a few cars scattered around the lot, likely belonging to the surfers she could see already on the water. The sandy beach also seemed somewhat empty; a couple running together were the only people she saw. Glancing at her smartwatch, she surmised it was too early and maybe too cool for most people to be out, staking out their territory with colorful beach umbrellas, blankets, coolers, and toys. Once the temperatures rose, however, the beaches would be packed.

The strong odors of salt, fish, and clumps of seaweed drying on the beach permeated the air while birds wheeled overhead, screeching and cawing as they scavenged for breakfast. Mia walked down to the wet, hard-packed sand, plugging her wireless earbuds in her ears and queuing up her favorite workout playlist on her phone. She completed a few yoga stretches to limber up before starting a slow jog to warm up. It wasn't long before she was one with her music, her feet pounding the sand in time with the beat, a gentle breeze pushing against her back. Foamy whitewash rolled in and back out, scouring the sand, clearing her footprints, and leaving clumps of seaweed along the shore. Towering palms with thick hula skirts shielding palatial homes built on the bluffs that overlooked the ocean swayed in the gentle wind.

The night's pent-up adrenaline and stress sloughed from her spirit and body. Sweat dripped from her chin and ran in rivulets down her torso as she found her rhythm. Her muscles moved fluidly, her brain and body responding to the release of endorphins. She became absorbed in the music, pace, and her body's motion, oblivious to how far she'd run or for how long. Slowing down to catch her breath and figure out where she was, Mia guessed she had run much further than usual, at least by a mile or two. Bent over, hands braced on her thighs, drawing deep breaths, she felt her legs quivering, a sure sign to turn back. Her muscles were loose, and heat radiated off her body. Mia felt like a furnace burned inside her, and she peeled off her thin windbreaker and tied it around her waist. She took it a little slower, walking back to her car, singing aloud with her playlist, unsettling the gulls that had descended onto the sand.

Just yards from where she started, Mia neared a group of people staring out at the ocean in horror. She stepped up to see what drew their attention and watched as a surfer and his surfboard were hurled up in the air, and a shark rocketed up out of the water beneath him. She watched, stunned, as they splashed back down in the water. It seemed like hours passed, though it couldn't have been more than a few seconds before the surfer bobbed back to the top of the water. A group of surfers and people on paddle boards made a lot of noise, pounding their surfboards and slapping the water to run the shark off so another surfer could get close, grab hold of the victim of the attack, and hold his head above water. She watched as they helped tow the victim to shore.

She pulled out her cell phone and dialed emergency services for an ambulance, giving the dispatcher as many details as possible, including her name and the name of the hospital where she worked, and letting them know she would help stabilize the victim until the ambulance arrived. Assured that help was on the way, she shoved her phone back in the pocket of her shorts and ran into the rolling surf to help bring the injured surfer on to the beach.

"I'm a doctor," she said, taking over and helping several people hoist the unconscious man out of the water. "Lay him down here, away from the surf washing up."

Blood drained from his leg and soaked into the sand, and Mia could see where the shark had bitten him, taking a chunk out of his calf. The surfer who'd brought him in kneeled beside her.

"Can you help him, Doc? Please, you've gotta help him," he pleaded, helping to lay the unconscious man out in the sand.

"I don't know yet. Can you keep the crowd back? They're too close. I need room to work, and I don't need them kicking up sand."

"Wait," he said, looking around, eyes wide, appearing terrified. "My friend… my other friend… I think he's still out there in the water. He was close to Josh when the shark came."

"Another surfer?" she asked, shocked since she hadn't seen another person being attacked. But he nodded, and she understood. "Alright, go see if your friend is okay. I've got this."

"Okay, yeah. Yeah. I'll be right back," the man said, turning away and searching along the beach. Obviously not finding his friend there, he ran back toward the water, calling to a group of surfers who'd just come onshore. Mia watched the surfers turn and run back into the water. A woman, wet from the ocean and still in her neoprene suit, came and sat down beside her.

"Hi, how can I help?"

"Can you help keep everybody back?" Mia asked, trying to rip the leg of the man's wetsuit so she could see the scope of his injury. Blood was gushing from his leg. The woman nodded and spoke to one of a dozen surfers standing in a group off to the side. The group then circled Mia, the woman, and the man, edging the crowd back and blocking several people who'd pulled out their cell phones to take pictures and video. Mia focused on what she was doing, unconcerned with the onlookers. The woman handed her a pocketknife, and Mia cut the neoprene suit. Blood drenched her hands as she worked. She ripped her jacket from around her waist, emptied her pockets, and used it as a tourniquet, folding and wrapping it around his leg, tying it in place with the arms.

"Okay, does anyone have any unopened bottles of water and blankets? Any with you or in your cars? I need to rinse this wound to see the full extent of the injury and wrap him in blankets to warm him up," she said, looking around at the people watching her. Besides severe loss of blood, she worried he might suffer hypothermia.

A few bystanders nodded and ran to their cars, bringing back dozens of bottles of water and several thick blankets. Mia layered the blankets over the man's torso to warm him while she cleaned his mauled leg, rinsing out any loose debris, including shark tooth fragments and vibrio bacteria that lived in a shark's mouth.

Unable to do a complete evaluation of his injuries in those frantic moments, she could, however, see that his leg was broken in two places. A large part of his calf muscle and flesh behind his knee had been ripped off, leaving ragged, mangled tissue. He needed massive doses of antibiotics to prevent infection and a few pints of blood. The paramedics would have some of both in their ambulance and if he lived long enough to make it to the hospital, they'd start an IV.

"I think I can hear ambulance sirens," the woman said. "They should be here in a minute. Do you think he'll make it?"

"I'm hoping so," Mia said, whispering. "I've done everything I can. The hospital's only a few minutes away, and he will receive good care there."

She sat in the sand next to the injured surfer and let out a long, shaky breath. They had all done everything they could there on the beach, and now shock was settling in for everyone. She stared out at the Pacific Ocean, an endless expanse of placid blue stretching to the horizon. But she knew looks could be deceiving. Beneath the hypnotic beauty lurked a world of predators—Great Whites, Shortfin Makos, and Threshers. Late spring into early summer was pupping season, and like clockwork, that drew the sharks closer to shore. The notion sent a chill down her spine, and she shook it off, directing her attention to the injured man lying in front of her.

Positioning herself between him and the blowing sand as best she could, cradled his head on her lap as he moaned. "You're going to be okay," she assured him.

The ambulance pulled up on the sand, and Mia moved back as the paramedics took over. Within minutes, they had the surfer in the ambulance and were speeding away with the sirens blaring. Mia stood in the sand next to the purple-haired woman, whose name she still did not know but who'd helped her stabilize the victim and watched the ambulance go.

"You did good, Dr. Thomas," the woman said, turning to Mia. "They're lucky you were here on the beach."

"Thank you. I hope he makes it."

"Me too. I'm Alisa Martin," she said, extending her hand. Mia grasped her hand, surprised at the strength and firmness of the handshake. "It's unfortunate to meet under these kinds of circumstances, but I'm glad to meet you. You come out here often?"

"Maybe a few times a week, just to burn off some energy. I work the night shift at University Hospital, and sometimes I can't sleep, so

I come out here and run until I'm tired enough to go straight to bed. But this is the first time I've come across an emergency out here."

"I've been surfing here for nearly a decade, and this is the first shark attack I've seen. I hope to never see another one."

"You're going back out there?" Mia stared at the woman, incredulous that she would venture back out there with a shark still in the vicinity.

"Yeah, but maybe not today." Alisa chuckled. She was still chuckling as she walked away. Mia hoped with all her heart that Alisa would never see another shark attack but, more importantly, become a victim of one. Besides, seeing one once was enough for her as well. And all things considered, this one could have been much, much worse.

The man who'd brought the victim to shore staggered toward her. He'd just come from searching for his friend; ocean water was still running off his hair and body in rivulets. He was shivering, his face had an unhealthy pallor, and he wore an expression of desperation that spoke volumes.

"Hey, Doc! Doc. Do you think he'll be okay?" he managed to get out between breaths.

Mia stopped to look at him. He was in bad shape and probably needed to go to the hospital as well.

"He's on his way to University Hospital. He's in good hands with them," she assured him. "Have you found your other friend?" she asked, her voice lowering to a near whisper.

"No. Not yet," he answered, bending over at the waist and taking deep breaths. "They're still looking, though."

"You need medical attention."

"No, no. I'll be fine. I have to find Colin, then check on Josh. I'll see a doctor later."

As if on cue, officers from the sheriff's department and members of the press swooped down on the beach, microphones extended and cameras flashing. Mia caught the man's eye, and they shared an unspoken agreement. It was time to withdraw, to distance themselves from the frenzied circus that had erupted around them. The man ran back out into the water. Mia followed him to the water's edge and kneeled, scrubbing her hands as clean as she could with clear water and wet sand.

CHAPTER THREE

Mia's eyes were heavy with sleep when the sound of her apartment door burst open. Chelsea, her best friend and a hurricane of energy, flew into the room.

"Mia, up and at 'em! You are front-page material, babe!"

Groggily, Mia fumbled for her glasses. "What's the emergency?"

Chelsea thrust her phone in Mia's face. "The guy you saved, well, he's like the Crown Prince of surfing, and you're his knight in shining armor now."

"What?" Mia squinted at the phone in Chelsea's hand. Photos of a ridiculously good-looking guy in surf gear splashed across the news app. "That's him? The surfer?"

"You betcha. And not just any surfer — a loaded, A-list, heart-throb surfer." Chelsea wiggled her eyebrows suggestively.

Mia quickly skimmed the articles. "Joshua Alan Brenner, elite surfer and son of Australian billionaire James Brenner, titan and CEO of Brenner Industrials... woah, this is surreal."

"I bet half the hospital staff is drawing straws to be his nurse right now."

Mia chuckled. "I just happened to be at the right place, Cee. Didn't even know who he was."

Chelsea grinned, pocketing her phone. "Well, you do now. And life as you know it, my friend, is about to get a lot more interesting. But I've gotta run now. I can't be late again. I'll give you a call later. You and I are going to have a long talk over food and drinks. I need all of the deets."

Mia sighed and laid back on the pillows. The tiredness evaporated, replaced by a newfound curiosity. After Chelsea left, Mia grabbed her phone again. She fell into an internet rabbit hole, gobbling up every article and social media post about Josh.

Waking up later that evening, Mia stretched and instantly regretted the phone that had slipped between her sheets and jabbed her in the back.

She rubbed the sore spot before tossing her legs over the side of the bed. Her mind, weirdly enough, floated to Josh Brenner, the pro-surfer turned daydream crush. She'd gone down a late-night rabbit hole, gorging on every piece of Josh content she could find. But as she glanced at her clock, reality sank in—work awaited. She calculated whether or not she had enough time to check on Josh Brenner before she had to report for work in the emergency room… and concluded that if she could get dressed quickly and leave in fifteen minutes, she'd have plenty of time.

She showered again, this time hoping to clear her head, and hurriedly dressed in scrubs fresh from the laundry before tackling her hair. She took the time to brush it until it hung down her back in fat, lazy spirals, though she couldn't leave it down. As thick and textured as it was, her hair swelled in the heat and humidity, and then the hairnets and caps she had to wear in the treatment rooms wouldn't fit. She pulled it into a ponytail and pinned it securely in a messy bun.

Staring in the mirror, she scrutinized her appearance. Her caramel complexion, smooth and blemish free; bright brown eyes—the color of weak tea, and deep, black irises; thick brows and the gentle slope of her nose indented by the weight of her glasses; and full, pillowy lips. Amazingly enough, her features had come together quite nicely. She decided to forego makeup, even the little bit she usually wore. She stretched her eyes with her fingers and squeezed two drops of the eye drops directly on her eyeballs, hoping to clear the light pink coloring and irritation resulting from lack of sleep. It was all she had time to do if she wanted to get to the hospital early.

Soon enough, she was ready to walk out the door. She picked her phone up off the bed and grabbed her charger. If she wanted cell service all night, she'd have to keep her charger with her. Her phone blinked on and revealed a picture of Josh Brenner, probably a selfie that she'd saved to her wallpaper. It was her favorite photo of the nearly half-dozen she'd saved. Chelsea had shown her that picture earlier that day, and it had sent shivers through her body. She felt he saw her—as if he were staring directly at her, and she'd saved it to her phone. Yes, it was a totally 'simp' thing to do, but then, it didn't matter because no one would see it but her. It was for her eyes only.

She clicked the screen off and slid the phone and charger into her tote. Her eyes were already starting to feel dry again, so she grabbed the eyedrops off her dresser, another necessity before the night was over. She hooked her purse and the tote bag over her shoulder and left the apartment. Tonight was going to be a long night if how she felt right now was anything to go by.

Mia ran the four flights of stairs down to the ground floor and out to the parking lot rather than wait on the elevator. Opening the passenger-side door of her SUV, preparing to throw her stuff onto the passenger seat, she gagged instead from the foul smell emanating from her running outfit and sneakers that she'd worn that morning. She'd forgotten she'd tied them inside a plastic bag and tossed them on the floor of the front seat. She covered her nose and mouth to keep from gagging any more as she scrounged around in her gym duffel for another plastic bag.

She tied the entire foul mess inside and tossed it in the garbage bins behind her building. She found a little tree-shaped air freshener in the center console between the two front seats and hung it on the rear-view mirror. Rolling the windows down to help air out the truck, she turned the truck on and pulled out of the parking lot. By the time she turned onto the main thoroughfare, she was feeling slightly nauseous and convinced the stench would never go away.

Mia arrived at the hospital's employee parking lot a few minutes early, swinging past the hospital's small plaza directly in front of the doors to the building. A small crowd had gathered, and Mia surmised the people were from local news media outlets, hoping to catch a scoop. Unconcerned, she parked near the back of the lot, far from her usual spot, not wanting anyone to catch even a whiff of her smelly truck. She left the sunroof open a crack, hoping it would air out even more while she was at work, and climbed out. She grabbed her lab coat off the back seat along with her purse and tote, pulled them onto her shoulder, and began walking towards the hospital. Intending to take a wide path around the news crew, she was caught off guard when she saw someone running towards her and calling her name. Thinking it was likely a co-worker, Mia waved and kept walking. Suddenly, Mia stopped and froze like a deer in oncoming headlights. It wasn't her co-worker but rather a reporter.

"Dr. Thomas. Dr. Thomas. Weren't you the doctor on the beach who saved the surfer, Josh Brenner, this morning? Do you have a moment? I'd like to ask you a couple of questions."

Mia clutched both her shoulder bag and lab coat to her breast as she tried to decide if she should run toward the hospital or back to her truck. If she continued toward the hospital, would they still be out there when her shift was over? Was there a chance to avoid them if they were? She was on shift for the next ten hours, but if Mia ran back to the truck, she wouldn't make it to work on time — maybe not at all. Before she could decide, two reporters caught up to her, bombarding her with questions.

"We received a video of you saving Josh Brenner's life this morning. How do you feel? Did you recognize him? Can you tell us in your own words what happened?" the woman fired at her, ready to record her answers.

Mia tried to answer some of the most straightforward ones that only required a yes or no for an answer, but then the horde of reporters joined them, jostling for position to hear her answers and get clear pictures and video. More people began shouting questions at her, and the situation devolved into chaos, reporters and camera people pushing and shoving each other — and her — to get a statement. The crush of people made it difficult to move forward. Mia needed to get inside the hospital or call off, but a glance at her watch let her know it was too late to do the latter without penalty. She put her head down and strode forward, forcing her way to the front entrance.

"No comment," she said, refusing to stop. "No comment."

Two security officers rushed through the hospital doors to escort Mia inside, and she felt relieved. The paparazzi continued to call her, trying to get her to look up so they could get clear photos and videos of her entering the hospital, and reporters shoved microphones at her, but she ignored them all, kept silent and her head down as the officers pushed the crowd back.

Deposited safely inside, Mia heaved a great sigh of relief as she tried to settle her nerves. She had not expected reporters to bombard her in front of the hospital and especially not call her by her name. She couldn't imagine why they would have any interest in her and hoped she wouldn't have to go through this every day for as long as Josh Brenner was in this hospital.

Irritated, she huffed and glanced at the clock, realizing she was late for her shift meeting.

"Is this my life now?" she wondered aloud as she shoved her bags inside her locker and clicked on her phone, taking one last look at it before sliding it into her tote. Josh's face smiled back at her from her wallpaper. Her phone buzzed, and a text came through from Elaine Smith, a buddy and fellow fifth-year. Where are you? We're in the staff conference room in the basement. Hurry. We have Reynolds tonight.

Suddenly, she felt like crying. Reynolds was a taskmaster, and he wouldn't hesitate, not for an instant, to make an example of her. She locked her things away and practically sprinted down the hall to where her colleagues were meeting.

CHAPTER
FOUR

Mia slipped into a seat at the back of the room, hoping she wouldn't be noticed.

However, when she looked up, Reynolds was staring at her. Grateful he didn't say anything, she gave him a timid nod and smile. Pointedly looking away, he clapped his hands together, focusing the attention of the group of eleven fourth and fifth-year residents before him. He picked up a manila file folder from the table in front of him, opened it, and skimmed through the contents before speaking again.

"It's been a madhouse in the ER all week, but it seems rather quiet now, so we're going to take advantage of the break and go upstairs for post-op checks. We have a full house — fifteen patients in critical care in both the general ICU and the post-op ICU, and it looks like eighteen more in stable condition on the ward, all of which came through our ER within the last seventy-two hours. We will do rounds, and afterward, we'll go into the treatment room for the rest of the shift. Are there any questions?" Reynolds looked at each doctor, and when no one ventured to ask a question, he put the folder down and slid his hands into the generous pockets of his lab coat. "Fine. Let's go."

Mia knew she was tired because rounds were a blur—a quick rundown of names and cases, questions by Dr. Reynolds and tentative answers by her resident colleagues. Normally, she enjoyed rounds. It made her feel like a real doctor. However, tonight, she was interested in only one patient.

As they approached yet another patient, this one in ICU, the name jumped out at her: Helen Ravenswood, the woman critically injured in a pile-up on Interstate 8. Mia had prepped her for emergency surgery. Dr. Adderley and his team had actually done the surgery, but Mia had been assigned as her primary when Ms. Ravenswood was brought in by paramedics. Mia felt a burst of pride for having done an excellent job. Dr. Engels, head of the ER night shift, had been the first to congratulate her.

As the group moved from patient to patient, Mia stayed in the back of the group, hoping to stay under Reynolds' radar. She continued to lag behind when Reynolds led them to another section of the ICU, going back out in the corridor, turning the corner and walking down another corridor. Passing the ICU nurses' desk, Mia spotted Rose, one of her closest friends, and Rose hurried to catch up to the group, falling into step beside Mia.

"Hey, superstar. I heard you saved Josh Brenner on the beach. Big news, huh?"

Mia rolled her eyes. "Yeah, it seems he's pretty famous."

"You guys on your way to see him now?" Rose asked.

"Looks like it." Mia's eyes darted ahead of the group to see where Dr. Reynolds was leading them. "Tagging along?"

"Of course. Never miss a chance to look in on our new patient," Rose said, grinning and bumping shoulders with Mia.

The team finally approached the area where Josh was being cared for. Instead of a ward, patients in this section had private rooms. Rose nudged Mia as they caught sight of a leg encased in plaster and elevated at an angle above the hospital bed.

"Let's get closer so we can see him," Rose whispered. Mia nodded and moved towards the front behind Rose. Standing closer to the bed, she was able to get a good look at Josh, and her focus on him was so intense the world around her blurred into background noise. While Dr. Reynolds discussed Josh's condition, Mia inventoried everything about the man lying in the bed.

His breathing was shallow, his complexion was exceedingly

pale, and an oxygen mask covered half his face. Machines beeped softly around him, a tangle of wires connecting him to monitors. *He looks so different,* she thought, comparing him to the glowing, robust figure captured in the photo on her phone.

"Dr. Thomas?" Dr. Reynolds's voice snapped her back to reality.

"I'm sorry. I thought he was waking up," she stammered.

Dr. Reynolds raised an eyebrow but didn't press further. "Would you care to recount your initial response when you realized Mr. Brenner was in distress?"

She cleared her throat, then gave an account of the events on the beach, aware of the intense interest of Rose and her colleagues. When she finished, Dr. Reynolds nodded, a subtle but clear sign of approval.

As they left Josh Brenner's room, Mia felt momentary relief wash over her. Whatever the rest of the day held, she had faced one of the most nerve-wracking moments of her life — seeing Josh Brenner lying in bed, barely recognizable from the man she'd saved — and come out the other side without making herself look foolish.

"Are you okay?" Rose asked, and Mia nodded, grateful for the friend who always seemed to know when she needed grounding.

"I'm fine," Mia assured her, though in the depths of her thoughts, she knew 'fine' was a far cry from how she really felt.

"I'll see you at lunch later, right?"

Mia nodded again and squeezed her friend's hand. Then, she hurried to join her colleagues waiting at the elevators.

Every chance she had, Mia made brief visits to check on Josh. She'd slip inside quietly, perch on a chair next to his bed, and look at him. Even in the dim light, she could see the toll the severe injuries were taking on his entire body. Sometimes, she spoke softly, filling the sterile air with mundane yet comforting chatter. The internet searches about Australia she read aloud to him weren't for his benefit as much as hers—it gave her hope, something to look forward to sharing with him when he finally woke up.

On the third night, she noticed his restlessness immediately. Josh seemed to be in the throes of a vivid dream, his blankets in disarray. Mia's heart clenched, but she carefully smoothed his sheets and resumed her seat. As she leaned close to speak, something shifted in the air. Josh's frenetic eye movements calmed; his breathing steadied. Could he hear her?

She reached out, her fingers tracing the lines on his forehead, then trailing down to touch the stubble on his jaw. To her amazement, he turned toward her, his lips curling into something—was it a smile or just a trick of the light? She pulled back, questioning whether to call a nurse, weighing the pros and cons while staring at his now peaceful face.

"I saw that, Josh Brenner," she whispered, allowing herself to bask in a moment of pure, unfettered joy. It was time to go, but she lay her hand lightly on his. "People are pulling for you. I'm pulling for you. You hang in there, and I'll see you tomorrow." With a lingering glance, she left the room, closing the door softly behind her.

CHAPTER
FIVE

Josh

Josh had been dreaming again, though his dreams were more like nightmares.

He saw it happen every time in vivid, terrorizing detail, and each time, his breath got stuck in his chest. The massive head of a shark rose out of the water beneath him, and then he splashed back down, helpless and battered. Before he could catch a breath, the animal broadsided him again and again. Josh felt an overwhelming pain in his side. He couldn't breathe. He knew he wouldn't be able to get away, although he was within swimming distance of the shore, but he couldn't give up. Giving up meant certain death. Panic surged through him as the shark came around for another pass, its eyes devoid of emotion, its jaws aiming for him. Adrenaline pumped through his veins as Josh fought for his life. His fists pounded the shark's sensitive snout and eyes as rows of sharp teeth embedded into him and ground against the bones and flesh of his leg. Finally, it let go of him, and Josh kicked to the surface, gasping for air, his lungs burning. He grabbed onto a broken piece of his surfboard, clinging to it as if it were a lifeline.

Josh kicked to keep his head above water, but his heart froze, seeing the shark's fin slice through the water as it shot straight for him, quicker than a bullet, and clamped down again on his left leg. This time, it lifted him and shook him, then pulled him down toward the ocean floor, the other half of his board dragging behind him by the leash around his ankle.

His lungs burning, Josh fought for his life with every bit of his remaining strength, knowing he would drown if he didn't get some oxygen in the next few seconds. He kicked and punched, then kicked some more, hitting the shark several times on the snout and in the eye closest to him. Seemingly toying with him, rather than trying to eat him, the shark let go of him and swam away, and Josh kicked for the surface. He sucked air into his fiery, oxygen-starved lungs, and when his board bobbed along close enough for him to grab on to it, he did so, trying to keep his face above water.

Each breath he took was excruciating. All he could do was pant, sucking in small, shallow breaths. His eyes closed and straining for any sound or movement of the water that might signal the shark's return for another shot at him, all he could hear was his own heartbeat pounding in his ears. *What the hell? A shark? Shit. Shit. Shit. Gotta get out of the water. We've gotta get out now.*

The thoughts raced around in his brain, but he couldn't get the words out. Water filled his mouth, and though he kept spitting it out, more replaced it. Just as he felt he could no longer hold on, he felt hands grab him, holding his head above water. Darkness rolled over him, and he had nothing left to fight with.

"Okay, buddy. I got you, Josh. I got you. Just stay with me. We're going to get you some help," he heard Sean repeating.

Grateful, he relaxed in his friend's arms, trusting him to get them both to safety.

Lying now in the strange bed, Josh fought to keep the darkness at bay and his mind from slipping away. Semi-conscious, teetering on the brink between reality and fever-induced dreams, faint sounds made their way to his foggy brain—footsteps, a door creaking. Then, the air around him filled with the scent of warm vanilla. He tried to focus, but his eyes, heavy and painful, resisted his attempts to open them fully.

Through a narrow slit of vision, he saw a blurry figure standing near him. A woman? Was it Dee? His mind was too cluttered to make sense of it. The woman moved to hover over him, eclipsing the soft glow of the room's light. Then she spoke. *No, not Dee's voice,* he realized. Dee would have been clucking over him like a mother hen, just as she always had. She'd been more of a mother figure than his nanny. But this voice was soft and melodic—angelic, even. This angel visited him often, her voice cutting through the delirium, though he couldn't grasp the words. It was like a cool breeze dispersing a cloud of mental smog.

Sometimes, she touched him. The sensation was gentle, and he longed for her soft caresses. His arm felt like a lead weight as he strained to lift it, to touch her back, to hold her hand to his cheek, but his uncooperative body betrayed him.

His eyes hurt and spun like free-floating marbles in his head. He squeezed them shut, but when he opened them again, she was gone. The room seemed to deflate, her perfume dissipating into thin air. He tried to speak, to call out to her, to ask her to stay, but his voice was as uncooperative as his limbs. The emptiness left him adrift.

The consuming darkness reached out for him once more, and this time, he couldn't fend it off. The fight had drained him, and he had no choice this time but to surrender to the void. But he tucked away her promise to return in his mind before being swallowed by unconsciousness.

~

Mia

The following evening, Mia drove through the parking lot, her truck freshly detailed and music floating from the open windows.

She was in a happy mood, much of it because she would have a whole hour to sit with Josh. She swerved into her regular space in the middle of the lot and climbed out. Reporters were again massed in the hospital plaza, and it looked as if their number had more than doubled. Both local and national news trucks were parked against the curb, with cases of audio and video equipment stacked in a heap beside them. Mia instantly felt something important had happened, something newsworthy, and her heart lurched in her chest. She hoped it had nothing to do with Josh and prayed he hadn't taken a turn for the worse.

She grabbed her things off the back seat and locked the doors with the key fob. Hesitantly, she started up the walkway toward the front doors, fully prepared to run if she saw a reporter so much as look in her direction. She made it through the hospital doors without incident and hurried to the women's locker room. She quickly stowed her belongings in her locker and then ran to the elevator. Surprisingly, when the doors opened it was empty, and she rode alone with her thoughts up to the sixth floor.

Mia immediately spied Rose standing in the waiting area reserved for patient families, talking with several men, and her stomach dropped when they all turned to look at her. She knew beyond a shadow of a doubt that they were Josh Brenner's family. Though the corridors were filled with medical staff and families huddling together, hoping to see their loved ones receiving critical care and praying for their recovery, the men stood out. As she stepped away from the elevator, giving plenty of room for a group of doctors and residents to get in, Mia heard someone call her name.

"Hey, Doc! Dr. Thomas. Your name is Dr. Mia Thomas, right?" A man called, waving as he jogged over, stopping in front of her. "How are you?" he asked, smiling down at her.

"I'm good. Thank you for asking. We met on the beach, right?" she asked, instantly remembering his marked accent and piercing, slate-gray eyes. He looked much better than the last time she'd seen him, if slightly different in his tortoise-shell glasses and dressed casually in cargo shorts and a T-shirt.

He clasped her hand in greeting. "Yeah, we did. I asked around

and found out your name. The media still calls you the Mystery Doctor."

Mia chuckled. "I'm glad to be out of the limelight, but I am sorry
about your other friend," she said, her voice filled with compassion.
"He hasn't been found yet, has he?"

"Thank you, and no, he hasn't. I know you're busy, but do you
have a moment? Josh's father and brother would like to meet you."

"Ummm, okay," she said, following him over to the two men who
were intently watching them.

Feeling self-conscious, she wasn't sure she wanted to meet them.
She wasn't comfortable when put on the spot by patient families.
They never failed to ask questions she didn't have answers to. As she
and Sean approached the Brenners, Rose caught her eye and gave her
a little wink, then held her hand up to her ear, pinkie to her mouth,
and mimed, *'Call me'* before slipping away.

"This is Josh's father, James Brenner, and his brother, Ian," Sean
said, introducing them. "Ian's name is James Ian, but we just call
him Ian," he added, nudging the brother before turning to her. "And
guys, this is Dr. Mia Thomas, the doctor who saved Josh's life on
the beach."

Mr. Brenner stepped forward and reached for her hand. "I can't
thank you enough, Dr. Thomas. We are grateful that you were there,"
he said, his English perfect, his accent barely perceptible. "I don't
want to think about what would've happened if you hadn't been
there." He held her hand gently in both of his, his grief and pain
clear on his lined face and in his crystal blue eyes.

"Don't give it another thought, sir. I'm just glad I could help. Try
not to worry. He's getting the best of care," she assured him.

"Thank you, Doctor, for everything," Ian said, also extending
his hand. His voice was equally smooth and cultured, with hardly
any accent.

Mia smiled at the two Brenners. Their resemblance was strong.
They had the same crystal blue eyes, a firm jaw, and dark brown hair,

though the older man's was starting to thin on top. Mr. Brenner was also a little heavier than his son, while Ian was taller and slimmer. They were both very handsome men. Mia looked from them back to Sean, who was as different from them as day from night. Sean stood out with his storm-gray eyes and long, dark hair, which he wore in a thick braid down his back.

"How long will Josh sleep? Is it normal for him to sleep around the clock like this?" Ian, the brother, asked.

"Yes, it's normal. Josh's body needs time to deal with the trauma. He has some pretty acute injuries, so he needs time, and we don't want to rush him. I don't know when he'll wake up, but if you have any more questions, Dr. Shaw is his doctor. He'll have more information about Josh than I do. I'm also sure you'll be able to meet and talk with Dr. Shaw when he does rounds."

"Thank you for everything you've done." He nodded, then looked to his father.

"My pleasure," she responded, turning to go back to the elevator. She didn't want to intrude on the family's time with Josh.

Rose saw her and came from behind the nurse's desk.

"Did you get a chance to see him?" she asked.

"No. I didn't want to go in there with his family waiting to see him," Mia shook her head, her arms folded tightly across her body. "I can come back later tonight after they've gone."

"We have a few minutes before they can go back in. Let's go around the other way."

"Okay." Mia nodded. "Lead on."

She followed Rose, slipping silently into the room. Mia gripped the cool bed rail, leaning forward to better inspect him in the dim light of the monitors beside his bed. Tiny blinking lights and soft blips emanated from the machines attached to him, providing a soft, discordant mixture of noise. He looked much improved, Mia thought as she got a closer look at him. She laid her hand on top of his, and his eyes flickered open—not much more than a slit — but it surprised Mia all the same, and she jerked back. For a split second, he'd looked at her.

What the heck, she thought. *He shouldn't even be the slightest bit conscious.*

She leaned forward again, careful not to set off any motion alarms attached to his bed. She was sure she saw his lips tip upward in a faint smile. Her eyes flicked to his, but this time his were closed. She straightened up but continued to watch him, deep in thought. Was he waking up on his own?

She searched for another sign, some indication that he was waking, but though he fidgeted, he appeared sound asleep. Mia decided she must have imagined his eyes opening. He moaned, and she reached over the rail to smooth the covers on his bed, hoping to calm him and assure him that someone was there, and he moaned again. This time, it was loud enough for Rose to hear, and Mia pulled her hand back, shoving it deep into her lab coat pocket.

"Hmmm," Rose said, moving up to stand beside Mia. After a quick glance at her watch, she checked his monitors and then pulled up his medical chart on her tablet. "It's almost time for his pain meds, but they're going to try to hold off until after his family has seen him," she stated with brisk efficiency, then turned to Mia. "Are you ready?"

"Yeah, I am. I've got to get back downstairs, too. Thanks for bringing me around."

"No problem. Come on. We'll go back the way we came."

CHAPTER
SIX

One week bled into two, and Josh's family remained at the hospital, hopeful that his condition would improve enough for them to take him back to Australia.

They came early each day and spent long hours in the hospital, taking turns to sit with him. Mia began coming later in the evenings, well after visiting hours, to see Josh. To avoid running into Mr. Brenner, his son Ian, sometimes Sean, and an entourage of men, often huddling in an empty family waiting area, conversing with each other or on their phones and laptops.

Also, since their arrival, Mia noticed the Brenners had pressed for changes in security and hospital protocols, ensuring no unauthorized person had access to Josh's room. A seating area was set up at the blind end of the corridor where men, undoubtedly a part of his new personal security team, could watch anyone entering or exiting any of the rooms along the corridor. The first night she'd encountered Josh's extra security, a giant of a man stopped her at the door. He towered over her, and she had to step back and crane her neck to look at him.

"Good evening, Doctor. May I see your badge, please? Mr. Brenner may only have allowed visitors." He watched her expectantly, his eyes shifting to the lanyard around her neck. Mia hesitated for a moment, not sure if he would turn her away, but she cooperated, lifting it without taking it off for him to read. He bent from the waist to read it, pausing and staring at her before sharing her name with a second guard, who checked it against a typed list of names on a clipboard. The second man nodded, and with a courtliness that she hadn't expected from someone so big, he stood upright and opened the door for her. "Have a good evening, Dr. Thomas." His smile was genial, and Mia returned it with one of her own.

Mia didn't realize she'd been holding her breath until it whooshed from her, releasing pent-up tension. She had been sure the guards would prevent her from entering Josh's room. Printed on her badge in bold letters showed she worked in the emergency room, down on the main floor. Mia could not fathom how her name came to be on the visitors' list or who had put it there. Still, she was appreciative.

The room was dark, full of shadows once she closed the door behind her. Besides the blinking lights on the machines, the only other light came from the muted television hanging on the wall and the fluorescent fixture in the toilet area. Someone had drawn the blinds and pulled the drapes closed on the large windows facing out onto the courtyard. A much more comfortable chair than the one she'd used in the ICU stood beside the bed, and she perched on the edge and turned so that she could see him through the rails.

She felt relieved to see him sleeping much more peacefully, no longer agitated, fidgeting under the covers. His eyes no longer flicked back and forth under the fading bruises on his lids. Reaching through the bedrails, she lay her hand on top of his. She'd never experienced such potent feelings for a patient before. *Had she first seen him in the ER, lying on a gurney in a trauma bay, like dozens of other patients she'd treated, would she have felt the same? Would she have maintained a strict sense of professionalism, treated his injuries, and moved on to the next?* Mia doubted she would've looked him up on social media, and even if she had, she wouldn't have saved his pics to her phone. And she would not have jeopardized her position to sit and watch him sleep, running her fingers through his hair, separating the curls as she smoothed them off his face, or rub the back of his hand and down his forearm to feel the texture and warmth of his skin. Mia had never had the urge to do this with anyone else. Her attraction for him was as enigmatic as it was compelling, yet she denied the urge to delve into the root of it.

As she sat beside him, her uncertainties melted away. Seeing him lying motionless in his bed compounded her desire to see, touch, and comfort him. Was it because she witnessed the horrific attack or that his rescuers had brought him to her, hoping she could save him? And what if her supervisor and coworkers got wind of her late-night visits with him? What would happen? Could they… would they dismiss her from the program? She knew she wasn't doing any harm. Her visits were no less innocuous than a visit to check on Helen Ravenswood. They couldn't prove she was more invested in Josh's recovery than in Mrs. Ravenswood's. Reynolds had told her to check on her while she was a patient, and Mia extended that privilege to check on Josh.

Rose and Chelsea had shared with her the gossip circulating: that Mr. Brenner had made a fuss about having Josh discharged so they could take him home, and if the rumors were true, Josh would be gone by the time she came back to work. It seemed the Brenners were eager to have him admitted into a top hospital and rehabilitation center in Sydney. Mia reached between the rails and took Josh's hand. It was cold and dry for the first time, and she clasped it in both of hers to warm it.

A glance at her watch reminded her it was time to leave. Time spent with him seemed to fly by while it slogged along in the emergency room. Feeling a bit self-conscious as she left Josh's room, Mia gave a tiny wave goodbye to the guards. Passing the nurse's desk, she checked for Rose. Not seeing her, Mia headed for the elevators. As she waited for an elevator, she saw her friend coming out of the Charge Nurse's office and waved. Rose strode over and looped her arm around Mia's.

"Hey girl, how are you? And how's our favorite celebrity?" she asked, leading her off towards the supply room, back to the rear corridor and the bank of freight elevators. "Do you have a minute? I want to show you something pretty awesome before you leave."

"Okay, yeah. But I can't stay long." Mia laughed as she let Rose lead the way.

"You guys have Reynolds tonight?"

Mia nodded, a bleak expression on her face, and they laughed again.

"This won't take long," Rose said. "You can tell me all about Sean Hargrove as we walk over. You two seem on friendly terms."

"Well, I don't know him like that. He carried Josh ashore after the attack, and we talked a bit. I tried to get him to go to the emergency room, but he wouldn't. From what he says, he and Josh are very close friends," Mia answered, remembering that fact from their brief conversation on the beach.

"Well, he is so fine, and half the staff drools over him. I might have done so once or twice myself. But I'll take any of them — Josh's father, brother, friend, even one of those bodyguards. If all the men in Australia are as fine as these guys, I'm ready to move over there."

"So, tell me, how *is* our favorite celebrity doing?"

"He seems better, don't you think?"

Mia nodded in agreement. "He was asleep when I saw him."

"Yeah, but he seems to be resting easier." They turned the corner and entered a large open space filled with rolling worktables and transport carts, stunned by the number and vibrancy of the balloons, plants, and fresh flower bouquets on every available surface, including the floor.

"What's going on here?" Mia asked.

"Isn't it cool? These have all come for Josh Brenner. They've been coming all day, every day, even late into the evenings. They'd still be coming if the shops weren't closed."

"Wow. These are all from fans?"

"Friends and fans from all over the world. We can't have too many in his room, so we've been bringing them back here. His father asked us to share them with other patients. The balloons are going to the Children's Hospital, and the flowers to the Cancer Center."

People in hospital transport uniforms loaded flowers and plants onto their carts and pushed them over by the rear freight elevators. Even more bouquets of balloons tied to long ribbons bobbed against the ceiling, and potted plants tied with bright ribbons sat on tables.

"This is crazy. It's like a million people know he's in our hospital. Is this normal procedure?" Mia asked, agog.

"What do you mean?"

"I mean, it seems like public knowledge that he's here in our hospital. How would we stop someone if one of his fans gets a little crazy and tries to force their way in here? This doesn't feel very safe to me. Did you see the reporters outside?"

"Stop worrying. Security is on it, and I doubt any *unauthorized* person will get past his new security detail sitting outside his door," Rose said, dismissing Mia's concerns. "Did they check you out?"

"Yeah, they checked my name to see if it was on their list."

Rose burst out laughing. "I wonder who put you on the VIP Visitors' list."

"I don't know, but I'm glad they did." The two of them laughed. "I'm glad other patients will get some joy from the gifts people send to Josh. It was nice of Mr. Brenner to suggest it. Look, I need to get back. Come walk me back to the visitor elevator," Mia said, turning her friend around to face the direction they'd come.

"Here, take this one." Rose motioned to an attendant, and they stepped inside the half-filled car. She used her key to release the elevator. "Kevin will ride down with you and bring it back up." Mia hugged her friend and stepped inside.

~

Josh

Josh floated on the ocean's surface, the sun warming him… the waves rocked him gently, the soft, continuous, susurrous sound of the ocean lulling him.

But the soft click of the door closing brought him out of his reverie, and he strained to identify the light tap of footsteps and soft, shallow breathing. Josh tried to turn his head toward the sounds, but it felt heavy, too difficult. A light floral scent preceded the silhouette of a woman who seemed to float rather than walk. He smiled and relaxed. He hadn't been sure she was real before this; so much seemed like a dream—or part of his nightmares, swirling around in his feverish brain.

The medicines they gave him kept him drifting in and out of consciousness. But sometimes, he felt like he could wake up because he was aware of things happening around him, especially when she came and leaned over to whisper in his ear. He couldn't understand her words, but he could focus on the sound of her voice, soft and throaty. How many times had she come to talk to him? He didn't know, but he had waited for her, longed for her to come and stop the chaos in his brain. To help banish the images that replayed over and over, like a movie clip that looped inside his head. He couldn't understand what the images meant or why they haunted him, but when she talked to him, they dissipated, giving him a respite.

She sat on a chair beside his bed, silent and calm, and he tried to watch her through his lashes, his eyes half-closed. It was a fight, however, to keep them from rolling around in his head like marbles. He saw her look over at him, her eyes following the contours of his blankets, traveling up from his face to his feet and back again. When her eyes settled on his face, she smiled.

He hoped she was going to touch him again. He liked it when she ran her fingers through his hair and caressed his cheek. She hesitated a moment before doing as he'd hoped. He struggled to turn his hand over and felt rewarded when she slid her hand against his palm. Moments passed, and she did not move, her hand clasping his. She was so still that Josh wondered if she'd fallen asleep. He lay still, not wanting to wake her if she had and not wanting her to pull away.

"This time tomorrow, you'll be gone," he'd heard her whisper. "Back to Australia so your family can take care of you." He tried to shake his head but only managed a slight movement. He tried to squeeze her hand.

"I hope you remember me when you're home and recovering. I hope you remember, and I'll never forget you." She turned his hand over and laid it on his chest, pulling the bedcovers over him. She was leaving. It was too soon, and he wanted her to talk to him. He tried to call out to her, to promise her he'd remember her, but his mouth was dry and his throat raw and painful. No coherent sound came out, so he pushed to open his eyes. But the effort was too much, and after giving in, he realized it didn't matter because she'd already slipped away.

CHAPTER
SEVEN

Josh came awake suddenly, the scent of lemon-scented antiseptic cleaner filling his nose.

The scent was so strong he could almost taste it in the back of his throat, and he tried to swallow to get the taste out of his mouth. He gagged as he tried to swallow. Looking around to determine his whereabouts, he hoped to see her, but no one was in the room with him. The room was foreign to him, small and bare. His bed was narrow and confining, a plain chair, and utilitarian blinds and drab drapery thrown wide over a single window. Bright sunlight streamed through the windows, making his eyes water and blurring his vision. He squeezed them closed, turned his head, and observed several small machines emitting spasmodic blipping sounds and flashes of colored lights. He picked out the drone of the air conditioner embedded in the wall as it forced cool air around the room and a television mounted beneath it, the volume muted.

He was uncomfortable in the bed, his shoulders and neck stiff and sore as if he'd slept wrong all night, and he tried to shift to a more comfortable position, though there was little room in the bed for him to change positions. Shock intensified as he realized he lay on a narrow hospital bed and that the leg suspended by some pulley system and swathed in mummy wrappings was his. He looked at his right arm and saw that a plaster cast that extended from his palm up past his elbow weighed it down. It lay limply on top of the blankets. He flailed, bringing up his left arm. Relieved that it was free of plaster, only tucked beneath the covers, he flexed his hand in a fist, testing to see if he could move it. It worked, though it was painful, and he stared at it. Beyond some swelling and bruised knuckles, it looked normal. He took a slow, intense inventory of the rest of his body to see what worked and what didn't. The left leg did not respond to his commands, while his right leg, propped up on a wedge and bent at the knee, kicked out. He could move his head, though it hurt and made lights dance before his eyes. His chest felt constricted, and he could not inhale fully.

What the hell has happened to me?

He took several shallow breaths and scrubbed his face, surprised at the rasp of the beard growing in. Moving lower, he found more bandages wrapped around his chest and began to scratch; the painful itch was maddening.

When he tugged the wrappings to get to the skin, a sharp, breathtaking pain exploded in his chest, cutting off his breath. It felt like a stab to his heart. The immediate bout of reflexive coughing and gasping for air made the pain even more excruciating, and he jerked around in the bed, causing his entire body to respond with unimaginable pain. Increasing pain levels wracked his entire body as alarms and pulsating beeps shattered the silence and his brain. His jerky movements in the bed had set them off.

A tall man built like a line-backer, dressed in scrubs, rushed into his room, and Josh squirmed to sit up. The man helped him to lie back down and raised the head of the bed so Josh could breathe through the spasms.

"Water, please," Josh croaked out, and the man nodded, pouring water from a pink plastic pitcher into a matching plastic cup, holding it so Josh could sip the tepid water through a paper straw. Even at room temperature, the water was delicious, and he would have drunk it all, but the man rationed it, only letting him have a few sips.

"Mr. Brenner. Good to see you're awake. My name is Theo, and I'm your nurse today."

A strangled sound left Josh's throat. It was excruciating to talk. His throat felt raw like a metal rasp had scraped his tonsils. He acknowledged Theo with a nod, and Theo lifted his head to straighten the pillow, then straightened him out in the bed and pulled his covers.

"On a scale of one to ten, ten being the worst, how bad is your pain?"

"Worse. Way, way worse," Josh croaked. *How could he have survived whatever had happened to him, and how could he be in so much pain? It was a wonder it hadn't killed him.*

"Okay, let me see if I can make you more comfortable." Theo picked up the rubber grip lying in bed beside Josh and pressed the red button on the top. "This administers your pain medication. When you need more, press here. You'll feel it in a minute," Theo said, wrapping Josh's fingers around the controller. "Now," he said, straightening up, giving Josh another once-over. "You have family waiting in the hall. Are you up to seeing them? They won't stay long."

Josh dipped his chin in response, remaining rigid under the blankets. He was unwilling to experience another sudden detonation of pain.

"Alright. I'll send them in. Push the yellow button if you need anything else, and I'll come right in."

Left alone for a moment, Josh tried to relax. He looked around, but nothing struck him as the least bit familiar. Theo had said his family was waiting in the hall outside his hospital room door, yet Josh had zero clues about where this hospital might be or how he came to be a patient. He drew a blank, unable to begin imagining what could've put him flat on his back, bandaged from head to foot, plaster casts everywhere, and his leg swinging in traction. Josh was even more bewildered when his whole family entered the room – his brother Ian, his father and his father's wife, Ellie; Rebecca, his twelve-year-old half-sister; and Sean. They came in and stood around his bed, their expressions somber.

"Son." His father lay his hand on the bed next to Josh's. "You're okay, yeah?"

Josh stared up at him, unaccustomed to seeing such raw emotion in his father's eyes or on his face. His usual poker face was totally crumpled.

Was he okay? Josh wasn't sure. Something had happened, though he couldn't remember what.

Ellie moved closer and gripped his fingers. "Thank God you're awake, Josh. We've been so worried."

"As soon as we can move you, we're taking you back home," his father interrupted.

"No," Josh ground out, his teeth clenched, anticipating more pain, but the medication Theo had administered had dulled his pain. It had gone from unbearable to uncomfortable.

"Of course we are. You can't stay here," his father barked, his deep baritone jolting everyone.

"James," Ellie said, turning to her husband, touching him on the chest with her fingertips and looking into his eyes. Josh could tell she spoke to him without words, and his father released a harsh breath. "Not now. He needs time to process everything," she whispered.

"What is everything?" Josh asked, staring, waiting, demanding an answer. Both his father and Ellie moved back as Ian stepped forward, touching his brother to reassure himself that Josh was okay.

"Hey," Josh said, though it sounded more like an animal growl, and Ian smiled.

"Hey. Do you remember anything?"

Josh shook his head, a slight movement meant to forestall the pain, and Ian continued. "We've been here for over two weeks. We came as soon as we heard about the attack."

Josh looked up, a questioning expression on his face.

"You're in an American hospital. In San Diego, California, to be exact."

Again, Josh was puzzled.

"We were on vacation, surfing," Sean said, stepping closer to the bed. His glasses reflected the machine lights, but Josh could see his eyes fill with water. "You, me, and Colin. A shark attacked you while you were sitting on your board. You were waving and calling to us, though I couldn't hear what you were saying. We don't know why the shark attacked, but the authorities said it was likely a curious juvenile white shark exploring—not looking for food. Colin was closest to you when it attacked. You were tossed around and bitten on the leg. We never… we haven't found Colin."

Josh stared at his best friend, and questions flooded his brain. *A shark attack? They haven't found Colin? Where would he be?*

Sean wiped furiously at the tears, too choked up to continue, but then he did. "You've been in the hospital sixteen days. You've had several surgeries to repair broken bones, and your leg… well, it was badly damaged."

"Colin didn't survive?" Josh asked.

"No. The authorities don't think he survived," Sean answered.

"But they haven't found his body?"

"No. The medical examiner believes he drowned and was carried out." Sean's voice cracked with emotion. "So… they've called off the search."

"No," Josh sobbed. He wanted to scream and cry and get up from bed. He wanted to grab Sean and shake him until he took it all back. Colin couldn't be dead. Yet, as much as he wanted to do these things, he lay frozen in his bed, hot tears rolling down his face. Rebecca moved to the head of the bed and blotted his face, then offered him some water. He took a sip, but the water caught in his throat and brought on a bout of coughing. Josh prepared for the pain, but it was minimal compared to before.

"Charlie?" he finally asked.

"I called him. I also let him know we were still in the States because you were in critical condition, and we would stay here until you recovered enough to go home. He said he would let Colin's mother know. He sends prayers for your recovery."

Josh nodded and looked away, imagining Colin as he'd last seen him. Always happy, carefree, always smiling. Josh closed his eyes. It was too much to process, losing his friend in a senseless shark attack. He grabbed the rubbery grip of the controller connected to the morphine pump and smashed the button, seeking the pain-free darkness, the oblivion that the medication delivered, and jammed the button down, over and over, though it would only deliver one prescribed dose. Josh laid back on his pillows, his eyes closed, though he could tell when Sean moved away. He could also hear his family whispering. Soon, everything faded, the edges of perception growing softer and darker, until the soothing numbness enveloped him, quieting all the thoughts and feelings that were trying to overwhelm him. As the darkness took over the last bit of consciousness, he smiled and embraced it.

CHAPTER
EIGHT

The next time Josh awakened, he noticed a small hand gripping his.

He felt disoriented, though he remembered he was in a hospital. Looking to one side, he saw Rebecca sitting in a chair next to his bed, holding his hand. He had no notion of how long she'd been there nor how long he'd been asleep, though, from the bright sunshine flooding through the window, he surmised he'd slept a full day. Josh smiled at her, and she smiled back, gently squeezing his hand. They were the only two in the room.

"Hey, kiddo," he greeted her, his voice rough and his throat dry. "Where is everybody?"

"They're out in the hall with your doctor. We just came over from the hotel. Dad says we're taking you home today."

"Oh, and they left you in here to babysit me?" His voice came out a whisper, and she leaned closer to hear him better.

"I suppose. I'm happy you're awake. Do you feel better?"

"A little. Well, no. Not much," Josh amended, giving her a boyish grin and squeezing her hand.

The door opened, and they both stared as the doctor, a distinguished-looking, older man wearing a pristine white lab coat, entered the room. A stethoscope hung around his neck, and he clutched a tablet to his side. Several more doctors followed him into the room.

"Hello, Mr. Brenner. I'm Michael Shaw, your doctor while you're here, and these fine people behind me are residents. Do you mind if they stay while we talk?"

"No, it's fine. Can I get something for my throat? It burns like hell!"

"Of course. Water for now, but I'll have the nurse bring you something."

A resident poured water from the pitcher into a plastic cup, stuck a straw in it, and held it for Josh to take a sip. Josh took the cup with his good hand. Though shaky, he managed to keep from spilling any on himself. The water was cold and refreshing, and he drank it all.

"Well, Josh, I think you're doing much better today. Better than I expected," Dr. Shaw began, accepting the cup Josh passed back. "Your vitals are not too bad. They've improved in the last twenty-four hours and are almost where they should be. How are you feeling?" He leaned forward, clicking his penlight and shining it into Josh's eyes.

The light felt laser-bright, and Josh's eyes watered. He flinched at it, blinking away the dark spots floating across his vision.

"How long will he be here, in intensive care?" his father asked, moving to stand beside the bed. "We want to take him home as soon as possible." Ellie and Rebecca had left the room when the doctors entered, but his father and brother had only moved back, giving them room. Now, he moved back to Josh's bedside.

"I wish I could give you a definite time frame, Mr. Brenner, but I just can't. Josh only came off the sedatives yesterday. We'll continue to treat his injuries and hope he hasn't suffered brain trauma." The doctor turned back to Josh. "Joshua. Do you remember what happened to you?"

"No. But I was told about the shark attack and my friend, Colin Mitchell." Josh watched the doctor tap on his tablet. He could still not process everything.

"That is to be expected," replied Dr. Shaw, looking up. "Don't force your memories. You've suffered a lot of shock to your body, and I kept you sedated to help you heal. We gave you intravenous fluids and antibiotics to battle infection and other complications. You also lost a lot of blood before arriving at the hospital, so we gave you a few pints to replenish what you lost. You've run a low-grade fever for a week, but it seems to be abating now—another good sign you're recovering. Your body has suffered a lot of stress, and your mind has locked away most of those painful memories. It's a coping mechanism while you heal. The pain medicines we gave you helped dull them, but things will return once they wear off." Dr. Shaw looked down at his tablet again.

"You had emergency orthopedic surgery when they brought you into the ER to repair three broken ribs, your fractured right arm, wrist, and some bones in your hand," Dr. Shaw read aloud, pointing to each of Josh's casts and bandages. "Your right fibula was broken in three places from the shark's bite, and it severed part of the gastrocnemius, soleus, and tibialis posterior muscles. You also had substantial tissue loss in the surrounding area. It's possible the nerves and blood vessels in your leg are irreparably damaged, which could affect your ability to walk. But we hope not — we won't know for sure for a while yet.

"We are monitoring your vitals and pain and closely monitoring your leg for signs of infection. You were intubated for a week or so, which may be why your throat is a little sore right now, but you've been weaned off most of the sedation medication, which is why you woke up a little disoriented. But all in all, I think you're doing great and are a very lucky man. It could have gone much, much worse. We'll expect your help now that you're starting to recover…"

"Help you how?" Ian interrupted, also stepping to the bedside. "What are you expecting him to do?"

"Josh can be instrumental to his care and recovery. We'll communicate with you every step of the way, Joshua, and you can tell us how you're feeling, what seems to work for you, and what doesn't. We need our patients involved in their care."

Ian grunted derisively in response. His father caught his eye, shrugged, then looked away while the doctor continued.

"I think you should think about talking to someone who can help you process everything that's happened, and down the road, think about some reconstructive surgery on your leg. Do you have any questions for me?"

Josh shook his head. He'd watched his father and brother as the doctor read off the list of devastating injuries and saw the shock, disbelief, and sympathy in their expressions and body language. Like Josh, they were amazed he'd survived, but he knew how dangerous surfing could be. It was an extreme sport, and surfers often suffered scrapes, gouges, lacerations, and broken bones. A good-sized wave could upend a surfer and dash them against the ocean floor or drag them across a coral bed before they could free themselves and swim back to the surface. Some drowned, and others died from their injuries. Shark attacks were infrequent, but they had happened.

Indeed, Josh was lucky to survive. His leg — but more specifically, the bite he'd suffered — was the most concerning. It didn't sound like that would heal as fast, and Josh wondered if he'd have to sit out the rest of the season. A simple break could heal in a couple of months, and he could be back on the circuit by late summer, but multiple breaks all over his body could take a while. Josh grimaced. He'd hate to lose out on the rest of the season.

Becca came back into the room and moved to pat his arm. "It'll be alright, Baby Brother," she whispered. "You'll be better in no time." Josh smiled at her. He would have given her the biggest hug if he'd been able.

"Now that he's awake, can you discharge him in the morning?" his father asked. "We need to get back home. We've been gone too long, and I want to take him back with me. He'll be well taken care of. When we land in Sydney, we'll get him admitted to an excellent hospital."

Josh tried to focus on his father as he spoke to the doctor. He seemed adamant about taking him back to Australia with them, but Josh wasn't sure he wanted to go back, especially not back to his father's house. He hadn't lived in his father's house in over a decade, even before Warren's death.

Warren was Josh and Ian's middle brother. He was killed during his last stint in the military. Their father had never really forgiven Warren for joining the Australian Special Forces and getting assigned to the front lines of embattled Middle Eastern countries. With only months left of a six-year tour, his commander reassigned Warren to a peace-keeping mission. One night, his unit had gone on patrol, and the jeep he'd been riding in rolled over a half-buried IED, killing all six soldiers. With Warren's death, his father pressured Josh to come into the firm, but Josh refused, which added to the tensions between him and his father. He was not about to live under his father's influence or be manipulated into returning to work for Brenner Industrials. Besides, *if* Josh were to return, Deidre could take care of him in his own home. Fortunately, he'd installed an elevator, so she wouldn't have to trek up and down three flights of stairs all day.

"I would not recommend moving him that soon," Dr. Shaw said. "I'd like him to stay put and improve a lot more before discussing his discharge, at least two or three more weeks. Once the casts come off…"

"A couple of *weeks*?" James Brenner sputtered, his face turning bright red.

"Excuse me," Josh said, remembering what the lady had told him before she disappeared. She'd told him he would leave, going back home with his family. He forced himself to speak over his father. "Is this a good hospital?"

"Yes, it is. We're a top-rated research and teaching hospital," Dr. Shaw answered proudly, looking over at the residents.

"Then there's no need for me to move just yet, right? I'll be fine here. What're a couple more weeks?" Josh said, settling the matter.

"Son," his father said, "you need to come home where you can get the best of care, where we can help you get back on your feet."

Dr. Shaw took a deep breath before interjecting. "Joshua's been through a life-threatening ordeal, and he will need a lot more healing, possibly more surgery, whether he gets it here or in Australia. But you don't want to jeopardize his health unnecessarily." He swung the tablet down by his side and prepared to leave. "However, it is your decision, Joshua. Have the nurse page me if you need me. We can talk more later. Do you have questions?"

"No, not right now. Thank you, Doctor," Ian replied, speaking for everyone, and stepped forward to shake the doctor's hand. Their father was staring at Josh, incredulous that Josh would choose to remain in the States.

Doctor Shaw nodded and shook Josh's father's hand before signaling the residents to follow him. Theo came in as the doctors left.

"Sorry, Mr. Brenner. I need a few minutes with my patient. You and the family can come back this evening. It's time for Josh's meds, and they'll make him sleepy. He'll probably sleep a couple of hours after them."

Josh's father nodded and squeezed his son's shoulder gently. "We'll get something to eat and come back later."

"Okay, Pop."

Ian also squeezed Josh's shoulder, and Josh noted it was the precise spot where their father had clasped and in the same way. His first thought was how much like their father Ian had become. His second thought was maybe they thought he would break if they hugged or touched him anywhere else. There was also the possibility, he amended, feeling sorry for himself, that maybe they thought he was already broken.

"It's going to be okay, Josh." Ian's voice was tight, the words sticking in his throat. "We'll get the best doctors to consult on your treatment. It won't matter if you come home now or stay a few more weeks; you'll get the best rehab available. I want you to come home. Pops wants it, too. You've been gone a long time, and though he won't admit it, Pops needs you. He feels a desperate need to make things better between you two. But whatever you decide, I'm here for you. We're all here for you, man." He exhaled a shaky breath.

"You gave us such a scare, Josh. I'm *still* shaking. I was so afraid we were going to lose you, brother. Get better, okay?" Ian wiped his eyes, unashamed of his feelings, and Josh had to blink back the tears that stung his eyes. Josh nodded at his brother, and Ian turned and left.

Once everyone was gone and the room was quiet again, a deep and abiding fear rose within him. Chilling scenarios crowded his mind. Though he'd come close to losing his leg, his surfing career might be in the toilet, and the crew was done. Suddenly, it felt like icy-cold fingers ran down his spine. Josh inhaled and closed his eyes. How could he be so selfish? How could he sit there and fret over his career when Colin had lost everything? By all reckoning, he was fortunate to be alive.

Josh sank back into his pillows and stared into space as memories of him, Colin, and Sean played across his mind while hot, burning tears rolled down his cheeks, dripped onto his chest, and soaked into his hospital gown. Colin had been a good friend, and Josh knew he would miss him. Though not strictly religious, Josh believed in a higher power, and at that moment, he felt unworthy of his friend's generosity. He vowed, then and there, no matter what he had to endure, to honor Colin's ultimate gift.

CHAPTER
NINE

Josh was propped up in bed, a cell phone in his free hand, the television remote in his lap.

The nursing assistant had come in earlier and helped him sit up, adjusting his pillows and the angle of the bed until he was comfortable and positioned to watch TV. Though he'd run through the available cable channels several times, nothing caught his attention. The one thing Josh was not familiar with was extra time and idleness. Boredom had never been an issue before, as Josh had always found something that attracted his attention, but now time weighed heavily. He had absolutely nothing to do—or *could* do. While the visits with his family had been a little strained, he had enjoyed them, but they had returned to Australia. He was also relieved the pressure was off—at least for now.

Because he was a fall risk, he had to stay in bed unless an attendant came to help him into a wheelchair. The chair was uncomfortable, and since they didn't take him out of the room, he found it much more comfortable to stay in bed. Sean had stayed behind when everyone else left, and Josh was happy to have his company.

"How're you doing, bro?" Josh asked. "You look beat."

"I'm fine. The Pipeline is this weekend. I was thinking of passing."

"Passing it up? Why?"

"Things have changed. You're in this hospital…."

"Yes, but you don't have to throw away your career."

"I know. But… I guess I'm just tired. So much has changed in such a short time. I want to be here for you, and what if there's some word of Colin?"

"It'll be fine. You'll only be there for three days. Then take a break if you want. I don't want you to miss a chance to do what you love, and you have the best shot of taking it all. I'll still be here when you get back."

"I dunno, Josh."

"Go. Bring back the top trophy. You can do it. Look how you took them all down in Huntington Beach."

"I need to leave tonight, then."

"So you were just going to let the competition slip by? You weren't going to mention it at all like it never happened?"

"Yeah, pretty much."

"Go. Catch your flight. I'll be fine."

"Okay. But call me if you need anything."

"Yeah, like what? I've got everything I need right here. Go before you miss your flight."

"Yeah, yeah. I'm leaving. At least I'll be sleeping in a real bed while I'm there."

"Maybe it'll help with the snoring."

"I do not snore."

"Yeah, you do, mate. You really do."

Sean stuffed his duffel bag until it bulged and removed all traces of his co-habitation in Josh's room. After spending a little more time with Josh, he left that evening.

Josh exhaled a breath of relief. He was glad Sean was going. He didn't want him hovering, worrying about him, and it would boost the other team members' morale, reminding them of the importance of sticking to their schedules.

Josh shouldn't have been surprised Sean had planned to skip the Hawaii event. He probably would have done the same if Sean had been hospitalized. They were like brothers — blood brothers, to be exact. When they were eleven, the second year Josh and his brothers spent the summer at their country estate, he and Sean had cut their grungy palms and smashed them together, fusing dirt, blood, and germs. Luckily, they hadn't contracted some illness while making the pact. Josh smiled as he looked down at the palm of his hand and the small crescent-shaped scar that remained. It had been a long slash in his eleven-year-old palm, but time had shrunk it until now it was barely visible: a slightly raised silver line less than two centimeters long.

With Sean gone, Josh sifted through his memories of the woman who had visited him while he'd been sedated. None were clear, and he hadn't been able to make out what she looked like, but some things stood out about her. He remembered her voice. She always talked to him as if they were having a conversation. And her touch. Each time she'd sit with him, she'd hold his hand and smooth his hair. Her hands were small, fitting inside his, comforting him as he lay trapped in his bed—and inside his head. But they were strong hands; they kept the fear and nightmares at bay. She smelled good, with a light, flowery scent and a lingering trace of vanilla. Josh had never been very religious, but he could think of no other way to describe her other than as his Angel of Mercy and Guardian Angel.

Josh was anxious. He hoped she wasn't a fantasy, an illusion his brain created to cope with the pain and delirium. He wanted... no, *needed* her to be real.

~

Mia

Mia pulled into the hospital parking lot after three days and nights off.

She noticed fewer media people, equipment, and vehicles parked outside the main hospital doors. News reports of Josh's recovery had also slowed to a trickle, most not even making the local evening news, and were finally absent from the front page of the tabloids. The search for Colin Mitchell no longer made news either, as the search for him had been called off. It seemed to Mia that everything and everyone had returned to normal. She hoped the reporters would also move on. A few tried to catch up with her and get an exclusive, impromptu interview, but Mia had learned how to fend them off. She no longer needed security to run interference. Instead, she refused eye contact and strode past them as if they weren't clamoring for her attention. Each time, fewer and fewer approached her.

Tonight, Mia was early. The ER was short-handed, and she'd been asked to come before her scheduled shift. She didn't have time to stop to see Josh before starting, but she knew he had been weaned off the strong sedatives and should have awakened from the induced sleep. It felt like a long time since she'd last seen him. Four nights ago, before her long weekend off, she'd sat with him for nearly an hour, observing him and committing him to memory. She had been happy his breathing had improved, growing stronger and more regular, and the dark bruises on his face and torso had begun to lighten and fade. He'd developed a healthier ruddiness, the pallor of sickness receding. He hadn't seemed susceptible to any major or life-threatening complications, though the lingering low-grade fever, signaling a possible infection, had been worrisome. He'd been prescribed multiple rounds of strong antibiotics, and she anticipated he would be much improved when she saw him later.

She'd expected him to be gone when she returned to work, but surprisingly, he was still there. She'd heard from Chelsea that the

Brenners had departed without much fanfare after creating a big fuss for his doctors to discharge him, and Mia hoped he hadn't suffered a setback.

Her chance to see him came well after midnight. She'd been seeing patients for seven hours straight, and there had seemed little relief in sight when Dr. Fields, the cohort's supervisor, sent the residents off for an extra-long lunch break. They'd scattered to various parts of the hospital to rest, get food, and possibly get in a quick power nap. Having brought her lunch, Mia stopped by her locker to get it and carry it upstairs. She punched the elevator button for the fifth floor, remembering Josh had been moved to a new room. Stepping off the elevator, she appreciated the silence and peacefulness. The floor observed visiting hours, and after the families left and the patients were in bed, most of the overhead hall lights were turned down, and few people strode the halls. The nurse's desk was vacant, but bright light spilled from the supervisor's office. Mia sped past, hoping not to run into anybody. Josh's room was at the end of the long corridor, and one man sat outside his door. Mia dangled her badge on the end of the lanyard, and he nodded to her. She knocked softly before entering.

"Come in." She heard the command, the voice rough but deep.

Mia entered and walked to his bedside. She stared mouth agape, astonished to see him awake and sitting up in bed. He looked a hundred times better.

"Hello, Doctor."

"Hello Josh… umm… Mr. Brenner. How are you feeling?"

"Pretty good, all things considering. It appears I'll live, as painful as that might be. Please, call me Josh."

"Okay. Thank you, Josh. I hope I'm not intruding. I just wanted to come up and see for myself how you're doing. I'm Dr. Mia Thomas, and I work downstairs in the ER. I've been pulling for your recovery, and I'm so glad you're doing so much better."

"Thank *you*. You're my Angel, aren't you? You visited me while

I was unconscious.”

“I… I did,” Mia answered, stammering, “But wait. What did you just call me?”

“I called you my Angel.” He gave her a wide, disarming smile. “And I thought you might have been a dream, but I’ve been hoping you weren’t and that you’d come back. My friend told me a beautiful doctor patched me up on the beach. That was you, wasn’t it?”

“Yes, I took care of you until the ambulance arrived. And I’ve checked on you a few times, except while your family was here.”

“They left a few days ago.”

“I know. I had the weekend off.”

“Hmmm. I’m glad you had some time off. Come. Sit. I miss hearing you talk to me.”

“You heard me?”

“Yes. I heard you. I don’t remember much of what you said, but I heard you. I felt you when you held my hand.”

“Really? Ohmigod. I didn’t think… I…” Mia blushed furiously and sat down in the chair next to the bed. It seemed no one had moved it. “I was just rambling. I wanted you to know someone was here for you.”

“And it worked. It was… comforting. Thank you.”

He smiled, and Mia was mesmerized by it; that and his eyes. They were the bluest she’d ever seen, a dark blue, almost indigo, and they crinkled at the corners when he smiled. They were fixed upon her face and made her feel bashful. She smiled and was rewarded with another beaming grin.

“I am forever grateful for your care. Tell me something about you, Dr. Mia Thomas.”

“I’m a fifth-year resident, and you already know I work in the emergency room. I was running on the beach when… when the shark attack happened. I’m really sorry, you know…”

“About my friend, Colin.” She nodded, and he smiled sadly. “They never found him. But I am glad you were in the right place at the right time to administer first aid."

"Well, what kind of emergency room doctor would I be if I couldn't offer a little first aid?"

"I owe you a jacket, I hear. You wrapped me up in yours, yes?"

"I did, but you don't owe me for it."

"Nonsense. I do, and I want to repay you for it. I owe you so much more, and that's the least I can do."

"I'm surprised you're awake. Most of the time I come by, you're sleeping." Redness suffused her face and neck, and she looked at the floor in embarrassment. She hadn't meant to say that. She hadn't meant to sound like she had stalked him. Then he laughed, and she looked up. He extended his hand, palm up, inviting her to put her hand in his. She slid her hand between the railing bars, and he clasped it, rubbing the back of her hand with his thumb, swirling the skin and raising gooseflesh up her arms. Mia flushed. The moment felt more intimate than when she'd held his hand during her previous visits.

"I thought I might have dreamed you up," he murmured, and she shivered. Though his words were sad, his pronounced Australian accent wrapped in his deep, gravelly voice was absolutely delicious; the sexiest sound she'd ever heard, and they sat together for several minutes as Mia searched for something to say. She was becoming uncomfortable with the silence and their connection, concerned that a nurse or P.A. might come through the door, but he seemed content.

"Why didn't you go home with your family?" she blurted out. "Before I left, I'd heard they were planning to take you back home."

"I wasn't ready to go back. I have things I still have to do here."

"Oh." She couldn't think of anything else, so she withdrew her hand and moved to stand up.

"Must you leave?"

"I have to get back. I only had a break."

"It was kind of you to check on me. Will you come back? Please." He watched her intently and smiled when she nodded.

"Yeah, sure. I'd like that a lot, but I don't know exactly *when* I might be back. It depends on how busy we are in the ER, and sometimes, I don't get a break or lunch until it's almost time for me to get off, which, depending on when I come in, could be between four-thirty and six-thirty," she said, the words spilling in a rush.

"That's fine. Come back whenever you can. As often as you want. I'm not going anywhere anytime soon. It would be nice to see you again.

He reached for her again, and she put her hand in his. They remained hand in hand for a long moment before she pulled away. She waved goodbye and hurried out of the room. That had been nerve-wracking and so much more.

~

Josh

Josh watched her as she walked away.

She had come back. He was thrilled. And she was beautiful. No one would have faulted him for staring at her the entire time. From what he had seen beyond her baggy scrubs—her face and hands were the only part of her exposed; he'd bet she didn't weigh more than sixty kilos, sixty-five tops. She had stared back at him through oversized tortoise-shell glasses perched precariously on her nose, ready to slide off with any motion of her head, her hazel eyes sometimes dreamy and other times nervous and edgy. She had pillowy pink lips, straight white teeth, and a wide, generous smile, and he'd had the urge to rub his thumb across her bottom lip, smoothing the bite marks she put there. Some of her hair had escaped the messy bun, the tendrils and wisps spiraling down the sides of her face, curling over her ears, and settling on her collar. He'd had the insane urge to brush his hand against her cheek, wrap the wispy curls around his fingers, pull her messy bun apart and wrap her hair around his hand. He wanted to feel the thick curls to see if they were as soft as they appeared.

He'd looked her up and down, as much as he could from his position in the bed, and he guessed she was of average height, not very short. He felt he might be nearly a foot taller, but he'd been unprepared for seeing her. He shook his head. She was more than he'd ever imagined. So sexy, even in those baggy scrubs. An angel? Yes. But now that he'd seen and talked to her, he revised his assessment. She was a goddess.

CHAPTER
TEN

Josh was awake most of the day now and could sit for a good long while.

In the mornings, PCAs and CNAs came and helped put him in the recliner and again in the afternoons to put him back in bed. He spent the meantime watching television and playing games on his phone. As days passed, he grew increasingly bored with the routine and looked forward to evenings when Mia visited.

Most evenings, Mia would stop by his room before her shift to visit for an hour or so. There was always a chair beside the bed, ready for her to come and sit, and the time would fly by much too fast as they talked and laughed together. Josh was a jokester, making her laugh at the silliest things, but he was also a good listener, drawing things about herself that no one, except maybe Chelsea, knew. She'd told him about her parents' death when she was four years old and having to live with her grandmother, her father's mother, and how much she'd loved and still missed her. Mia doubted she'd ever articulated to anyone the promise she'd made to her grandmother to let nothing stop her from achieving her lifelong dream of becoming a doctor. She'd never had to explain it to Chelsea, as she shared the same drive. As she talked to Josh, she felt an instant kinship. He seemed to understand when she'd told him she intended to become one of the premier surgeons in her field. And Josh did understand. He knew the kind of ambition it took to be at the top. It was what made him rise to the top of elite surfing. It was a hunger that drove one to be better than everyone else.

Josh also shared some of his background—funny stories about

growing up as the youngest of three boys, his older brothers Ian and Warren, and Sean, whom he practically adopted when they were eleven years old. Josh's family lived in a stately, old mansion in the heart of Sydney, close to the Central Business District where his father worked. Josh often had to amuse himself when not in school; his brothers were much older and not inclined to have him tag along. His father worked long hours and traveled at length, leaving him and his brothers in the care of their nanny, Deidre, and Virginia, their cook.

James Brenner had turned the small mining company his father had built into a mega-company by the time Josh was eight and decided his boys needed to spend time away from the city. Ian was sixteen, and Warren was fourteen, and they had their own friends and pastimes, which included sports, friends, and girls that they were unhappy to leave for months at a time. But their father was adamant and bought a country estate. He sent them to the country every summer until Ian went to university, followed by Warren. Not much changed for Josh as he learned to entertain himself around the estate. One of the workers had had a mutt of an indeterminate breed that they called *Dog*, and he had taken an instant liking to Josh and followed him everywhere. Josh and the old dog liked to play fetch with thick, broken branches as they walked and explored the estate.

Emboldened by the dog's company and nothing much else to do, Josh ventured well away from the house and outbuildings one afternoon and found himself down by the Ambling River, which was more of a lazy creek as it cut across the back meadow of the Brenner property. Josh had never been that far out before and had only heard about the Ambling River, but seeing it, it appeared to be a good place to hang out — maybe do some fishing, which Josh knew nothing about, and swimming, which he loved. As Josh and Dog explored the banks of the river and considered taking a dip in the cool water, he heard a shout. It sounded like a kid's shout, and a very angry kid at that. Josh looked around but didn't see Dog, so he ran toward where he thought the shout had come. As he got closer, he saw Dog, then a boy about his age, standing on the riverbank. The boy had a small fish dangling off the end of a length of fishing line, wrapped around a thick stick similar to those Dog and Josh played with, and apparently, Dog wanted that stick.

"Down, Dog. Down!" Josh yelled and ran to collar Dog.

"This is your mutt?" the boy asked. "He's trying to take my fish."

"Sorry," Josh said, grabbing Dog by the frayed rope around his neck. "He's not my dog, but we were playing fetch, and he must've thought you had his stick."

"Whose dog is he, then?"

"Glenn McKenna's dog, I think, but he just hangs around our house most of the time. He follows me."

"Does he eat raw fish?"

"I don't think so. How many fish have you caught?"

"About three or four so far."

"You caught them with that?"

"Of course. How else could I have caught them? With my hands?"

"A fishing pole, more like." Josh shrugged a shoulder.

"This *is* a fishing pole. It's good and strong, and I caught all those fish with it. I almost caught a giant fish with it. There's some monster-size fish in this river!"

"I don't believe that."

"Suit yourself, but don't say I didn't tell you about them when I catch one."

"Can Dog and I sit and watch you catch one?"

"Sure, but it's more fun when you do it yourself."

"I don't have a fishing pole."

"Go find a stick like mine, and I'll rig you a line."

"What are we going to do with all the fish we catch?"

"Cook 'em and eat 'em."

"Maybe Ginny can cook them for us. I'm not allowed to cook

anything.”

“Well, me and Lizzie cook all the time. I know how to cook fish.”

“Okay. I’ll be right back with a stick, and you can show me where the biggest fish are,” Josh said, skipping off behind Dog, who already had his nose to the ground, apparently ready to sniff out a few good sticks.

Mia laughed until her stomach hurt as Josh told her the story. “I can imagine you two trying to clean and cook your fish. Did you?”

“Oh, heck no. Ginny cooked them. I think Sean and I ate at least three of them—they weren’t very big, and she sent the rest home with him. Those were the best fish I ever ate. I still remember how good they were.”

Josh also talked about his summers hanging out with Sean all day, every day, on the estate and in the township of Palmer near the Brenners’ country estate. Once it became apparent that Sean was with Josh and Dog, no one seemed to worry about the boys or what they were up to.

Mia also heard the sadness, and even loneliness, in his voice when he talked about Sean’s family and having to go back to Sydney. Sean lived with his mother and sister in Palmer, and Sean’s mother worked several jobs and long hours to support the family. She relied on Elizabeth—Lizzie for short— Sean’s older sister, to keep an eye on him, but Sean was able to escape Lizzie’s supervision most times, and he and Josh disappeared for hours, only returning home before his mother got home.

Mia listened when Josh told her how the two of them had become inseparable and had set out to convince Josh’s father and Sean’s mother to let Sean attend St. Clements Academy in Sydney with Josh. The boys had figured out that Sean would stay with the Brenners in Sydney during the school year and spend their summer and school breaks in the country. Surprisingly, their parents agreed to try it out — but from that moment on, everyone accepted that

Sean was a permanent part of the family.

Mia enjoyed her time with Josh in the evenings. He made her laugh, and his stories were amusing, even when he talked about surfing and the exotic locales he traveled to. She decided that, down the line, maybe once she finished her fellowship, she'd visit some of the places he described. Josh, being the impulsive and confident sort, invited her to come with him once he was discharged and could travel again.

Mia checked her watch again. She was tired, hungry, and hadn't had a real break since coming to work almost eight hours ago. She'd been called in early. The ER was short-handed, and residents had been called to fill in. Unless things got better, or she got lucky, and Dr. Neal sent them home early, she still had four hours left of her regular shift.

Mia rode the elevators up to the fifth floor, intending to sit with Josh for a few minutes and then find something to eat before returning to work. The floor was quiet, as was the nurses' desk, and Mia strode down the deserted corridors. She approached Josh's room door and waved at Sam, his security guard. Sam had become a fixture outside Josh's door at night and seemed friendly. He'd come to recognize her and never requested to see her badge after their first meeting. At first, two men had sat outside Josh's door, but Sam had been the only guard for the past few nights. Tonight, he was lounging on a small leather sofa, his motorcycle boots crossed at the ankle and his long legs lying across the seat of a chair he'd pulled over. He didn't look especially comfortable, but he seemed interested in whatever was playing on the television mounted on the wall. Though the volume was low, it sounded to her like a basketball game was on.

"Hey, Sam. How are you tonight?"

"Fine, Dr. Thomas. Been kinda quiet around here."

"I'm sure the staff appreciates that."

"Yeah. I suppose so."

She eased the door open, hoping Josh was awake. She could hear him talking loudly over the television in his room, and she hesitated, wondering if he was on his phone. Entering, Mia noticed no one was in the room with him; the television was muted, and he wasn't on the phone. Instead, Josh lay crooked in his bed, his hospital gown drenched in sweat. He was talking, even yelling, in his sleep. As she got closer, she saw him thrashing about, obviously having a vivid dream. The monitor beside his bed was blinking red lights and emitting frequent beeps, and she wondered if a motion alarm was going off at the nurses' desk.

"Josh? Josh, wake up," she whispered, touching his shoulder gently, not wanting to frighten him further but wanting him to open his eyes. Instead, his one unencumbered arm and leg flailed against the bed covers in earnest. She touched him on the arm and called him again. He woke up, seemingly disoriented, his eyes and mouth opened wide.

"Wha…?" he started. "Mia?"

"Are you all right, Josh?"

"A dream… I was dreaming."

Mia looked into his eyes and pressed his wrist to get his pulse. His eyes were glazed, but within a few moments, the fog slowly began to recede from his eyes.

"More like having a nightmare, I'd say," she replied. "Lie back. I want to raise the head of the bed. I need to wrap you up in your blankets; your gown is wringing wet. Here, let me help you take it off."

Sam entered the room behind her and came over to help.

"Thanks, Sam," Mia said once they'd pulled Josh up and straightened him out in the bed.

"Is he okay, Doctor? I'd checked on him a little while ago, and he was talking on his cell phone. When I heard him a few minutes ago, I thought he was still on it."

"Well, he seems to be fine now."

Josh had awakened but still seemed groggy. A nurse and a personal care aide arrived as Mia scanned the flashing lights on the monitor behind his headboard. Mia didn't know any staff on this floor but nodded to them and stepped back, giving the nurse room to check on Josh while the PCA went to the opposite side of his bed and checked his blankets.

"He needs a fresh gown and bedding, Cathy. These are wringing wet," the PCA said. The nurse nodded as she reset the motion sensors and adjusted the monitors attached to his bed. Returning to the side of the bed, she looked down at Josh and very matter-of-factly asked, "Another nightmare, Mr. Brenner?"

Josh shrugged one shoulder. "They come and go."

"Well, this one seemed to be pretty bad. While Lisa gets you all nice, dry, and settled, the doctor, I, and Mr. Hoecke will step outside. We'll be right outside the door until she's done."

Josh acknowledged her with a slight chin dip, never taking his eyes off Mia as she was led away.

"This didn't surprise you, did it?" Mia asked once they were out in the hall. "Does he have these kinds of episodes often?"

"He has one almost every night. We've reported them to Dr. Shaw, but this one may have been his worst one yet. He's never set off so many alarms before."

"Really? I've never seen him this agitated. Does he have something to help him sleep?"

"Dr. Shaw ordered a mild sedative, but he won't take it."

"He won't? Why not?"

"He says he doesn't want to be drugged to sleep again."

The door opened after a few moments, and the PCA came out. "I'm done, Cathy," she reported.

"Thanks, Lisa. You can go back in if you'd like, Doctor. I've got to get back, but I'll look back in on him again after you leave."

"Thank you. I can only stay for a moment. I want to make sure he's okay first."

The nurse and the PCA left, and Mia went back inside Josh's

room. He was lying back on fresh sheets and pillows, fresh blankets tucked around him, and the head of the bed was raised to a slight incline. He looked comfortable. The PCA had also removed his damp gown and bedding, leaving his room neat.

"Hi," he greeted Mia.

"Hi. Feeling better?" She sat down beside the bed and turned to him.

"Yes, now that you're here."

"Do you have nightmares like that very often?"

"Sometimes, I guess. Often enough."

"Does your doctor know?"

"I imagine the nurses have let him know since I seem to set off all sorts of alarms pretty regularly." He smiled at her and reached through the rails for her hand, but she ignored his overture, clasping her hands in her lap instead.

"Maybe they can give you something to help you sleep."

"No thanks," he said, letting his hand drop to the bed. "I don't want more pills. Maybe the dreams will go away after a while. It's nothing to worry about."

She heard his sigh but focused on the monitor displaying his vital signs. She wanted to hold his hand but was wary of someone else, maybe the doctor on call, showing up to check on him. She didn't want to be caught holding hands with him, like some lovesick girlfriend. Instead, she asked, "You're reliving the shark attack, aren't you?" It had come out more of a statement than a question, but then she was sure that was what was happening. "We can talk about what happened if you want. It might help with the nightmares."

"Not necessary," he responded a bit brusquely. "I'd rather talk about something else unless you're having nightmares, too. You were there; you saw it as well."

"I did, but I don't dream about it."

"Then, I'd say you're good, and we don't need to talk about it."

"I've never seen a shark attack before or treated anyone bitten by a shark, but I've seen some pretty terrible injuries come through the emergency room. Some people react differently to extreme trauma. I think your nightmares are your way of reacting to your trauma."

"Don't start psychoanalyzing this, Mia. I get enough of that from everyone else."

"I just want to help."

"And you do, just by sitting here with me." He reached for her hand again, and she smiled, sliding her hand through the bars. He grasped it and began softly massaging the skin on the back of it.

"I guess I am trying to process that Colin died in the shark at- tack," Josh said, closing his eyes for a second. "When I sleep, I see this gigantic black eye staring at me. It's like a black hole, but it's not empty. It's sentient, and it seems to know me."

"I stayed with you while your friend and the lifeguards went out to look for him."

"Sean told me. Did you know authorities called off the search after a few days?"

"I did. Could you talk to someone, not necessarily a doctor, about that? Everyone grieves differently, and it's okay to talk about it."

"I don't need a shrink, though. That's a waste of time."

"It could help, but you're right. It would be a waste of time if you didn't want to talk to him. Do you think you can get some rest now?"

"Yes. Of course. I'm good now. I'm sorry for scaring you."

"No, it's okay. It was just unexpected. I didn't know you had night terrors, but it's to be expected. You've gone through a lot."

"I'm okay now. I'll probably watch television for a while and nod back off."

"Okay. I've got to go. I'm already late, and my supervisor will send a search team after me if I don't show up soon."

"Go. Go. I'll be fine. Don't worry about me."

"It's not a problem. If you ever want to talk, I'll listen," Mia offered.

"You always come to my rescue." He laughed wryly. "You really must be a Guardian Angel."

"I wouldn't say that, but I am glad to help." She brushed the back of his hand with her fingertips and smiled before walking away.

In the elevator, Mia smiled to herself. She didn't know why seeing Josh and talking to him made her happy or why he liked holding her hand, but it did. It made her feel giddy inside, like champagne bubbles in her stomach and chest. He seemed to like her—a lot, and not just as a friend. He flirted with her constantly and always wanted to hold her hand.

Mia shook her head to clear her mind and regain her senses. Whatever was going on between them, it would have to stop. Hospital gossip would slay her reputation, and Dr. Reynolds, who didn't seem to like her anyway, would have plenty of ammunition to get her dismissed from the program. She only had a few more months of this and the following spring rotation to get through, and she'd be done. She couldn't let a silly infatuation get her kicked out.

Besides, it *was* silly of her to think there could be anything between her and Josh. He was a patient, and she needed to stop *wool-gathering*, as her grandma used to say whenever she was caught daydreaming.

She laughed. She wondered what her grandma would think and say if she knew Mia was attracted to somebody like Josh Brenner. Despite knowing better, despite her best intentions, and even knowing her supervisors and colleagues would frown upon any relationship between her and Josh, Mia couldn't help herself. She liked him and wanted to be around him.

Her thoughts drifted, and she wondered how successful she'd been in keeping her visits with Josh under wraps. She'd tried to be professional about it as if she was checking on any other patient, but she wasn't all that confident it had worked. The nurse, Cathy, hadn't seemed surprised to see her in Josh's room, and she certainly hadn't treated her like she was his doctor. Neither had Lisa, his PCA. Cathy had treated Mia like his love-sick, overly worried girlfriend. The image that came to mind made Mia cringe, and she hurriedly shifted gears, pushing all thoughts of Josh away. When the elevator doors opened, she practically plowed into the group of doctors waiting to get in and hurried toward the patient treatment area.

CHAPTER
ELEVEN

The night terrors were becoming more vivid and frightening, and Josh certainly hadn't convinced anyone, especially Mia, that tonight had been just a normal dream.

As clear as day, he had seen a giant black eye staring at him. He'd also seen the immense fish rise out of the dark, swirling void, slam back down, sending a torrent of water over his head, and circle him, its dorsal fin cutting through the water. He felt its rough skin pushing against him, closing in with every circuit. He stared at his hand, opening and closing his fist, flexing his fingers to loosen them. They'd been tightly balled in a fist, and his palms had hurt where his nails had dug into his palm, leaving deep, red imprints. He remembered beating his fists against the shark's body as it passed him, to no avail.

He squirmed, trying to get comfortable, but the movement was painful, and he held his breath. His chest ached; his broken ribs were still healing, and he rubbed at them, picking at the bandages wrapped around his torso. They were wrapped tight to keep his ribs from moving out of place while they healed, yet the bandages had felt like a vice in his nightmare, restricting his movement and breathing.

Before Mia arrived, he'd fought to wake up. Josh knew he was panicking in his sleep, believing he'd die if he didn't wake up, and he struggled to regain consciousness. He'd felt her touch and heard her call his name, taking him out of the dream's grip. Awakening, he saw it was really her but immediately needed to fill his oxygen-starved lungs. They felt like they were on fire, and he sucked in great gulps of air and choked on them.

Uncomfortable but at least able to sit up, he saw most of his bed covers on the floor where he'd obviously kicked them in his sleep, and it had taken both Mia and his guard, Sam, to help him get disentangled from his sheets. The room lights were on, banishing the shadows, but other lights flickered, and alarms blared. His leg, still in traction, swung uncontrollably like a pendulum, and his arm, weighed down by the plaster cast, felt like lead.

He'd obviously frightened Mia, flailing around in the bed. She undoubtedly thought something had happened to him. He usually tried to stay awake until after Mia's visits because he didn't want her to see him like that. He didn't want her to know that he fought off terrible demons when he slept. It was the main reason he refused drugs that made him sleep. Then, the nurse came in and asked him if it was another nightmare. Mia looked surprised, then even more worried. Now, she knew he was not only physically damaged but mentally as well.

Heat and embarrassment suffused his face. He hated being unable to do things for himself — needing someone's help to get up, sit up, wash his face, comb his hair, and raise or lower the head of his bed, although there was a button on the panel on the side of his bed. It was a blow to his ego that he couldn't even get a glass of water by himself. He'd never been this helpless before, and if the doctors were right, he would need a lot more assistance to help him get around and see to his needs.

He didn't want her pity. He didn't want her to look at him like he was less of a man. Anger and frustration came on the heels of his embarrassment, as well as thoughts about his career. He couldn't help wondering about what was going to happen to him. Surfing was his life. It was *who* he was and *what* he did. If he couldn't surf, what would he do?

The thoughts and emotions churned within him until he finally felt drained. The whole situation sucked, and there was nothing he could do about it. Not wanting to think about his future any longer, he focused on his feelings about Mia. Despite everything, he was glad she visited him in the evenings. He'd come to depend on her visits to relieve the monotony of lying in bed. He was sorry she'd been upset at seeing him like that, and when he'd reached out to her, wanting to hold her hand, feel her soft touch, *and* mollify her, she had shut down. He smiled.

There were so many mixed signals radiating off her, like waves. Josh understood her reluctance. He felt she cared about him, maybe even liked him more than just a patient, but she was skittish about showing it. He knew she worried about what her coworkers would think and say and what her supervisors would do if they found out something was going on between them. But in his gut, he knew there was chemistry between them. It was in how she looked at him, worried over him, and he was rather keen on the attention. Her strange, hot and cold behavior didn't bother him in the least. It was rather endearing, and he wanted to pull her into his arms, or at least his one arm. He now had another reason for staying in the U.S. When he was finally discharged, he would see how this thing he had for Mia Thomas would play out.

Early the next morning, Dr. Shaw visited Josh, and surprisingly, there were no interns or residents with him.

"Hello, Josh. How're you doing? Sitting up okay for a couple of hours?"

"I am, thank you. But I'm ready to get out of this bed. I might go crazy if I have to lay here much longer."

"We might be able to get you out the bed, but you're not ready to move around too much yet. You still need the casts for now, and I put in an order a couple of days ago to have Dr. Cassidy come in to see you, though you were against the idea. But after last night's episode, I think it's best you talk with someone who can help you with the nightmares. They're getting worse and more frequent. You've had them every night this past week."

"What can a shrink do for me? Give me a lobotomy?"

"I doubt we need to go that far, but have the conversation. It can't hurt. He works mostly with veteran patients through the VA, so his schedule is always packed. But he said he'd try to get you in in a day or so."

"I won't take more pills."

"He may have some other options than amitriptyline or mirtazapine. Lay back now; I need to see how you're doing." He lowered the head of the bed until Josh lay flat, shivering from the stethoscope's cold touch and Dr. Shaw's brief examination. "Well, it's been, what… four, going on five weeks since you got those casts and your last set of X-rays? The swelling has gone down, so I'm ordering new X-rays, and maybe you can be switched to a soft cast and have your leg taken out of traction. You should be able to get a soft cast on your hand and arm as well. No pain?"

"No. No pain."

"Good. And no fever. I'm confident your bones are mending well, but I want them to have a look at that wound area. We don't want any surprises that could keep the skin from healing properly," Dr. Shaw said, making extensive notations on his tablet.

Josh agreed. "When do you think I can get out of bed? I'm done resting on my laurels."

"We'll try to get you in for the new X-rays this afternoon, and if they look good, you may be able to have those casts removed and get the soft casts by tomorrow. Once that's done, you should be able to get out of bed. You'll have to sit down, though. Maybe in that recliner over there or in a wheelchair. I don't want you to walk on that leg until it's completely healed, or you'll have a terrible limp."

"Yeah, okay. I can come and go around here in a wheelchair, can't I?"

"Yes, yes. You could be wheeled out to the solarium for a couple of hours. I'll order some occupational and physical therapy for next week. I want you to take it slow, rebuild your muscles and stamina."

"That sounds good to me."

"Good. I probably won't be back up to see you again today unless I see something on your X-rays, but I doubt I'll find anything untoward. You have a good rest of the day, and I'll see you tomorrow."

"Thanks, Dr. Shaw. You too."

Josh picked up his phone, texted Sean the good news, and then checked his calendar. He had several international calls scheduled over the next few days. One was with his business manager, who needed several necessary authorizations, and another with an important team sponsor. He'd also agreed to an exclusive interview with a sports magazine from his bed to reassure the world that he was alive and on the mend. Josh thought it was ridiculous, but his PR agent had impressed upon him the importance of keeping his fan base and sponsors apprised of his progress.

Josh pushed the rolling tray-table away from the bed. He'd barely touched his lunch. They'd served chicken pot pie today, and he swore he wouldn't eat another chicken or turkey pot pie if his life depended upon it. He'd tried to eat the bowl of fruit that came with it, but the fruit was tasteless, and he doubted it was fresh. More likely, it had come from a can. He settled back against his pillows and turned on the television, hoping to find something good to watch. He liked American spy thriller-type movies and had binged James Bond movies with Daniel Craig, the Bourne trilogy, on his tablet. Just as he'd settled down to check out *The Equalizer* with Denzel Washington, his cell phone buzzed, vibrating on the nightstand. He answered, surprised to see Teagan's name and picture on the screen.

"Josh? Wow. I can't believe I finally got through. How are you? I've called at least a hundred times, and I've never been able to get through to you."

"Yeah, I have my phone now. I'm doing better, Tea. How're you?"

"I'm good. I miss you. I want to come there to see you. I tried before, but the hospital only let family in to see you. I spoke to Sean, and he said you had been in a coma after surgery but was doing better. I feel so bad. How awful to be attacked by a shark, and poor Colin…"

Josh frowned as he listened to her gushing monologue. He'd heard her voice mail messages and seen the texts from her and so many other people, including his team members, sponsors, and business partners. He'd stowed his phone, tablet, and other belongings in the truck the day of the accident, and Sean had taken care of them until he could drop them off at the hospital. When Josh emerged from his deep sleep, he hadn't thought about talking to anyone or reading his messages. Then, it took several more days to remember the code to unlock his phone. That was weeks ago, and he still hadn't gotten around to responding to all the well-wishes.

"I have a trip planned for a few weeks in the States next month. I want to see you then. Do you think you might be out of the hospital by then?"

"It doesn't look like it, Tea. I was pretty banged up. Where are you now?"

"At home in London. My father had a minor heart attack, and I had to rush home instead of going to Saint-Tropez like I'd planned. But he's better now, home with my mother, who's fussing over him like he's fragile. I'm returning to France at the end of the week, then I'll come to the States."

"Sorry to hear about your father, but I'm glad he's getting better and back home. But Tea, I don't want you to come and check on me."

"But I miss you, Josh. I need to see you. Don't you miss me?"

"I'm sorry, Tea, I can't… I'm not ready to see anyone. My family just left, and… I,…I need time. I have a lot to deal with right now."

"I could be there for you, Josh."

"I appreciate that, Tea. But I need time to process what happened to me… and Colin." He took a deep breath. "Look, I have to go now. The doctor's here," he fibbed to get off the call. "Goodbye, Tea."

"This sounds like goodbye *for real*, Josh."

"I think it's best. Take care of yourself, Tea." He exhaled as he disconnected and stared at the phone in his hand. He'd been truthful when he'd told her he had a lot to process and wasn't ready to see her, but the real reason was he hadn't thought about her once since leaving her in Biarritz. He felt a little guilty about that, but everything had changed. His feelings had changed. His life had changed. Like a flick of a switch, everything in his life stopped, and when the lights came back on, he faced entirely new circumstances. Nothing was the same. And now, there was Mia. If things went how he wanted, he couldn't see Teagan in his life ever again.

CHAPTER
TWELVE

While Josh watched from the big reclining chair the physical therapists had put him in after his morning exercises, Robb Cassidy pulled up a chair, sat on it, and drew his ankle over his knee.

Cassidy was a tall, slender man, a little older than Josh. He was dressed in comfortable loose jeans and a button-down shirt, the sleeves of which were rolled over the sleeves of his white lab coat and pushed past his forearms. His white-blond hair was short and neat, as was his mustache and beard. He had what appeared to be an old scar that split his right eyebrow and blue eyes. He also had a friendly, easy-going smile that put his patients at ease.

When Josh first met him, he wasn't sure what to expect. He was already geared up to dislike the man and refuse further sessions, but one conversation led to the next, and by the third session, Josh was eager to discuss the elephant in the room.

"I looked up PTSD and think I may have a little of it. Maybe," Josh started as soon as Cassidy got comfortable.

"What makes you think that?" Cassidy asked, getting comfortable and opening his notebook.

"I've been reading a lot about it, and I check a lot of the boxes," Josh answered.

"Okay. Well, what symptoms do you have?"

According to the online articles he'd read, Josh suffered most of the symptoms, and as he ticked them off, Cassidy wrote them down.

"That's a pretty impressive list, but if you had all that going on, I'd think you'd have PTSD a lot, not a little, plus a few other things."

"Yeah, okay, but what are we going to do about it?"

"Well, first, I have to determine if you have PTSD, then figure out a treatment plan, which might include some meds you'd need to take. Dr. Shaw said you refused to take the pills he prescribed."

"I can't. I tried, but I can't wake up when the nightmares start. Then, when I do, I feel like a zombie the next day."

"It takes time for your body to adjust to the medicine."

"I have no control over myself… or my actions. I can't move. I can't wake up. I feel like I'm in danger, and my heart feels like it's going to burst out of my chest."

"The medicines we prescribe only help you sleep. They turn your brain off so you can rest. They don't knock you out; they don't incapacitate you. I may be able to prescribe something different, but you'll have to take it for at least a week to ten days. They need to get in your system."

"I don't like the drugs, Doc. I don't eat crap food, and I don't believe in putting a lot of chemicals, drugs, and stuff like that in my body. You know the side effects can be worse than the condition they're supposed to be helping. So, no. No drugs. What else can we do?"

"Well, aside from that, we'll continue to talk and unpack the trauma you've suffered.

"I don't understand. I don't remember very much. I know what I've been told, so I don't know why we have to keep bringing it up."

"The thing is, Josh, I believe you might be experiencing selective amnesia."

"What's that? You think I don't want to remember?"

"Maybe not consciously. You remember everything from early childhood until the day of the attack. Your nightmares could be manifesting what you're trying to suppress—everything that happened during the attack."

"Selective amnesia, huh. So how do you treat that?"

"We could continue to talk about it, go into detail about what you see and experience in your dreams, and if you've repressed so deeply that you truly cannot remember, hypnosis could possibly help."

"Hypnosis? Like making someone walk around and quack like a duck? I think not."

"I could never make you walk around quacking like a duck. But let's talk about your dreams for now. I want you to walk me through every detail."

Josh sat back and recounted what he could remember of the nightmare he'd had the night before. He described how his dreams would shift from bright and clear, like day, to dark and muddy, almost viscous, as he moved in slow motion. Then, something big would loom over him. Cassidy took notes on his tablet, letting Josh talk past their hour-long session until he'd run out of words. Josh felt drained afterward.

"I think we've made some significant progress today, Josh. Thank you for sharing all of that with me. I'll think about what you've told me over the next few days and maybe come up with a game plan for our next meeting. You'll start the medicines tonight that I've prescribed, okay?"

"Everything in me says no, Doc. But maybe. We'll see."

"Do it, Josh. You need to get sufficient sleep, deep REM sleep. When you're sleep-deprived, that brings on its own set of problems. Once you're sleeping better, we can get to the root of your other problems, but things could start resolving themselves once you're well-rested." Cassidy stood and extended his hand, which Josh shook. "Thanks for meeting with me. I'll be back Thursday afternoon, and we'll go from there."

"Okay, Doc. See you then." Josh was tired and ready to stretch out in bed. A nap even sounded great. He couldn't remember the last time he'd felt well-rested or had slept through the night. He hated the idea of taking sleeping pills, but if Cassidy was right and the pills he prescribed only turned off his brain, it might be worth a try.

Josh had expected Mia to stop by earlier that evening, but she hadn't come before her shift or at her usual break time. In fact, she didn't get a chance to see him until the wee hours of the morning. When she'd crept silently into his room, Josh could see she was exhausted. He'd been dozing when she slipped in quietly and pulled up a chair beside the bed. He watched her without speaking as she took off her glasses, laid them on the bed beside him, and laid her head on her crossed arms.

"You're exhausted, aren't you?" Josh asked as he reached over and splayed his fingers in her hair. He gave her scalp a gentle massage. The texture of her curls delighted him, soft but springy, the tips spiraled around his fingers of their own accord.

She grunted. "I am. It's been a tough night. It seems to be worse when there's a full moon."

"You think there's any truth to that old myth?

"I don't know, but it seems to fit the pattern. My team lost two babies. We worked all night and did everything we could, but neither one made it. One of the older kids was trying to light a candle with matches, and either the candle fell over or the matches started the fire, but the bed where the little kids were sleeping ignited. It spread in the room within minutes, then throughout their house."

"Ah, Babe. I'm sorry for that." Josh continued to massage her scalp, but he wished he could hold her. It said a lot that she'd sought solace with him. He could very well imagine losing kids was tough.

"There were seven small children and three adults in the house. Three children, five-year-old twin brothers and a two-year-old girl, were brought here by ambulance, along with the little girl's mother. The other members of the family were taken to several different hospitals."

"You're so strong, Mia. I don't know how you deal with things like that."

"It's hard to lose little kids. The baby and one twin didn't make it. The other twin is in critical condition. The woman is holding her own. It'll be touch and go for a while."

"That's good. You're my hero."

"I don't try to be a hero. I want to help."

"What made you want to become a doctor?"

"I've always wanted to be a doctor, but I didn't want to become a trauma surgeon until after I entered med school," she murmured, sounding half asleep. Josh tried to get situated in the bed to reach Mia better, and she shifted, giving him more room.

"You take care of everyone, Mia Thomas, but who cares for you? Who gives you hugs and a massage? Who makes sure you eat when you get home? Do you have a pet? Like a dog or cat or a little fish?"

"Nope. I work, eat, sleep, and repeat. I don't have time to take care of a pet. It's just me and my one-bedroom apartment," she murmured.

"I think you need someone to take care of you, to be there for *you*."

"I suppose that would be nice, but I spend most of my time here at the hospital, so I'd rarely be at home to take advantage of all that attention."

"If they did it right, you'd spend much more time away from the hospital."

"Mmm," Mia hummed, and Josh had no idea what that meant, but rather than continuing to question her, he massaged her scalp and the back of her neck. It seemed to soothe her, and soon, she appeared to have fallen asleep. Even if Mia didn't realize it, Josh believed she was the strongest person he knew—superhero strong. She wore scrubs and a lab coat instead of tights and a cape. Her talent and medical skill were her superpowers, and Josh swelled with pride.

"Can you stay a while?" he asked when she stirred.

"Only if you promise to wake me in fifteen minutes. I need to close my eyes."

"Okay, lie still. I'll wake you. I won't let you oversleep."

"Um-hmm," she responded, already half-asleep.

He was happy he made her feel better and enjoyed playing with her hair, but he could do so much more than give her a good scalp or foot massage. He could open doors for her and smooth her pathways, but would she let him? Would she just let him be with her?

CHAPTER THIRTEEN

Mia

The doctors were pleased by Josh's improvement, and the lead therapist on his PT team suggested he spend some time outside and get some fresh air and sun.

The weather cooperated, offering a bright, sunny, warm afternoon, beautiful for late July. The temperature hovered in the eighties and drove the stiffness caused by the constant cold from the air conditioners from his body. A hospital aide pushed Josh in his wheelchair to a quiet courtyard behind the main hospital, with Mia and Sam following. The courtyard overlooked a lush, landscaped garden with verdant grass, trees, and profusely blooming flower beds.

Mia had worked the night before, ending her shift that morning just before daybreak, but had gotten a few hours of sleep before returning to spend the afternoon with Josh. She'd fussed over her hair and outfit, hoping to surprise Josh, choosing a silky, grayish-green wrap skirt with vivid hand-printed and oversized floral graphics, a sage green chemise that she thought looked perfect with it, and flat, silver thong sandals with decorative seashells and glass beads on the straps. Brushing her freshly washed hair until it fell in soft waves down her back, she smoothed it into a tight ponytail, gelling down the fly-away edges, and applied her makeup with a light touch and added lip oil. She wanted to look as lovely as she felt, a stunning butterfly emerging from its drab cocoon.

~

Josh

Josh sat in his wheelchair, his leg encased in the new plaster cast propped up on the stirrup; his other foot was flat on the floor.

He hated having to sit in the chair and, even more, hated waiting for an aide to wheel him around, but he couldn't fool himself. He'd never make the trip on his own, so there was no reason to complain. He had, however, showered and dressed by himself before his aid arrived, putting on comfortable, loose-fitting pants and a pullover shirt. He'd brushed his hair back in a wolf's tail. It had grown a lot in the weeks he'd been in the hospital, and the hair on his face had also grown out and thickened into a substantial mustache and beard. Carlos, a PCA on the floor, brought clippers and trimmed Josh's facial hair for him. Once again, Josh felt human. He was fussing with the dressing on his arm when Mia knocked and entered the room. His eyes opened wide as she came to stand in front of him.

Heat flushed through his chest at the sight of her. She looked transformed. She was usually beautiful in her baggy scrubs and lab coat, her feet in bright, colorful clogs, and her hair pinned precariously on top of her head… but now, she was even more gorgeous. The sleeveless top tucked into the wrap skirt emphasized her small waist, flat stomach, full, rounded breasts, and long, toned arms. Her unblemished skin glowed like polished bronze.

"You like?" she asked, making Josh realize he was not only staring but also practically salivating. She blushed under his scrutiny.

"You look stunning. Absolutely beautiful."

"Thank you," she murmured shyly.

"Please, come here," he asked, reaching for her hand and tugging her gently to sit in his lap. She stepped forward but hesitated to sit. "Please," he beckoned, and she let him pull her closer to him. He wrapped his arms around her and held her for a moment. This was the closest they'd ever been, and he could feel her tremble. He inhaled her delicate perfume, his lips hovering over the curve of her neck, and she gasped in surprise when he kissed and licked the soft skin.

"You smell delicious. Who knew you looked like this under those baggy scrubs?"

"Scrubs are perfect for the work that I do. I'm no supermodel, you know."

"Who needs supermodels?" he retorted, sliding the strips of fabric holding up her top off one shoulder and dotting kisses at the nape of her sensitive neck and across her shoulder. He could feel her shiver and heard the soft moan that rose in her throat. Turning her around to face him, he stared at her, her beautiful hazel eyes mesmerizing. "Don't kiss me," she whispered, looking away.

"I want to," he whispered back, holding her gently, bringing her face closer.

"We can't."

"We can." He touched her lips with his, testing to see if she would pull away. When she didn't, he kissed her gently before turning more demanding. She responded, kissing him back, giving him access to her mouth, and his body ached for more. She tasted like peppermint. The kiss was searing, and he felt dangerously close to losing control. Pulling back, he drew a deep breath, feeling his heart racing.

"God, you don't know how long, how much I've wanted to do that."

She stared at him, her lips parted and reddened by his hungry kiss, apparently as overwhelmed by the urgency and intensity of the passion between them as he'd been. She pulled away and stood, smoothing down her dress. "I can't… we can't do that again."

"We can. We should. I know you felt what I felt."

"I did, and that's why we can't."

"Don't be afraid, Mia. I won't hurt you."

"I think you should call your attendant, or we won't make it downstairs," she ordered breathlessly, changing the subject.

"That's fine by me," Josh quipped, more than halfway serious. "Maybe we should stay right here the rest of the day."

Bougainvillea vines and blooms climbed over and through a pergola sitting in the corner of the courtyard, the interior cool and shaded from the sun. It offered a panoramic view of the gardens and the Quad, the open park-like area closed off to vehicle traffic, perfect for walking, sitting, reading, and sun-worshiping. Wide walkways took pedestrians across the hospital campus in four directions: northeast led to the Children's Hospital, northwest to the Cancer Research Center, southeast to the Women's Health Pavilion and Professional Building, and the main hospital building sat southwest. During the day, there was always heavy pedestrian traffic between the different buildings, people hurrying between the hospitals and professional buildings to the parking lots and structures beyond. But the courtyard itself was usually empty, a quiet, idyllic, and green space.

Carrying his phone and a book, Sam found a bench some distance away, giving Mia and Josh privacy while remaining close by. Mia and Josh settled under the pergola, partially hidden by purple and pink bougainvillea bushes and thick, creeping vines. Josh luxuriated in the afternoon warmth, as comfortable as possible in his chair, and Mia rolled out a small blanket and sat down, her body turned to face him.

"This is nice," Josh remarked. "We should have done this long ago. I think I was going mad inside every day, all day."

"You've made so much progress; maybe you'll be discharged soon."

"I hope so. I think these casts and PT are the only things holding me back." Josh reached for her, and Mia slid her hand into his.

She liked how he held her hand, clasping it and rubbing circles on the skin with his thumb. It seemed like a reflexive motion, but Mia knew it was his way of connecting to her. She used to worry her hands were too rough. The harsh hospital soap dried out her skin, but he never seemed to mind. She felt like they were on a date; sitting out in the open like this was more telling than slipping up to his room every chance she got. There was no denying they had a special attachment and regard for each other.

"Will you go back home once you're discharged?" she asked, raising the subject that seemed to be on her mind a lot.

"No, not right away. I'll still need rehab on this leg, and there are still surf events here that I have to attend, even if I can't participate. My team is still participating, and I have to meet with our various sponsors. But I was considering staying here, in San Diego, for a little while."

"Yeah?"

"Yeah. I want us to get better acquainted. I care about you—a great deal, in fact."

"Josh…"

"Wait, wait. I know," Josh interrupted her, holding his hands up. "I know how you feel about your supervisors and co-workers, but if I can rent a place, we'd be away from the hospital. I could do outpatient rehab, and we could hang out together."

"It sounds nice, but I don't know…"

"Jeez, I'm crazy about you, Mia. I think about you all the time, and not like a friend or my doctor. I know you feel something similar for me."

"I do, Josh. I do care about you, Josh, and I love spending time with you. But…"

"I feel the same. I don't want to be your *friend*. I don't want to keep things purely *professional* between us. I don't want you flinching whenever I want to hold your hand. I want to touch you in public, like now," he said, kissing the back of her hand, "and I desperately want to make love to you."

"We… we can't." She blushed furiously, the image of them together looming large in her imagination.

"I know. That'll have to wait. I don't want our first time to be rushed, fumbling around in a hospital bed," he said, grinning. "Although I would gladly accept it if you offered."

"Absolutely not. You hardly fit in that bed by yourself, and your door doesn't lock."

"It doesn't? Well, I'll make sure we have privacy and a California King bed so we have plenty of room to roll around in." He gave her hand a squeeze.

CHAPTER FOURTEEN

Mia

Mia smiled, but instead of feeling elated, she felt as though she teetered on a sharp and dangerous edge.

The picture Josh had painted sounded great, but it also made the hairs on the back of her neck stand up. He was the darling of the paparazzi who clamored for pictures of him that magazines and news outlets paid handsomely for. For heaven's sake, he needed a bodyguard to keep people from getting too close. It made Mia cringe inwardly at the thought of being constantly followed everywhere by reporters and photographers, not to mention total strangers — fans of his, wanting to get close to her. Her life would be on public display, and if she couldn't handle gossip among her colleagues, how would she handle seeing herself and Josh splashed on the front of tabloids?

"Good," Josh said, squeezing her hand. "I can't wait until I'm discharged."

Mia also had to admit it was a heady feeling that this beautiful man wanted to be with her. It felt surreal. She'd been stunned by the rush of excitement that flooded her body, the flare of desire he'd ignited with his kiss. She'd never been so aroused by a single kiss before. He'd been careful and tender but also intense, hungry, and demanding. She had tried to fight the feelings he stirred, but it felt so much better giving in to them. She had dreamed of kissing him, wishing there could be something between them, but she'd been unprepared for the onslaught of desire, the primal need that burned deep in her core.

Thankfully, he'd regained his senses and broke off the kisses. She'd been lost in the feel of him, the taste of him. Concerns regarding her colleagues and supervisors—anyone who could have caught them kissing—had faded away under his touch. Now, however, under stark scrutiny, she realized she'd lost her head, and the consequences could have ruined everything. The heat of embarrassment suffused her body. Mia's thoughts swirled chaotically in her head, and she forcibly pushed them down, stuffing them away to examine later. She hated to spoil Josh's first outing. Feeling more in control, she glanced up and found him staring at her.

"What are you thinking?" He seemed to see through her, and she pulled her hand away, smiling as she clasped them in her lap.

"Nothing. I'm fine."

"I know that look, Mia. You're overanalyzing things."

"No, really. I'm not. I don't think… I'm not sure this… *us*, is a very good idea."

"Why not?" His gaze was so direct and piercing that she began to squirm.

"Well, for one, we're so different. Josh, you know what my life is like, and it's as different from your life as night is from day. I plan to become a surgeon, with at least three more years of training ahead of me. You have bodyguards. I've never met anyone who needed bodyguards."

"I don't always have bodyguards. They're here mostly for security while I'm in this hospital. The paparazzi can be relentless."

"But that is *exactly* what I mean. That's scary. Hordes of media people want to know every little detail about your life. Your face is always on a magazine cover or newspaper somewhere in the world. You're rich and famous. Millions of people follow you on social media. That's not my life. I work in the background. I rarely meet the people again once they leave the ER."

"You're super smart, compassionate, beautiful, and what can

I say? You're just awesome. I can't wait to show you how much you mean to me. You see me, *the real me*, not the rich asshole or meal ticket people think I am, and you care about the person I am. At least you make me think you do."

"I do, Josh. I see a wonderful, kind human being who has accomplished so much. Compared to yours, my life is boring."

"Stop it. You are going to be a brilliant surgeon. It's a sorely needed job that I could never do. You save people's lives."

"But I'm boring. All I do is work."

He sighed and picked up her hand, holding it in both hands. "Okay. Anything else? Any more reasons why we can't do this?"

"Well, no. Not off the top of my head. But those are pretty big reasons."

"I don't think so. I want this with you, Mia, but I can't make it happen by myself. If you don't want this, let's stop it now. I leave it in your hands."

"I want to be with you, Josh, but you'll get tired of me and my lifestyle sooner or later," she whispered. *When,* not *if* he left her, it would decimate her, and the thought felt like a stab in her chest. She couldn't breathe.

"I would never leave you, Mia. I would never hurt you. You probably don't believe this, but I've never felt this way about anyone before. Not ever. I can't imagine walking away from you and purposely hurting you. I give you my word." He looked so solemn that Mia couldn't help but smile and get up on her knees. She put her arms around his neck and laid her head on his shoulder.

"Pinky swear," she whispered, holding up her little finger.

"Pinky swear." He gripped her finger tightly.

"We're really going to do this?"

"Yes," he said, his eyes staring into hers. "And don't worry. Everything will be fine. Hunky-dory."

"Are you serious? Hunky-dory?" Mia burst into laughter.

"As serious as a heart attack."

CHAPTER
FIFTEEN

Josh

After breakfast, Josh pushed his tray away. He held the button on the bed panel until the bed lowered enough for him to put his feet flat on the floor, then raised it until he could easily stand.

It was his trick for getting out of bed by himself. He ignored the leg brace the therapists had him wear in place of the cast. He was supposed to wear it all day, only taking it off to sleep. He hobbled to the bathroom to relieve himself, then eased back into the reclining chair. Though the staff frowned upon him doing things by himself, preferring he'd wait until someone came to help him, he never did. They took too long to come get him out of bed. He let them dress him, as he still had difficulty doing that, but it felt good to do some things himself.

It also felt good to be out of the immobilizers for a while. The immobilizers were basically splints and braces that could be removed, like when he lay in bed. The first thing the PCAs did when they came in was strap the leg brace on, tighten it up past his knee, and then put the brace on his arm. They'd taken the wraps off his chest not long after waking from the sleep-induced coma, letting his ribs heal naturally. Only when he moved wrong or used his core muscles to sit up did he experience twinges of pain shooting throughout his torso. Otherwise, he was starting to feel almost normal.

Also, since the hard plaster casts had been switched for the immobilizers, Josh had made great progress handling the crutches and building upper body strength. He also had better dexterity in his hand and arm. He was champing at the bit to be discharged soon. He'd been admitted on June fifth, and they were now at the end of August. He'd been in the hospital for almost three months, and his business interests were starting to suffer.

Brenner's Mavericks was a high-performance team and a strong brand, but now that he was taken out of the equation, things were taking a big financial hit. The longer he stayed confined to the hospital, and his future in surfing remained uncertain, the more nervous sponsors became, and a few jumped ship. Van Niekerk immediately pulled the plug on the promotional tour before Josh even regained consciousness, and the Pretorius Corporation dropped its endorsement last month. Meyer Surfboards continued to honor their commitment to the team, but they were more parsimonious with their sponsorship dollars.

Josh knew that he would need to go after more sponsors as soon as he could move around. He'd lost a chance to woo American companies when he'd missed the Hawaii Pipeline and the Ventura Beach competitions several weeks ago, but the Huntington Beach competition was coming up in September, and he hoped to be out of the hospital by then. Other things were slipping through the cracks, and Sean was trying to handle as much as he could, but some things Sean couldn't take care of. His business manager, Monica Ackroyd, needed him to review contracts and authorize bank transfers. Money was being tied up, and checks, payroll, and hospital bills were coming in, but the account was becoming underfunded. Josh had transferred a big chunk of money to the business account that morning, per Monica's request, but he knew that was only a stopgap, not a solution.

Someone knocked lightly on the door before entering his room. It was Carlos, and Josh grinned at him. He liked having Carlos as his PCA much better than the young female aides who twittered and gushed so annoyingly. Carlos hovered, as that was part of his job, but he and Josh could talk about stuff that interested them both, like surfing and street racing. Carlos was into street racing and was restoring a vintage Dodge Charger during his free time that he intended to race. Though Josh loved shiny new sports cars with high-performance engines and luxury appointments, he could understand the appeal. Cars were cars, and the two men found common ground through their love for them.

Carlos set a pile of clothes on the edge of the bed, and Josh took the loose, navy sweatpants off the top and pulled them on the way the occupational therapists insisted. He tossed the two hospital gowns he'd pulled off and tossed them at the younger man and wrangled into a long-sleeved Henley shirt, leaving the front, three-button placket undone. Josh grinned at Carlos, confident he'd beat his best time for getting dressed, and sat patiently while Carlos put on the brace and splint. Josh was in a good mood, surprisingly. He'd started doing things for himself for the past two weeks, and it felt good not to need much assistance.

"Where would you like to sit this morning, Josh? It's beautiful in the Solarium. You can have your lunch there and meet with Dr. Cassidy later."

"I think I'll stay here for a couple of hours, and you can come get me around lunchtime. I need to make a few calls first."

"Yessir. I'll come to check on you, then we'll go into the Solarium at eleven."

On his last visit, Sean had dropped off a new ultra-light laptop. Josh pulled the rolling tray table in front of him and opened it. It was ultra-fast, connecting to the hospital's internet in seconds. Josh switched on the encryption app and prepared for the first of his video conference calls. This one was with his PR agents, Bancroft and Bolls. It was almost five PM in London but just after eight AM in San Diego. Their job was to help quell as many concerns and rumors as possible that had persisted since he'd been attacked by the shark two months ago. They'd done an excellent job putting out accurate information and updating his social media with new photos and videos, especially an interview from his hospital bed. But the next phase was to focus on promoting the team. There were nine—or seven, now that Colin was gone—and as he was unable to compete anytime soon, Josh wanted the Maverick brand to remain strong on the circuit. Sean was their top earner, but the others, including Will Meyers, Joey Maldonado, and Gilly Brownlee, were surging up the ranks, and he wanted the PR firm to capitalize on the team's successful record.

After meeting with Dr. Cassidy, he had the second important call of the day. Sydney was sixteen hours ahead of Pacific time, and Monica had arranged to have Josh's business advisors, attorney, and accountant on a video conference call. Evalynn Bancroft could join them on the call, depending on how much they accomplished this morning.

Finally, he made a note to call Tommy Walters of Walters Industries that evening. Walters manufactured wetsuits, and he, Sean, and Colin had been testing out the new ones the day of the shark attack. He wasn't aware of—or cared—how Tommy Walters had gotten hold of his shredded wetsuit, but Sean had informed him that they were developing a design that used flexible steel mesh to protect surfers during a shark's exploratory attack. The Bancroft and Bolls had done an excellent job keeping Walters interested in Josh as their spokesperson for the new suits once they went into production.

However, Josh wasn't sure he still wanted to be a Walters spokesperson. Or anyone else's, for that matter. He was, or at least he had been before the accident, a surfer. Not a model, envoy, or somebody's good luck charm. Even if he could no longer surf, modeling and hawking wetsuits didn't seem appealing. However, Walters wrote big checks, and Josh needed to hear them out. Maybe he could put one of the other team members up for the job. Gilbert Brownlee looked like a model, and he was hot right now. Maybe they could put a deal together with Gilly as their new spokesperson.

"Hello, Josh. Can you hear me?" Evalynn's sultry voice came

across loud and clear, bringing Josh out of his ruminations.

"Yes, I can. How are you, Eva?"

~

Mia

Mia squealed when she arrived during her lunch break.

It was after midnight, but Josh was still awake, propped up on pillows, his bed cranked up at least forty-five degrees. She should not have been as astonished at the change in Josh's appearance, as she had plenty of pictures of him on her phone — some taken from his social media posts, others selfies they'd taken in his hospital room. His PCA had taken on the job of keeping him freshly groomed, and though Mia liked the way he looked with his hair growing out thick and full, hanging long on his neck, she couldn't help but appreciate his movie-star good looks after a fresh cut. She couldn't help but appreciate how lucky she was that he was hers and she was his.

She flew to his side and kissed him, a hungry, possessive kiss. A husky groan rose in his throat, and his fingers splayed in her hair, holding her tenderly, cradling her head as he deepened the kiss. Josh took her breath away. His kisses were scorching, intoxicating, and addictive. When they kissed like that, it set off explosions of sensation inside her. She staggered back when he let her go of her. "Wow. Ummm, sorry, sir. I'm so embarrassed. I thought you were my boy

"You'd kiss a Hemsworth like that?"

"No, of course not. Okay, maybe. But that was a damn good kiss. Can I have your autograph?"

"Absolutely, but it'll cost you another kiss."

"Oh, no. My boyfriend would have a conniption if he knew I was kissing strangers."

"I won't tell if you don't," he mumbled. She leaned over and gave him another scorching kiss. She heard the rumble start in his chest as his tongue slid inside her mouth. She pulled back, ending the kiss prematurely, seeing the frustration momentarily etch his features. She smiled, bending to put her lips against his throat, feeling his racing pulse.

"Josh?" She whispered.

"Hmm?" His voice was husky and rough, and his throat vibrated against her lips.

"You clean up soooo good."

"You think?"

"Um-hmmm. And you smell divine." She leaned back, a happy grin on her face.

"Today was shower day," he quipped. "If I had known you preferred the preppy look to the beach bum look, I might have had Carlos take his clippers to my hair and beard a long time ago."

"Umm," she said, taking another big sniff before straightening up. "I don't know which one I like better."

"But it was worth it, yeah?"

"Without a doubt." She hopped up onto the bed beside him and laid her head on his chest. Being next to him made her entire body hum with awareness, and listening to his strong heartbeat in her ear and against her cheek made her own heartbeat erratically. She'd never been as affected by anyone as she was by Josh. In fact, she was so distracted by her feelings that it startled her when he'd lowered the bed and the rails and swung his legs off the bed so he could sit with his arms around her.

"Look at you," she grinned happily. "You really are determined to get out of here, aren't you?"

"It can't come soon enough. I think I'm about done with these immobilizers, yeah?" he asked, lifting his arm off the bed to scratch inside the brace. His arm had shrunk a lot with the dissipation of swelling and mild muscle atrophy.

"Don't scratch," she warned, noticing him digging inside the brace. "You could break the skin and cause an infection."

"It feels like a colony of ants is crawling under my skin. You could rub some of that lotion over there on it, couldn't you, Love?"

"Okay, but I'll bring some moisturizing cream tomorrow. You'll be itchy, peeling, and scaly under the braces until they're off completely. I've got some thick emollients you can use. It'll look and feel better."

"I wouldn't mind if you rubbed emollients all over me. I have such an itch." He pulled her gently, guiding her down beside him on the bed.

"I mean, like, if you're offering me a paid position or something," she murmured against his lips, "I might consider it, but it could cost a lot. Maybe a couple thousand bucks a pop."

She let him nuzzle below her ear, down her neck and across the top of her scrubs. She shivered as his fingers slipped inside her waistband, rubbing the soft skin of her belly. Thankfully, he didn't go any further. She didn't want him to push his fingers inside her panties, though admittedly, she ached for him.

"It would definitely be worth thousands to have your hands rubbing all over my body," he growled, his gaze darkening and his smile turning roguish.

"I'm just going to rub one arm and leg, Josh. Not your whole body."

"No, that's not fair. What about my other arm and leg? I need emollients on both."

"I don't know. I might have to charge double." She exhaled a shuddering breath. She smiled. It felt so good to be this close to him, his face in the crook of her neck, his lip kissing and sucking the delicate skin there. She slid her hand under his gown, noting he wore cotton pants and a drawstring and smoothed the strip of hair that disappeared below his waistband before swiping slowly back up to his chest.

"Done." He caught her hand and forced it lower, grinding against it. "See what you do. I had no intention of mauling you on this bed."

"Good," she said, laughing as she rubbed the palm of her hand against the thick swell constrained inside his pants. She squeezed lightly, making him moan. "Let me up. I've got to get back to work."

"Don't you have a few more minutes?" he asked, pushing up against her palm.

"Maybe two more."

"Good. Come, this won't take long."

She let him push her back on his bed, and he twisted around to put his leg over her, tucking her tightly against his body. Then he kissed her. Mia loved his kisses and the way his hands roamed her body. She didn't resist when his hands slid beneath her top and worked to unclasp her bra. Yearning rose up from her core, and she matched the urgency of his kisses. He pushed her top up, freeing her breasts from her bra, and her nipples hardened as he licked and blew on the aureoles before sucking them, one then the other, hungrily into his mouth.

She sucked in a sharp breath, feeling a liquid throb between her legs, a deep ache building in her core. A low, rolling moan escaped from her as Josh switched breasts, from one to the other and back again. Her body began to tremble, and he moved lower to kiss and suck the soft skin of her belly. He continued to knead and cup her breast before pulling her top back down and straightening up to kiss her lips.

Shaken, her heart pounding furiously, Mia realized anyone could have walked in and quickly sat up, refastening her bra and smoothing her clothes. She climbed off the bed, feeling winded and unsteady on her feet. She'd never felt so needy for anyone else before, not the way she ached for Josh. He made her forget everything, losing herself in him and the sensations he wrought.

"Just for that, triple."

"Done."

He sat up and reached for her again, pulling her to stand between his knees. His fingers tugged at her hair, and it fell apart like a dark, velvet curtain. He cradled her head, holding her as he kissed her again. She gave him access to her open mouth, curling her fingers in his hair. When they broke apart, she stared at him, seeing his breath was as ragged as hers, his chest heaving beneath the thin cotton hospital gown. His eyes were dark and narrowed, and he licked her bruised and swollen lips.

"What?" she asked, pulling back.

"You look thoroughly kissed."

"Look what you've done to my hair." She scooped it up and twisted it into a ball, trying not to look at him. He smiled as she snatched the pins off the mattress and pinned her hair securely. "Why are you staring at me?"

"It's your lips. They make me want to kiss you again."

"You can't. I can't. I'm going to be late." She stepped back. "I'll try to see you later if I can." As she pulled away and headed for the door, he called to her.

"Can I get a goodbye kiss before you go?"

"No way," she answered, shaking her head and preparing to slip out the door. "I'll never leave here if I come back over there."

Josh laughed as the door closed behind her and then exhaled. Kissing Mia was like playing with fire, and they stoked the heat and flames higher, brighter, and faster each time. And each time, they came a little closer to being consumed.

CHAPTER
SIXTEEN

Josh

The days passed quickly now that Josh spent less time in bed.

It had felt like a prison reprieve when Dr. Shaw gave the go-ahead for him to start physical therapy. For two months, he'd been bound to a bed, his body wrecked, his spirit all but broken. But the hard work demanded by the exercises gave his mind something to latch onto and his body the needed release of the sexual tension that built up whenever he and Mia were together. He focused on rebuilding his strength and stamina, particularly in his upper body, knowing it would take more time for him to feel steady and strong on his feet.

From the articles and pictures published in the tabloids, one would believe Josh lived a capricious lifestyle, but actually, he was very focused and disciplined, and he believed in taking care of his body. He'd even begun enjoying his mornings with the physical therapists who tailored his workouts, adapting isometric and isotonic exercises so he could do them in a wheelchair. As an elite athlete for so long, Josh had been skeptical about working with the thin elastic bands in a wheelchair—until his sessions left him exhausted and sore. But he relished the soreness, as it let him know his body was responding to his efforts.

In the afternoons and early evenings, he communicated with his business advisors and team members, as Sydney was eighteen hours ahead of San Diego. Four o'clock on a Monday afternoon was eleven o'clock Tuesday morning there, so Josh had to be meticulous in scheduling calls with his advisors, sponsors, and business partners, who were not only in Sydney but around the world. His biggest sponsor, based in South Africa, was ten hours ahead, giving Josh a window between five and eight in the mornings for conference calls and meetings.

Also, in the evenings before her shift started or during her first break, Mia would come by; he'd watch television and play boring but supposedly mind-sharpening games on his phone while waiting. Sometimes, he'd feel tired enough to sleep a few hours. The nights were rare when he slept straight through without dreaming. However, Josh continued to refuse the medicines to help him sleep, fearing that the nightmares would take over once he fell into a deep sleep. Without the meds, he could feel the dreams coming on and could wake himself. He'd trained himself to recognize the feeling preceding the nightmares and learned to shut them down. With the pills, Dr. Cassidy and Dr. Shaw prescribed, Josh knew he would fall into a deep sleep and become trapped in his dreams. By how they made him feel, he worried he might die without waking up.

Cassidy asked him to meditate at least twice daily, telling Josh it would help him relax and refocus his attention, especially before bed. It would help him cope with the stress of falling asleep and replace his anxiety with a sense of calm, peace, and balance. Josh had given it a try. Since seeing Mia in the flesh and confirming he had not conjured her up, focusing his attention on her had become easy. He would replay conversations they'd had in his mind and think about things he wanted to ask her or tell her when she came back, and sometimes that would work. But after weeks of meeting with Dr. Cassidy every Tuesday and Thursday afternoon, Josh didn't feel they'd made much progress. The nightmares continued to plague him, forcing him awake, oxygen-starved and drenched in sweat, and he rarely went back to sleep, even if he'd only gotten in a couple of hours beforehand.

Robb Cassidy arrived one afternoon while Josh sat in his reclining chair, enjoying the warmth and dappled sunlight in the solarium. The attendant had parked him near the floor-to-ceiling windows overlooking the hospital courtyard. It was a beautiful view, Josh's favorite.

"Dude, look at you. No immobilizers? Now that's progress, if you ask me," Cassidy said, giving Josh a once-over.

"Yeah, it is. I've advanced to trying to get around on a cane. How are you?"

"Great. And busy. I like this spot. It's a nice, quiet spot to sit and talk and relax. Is it alright if we stay here, or would you like to go to your room, where we can talk freely?"

"This is fine," Josh said, looking around the big space. There were only a few other patients in the room. Cassidy pulled a chair over and sat down.

"I was wondering if we could discuss what's next for you. I hear you're progressing very well and likely to be discharged in a few weeks," he started, settling his tall, lean body in the chair.

"Yeah, well. They haven't said anything to me."

"Okay. Well, let's talk about your plans once you're discharged."

"I haven't made any solid plans yet. Sometimes, thinking about the future gives me headaches. I know one thing, though: life's given me a bunch of lemons, and I don't want to make lemonade."

"I understand. So, let's figure something out for when you're on your own after discharge. You've come a long way in a short time, but even after you're discharged, you won't be one hundred percent. Maybe not even fifty percent, compared to where you were before the accident."

"Yeah, I know. Dr. Shaw told me I'll need more physical therapy, and when I'm further along, I might want to consider more surgery on my leg."

"Okay, good. You understand that it might take time to feel comfortable out on the ocean, even after you're able to surf again."

"I don't understand. What do you mean?"

"Well, it's like falling off a horse the first time. There's always some trepidation about getting back on it."

"Okay. But I've been surfing almost all my life."

"This is your first shark attack?"

"Yes."

"And your friend was killed in the attack?"

"Yes."

"So, you might, and I only bring this up because of the possibility that it might happen, experience some anxiety about going back into the ocean."

"Hmmm. I don't know, Doc. I plan to compete in November if my leg is completely healed."

"Okay. So, do you have some idea where you'll do outpatient therapy? I understand your family was hoping you'd return to Australia."

"They are, but I'm not ready to go home, at least not yet. I've been looking at an advanced rehab clinic in Los Angeles. The Listerman Institute, I think it's called. A buddy of mine recommended it. He said professional athletes and Olympian hopefuls go there after an injury to get back their competitive form. I also talked to Dr. Shaw about it, and he says he can help speed up some of the transfer paperwork." Josh fumbled distractedly with a paperclip lying on the table between himself and Cassidy.

"Hypothetically, what if you can't compete again?"

"That is the million-dollar question. The answer is, I don't know. My life is tied up with surfing. The money I personally earn goes to support the team enterprise. Then some sponsors support our brand, like Walters Industries, which manufactures our wetsuits and other gear, and Harrier Manufacturing, which supplies our boards and wax—things like that. I have my own endorsements, a few other members have some, and the team has a few collective ones. We all promote things like surfing gear, breakfast cereals, sports drinks, soft drinks, and all kinds of stuff. We're especially big in Australia and Europe. I do promotional tours and shoot surf videos. Two years ago, I got a fifteen percent stake in a high-fashion line of beachwear and accessories by Ken Silver. I also have a twenty percent interest in a different company's fashion, sports, and leisure wear lines. They're all doing amazingly well, sold through upscale retail outlets and online. So, overall, surfing can be pretty lucrative. But for me, it's the challenge, you know? I love surfing, and I don't know what I would do if I had to give it up."

"I see. So, you could focus on building your business portfolio."

"I guess so. I mean, I could, but I don't know if I'd still want to."

"You lost a big chunk of leg muscle in that attack, which might very well affect your ability to compete in November or even next year."

"I try not to worry about that while I'm laying here. I do whatever they tell me to, so I'm in decent shape when I leave here, and then I'll train to be ready in November. Until then, I work the business side and take everything else one day at a time."

"That's a good plan."

"Yeah, and maybe if I have to retire, I'll become an eccentric and live the rest of my life on an island on the Barrier Reef. I can donate all of my money to philanthropic organizations—if there's anything left after these medical bills. This place is pretty pricey."

"Now that sounds idyllic, living off the grid on a tropical island. My wife and kids wouldn't like living like that for too long, and I don't imagine I would either, but an extended vacation there sounds nice."

Memories of living on the beach, sleeping in the sand alongside Sean and Colin, and learning to surf from Colin's uncle Charlie entered Josh's mind. Charlie Miele was an icon of surfing back in the day, but he'd hit rock bottom and became a beach bum, living in his van. Josh smiled. He was fifteen when he and Sean had run away from home and hooked up with Colin Mitchell and Charlie. His father had been furious, but those were some of the best times of Josh's life. Now, though, Josh was beyond sleeping in the sand and living like a beach bum. They had ended nearly a decade ago—when he'd won his first World Championship at eighteen, the youngest to ever win the title.

"Yeah, maybe a vacation, a couple of weeks, maybe. It might drive me crazy to live off the grid for more than a month. And I doubt my girl would be happy on a remote island for very long. She's an American, and she has a strong independent streak."

"And, there is that. I learned the hard way that a happy wife makes a happy life. Now, I say *'Yes, Dear,'* to whatever she's talking about." Cassidy laughed.

"I'll have to remember that," Josh said, laughing with the doctor. Josh had come to like the man. He was easy to talk to, and their sessions together often left Josh in a philosophical mood.

Cassidy looked at his watch and stretched out his long legs before standing. "What do you think about meeting here in the Solarium next time, Josh? It's pleasant out here."

"Yeah, I'm pretty sure we can. I'll have the aide bring me."

"Great. I hope you think about some of the things we discussed, and we can hash out some of your ideas next time if you like."

"Sounds good, Doc. Have a good day, okay?"

"Thanks, I will. See you on Thursday."

Josh remained in the atrium long after Dr. Cassidy left. He didn't want to consider a Plan B or a Plan C, but he understood the rationale behind Dr. Cassidy urging him to do so. Josh laughed aloud as he pictured Mia's reaction to giving up her career as a doctor and her dreams of a Fellowship to go live on a primitive little island off the coast of Australia. She'd be convinced he was crazy for even suggesting it, but it could be nice, just him and her, and maybe a kid or two…

Josh's humor subsided with that thought. He could easily envision them together, married, and having kids. Maybe not living on a deserted island but traveling and enjoying life. He had enough money to last them several lifetimes, the income from his trust and the accumulated dividends he'd received from Brenner Industrials since he was fifteen. He wasn't sure how Mia would feel about not having to work another day in her life. She was ambitious and driven, and she would likely reject a pampered life, as it wouldn't provide the outlet she needed to channel her energy and intellect. He understood. Surfing had been that important, challenging outlet he'd needed. It was why he understood how her career as a doctor gave her fulfillment. Being a wife and mother would add to the fulfillment of her life as a doctor, not replace it.

That evening, Josh was sitting up in bed when Mia stopped by for a visit. He gave her a bright and cheerful smile, reaching for her with his right hand instead of his left.

"Hey, they took your casts and braces off," she said, sliding her cool hand onto his warm palm and lacing her fingers with his.

"Yeah, and I feel like they've finally set me free," Josh answered, holding aloft their clasped hands. "No casts or immobilizers."

"Your leg, too?"

"Yeah, and it's terribly itchy, scaly, and peeling. I'm going to have an ugly scar."

"No, don't say that. It's going to be perfectly fine. A little nip here and there, and voilá, perfection. Let's celebrate. I brought your favorite." She lowered the roll-away tray table so that it rested above his lap. She pulled several little plastic containers from her coat pocket and set them out, ripping the lids off two.

"Gelatin shots," she crowed, handing him a plastic spoon. "Take your pick. I snagged orange and strawberry."

"Gelatin shots? With vodka or rum?" He picked up the orange cup and stared at it.

"Neither. Just plain old gelatin." She clinked the strawberry cup against his. "Cheers."

"How is plain old gelatin my favorite?" he whined.

"Don't be a sourpuss. We're celebrating." She dug into the cup of gelatin, scooping up a big spoonful, and he watched her put it in her mouth and savor it. He followed suit. It tasted orangey and jiggly and gel-like in his mouth. He would have spit it out if she hadn't been watching him. Instead, he swallowed it before it fully melted, doubting that rum or vodka could have improved the taste.

"So, now that you're out of the casts, it won't be long before you're toddling around on a cane, Mr. Brenner."

"No way, Dr. Thomas. I'll be in peak condition in a few months, and you'll be out in the crowd watching me conquer a twenty-five-foot wall of water as it rushes toward shore at breakneck speeds," he huffed in mock offense. "Biceps of steel." He showed off his bicep, and she smiled. It had atrophied a bit while in the cast.

"I'm sorry. You're right, and I apologize. Here's a peace offering." She giggled, lining up the remaining cups of gelatin on the table in front of him. "Two more oranges and one strawberry for later. I can't stay. I'm supposed to be doing rounds in the surgical ICU, but I wanted to see you, and I'm glad we had a chance to celebrate."

"Think you'll be back?"

"Hard to say. The ER is busy as usual." She smiled, tossing their trash away.

"Come here, please," he said, taking her hand and pulling her closer. "I need something from you."

"You do? What?" she asked naively, stepping closer to the bed. He took her hand and wove his fingers in between hers. She was so beautiful. She was a feast for sore eyes, even looking like she might jump out of her skin at any moment.

"I need to hold you with both arms and kiss you. The plaster and immobilizers are off, and I want to feel you in my arms. The waiting has almost driven me crazy. Can I?" Josh whispered, looking into her lovely hazel-colored eyes.

"Wait. What if… I mean…"

"No one's coming," he interrupted, pulling her closer until her face was only inches away. She remained closer, her eyes staring into his, and he leaned forward and kissed her. Sliding one hand into her hair and angling her so he could deepen the kiss, he deepened the kiss, demanding access to her mouth with his tongue, and she opened to him. Cradling her in his arms, he kissed her like a starving man, devouring her mouth. She whimpered, yielding to his hunger, and he grew harder and more needy beneath the blankets. It was deliciously painful to be this close to her, only able to kiss her when he desired so much more.

Pulling away, she staggered as if drunk on his kisses and touch, which made kissing her that much more satisfying for Josh. He could only imagine how deliciously gratifying it would be to make love to her. Watching her gain her feet and wits, he was mesmerized as her hair slowly slid from the pins and fell in a mass of waves, tangles, and thick spirals. Hairpins landed in his lap, and Josh gathered them up, grinning as she took off her glasses and hastily fixed her hair. He picked up her glasses and looked through them. The lenses were completely smudged from being pressed between their faces, and breathing hot vapor on them, he cleaned and polished them with his soft bedding. Mia blinked myopically at him as he carefully slid them on her face, making certain they were in place over her ears. He brushed his thumb over her reddened and swollen bottom lip.

"Look at me, Josh. My hair is a mess, and you took off all my lip gloss," she fussed at him, knowing it was as much her fault as his.

And he did look at her. At that moment, he thought she was the most beautiful, most sexy woman he'd ever seen.

"What if someone walked in while we were… making out like teenagers?"

He grinned even harder. He knew she never felt comfortable when he kissed her like that, but she always gave in, giving him everything.

"We're consenting adults, Doctor. At least I am, but I haven't seen your driver's license, have I? Still, I hope you are. Besides, Sam wouldn't let anyone barge in here while you're here."

"What…?" She sounded surprised.

"He won't let anyone come in here until after you leave."

"I…I never noticed that."

"No? Well, it's true. He knows we're in here making out like teenagers."

"What?" She turned to face him, horrified.

"He knows how I feel about you."

"How you feel about me…," she repeated. "He thinks we're in here making out?"

"I'm sure he suspects it and guards our privacy."

"You're kidding."

Josh watched Mia turn several deep shades of red, staring at him, eyes wide and a little fearful. "Why are you looking at me like that?" he asked, grinning.

"I can't look him in the eye anymore. How am I going to walk past him when he thinks…"

"Don't worry about what he thinks. I'm sorry for upsetting you. Please, come here."

"Uh-uh. He probably thinks I'm a… a…" she stuttered, unable to get the word out.

"He does not. Please come here," he asked softly. Mia narrowed her eyes and tilted her head, warning him not to try anything, then slipped her hands in his. "Jeez, woman. He's happy for us. That's why he guards the door and won't let anyone enter. He knows the nurses' and doctors' schedules and will let me know if anyone needs to see me. You'll have time to hide in the bathroom."

"I can't hide in the bathroom. I usually can't stay that long," she said in a near-panic.

"I want to hold you and kiss you again, Mia. I don't care who knows or sees us, but I promise we'll be more circumspect. Just know that once I'm out of here, nothing and no one will stop me from being with you openly and publicly. I can't wait to spoil you."

"I don't know, Josh. I'm… I guess I'm not good at being a celebrity girlfriend."

"Good. Continue being you. It's what drew me to you. And come all the way over here, please. I promise I won't bite this time," he said, pulling her closer.

"You're going to kiss me again?"

"Yes," he acknowledged, giving her his best disarming smile.

"Okay, just one. A quick one. I'm supposed to be doing rounds."

"Um, I don't know if one will be enough. And no quickies. We're never, ever going to have quickies."

Mia blushed. "Just one, Josh," she insisted, trying to look fierce, but she didn't back away. "What's gotten into you, Brenner?" She laughed this time, and it was music to his ears.

"You got to me, and I like it." He held her, nestling her against his chest.

"I think I might like it, too," she admitted. "Just one more, then I have to go," she said, raising up to kiss him.

"Okay, just one more," he bargained, knowing it would never be enough, and if it was left up to him, she would be late, *really, really late,* getting back to work.

CHAPTER
SEVENTEEN

Dr. Shaw knocked on the door before entering Josh's room, and Josh pressed the button to raise the head of his bed to a sitting position.

It was early afternoon, and he was resting, finished with his morning therapy sessions. He was not, however, tired enough to sleep.

"We should stop meeting like this every day," Josh teased.

"You think so, hmmm? How're you doing?" Dr. Shaw asked, taking the stethoscope from his pocket and coming over to examine Josh.

"Pretty good. How about you?"

"Couldn't be better. I've brought some good news," Shaw said, pressing the cold scope against Josh's chest.

"Hmm," Josh grunted. He knew the drill. To speed things along, Josh needed to be quiet and still while Dr. Shaw completed his exam, even if Shaw asked him a question, or it would take forever.

"I think you're about ready to get out of here; maybe the day after tomorrow?"

"Ohmigod, I am so ready. I like your luxury accommodations, but yes, I am ready to get out of here."

Dr. Shaw laughed with Josh. "Okay, well. I haven't received your OT and PT assessments yet, but I hear you've progressed beyond expectations. So once I have them in hand, which I expect to happen sometime tomorrow, I can recommend your discharge. You'll need physical therapy on an outpatient basis, and I want you to continue seeing Dr. Cassidy. He seems to be helping, yes?"

Josh shrugged. "I guess. I still have nightmares, but you already know this, don't you?"

"Yes, the nurses have to notate each episode in your chart, but hopefully, that can be resolved in time. Here's the number for Cassidy's office. You can call and set up a few outpatient sessions for next week. Anything else?"

"I've been researching Listerman's Rehabilitation Clinic in LA. I may have to work with another doctor up there."

"Ah, yes, thanks for reminding me. The Institute for Sports, Orthopedic, Rehabilitation, and Specialty Surgery of San Diego is just a few miles from here. They call it *SOARS* because it's quicker and easier to remember than the full name, but they provide in-patient and out-patient services. Check out their website; you can probably talk to someone on the phone. You can also ask your PT team about it. They should be pretty familiar with it. You can let me know which clinic you prefer, and I'll start the paperwork on this end. We'll shoot for Thursday. How does that sound?" Dr. Shaw stood, folded his scope, and stuffed it in the deep pocket of his lab coat.

"Sounds great. Thank you, Dr. Shaw. For everything." Josh extended his hand.

"I'm glad to see you walking out of here, Josh. You've come a long way," he said, shaking Josh's hand.

Josh let the head of the bed down and picked up his phone to check the time. It was still early in Sydney, but he quickly emailed Monica Ackroyd. She'd see the message first thing and find him a rental quicker than he could. Satisfied, Josh lay back and tried to relax. He was finally being discharged after three long months cooped up in this room, in this bed. The only bright spot in the last three months was meeting Mia. She would be so excited and relieved. They wouldn't have to hide anymore, and she wouldn't have to worry about her colleagues catching her coming and going from his room. He couldn't wait to tell her the great news and considered texting her, but decided to wait until she came by that evening. He wanted to share the news face-to-face.

Josh prepared for his final session with Dr. Cassidy the next afternoon. Now that this hospital stay was coming to an end, he was anxious to discuss the progress Cassidy thought they'd made. As far as Josh was concerned, their sessions had not progressed beyond Cassidy's irrelevant questions and Josh's rambling answers about his family, childhood, close friends and associates, surfing, and the business side of his surfing brand. Josh hadn't figured out what his future might look like, and therefore, he didn't have a plan B or C if plan A fell through. Josh was, or at least he had been, meticulous about the things he put into his body—from the food he ate, which had to be organic, pesticide- and preservative-free, and minimally processed, even when he was traveling, to refusing most kinds of drugs. He'd seen the damage an addiction to prescription drugs, like painkillers, could do to a surfer's career. Surfers put a lot of stress on their bodies, and injuries were common. Frequent visits to an emergency room could net a surfer any number of codeine and morphine derivatives prescriptions, yet Cassidy's best option had been sleeping pills.

To his credit, Cassidy had suggested Josh try meditation and hypnosis to help him cope and eventually overcome his PTSD diagnosis. He'd also tried to temper Josh's expectations after leaving the hospital, wanting him to consider he might not be ready or able to compete—both physically and mentally—again. But Josh knew if he had accepted that line of reasoning, failure would be all but assured.

Josh still could not talk about the intense and irrational fear he experienced during his nightmares or the events leading up to or immediately after the shark attack. He hadn't fully processed Colin's death. Though he'd heard the facts from Sean and read the little information published in the news and on social media, Colin's death still felt surreal. Josh had difficulty wrapping his head around any and all of it. This meant, in his estimation, the counseling had been ineffectual, and he had no intention of continuing it after leaving the hospital. He hadn't admitted as much to Dr. Shaw, but rather, he'd kept his own counsel.

Josh felt once he left the hospital, the dreams would stop. Getting back on the ocean and finding his Zen again could be all the therapy he needed. Ever since he was a teen, he'd surfed up and down Australia's Sunshine Coast, infamous for the sharks that inhabit those waters, and he'd never even seen a shark close-up before. What were the odds of being struck by lightning twice?

Josh didn't expect much from the final session with Cassidy to change his mind, so he decided to spend the hour before they met with a catnap. As he settled comfortably against the pillows, his phone buzzed, and a picture of Sean and the notification that it was a video chat came up on the screen.

"Dude, can you hear me fine?" Sean asked, a big grin on his face.

"Yeah, I can hear you just fine, Dude. How are you? I was planning to call you later."

"Yeah? I've been up a while. And you know what they say, *'Great minds think alike.'* How're you coming along?"

"Doing great. I'm being discharged in a couple of days."

"Great! Your pop and Ian know? You coming home?"

"No, they don't know yet, and no, I'm not coming home. The doctor just left, and he thinks I'll need a lot more therapy, so I'll be staying here a while longer."

"What? You're staying in the States?"

"Yeah. I'll do some therapy here while I figure out what's next."

"Okay, but why aren't you coming home? But hey, wait. A question for you. Have you met the beautiful Dr. Thomas yet? She's the one from the beach."

"Oh yeah, I've met her. She's going to be my future wife."

"Yeah? Seriously?"

"Yeah, seriously. And I'm also going to compete in November. Can't do Huntington, though. It's in three weeks. Too soon, but I'm thinking I should be able to do the Master's in November."

"Wait, wait. You think you'll be ready in, what, three months?"

"I'm going for it."

"Wow. Well… okay. That'll be awesome. I've got about two weeks free before the meet in Huntington Beach, and I thought I'd come and hang out with you, then rent a car and drive up there. If you're out of the hospital, maybe you can come with me and hang out with everybody. Most of the team will be there."

"Sounds great. Monica's finding a place for me. When she does, I'll send you the address. You can stay with me."

"Really glad you're better, man. Can't wait to see you."

He and Sean talked for a while, catching up, until it was time for Josh to meet with Dr. Cassidy. Josh sat up, raising the bed until he could stand with no trouble and moved to his recliner. He'd only made himself comfortable when Cassidy knocked and then entered the room.

It was still dark when Josh woke up with a start. His eyes scanned his room and settled on Mia curled up in his recliner. She appeared fast asleep, softly snoring. Josh felt disoriented, wondering when she'd come in and how long he'd been asleep. He reached for the pitcher of water beside the bed and the cup. The water was still cold, ice floating in the pitcher, and he emptied the first cup and poured another. He'd felt a nightmare coming on, and he'd awakened himself. He was glad he did, as he might have missed her visit if he'd slept much longer. He noticed her breathing had changed; her soft snores had stopped.

"It's rude to watch people sleep," she mumbled, unfurling her body in the chair and stretching.

"I enjoy watching you sleep."

"What time is it?" she asked, standing and arching her back, rubbing the base of her spine.

"A little after five. The sun will be up soon," he said, looking at his phone.

"Shit." She rolled her neck. "I only sat down for a minute and was out like a light. I got off shift this morning at three-thirty."

"Bad shift?"

"The usual."

"Come over here with me; there's room," he said, moving over and patting the bed."

Mia shook her head but was smiling as she reached into her bag for some gum.

"I want to hear what happened that was the best part of your day and then the worst."

"No, Josh. My day is nothing special."

"That can't be true, so humor me. I'll start." She climbed up on the bed and squeezed in beside him. He pulled her into his embrace and started. "The worst part of my day—any day—is waking up and realizing I can't go out on the water. I used to go out almost every day, spending hours on my board, feeling the water rock me as it swells, as a huge wave twenty, maybe twenty-five feet, forms up. You can tell if it's going to be a big one. You can feel the difference. Then, I'd paddle as hard and fast as possible to catch it. You can't imagine the feeling, the adrenaline rush that takes over as you ride that monster as it barrels toward the shore. It feels like catching the wind, like flying. Then I woke up. It's hard to think that those days might be over."

"And the best?" Mia asked, rubbing his chest, tangling her fingers in the hair there.

"Seeing you. I practically live to see you." Josh took her fingers, brought them to his lips, and kissed the tips. "Now, your turn."

"Every day is different, but the worst part of last night was telling a woman and her adult children that the man she'd married and lived with, raised a family with, for over forty years, was gone. He'd had a massive heart attack, and we couldn't resuscitate him. She was heartbroken. The family was heartbroken. It's hard to comfort the family when their loved one dies."

"Tell me the best part?"

Mia snuggled closer, blinking back tears that pricked her eyes and threatened to spill. "Right now, the best part is being with you like this."

"Well, Doctor," he said, kissing her gently on the lips and the sensitive skin beneath her ear. "Have I got news for you.

PART 11

CHAPTER EIGHTEEN

Josh

Josh stared out of the hospital window at the beautiful panorama.

It was still early, but the sun was laser-bright in the clear azure sky. There wasn't a single cloud as far as he could see, and the hospital grounds stretched into the distance, a sea of greenery bisected by white walkways and vibrantly colorful flowerbeds. He could see people hurrying in all directions. Beyond the tops and through the gaps between buildings, Josh could see the deep blue color of the ocean. He was mildly surprised. He didn't know the hospital was close to the ocean. However, it made sense. Ambulance drivers usually took patients to the nearest hospital, and ninety-four days and who knew how many hours or minutes ago, he'd been brought here in critical condition by ambulance. Though he didn't remember any of it, he smiled. Today, twelve weeks later, he was leaving under his own power.

Josh felt humbled. He owed much to the hospital staff, who'd done all they could to make his recovery successful, but he owed even more to Mia, including a completely new jogging outfit. Without hesitation, she'd ripped her windbreaker jacket into strips, using part as a tourniquet and stop the bleeding, another part as a splint to hold the gaping wound and broken bones in his leg together, and the rest as bandages to keep sand and debris from further infecting his injuries. From what he'd heard, he'd destroyed her clothes, bleeding on her and soaking the sand around them as she worked to save him. Because of her quick thinking and selflessness, he'd survived long enough to make it to the hospital.

Josh turned away from the window, knowing he would make that, and so much more, up to her. She deserved it, and it would make him happy to provide it. He looked around the bare hospital room. Everything of his that had begun accumulating over the months had been cleared out. This morning, he'd awakened early, showered, and dressed in regular clothes. He'd shopped online for the dark gray linen slacks and a collarless dove gray linen shirt. The store delivered them on hangers, impeccably steamed and pressed, along with briefs, a belt, black canvas slip-ons, and a pair of polished, gunmetal Ray-Bans. Fully dressed, he relished the feel of real clothes against his skin, glad to be done with the rough, homespun cotton hospital gowns and the rough-dried sweatpants and tee shirts he'd worn for therapy. Having arrived at the hospital in what was left of a torn and tattered neoprene wetsuit, Josh gladly paid for the premium service.

When Carlos, his PCA, arrived, he was surprised to see Josh up and ready to leave.

"Mr. Brenner. You know it's hospital policy for us to be in the room with you when you shower. Why didn't you use the call button?"

"I am leaving today, Carlos. I'll be at home, showering and dressing myself from now on. Better to start doing things for myself now rather than later. I didn't slip, trip, or fall."

"Well, that's good. Are you finished packing?"

"Not much to take with me." Josh scooped up a leather case from the tray table and tucked it under one arm. Inside were his phone and laptop. "I'm ready if you are."

"Wait, you can't just leave, Mr. Brenner. You have to wait for transport."

"Transport?"

"Yes. You have to be transported downstairs. Hospital policy."

"You're not serious, are you?"

"Yessir. Someone will come up and take you downstairs in a wheelchair…"

"Absolutely not."

"I'm sorry?"

"You're here, and I'm dressed and ready to leave; why can't you and I just go downstairs?" Josh stared at the young man and saw stark confusion on his face. He grunted disparagingly. Obviously, no one had ever refused transportation to the front door before.

"More hospital policy?"

"Yessir. I'm sure it won't take but a few minutes. Do you have your discharge papers?"

"No, I don't have any papers."

"Whoever comes up from Transport will take you to the business office first, then to your ride."

Disgruntled, Josh pulled the chair that Mia normally sat in over to the window and sat down. He inhaled and exhaled deeply to calm himself, mindful that this was no luxury hotel where he could express check out and leave when he was ready. Besides, Carlos had a point, or at least the hospital did, in that Josh had never walked from his room to the front lobby before. He knew the elevators were down the hall and around the corner, but he wasn't sure how far it was or how long it took to get to the front lobby. He sat and brooded while Carlos double-checked the room for anything Josh may have missed. Finally, Sam entered the room, followed by a woman pushing a wheelchair.

"Hello, Mr. Brenner. I'm Millestine from transport, and I'm here to take you downstairs."

Josh looked from Sam, who was grinning, to the petite Black woman at least half his height, a third his weight, and undoubtedly twice his age. She wore a shocking pink uniform similar to the nurses' scrubs and a white cardigan sweater, her badge dangling from a blue lanyard around her neck. Nope, he thought to himself. *No way was he going to let this little old lady push him in a wheelchair.* He glared at Carlos.

"Hey, Millie," Carlos said after giving her a big hug. "Mr. Brenner doesn't like wheelchairs. He wants to walk down."

A furrow deepened in the woman's forehead as she scrutinized Josh. "Nope," she said after a few seconds. "It's hospital policy that you ride in this here chair, Mr. Brenner," she said, tapping the back of the wheelchair. "Can't have you stumbling and tripping, or you'll be right back in here. Besides, it's a quick ride. Okay?"

"How will I know if I can walk that far if I don't get the chance? Maybe I could walk behind the chair, holding on?" Josh suggested. But Millie shook her head, making her steel-gray curls bounce around wildly.

"Nope, that's my job. I walk behind the chair, and you sit and ride."

"Hospital policy?" Josh asked with barely disguised sarcasm.

"Hospital policy."

Resigned, Josh sat down in the chair, tucking his feet on the little stirrups, his electronics case on his lap and his cane between his knees. Carlos held the door for Millie to maneuver the wheelchair into the corridor and waved goodbye as they proceeded to the elevator. Sam, a silly grin on his face, followed them. As Millie pushed him in the wheelchair down the hall, Josh reevaluated his opinion of her. She seemed much stronger and had more vigor than he'd given her credit for. She maneuvered the wheelchair in and out of the pedestrian traffic while rolling it at a fair clip, nodding and greeting people as they passed. Millie must have said *Good morning... Hello... Have a good day* a hundred times by the time they reached the lobby, and though he would never have admitted it aloud, even under duress, the ride had been pretty fun.

As Carlos had predicted, Millie took Josh to the business office first, a clear glass office cubicle marked Billing and rolled him up to a woman seated behind the desk. It didn't take long for him to settle his bill, and when he was done, Millie pushed him out of the office and back to the lobby.

"Do you have a ride waiting, Mr. Brenner?" she asked as they neared the lobby doors.

"Yes, but I'm not sure she's here yet. She hasn't texted me yet."

"We can wait in here until she comes, or we can wait outside if you like. It's a little warm out, but it's nice. We have a little sitting area that's shaded and cooler right outside these doors."

"Okay, let's go outside."

Millie pushed him through the automatic doors and swerved around the north corner of the building to a cobblestone piazza with colorfully painted picnic tables, benches, and toadstool chairs and tables. Tall trees, lush landscaping, and flower beds filled with profuse and vibrant blooms completed the welcoming setting. Millie parked him near a vacant bench, and Josh slid from the wheelchair to sit on it. Sam took a seat on a toadstool across from him.

"You can leave me here, Millie. Sam won't let anything happen to me."

Millie tilted her head towards Sam, giving him a thorough once-over. Sam read her expression and grinned at her. "I'm actually his bodyguard, Miss Millie."

"Bodyguard, huh? Well, I guess it'll be okay, then."

"Thank you, Miss Millie. It has been a pleasure meeting you," Josh said, patting the hand still gripping the handles of his wheelchair. "Our ride home should be here in a few moments."

"Good meeting you too, Mr. Brenner." She returned the gentle pat on his shoulder. "You be safe and take care of yourself. No more shenanigans that'll land you right back here. And you," she said, squinting at Sam, "If you're his bodyguard, then you'd better do a better job watching out for him, okay?"

Sam laughed. "I'm on it, Miss Millie."

She waved and left, deftly pushing the empty chair around the clusters of people gathered in front of the hospital.

"I can't believe I'm out of there," Josh crowed.

"That was a long stretch. A juicy job for me, though," Sam said, laughing. "All I had to do was keep a bunch of staff from peeking in on you. Most of them acted like teenagers at a boy band concert."

"Well, good job then, Sam." Josh burst into chuckles. "But right now, it seems like your job is about to get a little more difficult if that woman stalking towards us is what I think she is."

"What? Where? Who…?" Sam stammered, jumping off the toadstool and looking around. Seeing the woman, he sneered. "A fucking reporter. Maybe we better get inside until Mia comes. At least there, they can't get to you."

"Yeah, maybe you're right. Let me call Mia and have her meet us at a different door. Something tells me we'll be mobbed by reporters before she arrives." With Sam's help, Josh stood and returned to the hospital lobby, ignoring the reporter as she stalked them.

The private road wound around the side of the bluff before circling behind a three-story mass of dark, weathered wood and glass. It was a contemporary home designed to look old and part of its environment. Only when Mia swerved the truck onto the private road that offered a better view of the house were they able to see the sharp angles of the building and the storied rooflines, towering plate-glass windows, and several tiered balconies. The front entrance was on the leeward side of the building, surrounded by verdant landscaping and short, fat palm trees. The windward side faced the ocean, a perfect scenic view of the golden-sand beach and endless ocean. Mia felt her jaw drop as she parked in the driveway.

"Wow. This place is incredible."

"Monica doesn't mind spending my money."

"I can tell."

Sam hopped out of the back seat on the driver's side and held the door for Mia. She put the key fob in his outstretched hand and joined Josh on the wide landing leading up to the door.

"She has super-nice taste," Mia whispered, taking in the amazing space and sumptuous contemporary furnishings. The interior could have been featured in *Luxe Homes or Architectural Digest.* Josh strode to a credenza directly across from the front doors and picked up a large envelope with his name scrawled across the front. Mia followed him inside, leaning forward as she tried to see through the soaring glass windows. Wow, she thought, this is how he lives? She'd had no idea this was what he'd meant when he told her he was renting "a comfy bungalow by the beach." She knew the residences along this stretch of the beach sold for millions, as coastal properties were some of the most expensive real estate in the state. As such, she'd never had the pleasure of visiting one, nor had she ever expected to be invited to hang out in one.

"This is the main floor, the main entertaining space, with a gourmet kitchen and open concept dining room, living room, and lounge. There's only one bedroom suite down here, but there are five more upstairs, each with its own ensuite," Josh said, reading aloud from a brochure and breaking her trance. "Let's see," he continued, walking further into the room.

"This place has a five-bay garage with a Jeep Rubicon, two ATVs, and two jet skis inside for our use. Coming off the garage is the mudroom and laundry. There's an exercise room with a steam sauna somewhere off the kitchen and a fully functional office off the living room. We can check those out later. On the next floor up," he said, laughing at her open-mouth reaction, "are four more bedroom suites. Here, you can look this over. I doubt I'll be upstairs much. We're taking the downstairs bedroom." He handed her the brochure to read and get a feel for the property.

"What? A movie theater on the top floor? And outside those doors," she said, gesturing to her right, "there's an infinity pool and spa off the veranda. It's fully furnished with comfortable outdoor furniture, a full-sized outdoor kitchen, and a fireplace." She gasped. "Come on, I've got to see that," she said, pulling him towards the back wall almost completely made of glass. Josh complied. Grabbing a slim bar along the side of a window, he slid four windowed panels to the side in a neat stack. Mia grinned happily and stepped outside.

So, this is how the rich and famous live? She thought as she bit her lip to keep her jaw from unhinging; it had dropped so many times already. She could hardly believe this was where Josh would live for the next few months. It was so beyond anything she could have imagined, and she also imagined it cost a fortune to rent.

"Look there. I think you'll love watching the breathtaking sunsets from here."

"And the ocean, Josh. You could sit out here all night, watch the stars, and listen to the ocean."

"We. I want to sit out here, watch the stars, and listen to the ocean with you."

"I'd love to come hang out with you sometimes. You know something? I think my apartment could fit inside that main room at least two-and-a-half times."

"Come on. Let's eat. I'm starved as I skipped the hospital breakfast, and Virginia has lunch ready for us."

"Who?"

"Virginia. She came in from Sydney. She's been with my family for a very long time. She's prepared lunch for us. Afterward, if you want, we can explore the rest of the house."

"Wait, she's like your chef?"

"Yeah, sort of. She supervises the cooks at my father's home. Dee cooks for me at my house."

"Wow. Who knew you were so pampered, Mr. Brenner. Come on, then. I can't wait to have lunch cooked by a private chef. I wish I'd known about your pool. I would have brought my swimsuit, and we could've taken a dip in it," Mia added. "It's beautiful out here."

"Don't worry. I can't wait to see you in a bikini."

After lunch and a quick tour of the house, Mia swam in the pool for several laps, then settled on the daybed next to Josh. They'd opened a bottle of champagne and talked for a while, lulled into a sleepy state by the champagne and the susurration of the ocean as it lapped against the shore. Mia fitted herself along Josh's warm body and closed her eyes. As the sun began to set, the breeze blowing in off the ocean turned cool, and she snuggled closer to Josh, seeking his body heat, waking him from a light doze. Josh felt her shiver, and he got up, pulling her up off the divan with him.

"Come on, Babe. Let's go inside. I'm sure the bed is even more comfortable, and I'll warm you up."

As they entered the main-floor master from the veranda, Josh walked Mia backward, his arms tight around her, his mouth taking full advantage of hers. As they entered the room, the back of her legs bumping against the edge of the mattress, Josh broke the kiss and let her topple back onto the bed. She laughed happily.

"I came prepared, you know, just in case," he said, walking to the big, upholstered chair where he'd tossed his clothes when he'd changed into trunks and reached into his pants pocket.

"I was never a Boy Scout, but they have a great credo—Always be prepared." He came back to the bed and began stripping off his trunks.

Mia rolled onto her stomach and watched him. She raised up on her elbows to see what he'd tossed onto the bedside table and saw the square foil packets. She watched him roll his damp swim trunks down, kick them to the floor, and unwrap a condom. Climbing onto the bed, he rolled her onto her back and straddled her hips, hovering just above her. His gaze roamed over her body, scantily clad in the bikini. He took in the smooth, unblemished skin, full breasts, and soft, womanly curves.

"Mia," he uttered breathlessly, inhaling the scent of her perfume warmed by her body's heat. "Do you know how often I've dreamed of being with you like this? To see your body without the scrubs, to touch your skin, and kiss you like this?"

"I know, Josh. I've dreamed of you just as often," she breathed.

"You are so beautiful. Let me help you take this suit off." He pulled the strings that held it up, and she raised her hips off the bed so he could remove it and toss it on the floor with his trunks.

A low growl escaped his throat as he ran his hands over her skin, and he crawled down her body, trailing worshipful kisses as he went, making her moan and squirm and reach for him. He kissed and licked and grazed her skin lightly with his teeth, making her shiver under his worshipful ministrations. His hands cupped her breasts, and her nipples pebbled under his attention, suckling one and rubbing the other between his thumb and forefinger before switching.

"Now, Josh," she pleaded, her voice deep and throaty. "Now. Please."

Balancing himself over her, he slid one hand to cradle her head and the other under the small of her back, lowering his face to inches above hers. He looked into her eyes, darkened with her desire, and lowered his mouth to hers. Her lips were soft, her mouth sweet from the wine, and he kissed her with worshipful, soul-searing tenderness. Hearing her ragged breath and feeling her heart pounding, he pressed a knee between hers and positioned himself between her thighs. She opened for him, and he nudged her legs up. She encircled his waist, locking her heels in the dip of his back. He aligned himself and slid slowly, deep into her body.

Josh was all hard maleness, his body lean and firm, and he was driving her crazy with his slow exploration of her body. He had long ago ignited a passion, a raging fire within her, and she felt on the edge of delirium by the time she felt him slide deep inside her. Once fully seated, they quickly fell into a primal rhythm that demanded everything from them. They could no more hold anything back than they could stop breathing. Josh thrust into her with long, deep strokes, and she arched up to meet him, both taking and giving in turn. She held him, kissing, licking, and sucking the skin of his throat, shoulders, and arms; every inch of skin she could reach and rode with him over the edge of reason. Mia exalted as she felt him swell, thickening and lengthening until she felt impaled. He was close, but she was ready, and looking into his beautiful face, the blue of his eyes so dark, almost navy, as they stared into hers, she let go, her mouth opened in an O, her body straining against his.

"Christ, Mia," he growled in her hair, one arm cradling her head, the other gripping her hip to keep her from moving. "You feel incredible. So good, so good," he echoed, moving slowly at first, grinding his pelvis against hers. He covered her mouth with his, slipping his tongue inside and tangling with hers as he thrust harder, picking up his pace.

She could feel him pulsating, and she held him, squeezed him between her thighs, her legs still wrapped tight around him. She no longer cared about the sounds that ripped from her throat or his deep, gritty growl that rose and reverberated against her breast as she felt him grip her tightly and his climax slammed into her.

CHAPTER NINETEEN

Mia

Bright sunshine and the screech and cawing of birds scavenging their breakfast in the sand and surf outside the bedroom window filtered into the darkened bedroom, pushing aside the faint shadows and quiet.

Mia opened one eye and ran her hand to the edge of the bed. It was cool and empty, confirming Josh's absence. She stretched languidly, feeling slightly tender throughout her body, before returning to the fetal position she favored in sleep. She snuggled deeper into the cloud-soft mattress and sumptuous bedding that was a far cry from the discount department store brands she was used to. She lay with the covers pulled tight beneath her chin and let her thoughts drift back to the most fantastic night she'd ever spent with someone.

She didn't know when they'd finally fallen asleep, but Josh couldn't have gotten much rest if he was already up and about. He'd been everything she'd ever dreamed of—attentive, tender, patient, insistent, and insatiable. His hunger for her had intensified from weeks of restraint, heated kisses, but chaste contact. Last night, Josh had made good on his promises, and she'd been caught up in the raging storm of his desire. Just thinking about it, remembering, made her crave his touch again and relive the excitement and wild passion.

Instead, she rolled out of bed, her body stiff and sore, her stomach rumbling. She took a quick shower and dressed in the white denim short-shorts, coral tee, and white thong sandals she'd packed in an overnight bag. She attacked her hair, bringing it under control and securing it in a low ponytail. Josh had plugged her phone into the charger and left it on the bedside table for her to find, and she picked it up. There'd been no calls or texts. She was surprised to find it was late in the afternoon and that Josh had let her sleep. Wondering where he was, she left the bedroom and followed her nose, which led her to a large kitchen, a gourmet cook's dream. Josh was seated at the island, talking to Virginia, with a large mug of coffee and a plate of fruit in front of him. Virginia saw her first and smiled.

"Good morning, Doctor. I hope you slept well. Come, have something to eat."

"Thank you, and yes, I slept very well."

"I can fix you some breakfast, eggs, bacon or sausage… waffles or pancakes… whatever you'd like. Coffee? Juice?"

"Coffee, please, but I'll have what he's having," she said, climbing onto a stool to sit next to Josh.

"He's already had breakfast. This is a snack," Virginia replied, smiling at Josh. "It's no bother. Let me fix you something."

"Okay. I like my eggs over easy, and one of those pastries over there will do," Mia said, pointing to a basket of fresh pastries. "No need to fix waffles or pancakes."

"I set the table on the veranda, under a nice umbrella, if you'd like to sit outside. I'll have everything ready and bring it out to you."

"I don't want you to go to any trouble just for me," Mia protested.

"No trouble at all. Shoo, shoo. Have your coffee outside. It's a beautiful day."

Josh grinned. Used to Virginia's bossiness, he picked up his plate and coffee cup, ushering Mia through the cantina doors onto the veranda. Virginia followed with a tray of coffee, a cup and plate for Mia, and a basket of pastries. She served Mia, replenished Josh's coffee, and returned to the kitchen.

"Hello, sleepyhead," Josh said, wrapping his arms around Mia and kissing her. "How do you feel?"

"Wonderful. This is like a mini vacation."

"Good. Virginia was right. It is a beautiful day. Would you like to walk on the beach after lunch?"

"That would be great. I think I'll need to walk a few miles, and often, if Virginia cooks big breakfasts on the regular. I don't cook much. It's too much effort to cook for myself. Ohmigod, this is delicious," she said, savoring the hot coffee.

"I think Virginia's going to enjoy spoiling you."

Mia had barely finished her coffee when Virginia brought out a mountain of food covered in shiny, stainless-steel, insulated domes. Mia watched, astounded at the amount and assortment of dishes she set in front of them. There was more food than she and Josh together could eat all day, and far too much for just one person.

"This is too much, Josh. I can't eat all of this."

"I'll eat a little. It's only my third breakfast, and I can keep you company."

"Third breakfast. How long have you been up?"

"I get up with the sun, Madam," Josh said, grinning as he handed Mia a warm plate and removed the dome covers. "I've had coffee, a couple of pastries, and some fruit to hold me over. I wanted to have breakfast when you woke up."

"You should have wakened me."

"No way. You need your sleep. But eat up. I want you to keep up your strength. Can't have you wimping out on me." He laughed, gesturing with his fork.

"Wimping out? We both fell asleep."

"You did. But I have an excuse—if I ever needed one, because I'm still recovering. In a couple of weeks, I'll be back in shape."

"Please, take as long as you need. I'm eager to see you at your best."

"Oh, you will, Doctor Thomas, and that's a promise. You know how *hard* I try to keep my promises."

Mia laughed as she watched him smirking across from her. It was her first time seeing him so happy and relaxed. He lounged comfortably in his seat, the vivid green, blue, orange, and yellow colors fighting for dominance on his baggy board shorts he'd paired with a plain white t-shirt and thong sandals. She noticed the rough, reddened, and puckered scarring on his leg, the missing muscle and tissue giving the leg a much thinner, distorted silhouette, and wondered if their activities had done any harm. But Josh didn't appear to be suffering any pain or discomfort anywhere.

"What?" he asked, seeing her give him a quick perusal.

"You."

"Me, what?" His eyes lit up, and a silly smirk spread across his face.

"Well, for one, I love your fashion sense."

"These pants are *fire,* aren't they?" he asked, looking down. "Can't miss me when I'm out on the water. Wow. Look. Here's a tiny bit of the color of your shirt. See? We match."

"Yeah, but I think we would've matched somewhere, no matter what I wore."

"That's because we're good together, even when we don't try to be," he said, tipping his glass to her.

"Who knew you had such a big ego?"

"*You* knew how big my *ego* was." He tilted his head and stared into her eyes, his brows moving up and down rapidly. Mia paused, her fork halfway to her mouth and stared back. She couldn't help but blush.

"You are cruising for a bruising, Mister," she threatened.

"You don't know the half of it, Babe."

After brunch, they went for a stroll along the beach. Being with Josh, away from the hospital, was nice, and Mia had to admit she also felt relaxed and well-rested.

"Thank you, Josh, for inviting me to hang out here with you," she said, squeezing his hand.

"No, thank you. I'm glad you agreed to stay with me."

"It feels surreal, you know? I've pinched myself at least twice already to make sure I'm not dreaming. My arm ought to be black and blue by now."

"Well, stop abusing your arm. You're not dreaming unless I'm dreaming, too. Then we're both dreaming, and two people can't dream the same dream at the same time, yeah?"

"Stop, you're so silly. Anyway, when I checked out your social media…"

"You checked me out on social media?" He grinned.

"A little. Just Instagram." She lowered her eyes and her voice. "And Facebook, and… maybe a few others."

"So, what did you discover that you didn't already know?"

"This was before I knew anything about you. When I found out who you were. Anyway, that was how I learned you've traveled all over the world, lived in the most luxurious homes and hotels, you party on gorgeous yachts, and you're just an average international celebrity and the world's most eligible bachelor. It's surreal that I'm here with you."

"Hmmm. Don't believe the hype, Babe. It's good to know that the ton of money I pay to my PR people is effective, but I'm just a hard-working surfer. I surf six or seven days a week and train eight to ten hours a day every day except when I compete, which is at least three or four times a month because I'm on two different circuits—the U.S. and the World circuits. Coming here was the first vacation Sean, Colin, and I had taken in years, and it was the longest time we'd ever been off the grid. We had ten whole days to relax and free-surf and get ready for the summer finals in Venice Beach. I missed them, of course, as they were last month, but Sean was there. And, as they say, the rest is history."

Josh stared out at the ocean, seemingly a million miles away, and Mia remained silent, giving him the time and space to come to terms with whatever he was thinking about. "How long have you lived here in San Diego?" he asked after several long moments, turning his attention back to her. "I've surfed in a few competitions held here, but I've never stayed long enough to visit the city."

"I've lived here four years, but I am a native Californian. My best friend Chelsea and I moved here from the Bay Area a few years ago. I love it here. You have to remind me to introduce you to Chelsea. She comes from a crazy rich Asian family, but she's my girl."

"Okay, and you can show me around, take me to some of your favorite places, and we can do things you like to do."

"I'll give you the whole VIP tour.

CHAPTER TWENTY

Mia pulled off the hazard gown she wore over her scrubs and the nitrile gloves and balled them up.

She shoved the entire bundle in the medical trash bin before scrubbing down and leaving the acute trauma area. She was tired and a bit wired from innumerable cups of coffee and exhausted, having come in three hours before the start of her regular shift. She'd done it to help take care of the crush of patients rushed in by ambulance after a busload of tourists on their way back from a day trip to Tijuana was involved in a crash on the freeway. Some suffered minimal injuries, including bumps, bruises, and lacerations, but most had bone fractures, several requiring emergency surgery. The influx of patients caused a major backup in the normal flow of the emergency room, and everyone in Mia's cohort had been called in.

A headache was starting to bloom behind her eyes, which also felt dry and gritty. She couldn't complain, however — it was her own fault. She'd spent her entire weekend off doing all sorts of fun things with Josh and getting little sleep when they finally crawled into bed.

She'd had a great time showing Josh around. Thursday night, she'd taken him to a craft beer 'tasting' at a local brewery and stayed to listen to live music. On Friday afternoon, they visited an exhibition of restored classic cars. Mia could tell he thoroughly enjoyed himself as he'd spent hours talking specs with the owners, getting up close and personal with the engines and custom paint jobs on dozens of classic American muscle cars, lowriders, and preserved vintage vehicles. She'd enjoyed the outing because he'd had so much fun.

Saturday afternoon, they'd stopped by a food festival in one of the city's oldest historic districts. The street fare was a mix of culturally diverse cuisines, and Mia had learned, to her horror, that Josh had adventurous tastes, having traveled around the world. She learned he would taste anything at least once, including fried crickets and other bugs. Somewhat appalled, more often than not, she left him standing in front of food booths sampling foodstuffs she had no intention of putting in her mouth, and instead, she would wander away to browse the beautiful handmade jewelry and accessories.

Mia had been concerned for a moment that, after months of bland hospital food, Josh needed to take it easy on all the culinary delights, but it appeared he had a cast-iron stomach as nothing seemed to bother him. Sunday morning, they'd slept in, missing a perfect sunrise and the start of the North Shore Regatta, the festive annual eight-hour parade of rowboats, yachts, and other seaworthy vessels that sailed from the northernmost point of the county, Lash Harbor, down to Coronado Island. They'd lazed about the rest of the afternoon until Mia needed to leave. She'd planned to take a short nap before going to work, but the call had come asking her to clock in ASAP.

Now, glad to be off the clock, Mia headed to the locker room to get her belongings. She was going straight home instead of to Josh's place and planned to sleep the entire day. She'd called Josh to let him know, and despite his wheedling to come sleep in his bed, she remained firm. She now understood the saying 'burning one's candle on both ends and looked forward to Me-Time—chilling out, popping a frozen entree in the microwave for dinner, turning on the TV, and burrowing under the bed covers.

Coming off the elevator of her apartment building, she decided to stop and check on Chelsea. She hadn't talked to her BFF but once all weekend, and that was a quick call to let Chelsea know she was staying over at Josh's. She hadn't wanted her worrying and looking for her. Mia knocked on her friend's door, but when she didn't get an answer, she unlocked the door with the extra key. Mia didn't go into Chelsea's apartment often with her key, but she considered this a well-being check. Mia stepped inside the apartment and called out. She could hear Chelsea's blow-dryer shut off, and her friend came running out of her bedroom, swallowed up in a terry-cloth robe and the front half of her hair still wet.

After giving Mia an enthusiastic hug, she asked, "Do I need to ask how things are going between you and Super Hunk?"

"No. But I had a good time."

Chelsea grabbed Mia's hands and danced about in her excitement. "Good? Just good?"

"Okay, it was the best," Mia admitted, squeezing her fingers.

"I want all the details. It'll take me about fifteen minutes to finish my hair and get dressed, then I'll be right over."

"Okay, come on over. I'm going to shower while you do that. I need something to eat before I crash, and I guess I could toss a load in the washer. You can keep me company."

"Put on the coffee, and I'll be over as soon as I get dressed," Chelsea replied, hurrying back to her room.

Refreshed from her shower, Mia decided breakfast was in order and set eggs, bacon, and a package of English muffins on the counter. Chelsea came in the door and set down a wedge of cheese and a fresh fruit salad.

"Mmm, we're eating fancy this morning. You put on the coffee while I get this together," Mia directed.

Mia arranged everything on a large tray and carried it out onto the balcony, where Chelsea was already sitting with a cup of coffee. *Virginia's rubbing off on me already. I'm picking up some classy habits just hanging out at the beach house. I might even have to get some of those stainless-steel domes that she uses to keep food warm,* Mia thought, smiling as she set the tray down on a tiny table between the two patio chairs and sat across from Chelsea.

"Okay, I'm all ears," Chelsea urged, seeing the smile on Mia's face. "Start from when you picked him up at the hospital."

~

Josh

Virginia spun around in the kitchen, hearing two loud voices and laughter coming from the office on the main floor.

Both were familiar, and she ran to peek inside the office from the doorway. Josh and Sean were throwing balled-up paper at one another, acting like boys instead of grown men. She was surprised to see Sean, unaware he was in the house. She hadn't heard him arrive, didn't even know he was coming, but she was happy nonetheless that he was there. He looked tired and even thinner than usual, but knowing him as she did, she doubted he ate much more than sweets—candy, baked goods, and fast food. He had a tremendous sweet tooth and also craved fast-food burgers with fries. He swore American fast-food chains served the best burgers and fries, better than anywhere else in the world. She took his word for it, not very interested in testing his theory for herself. She returned to the kitchen and pulled food from the refrigerator and the pantry, humming happily as she gathered everything that she needed to prepare a special lunch for her boys.

Virginia pushed the handcart loaded with a mountain of food, a pitcher of iced juice, and two glasses into the conference room. Sean and Josh were calmly sitting down, their ankles crossed and the heels of their shoes resting on the polished conference table, apparently relaxing after a busy and productive morning. The conference table was littered with electronics, pens, markers, and pads of paper. She pushed everything aside, including their feet, and spread a white linen tablecloth across half of the ten-foot-long, oval table, then arranged the plates, silverware, water and juice goblets, and platters of food. Sean was happily surprised at seeing her, both because they hadn't crossed paths in a while and because of the amount of food she'd brought in. He gave her a one-armed bear hug before turning back to grab a plate. Josh slid their papers and electronics into a neat pile at the far end of the conference, then came around the other side of the table to grab a plate.

"This is great, Ginny," Sean said, fixing his plate and sitting down. "So glad you came to San Diego to feed this big lunkhead. No one takes care of us like you," he added before attacking his food.

"Of course. With him just getting out of the hospital, he needs good food to heal," she said, nodding at the moderate amount on Josh's plate. "Not everyone can subsist off fast food."

"I never eat fast food, Ginny," Josh murmured, sitting down across from Sean as he began attacking his food.

"I wasn't referring to you."

"Well, if you would come to cook for the team while we're traveling, we'd all eat a lot better," Sean retorted without looking up.

"No, thank you. I actually have a job I like. But tell me something, Sean Christopher Hargrove — just how long are you planning to stay?" she asked, staring at Sean, one hand on the cart handle, the other on her hip.

"I just got in today, and I'm in trouble already?" Sean whined.

"She only calls you by your whole name when you're out of favor."

"Two weeks. I squared it with the Boss."

"Hmmm, that means I need to order more groceries," she said, inclining her head towards Sean as she spoke to Josh. "That one will eat us out of house and home, and yet he doesn't put on a single pound. Oh well," she sighed as if giving up on Sean, "if you want anything special for dinner, let me know." She leaned over and gave Sean a pat on the shoulder before pushing the handcart back to the kitchen.

"Whatever you fix will be fine, Ginny. Mia is working tonight, so there is no need to set a place for her. Thank you." Turning to Sean, he said, "You're staying until you go up to Huntington Beach, the end of the month, right?"

"Yeah, Mate. I'm hoping you'll be able to ride up with me."

"I should be able to go by then. So, tell me, who'd you submit on the new roster? I presume Colin and I have been replaced."

"Will Meyers picked up your slot, but I still need to fill Colin's so we'll have a full team roster. You have any ideas who to put in Colin's spot?"

"Maldonado looked good. Steady performance, lots of skill and technique, and the fans love him."

"The female fans, you mean…"

"Maybe a few men too. He's a good-looking bloke. Not my taste, of course."

"Of course."

"You'll be around for some PR and schmoozing a few sponsors, right?"

"Yeah, not a problem."

They ate in silence for a while, and then Josh looked up at his very best friend. "I'm sorry, Bro. Everything kinda fell on your shoulders. Thank you for looking out. You did a good job of it."

"Hey, no problem. You know I got your back."

"I know. I want you to know how much I appreciate it."

"Always, Brother. Always."

Josh and Sean talked about the team and the business as they finished eating, although Josh was finished long before Sean got full. It seemed, compared to Sean, his stomach must have shrunk significantly while he'd been confined to the hospital.

"I wanted to talk to you about something," Josh said, pushing back from the table.

"Yeah? You need some advice on what to do with that beautiful doctor, right? Dr. Mia Thomas. She's right gorgeous."

"Not even. I know exactly what to do, and yeah, she is right gorgeous. No, seriously, I need your thoughts, as limited as they might be, on something else."

"Don't be so testy," Sean teased back. "Run it by me."

"I intend to surf in the Masters in November. I need a good trainer to help me get back in shape. I've got outpatient PT twice a week at a good rehab clinic to help me build up some strength and stamina in this calf, but I also need to train on the water at least a couple of hours a day to get back in shape."

"Yeah? Well, yeah, I can make some calls. I think Naghee Nomura is back in the States. I heard he was staying down by the border."

"He left Hawaii?"

"That's what I heard."

"If I could get Naghee, that would be great. Can you see if you can track him down?"

"Yeah, no problem. I'll make some calls. But do you think you'll be ready in four months?"

"I intend to try."

CHAPTER
TWENTY-ONE

Josh awakened abruptly in the expansive bed, anxious and disoriented in the unnerving stillness and overwhelming dark.

He lay frozen, reaching out with his senses, searching for something familiar to alert him to where he was, and was rewarded with a soft snore to his right. He ran his hand across the silken sheets and touched her. Mia was curled onto her side, knees drawn up, her hands under her chin, and her back to him. Her hair had come down from the loose braid and pins she'd worn to bed, and he rubbed a few of the soft strands between his fingers. *Waking up disoriented was a lot better than waking up to night terrors,* he thought to himself, although truthfully, his heart was still racing. However, he had not had a nightmare in the two weeks since his discharge, which he attributed to Mia's presence in the bed beside him.

At ease, Josh checked the time on his watch, noting it was four-thirty. Though he knew he wasn't going back to sleep, he laid back on the pillows, careful not to wake Mia. Folding his hands on his chest, he heaved a deep breath. Today was a big day. It had taken Sean nearly a week to find and contact Naghee Nomura and several days for Nomura to get back to Josh, but today was their first meeting. They were going out on the ocean so Naghee could assess how much work Josh needed to do to get back in shape.

Unable to stay in bed any longer, he got up and moved silently around the bedroom. Showered and dressed in colorful board shorts, a rash-guard top, and rubber thong shoes, Josh headed to the kitchen to put on a pot of coffee and find some leftovers. The house was quiet and dark, but the lights were on in the kitchen, meaning Virginia was already up, preparing the day's meals. He could smell the aroma of the strong coffee as he approached the doorway, and Virginia was at the island, tipping freshly baked breakfast pastries into a basket lined with a linen napkin. She'd also chopped up various fresh fruit and put it in a crystal bowl. Surprisingly, Sam was awake and sitting at the island, a half-eaten pastry in one hand and a steaming cup of coffee in the other. Dressed in crisp khaki cargo pants and a white pullover, it was evident that he'd been up for a while.

"Good morning, Virginia. Sam," Josh greeted them, grinning cheerfully.

"Good morning, Joshua," Virginia responded first, pouring a cup of coffee, then placing a warm croissant and chunks of peach, guava, and mango on a small plate. She set them both on the island in front of him.

"Seems like I'm not the only early riser around here," he said as he sipped the hot coffee, relishing the heat and strong dose of caffeine igniting his system.

"Nope. We've been up a while," said Sam cheerily. "Even Sean is up, and he asked me to tell you that he'll see you and Naghee later. He went out with his surfboard about thirty minutes ago."

"The dawn patrol," Josh murmured. Dawn was prime time for catching the big waves. "Okay, but why are you up so early?" he asked, turning to Sam.

"No reason, Boss. I don't usually sleep more than five or six hours at a time. I smelled these pastries and coffee Miss Virginia was making, and I couldn't resist coming down to see if I could have some. You look like you're ready to go surfing."

"Actually, I am. I start training today. A friend of mine has agreed to help me get my sh… uh, crap together," he amended, looking over at Virginia sheepishly; to his relief, she ignored him.

"It's not too soon, is it, Joshua? You'll be safe, yeah?" she asked, not looking up.

"I hope not, Ginny, and yes, I'll be safe. I have to work on getting the strength and stamina in this leg, or it'll never come back. Thanks for breakfast. I'm going out on the back patio; maybe I can catch a glimpse of Sean out there."

"You need me to come with you, Boss?"

"Nah, Sam. Enjoy your breakfast. I'm just going to sit right outside."

Josh took his coffee and food out to the lounge chairs, where he could see from one end of the sandy beach to the other and enjoy his breakfast, the morning solitude, the beach view, and the fresh ocean breezes.

As he sat, Josh watched as the darkness and light cloud gave way to a brilliant, white sunrise, and soon after, he could make out the dark silhouettes of surfers and paddle boarders in the distance. Try as he might, he couldn't pick Sean out among the surfers, but the urge to join him was nearly irresistible. He almost convinced himself to take one of the boards from the garage, paddle out, and wait out on the ocean for Naghee to show up, but then he stared down at his leg.

The front wasn't quite as bad as the back, where the pink, raised skin was pulled, wrinkled, and scarred—from his heel to the back of his knee. The doctors had only been concerned with patching him up, not overly concerned with making the leg, where two-thirds of his gastrocnemius and maybe half his soleus muscles were missing, look presentable. The bone had healed well, and the doctors assured him he'd keep the leg, though he'd have a slight limp and may have to walk with a cane the rest of his life. However, they didn't believe he could return to surfing on any competitive level.

Josh, however, was determined to prove they were wrong and that he would be as good as new after a few months of training.

Several days ago, he'd taken his first exercise in the ocean, though he hadn't gone further than knee-deep. Walking against the ocean's pull, shuffling in the loose, deep sand, had been much more tiring than he'd expected. He'd only stayed out about fifteen minutes, but it had been enough to cause a bone-deep ache to radiate from his foot to his hip. It also caused Josh to wonder if, indeed, returning to pro surfing was a pipe dream. The thought that his leg, unable to take the abuse that surfing posed and possibly collapsing at the wrong time, had him second-guessing bringing Naghee to San Diego to train him.

Giving in to his worries made his leg ache, and Josh put his heel up on a nearby stool. As he massaged it, he grimaced. The skin felt rough and lumpy under his fingers. The hair had not grown back, and he doubted it ever would. Dr. Shaw had suggested cosmetic surgery sometime down the road, but eager to leave the hospital, Josh hadn't given it any more thought. It was unsightly compared to his other leg, but neither Mia nor the hospital staff were concerned about how bad the leg might look, intent as they were on how well it healed. Once the casts and bandages had come off, Mia had up-held her promise to massage the dry, scaly skin with a moisturizing cream, but he didn't see or feel where it had made much difference.

Dr. Shaw had been confident that some cosmetic surgery could make the jagged flesh and thick, red scar tissue feel and look smooth-er and more normal. *And maybe,* Josh added, *a little electrolysis on the hair of the other, good leg, and a nice deep tan might make them match again.* Josh chuckled aloud. *Vanity, thou name is Joshua Brenner.*

He got off the chaise, went inside for a coffee refill, and returned to his seat. The day promised to be beautiful, a perfect SoCal day, warm and dry. The sky was a clear, azure blue, and thin white clouds devoid of any moisture scudded across the sky. *It must be true,* he thought; *It never rains in Southern California.* He hadn't seen a sin-gle rain shower in months.

The veranda was elevated, overlooking the beach, and the per-fect spot for people-watching. More and more people came out, strolling along the beach, and Josh could see more surfers on the ocean. It was starting to warm up, and Josh had moved from the tilt-back loungers into a chair beneath an umbrella when he noticed a tall, dark-skinned man walking in the sand close to the houses that, like Josh's, backed up to the beach. He wore faded orange and yellow board shorts, a faded Hawaiian shirt in similarly faded colors, unbuttoned and flapping in the breeze, and rubber flip-flops. Josh immediately noted that he carried a longboard in one arm of exceptionally high quality and appeared to be searching for someone, or someplace, in particular, though he didn't seem to be in any hurry.

Somewhat curious, Josh watched the man as he came closer, then grinned as he recognized the long, bushy beard that covered the bottom half of his face down to his chest, the long, thick braids that were now more salt than pepper hanging over his shoulders and down his back, and the intricate, tribal-style tattoos inked on the clean-shaven sides of his scalp. The man was almost at the steps when Josh jumped up, gave a whoop of excitement, and burst into a smile.

"Naghee? Wow, my man. Is that you?"

"It is." The man nodded. "What are *you* doing here, Josh Brenner? This is the wrong side of the Pacific for you, yeah?"

Josh took the steps down as fast as he could and greeted his friend, who all but lifted him off his feet in a bear hug and slapped him on his back. "I'm waiting for you."

"For me? What can I do for the best surfer on any circuit? I know about your wins this season."

"Ah, my friend, flattery only gets you a cup of coffee around here." Josh laughed at Naghee's teasing. "I want you to train me like I'm an Olympic hopeful."

"Well, here I am. Are you ready to get out there so I can see what you can do?" Nomura asked, pointing toward the ocean over his shoulder with his thumb. "I don't have all day. I got *real* Olympic hopefuls to train."

"Let me grab a board. I'll be right back."

Josh ran out onto the sand, carrying a decently crafted surfboard, most likely belonging to the house owners. He was beyond excited, anticipating the rush and power of the waves. It was his first time out beyond waist-deep water since the accident, though he had imagined himself going out with the other surfers numerous times. Naghee ran ahead and was already on his board when Josh reached the waterline. He stepped into the cold ocean water and prepared to push off the bottom, sending himself and his board out to where Naghee waited.

But a tiny, cold frisson of fear crawled up his back, and the hair stood up on his neck and arms. He stopped in his tracks, his body frozen, his hands in a death grip on the surfboard, and his eyes focused on the clear blue water, searching for shapes that might be skimming below. He could not help the panic that slithered up his spine and settled on the back of his neck and in the center of his chest. He began to hyperventilate. In seconds, the initial dread escalated to terror as he remained immobile in the water, the rolling surf pushing against his thighs, unable to move forward or turn back toward the beach. Naghee motioned for him to come out, but Josh shook his head. He was already further than he wanted to be at that moment. The sun sparkled on the white caps and the water, and tiny prisms of light glimmered in the spray, but it was all lost on Josh. There was danger lurking below the surface, and Josh knew he couldn't go any further. Naghee noticed that Josh did not seem okay and paddled toward him.

"What are you thinking, my friend?" he asked in his deep, rumbling voice.

"I can't do it."

"No?"

"No. I thought I could. I wanted to, but now, I can't help thinking about the sharks. I never cared before, but it's all I can think about right now."

"Would it help if I told you there are no sharks nearby?"

"No, I don't think so. Besides, how would you know?"

"Too many boats are out," Naghee said, pointing to the sailboats, speedboats, and small yachts farther out. "The noise runs them away. But if you want to make sure, you and I can swim and look around."

Josh stared out as if transfixed, then looked at Naghee. "No," he shook his head. "I don't want to do that, either."

"Okay. Then maybe we should sit here and enjoy the beauty and peace of the ocean. Let it ease your mind and your spirit. There is no rush."

"*I* was the one in a rush," Josh murmured. "I wanted to compete in November."

"Ah, for the U.S. Surf Association's Championship, yeah?"

"Yeah. Everybody thought I was crazy, but I believed I could do it."

"I wondered if that was your goal. Sean mentioned to me you were looking to train hard. You were top-seeded to win at Venice last month and the one everyone needed to beat next month in Huntington Beach. You'd just won Ultimate Surfer before your accident, yeah?"

"Yeah. Now look at me. I'm shaking like a leaf, and I haven't even left the beach," he said, holding his hands up, letting Naghee see the tremors and his knuckles turned white from gripping the rails of his board.

"It's normal, a natural reaction, Josh. You've been through a lot already."

"Everyone tells me that, but I couldn't imagine not surfing again. I thought I could get back up on my board, and it would be like nothing ever happened. I'd find my peace, my center, once I got back out here. But all I feel is fear. I'm terrified another shark could come and finish the job." Josh looked around, his eyes skimming across the water. "But I'm also angry, Naghee."

As he spoke, a wave of anger and depression engulfed him. The most important part of his life was over, stolen in a random act of violence. A freak accident had taken everything from him, even his affinity for the ocean.

"You give the animals too much credit," Naghee admonished. "They are animals. Yes. Dangerous? Yes. To be respected? Absolutely yes. But they do not deserve as much credit as you've given them. Let's take it slow and sit here for a bit. Find your spirit first. We'll try again tomorrow and every day until you're ready."

Josh nodded and looked out over the ocean. The vista of blue and turquoise water was no less magnificent and awe-inspiring than before. Tall waves broke against the shelf into smaller and smaller whitecaps that rolled past him toward the shore. The ocean had once been a siren's call to his soul. Now, it was part of his nightmares. He backed up through the water, moving back onto the sandy beach. He shivered, trying to stop violent shaking and dislodge the images that flashed through his mind. His feet on the edge of the rolling surf, he exhaled, and a deep, sorrow-filled moan rose from his chest. He didn't want to sit in the water. He didn't want to find his spirit.

Naghee watched him turn and trudge back up the beach toward his house without a word. Naghee picked up his board and followed him.

When Josh returned to the house, Mia was still asleep, but he needed her calming presence to silence the turmoil in his heart, mind, and soul. Josh entered the room quietly and went directly to the ensuite. Adjusting the water in the shower, he stepped inside, kicking his wet shorts to the side. He'd felt his heart seize in his chest, and lights had exploded before his eyes. It had been a foreign, debilitating feeling that terrified him more than he was willing to admit.

He scrubbed the salt water from his skin and hair, then stepping from the shower, he wrapped one thick cotton bath sheet around his waist and dried his hair with another. He swiped steam from the mirror and looked at himself. He looked haggard, even to himself, and he knew that if this morning was any indication, it would take a lot more time and work to get back in shape. And he had little time to do it if he was going to surf the finals in November. He didn't know how long it would take to get over this crazy new fear of the ocean.

~

Mia

Mia felt the bed shift as Josh slid into bed behind her, and he tightened his arm across her stomach.

She shifted so she could feel his naked body pressed against her back and breathed in his fresh scent. Burrowing deeper into the sheets and more firmly against him, she luxuriated in the feel of his hands on her body. She rolled in his arms, sending fluttery caresses over his cool, slightly damp skin. He smiled as they stared at one another, and he kissed her. She let him press her onto her back and slide over her. She splayed her legs, letting him settle between them.

"Good morning."

"Good morning," she replied, wrapping her arms around his neck. "How did it go?"

"Okay," he answered, ducking to kiss the sensitive skin beneath her ear, down the side of her neck, and moving down to pay particular attention to her breasts, the nipples already pebbling against his skin. She moaned as he teased her, bringing her to a feverish pitch, and she arched off the mattress as he reached beneath her, lifting her up so that she lay within his arms and slowly slid inside her. Mia looked into his eyes and saw such desperate longing there; it ignited a fire that threatened to consume her. She loved him so much. He began to rock with her, and this time, their lovemaking felt different — a raw, almost desperate need about him and the unquenchable fire raging inside her. She held him, giving her body and heart to him. Accepting everything he was trying to tell her, to show her as he held her, she met him stroke for stroke until slowly, deliciously, they came apart in each other's arms.

CHAPTER
TWENTY-TWO

Mia stopped on the way home and purchased two frozen smoothies and a bag of breakfast muffins.

She knew it was Chelsea's day off, and Mia wanted to surprise her with breakfast. Besides, she really needed Chelsea's advice, and the smoothie and muffins would make up for the early morning wake-up.

"Ummm, delicious," Chelsea said, tasting her drink. "What's in the bag?"

"I brought you an orange-cranberry muffin."

"Uh-oh, you're making me suspicious with all my favorite things first thing in the morning. What's going on, Thomas?"

Mia grinned and handed her a small pastry bag, then sat in an oversized chair across Chelsea's bed. "Well, I need your advice on something," she started, bringing her legs under her and setting out her food. "Josh wants to take me out on a real date, mind you, with dinner and dancing, 'all the bells and whistles' as he put it, before he goes to Huntington Beach. But I don't have anything to wear, so I thought you and I could… well, you know, go shopping. I want to look like the women he usually dates, not like me," Mia stammered.

Chelsea sat up straight, intensely focused, especially since Mia mentioned shopping.

"Okay. Who do you have in mind if you don't want to look like you? Do you want something like haute couture and designer?"

"Well, yeah. I guess so. I don't know. I don't want to look plain like I usually do."

"I seriously doubt he thinks you look plain. When is he going?

Where's he taking you?"

"He's leaving for Huntington Beach in two weeks and wants to surprise me on our date. He offered to buy me a dress because he wants us to dress up."

"Hmmm, money's no object, then. That's good."

"I can afford my own dress, Cee. I told him I hadn't been out dancing in a long time, so we'll probably do that."

"Umm-hmm," Chelsea said, nodding, deep in thought. As she sipped her smoothie, she considered her options. "What else do you need? Shoes? Of course, you'll need new shoes to match your dress. And underwear."

"Yeah, I need some new underwear, maybe some nighties, a robe… you know, for nights when I stay over, and another swimsuit. I bought a few nice things online because I didn't want to wear my comfortable granny panties and t-shirts, but I need more," Mia muttered. She hated shopping and didn't have Chelsea's taste or flair for the dramatic, so she was willing to let her friend take her in hand.

"Of course. You're going to need new thongs, bras…" Chelsea said as she thought aloud, taking control as Mia knew she would.

"Thongs are uncomfortable, especially under my scrubs."

"You have to get used to them, and to do that, you have to wear them until you don't even think about them." Chelsea dismissed her claim, waving her tumbler in the air. "But I'm sure we can pick up a few pairs of the sexy bikini panties. I'll see if I can get you an appointment with Phillipe. We need him to work his magic on you, trim your ends, and maybe put in a few highlights. Then let Jolie do your mani-pedi and Brazilian wax."

"Nope. I draw the line at the Brazilian. I've spent many nights with Josh already, and I don't need a wax."

"Nonsense. Of course you do. You have to be smooth under your clothes," Chelsea interrupted. "Then, we'll stop by Maxine's. You remember that fabulous little boutique where we bought your last dress, right? She carries some pretty exclusive designs without charging an arm and a leg.”

"Just an arm *or* a leg. This sounds like it’s going to break the bank.”

"You’ll need that AmEx card you’ve been holding on to. Girl, it costs to be beautiful. As a matter of fact, I have a couple of new dresses I bought from her. They’re still in the garment bag in the back of my closet. Pull them out and see if you like them.”

Mia got up and opened the door to Chelsea’s walk-in closet. It was packed wall to wall with clothes, but it was organized, and Mia could see the long gowns and evening dresses hanging in the back. Though Chelsea was shorter and thinner, Mia agreed that looking at her dresses might inspire Mia to choose a style and a color for herself.

Mia stepped into her stilettos and shimmied into a dark green, strapless, backless cocktail dress that looked almost black in some lights. It crossed at the waist, held together with a lovely floral pin, and showed her long, sleek legs when she walked. She put on her jewelry while Josh zipped it to the top of her buttocks, getting in a feel as he did. Mia shivered as he pressed his nose against her skin, inhaling the decadent perfume he’d given her, and kissed her bare shoulders and back.

"You look beautiful, love.”

"Thank you.” She smiled, turning in his arms. She felt beautiful. "And you look very handsome.”

"You like?” he asked, dropping his hands and stepping back so she could take in the tailored black suit, white shirt, dark green patterned tie that matched her dress, and emerald and onyx cufflinks sparkling at his cuffs.

"I want to get a picture of you,” she said, picking up her phone and stepping back to get all of him in the frame.

"Alright, then I’ll take pictures of you, then we can take selfies of the both of us.”

"So, where are we going?” she asked as she clicked the camera on her phone several times. He'd kept the plans for the evening to himself, telling her he wanted to surprise her. He smiled and wagged his eyebrows as he took her phone and clicked at least a dozen times. She put her arms around his waist beneath his suit jacket and smiled at the camera as they took at least a dozen selfies.

"You're still not going to tell me?" She looked up at him and gave him her most formidable look. She'd tried to get it out of him all week, but he'd refused to share his surprise. It had become a game between them, with her sneaking in her questions whenever she could and him easily evading them.

"I'm sure you'll be pleased with my choice, so just trust me," he answered, kissing her lips and taking off most of her lipstick. She frowned at him, knowing he'd purposely done it.

"I do trust you, but I still want to know." She decided not to reapply more lipstick and tossed the tube in her tiny purse with her phone.

"You'll know soon enough."

He took her hand and escorted her out to the car. Sam was driving them and waited beside a luxury sedan, holding the door for them. Mia slid in first, and Josh followed. It was a short drive along the scenic coastal highway; the two-lane road cut directly into the mountainside, the sparkling ocean pounding against the irregular coastline. Soon after turning off the highway at a small, sleepy village with cobbled streets, brightly painted Spanish-tiled buildings, and moss-draped trees, Sam pulled the car to a smooth stop. They were in front of a lovely, mission-style building with its distinctive stone exterior, quatrefoil windows, red tile roof, and small bell tower. As purple and pink twilight gathered, thousands of fairy lights began twinkling, illuminating the building, grounds, and the thick gnarled branches of the grand old trees in the expansive front yard.

"Oh, this is beautiful, Josh. How did you find out about this place?" Mia looked about, amazed at the quaint building and beautiful grounds.

"A friend suggested it. They said the food is five-star," he answered, taking her hand and leading her inside.

The building's interior was as authentic as the outside, with Saltillo tile floors, stucco walls, and heavy wooden tables and chairs with carved backs and legs.

"Welcome to Mission Vineyards Restaurant and Winery," the host said as he led them to their table near the outdoor garden. It was beautiful and intimate, with more tiny fairy lights flickering in the shrubbery and ornamental trees. A floral centerpiece and thick candle pillars sat in the center of the white cloth-covered table, set for two. Josh held Mia's chair for her as the host placed a menu detailing the special five-course meal on the table, one in front of her, the other in front of Josh as he took his seat.

Once they were settled, a short, rotund man with thinning dark hair gelled straight back and dressed in dark pants, a white shirt, a bow tie, and a black apron tied around his middle came over to their table. He had a megawatt smile and a thick accent, and Mia couldn't tell if it was Spanish or Italian.

"Good evening, Mr. Brenner, Miss Thomas. We are honored to have you. My name is Francisco Chauvrin, but my friends call me Franco. I would be honored if you would call me Franco as well," he said, bowing slightly before continuing. "I am part owner, manager, and sometimes cook, and tonight we have a special meal planned just for you."

He turned up the wattage of his smile, and Mia gave him her attention as he opened their menus and described their meal for the evening. Each course was paired with a wine selection that had been produced and bottled on the estate.

As Franco described their meal, another man, a younger image of Franco, poured the wine paired with their appetizers. Josh thanked them both, and soon, he and Mia were alone in their alcove. He reached across the table and took her hand, his thumb rubbing the skin gently on the back.

"You approve of my surprise?"

"Absolutely. This is gorgeous, and I'll never question your surprises again."

"You are gorgeous. I like looking at you in your scrubs, and I love looking at you with nothing on, but I am awed at how beautiful you are right now. We should do this more often so I can sit and look at you."

"You're making me blush."

"Just another appealing thing I love about you."

She smiled and picked up her wine, holding it, preparing to toast the evening.

"Cin Cin," Josh said as he clicked her flute with his own, the Italian rolling off his tongue. "Alla nostra salute."

Mia smiled, "How many languages do you speak?"

"Fluently? Four. English, of course, but also French, Spanish, and Italian. I understand some German, but I'm not fluent in it."

"You never cease to amaze me."

"Good. I never want you to get bored with me."

"I doubt I ever would. You picked up the languages while surfing?"

"No, my brothers and I were tutored. But they came in handy while I surfed."

"So, tell me about Huntington Beach. Will you surf a little while you're there?"

"Nope, I'll be working. I've got to show my face, give a couple of interviews, stuff like that. Everyone knows about the shark attack, so people are speculating if I can come back after this accident. No one on the U.S. or the International circuit, including our sponsors, has seen me since I won in Biarritz, France, back in May, so rumors of my untimely demise are spreading everywhere."

"Then, they'll be glad to see you're alive and well. And Sean is competing, right?"

"Yes. He and two other guys on our team will give them a run for their money for the top prizes in several categories, but Sean should take the title with me out of the running."

"Are you okay with not being able to compete this time around?"

"I have to accept that I'm not ready to compete, though I had hoped to in November. That was why I hired Naghee to train with me. But it's clear now that that isn't going to happen. It's too soon."

"I'm sorry. I know how badly you wanted it. How's the training going?"

"Not good enough, I'm afraid. Naghee is a great trainer. He retired at the top of his game several years ago and knows what I'm up against. I trusted his skills, but I was pushing myself because I needed to know if I *could* do it. If there was any way possible, Naghee would have been the one to help me do it."

"That makes sense. So how is it coming? I can tell sometimes when you're in pain, though you try to hide it."

"No pain, no gain. But I let Naghee go. I have too much to work on before I'm ready to get out on the water. I have to rebuild the little muscle I have left and get rid of the cane. I have a cardio and weight trainer and a masseuse to come to the house five days a week after I get back. I will make good use of that exercise room and sauna after my workouts."

Mia was surprised. She'd assumed he was still training on the water. He couldn't have let Naghee go all that long ago. Hadn't it only been a few days ago that he was excited about surfing again? She gave Josh a questioning look, but he looked away, and Mia could tell he didn't want to talk about it anymore. The mood was lightened as the waiter brought their meal in courses, setting a new dish down after clearing away the dishes of the previous course. Mia enjoyed the different paired wines, finding she liked the whites over the reds. She also enjoyed listening to Josh talk.

"So, tell me about the surf competitions," she said, picking a new topic. "How do they work? How are you judged?"

Josh seemed to relax as he explained it to her, his expression and posture softening. She wasn't sure she understood everything he talked about, but she could see how much he loved the sport. Josh put his napkin on the table when they finished their main course and reached for her.

"Would you like to dance?"

"I'd love to dance with you, Mr. Brenner."

He pushed away from the table and took her hand as he stood. They moved to the small dance floor, where a quartet was set up. The dance floor had likely been a central courtyard back in the day but was now separated into several dining rooms. It was open to the night, and a bright crescent moon and innumerable stars filled the sky. As he led her around the dance floor, Josh grinned at her. She was surprised by his fluid dancing. He'd left the cane by his chair, and Mia had forced herself not to bring it up. She didn't want to coddle him, but she didn't want him taxing himself.

"Are you impressed?"

"Actually, I am. I remember telling you I hadn't been dancing in forever, and now I get to dance with you."

He squeezed her waist and spun her, listening to her breathless laughter as she followed his lead.

Josh was glad he'd decided to take her out on a date. He had wanted to impress her and court her in the old-fashioned way. He didn't want her to think that sex was the only thing between them, and that fact rocked him. It was the first time he'd felt that way about any woman, and he realized he loved her. They danced a bit longer before returning to their table for dessert.

By the end of the evening, Mia had eaten her fill, drank far more wine than usual, and was only slightly bubblier than the champagne they'd finished off after dinner. Sam met them with the car, and Mia climbed inside and snuggled against Josh when he settled beside her. Wrapped in Josh's arms, the drive back felt quicker, and before she knew it, Sam was helping them out of the car. Josh put his arm around her waist and led her up the steps and into the house.

Mia felt frivolous and impulsive, buoyed by the rich food, dinner wines, and champagne, and she started giggling, holding on to Josh, her arms around his neck. He nudged the door closed with his foot, holding her against him before turning her so her naked back was against the cool door. Her hands slid down, palms against his chest, one knee bent between his legs, and she stared into his eyes. The pose was intentionally seductive, and heat flooded through him. He stared at her open mouth, her lips wet and glistening, and ached to touch her, to run his fingers through her hair and cup her ass as he pressed against her. He wanted her to feel how much he wanted and needed her.

Unable to resist any longer, he gave in to his desire, staring into her beautiful eyes, much darker in the low, ambient light of the foyer, as he ground his hips into hers. When he bent to kiss her, her arms circled his neck, and she arched against him. His tongue demanded entry to her mouth and she complied, allowing him to shift their bodies until she was pulled standing between his splayed feet.

"Do you want to go out on the veranda, maybe get in the hot tub and have some more wine?" he asked against her mouth.

"No. Not now," she whispered.

"Would you like some more wine, maybe in bed?" he asked, trailing kisses from her lips to the tops of her breasts, though more wine was the last thing on his mind.

"No, thank you," she shook her head, leaning her head back so that her hair fell down her back, giving him greater access to her neck, throat, and the tops of her breasts. She was so sexy, and Josh imagined unzipping her dress and letting it fall to the floor. He knew she only wore a skimpy piece of satin under the dress.

"What do you want, then?"

"Ummm. I want you. I want you to keep doing what you're doing and more." She pulled his mouth back to hers, and he tasted the lingering sweetness of the wine. She speared her fingers into his soft hair, gathering it in her fists, and a soft moan escaped her lips.

It was the sexiest sound he'd ever heard. She took his breath away, and he knew if they continued this way much longer, he would end up making love to her in the foyer. A possessive growl rumbled deep in his chest, and her eyes focused on him. She smiled and stepped out of his embrace. Taking his hand, she led him to their bedroom.

CHAPTER
TWENTY-THREE

Huntington Beach, California, USA
Master's Cup Championship

Josh

Josh climbed out of the car, followed by Sean, and proceeded to the hotel lanai while Sam stayed behind to oversee the unloading of their duffel bags, electronics, and surfing gear, including a half-dozen custom surfboards.

Entering the lobby, Josh immediately felt the buzz of electric excitement in the crowded room. He scanned the crowd and recognized many of the faces. Besides plenty of competing surfers, there were media people from dozens of magazines, newspapers, and television outlets, and quite a few executives from big-name surfing equipment and apparel companies milling about, no doubt wrangling interviews and pitching deals. Josh had also arranged a few meetings with several of those same execs for the weekend.

Amid the crowd, he felt at home. People called his name, waved, or slapped him on the back in greeting, and he stopped here and there as they engaged him in conversation. Most seemed genuinely happy to see him back in action. His phone pinged more than a dozen times, emails and texts coming through from teammates, friends, and business associates, asking if he'd made it in, where he was staying, and sending invites for dinner or drinks. Josh tried to answer as many as he could while others, seeing him in the lobby, approached him to chitchat. Sean caught up with him as Josh waited for the elevators, jiggling the keys to his hotel room in his hand.

"Do you want to get the guys together, maybe have lunch set up in a conference room or small dining room?" Sean called to him, catching his attention over the noise in the room.

"Yeah. Let me drop my bag in the room, and I'll meet you back down here in ten."

"Sounds good." Sean nodded before turning away and heading back toward the registration desk.

Ten minutes later, Josh entered the small private dining room where Sean and several of their teammates were sitting around the table, talking and laughing. Josh smiled. He hadn't seen any of them, except Sean, in months. Some had come to the hospital after learning Josh had been injured and Colin was missing, but Josh had been in no shape to see them then. He grinned as he circled the table, gripping hands and arms in greeting, slapping them on their shoulders and back. When he reached the seat held for him, he was in a festive mood, happy to see them all.

"Hey, I have an idea," Jordan Smith, one of the younger, newer members, said as they talked around the table, eating their lunch. "What about a paddle-out this evening? Colin's family had a memorial for him, but many of us couldn't attend. If we had a paddle-out tonight, we could all pay our respects together as a team." The group was silent for a moment, everyone considering Jordan's suggestion.

"Yeah, we'd have to do it tonight because once the competition starts tomorrow, we won't be able to until Sunday night," Grayson Pierce, another team member, responded. The suggestion started a flurry of questions and comments. *Can we get enough leis? Should we let anybody join us? Can't they just meet us on the beach? Can we get it organized this quick?*

Josh leaned back in his seat as the logistics were worked out, watching Jordan and Gray. It appeared they'd given the topic much consideration and had great solutions for most questions, and when everyone was satisfied, Josh nodded. The team would have a paddle-out at sunset.

Josh cringed at getting on a surfboard and paddling out on the water, though he tried hard to hide his feelings. He'd spoken only when asked a question, forcing a plastic smile as the team talked excitedly. When he'd first sat down, he'd been hungry enough to eat the big lunch entree he'd ordered, but now he felt queasy, unable to drink even a sip of water. A paddle-out was the last thing he wanted to do, especially not at sunset when they would be yards out from the shore, and it would be impossible to distinguish creatures moving about in the water. Even as the discussion moved on from this evening's paddle-out to details regarding the competition taking place over the next three days, Josh remained quiet and aloof. He wanted to go up to his room, fix himself a stiff drink, and calm his roiling nerves. They had about four, maybe five hours until sunset, and he knew his nerves would only get worse.

As he struggled with his feelings, he felt Sean watching him. And though Sean said nothing, Josh knew he could sense something was wrong. If Josh slipped away, Sean would come looking for him, and Josh wasn't ready to answer any of his questions, so he kept the fake smile plastered on his face, pretending to be interested in the conversation, and picked at his food.

That evening, the paddle-out had grown beyond the eight-man team to more than a hundred participants. Jordan had secured more than enough flower leis for the team, with some extras to pass out to people who hadn't shown up with their own. Sean handed Josh a surfboard, and the group filed into the water, some swimming, others paddling away from the shore. Once they reached the spot Jordan and Gray had chosen, they joined hands to form a circle. In formation, they chanted, splashed, and churned the water, which caused Josh to panic. The fear cut off his air, and he gripped the sides of his board so tight his hands felt frozen to the rails. He was certain he was going to pass out. He inhaled several times through his nose, exhaling through his mouth, trying to remember and apply some meditation techniques Naghee had taught him to calm down, but he was having difficulty. He forced himself to loosen his grip on the board and center himself so he wouldn't flip his board over, and nearly flipped it anyway.

By the time they had spoken a few words in honor of Colin and placed the flowers inside the circle formed by the noses of their boards, Josh was nauseous, lightheaded, and swaying on his board against the motion of the undulating water. He was trying to keep his gorge down and stay upright at the same time. Several times, he'd closed his eyes to calm his stomach, but not being able to see what might be out there was far worse than seeing it coming, and his eyes snapped open each time. He could not suppress the urge to search the surrounding water, to scan the depths, which only got darker and more ominous as the sun descended and twilight gathered. He was ready to call it quits. But fortunately, the ceremony wrapped up, and participants started turning around and heading back to shore. Josh skimmed through the water, lying flat on his board and propelling it with powerful, coordinated strokes past them. Reaching the banks, he left the surfboard for Sean to retrieve and found a secluded spot where he could retch privately. When he felt better, he saw Sean leaning against a boulder nearly as tall as him, holding both of their boards and waiting for him. Feeling sheepish, Josh nodded.

"I don't suppose you want to talk right now," Sean said, more of a question than a statement.

"No. Not now," Josh replied, shaking his head.

Sean tipped his chin and said nothing more as he climbed off the rock. He passed Josh a board and turned to walk away.

CHAPTER
TWENTY-FOUR

Opening Day of the U.S. Surfing Federation's Champions Cup the next day was as thrilling as anyone could have expected.

Josh was probably more excited than he'd been in years, having taken part in both International and American championship competitions. Twenty-four teams entered the Big Wave Competition, some with three entrants and others with four, including Josh's team. His four men were Sean, Will Meyers, who'd replaced Josh; Joey Maldonado, who had replaced Colin; and Lloyd Carter, who'd moved up to get the last slot on the roster. Sean and Will Meyers were long-time veterans and two of the most experienced of the remaining members on the team competing for the title in championships, while the nineteen-year-old cowboy, Maldonado, and twenty-three-year-old Carter, were much less experienced but excellent choices for substitutes. Although they had fewer pro competitions under their belts and no top-ranked competitive wins, they were no less fierce competitors. Josh had faith in the selections Sean had made.

At the end of the morning session, all four men had survived the first cut, earning a place in the afternoon line-up. There had been a momentary ping of envy and self-pity that morning when Josh realized he was sitting out the rest of the year, but as he watched the men pull out their best efforts and dominate their heats, pride replaced those painful, negative feelings.

A few of the teammates wore their wetsuits while standing in waist-high water, while the others stayed mostly onshore and wore board shorts and rashguard shirts with the team logo. It was a black-and-white reef ray embroidered on the right side of the chest and two armbands, one black for their deceased teammate and a green and gold one for Josh. It made it easy for reporters and paparazzi to spot them by the waterline. Josh had given several impromptu interviews all morning, and when a representative of the television press approached him, Josh was more than happy to oblige them.

The crowd roared, and Josh could feel their excitement and energy as he stepped onto the towering announcer platform. He waved to the thousands of surf fans below and those who watched him via televised programming. He waved to the fans who'd hoped to see him make a comeback in the U.S. after winning the Ultimate Surfer Title in Biarritz in May and having the subsequent near-fatal accident. He felt exhilarated. The crowd's adulation was like a physical vibration swelling up inside him. There was nothing like the adoration of fans, and Josh basked in it before turning to the three men who'd invited him up. Kevin Collier, an old friend and retired surfer, had spotted Josh as he cheered for his crew at the waterline and invited him up for an impromptu, televised interview. They grasped each other in one-armed hugs, like long-lost buddies, and Kevin pulled him into the circle of chairs in front of the television cameras. Josh greeted and shook hands with Lonnie Davis, a prime surfer he'd competed against many times before a bad injury had forced him to retire, and George Durant, a national sportscaster for the Sports Channel. Each of the three commentators seemed genuinely happy to see Josh up and about after news of the shark attack.

"How are you, man? I heard about the accident and wondered how you were doing," Kevin said, handing Josh a microphone and positioning him so the audience could get a good look at him.

"Doing pretty good now, Kev. The leg is mending, feeling much stronger, and I've picked up my training regimen."

"How long before you come back out to compete?"

"I can't say right now. I got back on my board about two weeks ago, and it's slow going, but I'm satisfied with my progress," Josh said with a straight face.

"That's great, Josh. Hope to see you back out here real soon. We all heard about Colin Mitchell, and it's such a loss, man. How's your crew doing? How are you doing?"

"Losing Colin was hard, you know. He was on the trip with me when the attack happened, as was Sean Hargrove, and we're just working through it, you know. He was a good friend and a great teammate, and what can I say? We miss him. Every day, I miss him."

"Yeah, and speaking of Hargrove. We saw him out there yesterday and this morning, and he looked fantastic. Looks like he's going to take top honors this year. Will Meyers is also looking good, and the youngblood, Joey Maldonado, might surprise everyone and make it into the finals."

"Sean deserves it. He's been working very hard. Will, Joey, all the guys are in good shape for this meet. I'm very proud of them and wanted to be here to support and cheer them on."

The other commentators vied with one another to ask Josh questions, extending the impromptu interview. When the time was up, Kevin stood and shook Josh's hand again, slapping him on the arm.

"It's been great seeing you and talking with you, Josh. We hope to see you back out here on the circuit soon, and as you can see, your fans are pulling for you."

"Thanks, Kev. I hope to be back out here soon." Josh shook hands again and gave Kevin a backslap before turning toward the crowd below. Cheers rose like a groundswell, and Josh raised up on the balls of his feet, stretching taller to become more visible, and waved both arms, a beaming grin on his face. The cameras swept up to capture him waving, and suddenly, he saw himself on the giant screens set up on the beach so the crowd could follow the action on the water and in the commentators' booth. Josh was still a star attraction, and the surfing world was happy to see him on his feet. Josh waved at the crowd for a few minutes before stepping down from the platform and heading back to the waterline.

Hundreds of people reached out to touch him on the arm and

back, and he knew his shoulders and back would be tender from the innumerable backslaps he'd received. The fans continued to surround him, impeding his progress as he made his way down to his team.

By late afternoon, the excitement that had flooded his body all day and the rush from being on the announcer's platform had subsided, replaced by exhaustion and pain in his leg. He'd worn a wide, cheerful grin all day, telling little white lies when needed, and now his face and cheeks ached from being frozen into position for hours. He needed to sit down and rest, take the weight and strain off his leg. He hadn't spent this much time on his feet in all the weeks since his discharge from the hospital combined, and even at the best of times, in the best of shape, it was challenging to walk or run on sand.

Josh started back towards the waterline, where he and his team camped out. The competitors had been whittled down to seven for this semifinal, and as expected, Sean was the one to beat. They would compete for first place and the championship cup the next morning. Halfway there, he turned away, deciding it was a good time to get away, and headed for the boulevard that ran parallel to the beach and led back to the hotel. He anticipated finding a taxi, as the area was packed with tourists, to take him back to the hotel.

As he neared the boulevard, he heard someone behind him call his name, then felt a hand on his arm. He turned around, and a woman jumped into his arms, her legs circling his waist and her arms locked around his neck. It was by pure reflex that he caught her and the shock that let her kiss him. Stunned, he put her down, but even as her feet touched the ground, her arms stayed locked around his neck, and he had to pry her off.

"Josh? Omigod, I'm so happy to see you. Where have you been? I've been looking for you everywhere. I've even asked Sean about you. Why haven't you called me back?"

"Teagan?"

"You look surprised to see me, Josh. How are you?" She tightened her arms around his neck and laid her head on his shoulder. "Where are you going? Back to your hotel?"

"I'm good, but how are you? How did you find me in this crowd?"

"I saw you up on the announcer's platform. Everyone in the world saw you. You'll be on every sports recap tonight around the world. I waited for you to come down, but you didn't see me waiting at the bottom, so I had to run after you."

"Oh," was all he could manage, looking her up and down. She wore a white bikini that showed off her perfect body and golden tan, flat white slip-on thong sandals, and a large tote hanging off her shoulder. She pulled a coverup out of her bag and slipped on a large pair of sunglasses, and he realized she had every intention of following him. Feeling uncomfortable, he looked around but didn't see anyone he knew, and he did not want to be caught on the street by reporters while he dealt with her.

"Did you miss me, Josh?" she gushed in her breathy, high-pitched voice. It had never grated on his ears before as it did now. "I missed you so much. Did you know I came by the hospital, but they wouldn't let me in? They only let family in, and Sean, of course, to see you. I told them I was your girlfriend, but they said no and turned me away. I thought we could work things out if we saw each other face-to-face."

"I'm sorry, Tea. You shouldn't have come all that way. And there's nothing to work out, you know."

"Of course, there is, Josh. We were dating the last time I saw you, and I thought we were growing close. I cared about you, Josh. That's why I tried to get Sean to make them let me up to your room. We needed to talk, but he refused. You should talk to him about that, Josh. He had no right to refuse to let me see you, right?"

Josh made sympathetic noises as she talked nonstop and fended her off as she tried to grab his arm or hold his hand. Josh lengthened his stride just enough that she struggled to keep up with him. As they walked, he thought back to all that had happened to him since he'd last seen Teagan Maddox. Had it only been four months since he'd met Mia, since the shark attack? It felt like a lifetime, and Teagan had never entered his mind. He wondered, even now, how to get rid of her before he made it to his hotel. He was definitely not taking her back to his room. He scanned the roadway, looking for a taxi, but didn't see one.

He'd tuned her out as they walked, which was something he remembered doing a lot of, and then he glanced back at her. She was scolding him because his assistant and the team had failed to keep up with their social media.

"It just fell into a black hole, Josh. That surely cost you followers, maybe even hundreds of them. Everyone wanted to know how you were doing during your recovery, and there was nothing on your page."

"Ummm," he hummed empathetically. It surprised him at how differently they saw their brief relationship together. Yes, they'd hung out together for a few months—more like a couple of weeks—off and on before the accident. Still, Josh had never been serious nor exclusive with Teagan Maddox, and she hadn't either. She often hung out with other 'friends' with whom she'd had 'benefits.' They hadn't once talked about a relationship—not even after attending a mutual friend's Valentine's Day wedding on Oahu.

Teagan was beautiful, smart, and successfully played at being a runway model. She'd been capitalizing on her beauty and sex appeal since she was sixteen, and in the last few years, she'd been trying to catch a wealthy husband. Josh suspected it had something to do with her trust fund. As far as he knew, she was well off in her own right, with old money passed down in her family. Along with the extravagant fees she earned from her sporadic modeling career, it was enough to support her lavish lifestyle, but it was nowhere near the type of money the men she went after had. Josh figured she'd only zeroed in on him because she learned of his family's wealth, but he lived frugally from monthly payments on the trust fund his mother had left to him. The Whitakers were nowhere near as wealthy as the Brenners, but that hadn't been true when his parents married.

James Brenner had taken the company his grandfather built and passed down to his children and turned it into a multinational megacorporation that ranked number two in the world in mining, engineering, minerals, and precious stones. When Josh walked away from his position in the company at twenty-two, his father had cut off access to the money. His checks were delivered into his account, but, as his father had said, outraged, it would stay there until Josh came to his senses. The money his mother had left was sufficient for his needs, and he occasionally infused a little cash into it from the most lucrative of the purses he won on the circuit. On paper, Josh was worth millions, maybe even a couple billions, but in reality, he lived much more economically.

Teagan didn't know that, though, and obviously believed the hype. Josh never intended to straighten out any misconceptions as they'd only had a casual hook-up, no different from other times and other women he had dated. Every woman he'd dated before Mia, including Teagan, had eagerly accepted Josh's terms—no strings attached, which was why this clinging, overly concerned posture Teagan exhibited felt extremely bizarre. Did she honestly think he'd lost his mind along with everything else?

Josh glanced back to see if she was still following him. She was, and he huffed, frustrated. He felt guilty and didn't know why, but he wished she hadn't seen or come after him. He was no longer interested in another string of one-night stands with her or anyone else. His heart belonged to Mia.

He slowed down so she could catch up, and they walked along the strip, lined with cheap, weather-beaten hotels and motels. He was still a mile or more from the luxury resort hotels where he was staying, but rather than allow her to follow him there, he led her to the lobby of the nearest one.

"You're staying here?" she asked, looking around, her nose wrinkled. Josh hadn't paid attention to the hotel. He'd been so intent on getting rid of her. It was a nondescript little place with little more to offer than cheap rooms at an exorbitant rate. But it appeared to have a decent-looking, immaculately clean restaurant that seemed to be doing brisk business among beachgoers.

"No, I just thought we needed to talk, Tea… privately." He took her arm and led her inside the hotel restaurant, requesting a table off to the side where they could talk without others overhearing them. Josh cleared his throat once they were seated in a booth along the back wall of the large dining room. After a few awkward moments, he blurted out his feelings.

"Teagan, I'm sorry, but things have changed, and we won't be seeing one another anymore. I met someone, and…"

"And, what? You're dumping me?"

"I wouldn't say I'm dumping you. I mean, I can't dump you if we were never… like that, and we never had that kind of relationship."

"But you're saying you're in a relationship now? What a joke. Who is she? Where is she? Why isn't she here?"

"It doesn't matter who or where she is. What's important here is there is no you and I. No. Us."

"Josh, honey, you can't mean that," she said, staring at him, her green eyes wide, her mouth open, and an expression on her face that most men would have swooned over. However, Josh sighed, hoping she wouldn't cause a scene. He hated drama, and Teagan was the queen of drama.

"Yes, I do," he said. "What's going on with you, Tea? What are you doing here in Huntington Beach? A little bit of a backwater for your tastes, isn't it? No glitz or glamor."

"Of course not, Josh. I've actually been in L.A. for a couple of weeks, staying with some friends in Beverly Hills, and I ran into Hunter Radcliff while we were out to dinner—you remember him, right? Anyway, he's competing too, and he mentioned you would be here. I convinced my friend, Marilee, to drive down with me. I wasn't sure you would be here, but I hoped to see you. You're happy to see me, right?"

"I'm happy to see you're doing okay."

"Yeah, me too. I mean that you're doing okay. Are you back to competing? I didn't see your name on any of the rosters."

"No. Not yet. I've been training a little, but I'm not back to form yet."

"Oh. Okay, well, this is where you're staying, right? I'm so excited to see you again. I'm hoping we can hang out again."

"That's really, uhm… nice of you, but I don't think so, Tea. I'm not planning to hang out while I'm here."

"That's okay. We could spend even more time together. You know, like we used to."

"Yeah, but no. We had fun times, but things have changed since Biarritz, at least for me. I don't hang out much anymore. But please, don't let me stop you from enjoying the competitions."

"I came to see you, Josh. What's going on with you? You act like you don't want to see me again?"

"We had this conversation already, Tea. And like I said, things are different now, Tea. I'm different. It's been good seeing you again, but I'm in a different situation now, and I've moved on."

"Moved on? In four months, you've moved on… from me? From us?"

"Look, I don't want to be the bad guy in this. I've met someone I care about, and we're seeing where things go from here."

"You? In love? I don't believe it…"

"Believe what you want. You and I are not happening. I think I'm going to have some lunch since I'm here. Would you like something to go?" Josh picked up the plastic laminated menu and scanned it while massaging his forehead between his thumb and forefinger to keep the beginnings of a headache starting to settle behind his eyes from worsening. He could tell Teagan was beginning to puff up with righteous indignation and was hoping she would not start a fight over this.

"So, that's it, Josh? You could have told me this at the beach. Why'd you bring me to this shit hotel?"

"This isn't my shit hotel, and you followed me. I stopped here so we could have this conversation. I thought it might be best to talk privately rather than having it out in the middle of the street."

Teagan looked away from Josh, but he thought he could see her turning things over in her mind. When she turned back to him, her expression was contrite.

"What we had was fun, Josh, and it could be fun again…"

He inhaled deeply, blew a long breath, and turned to look at her. He hoped he could get through to her without things turning ugly.

"I'm sorry if I hurt you, Tea. I never meant to, but things happen, and life changes. We have to change with it to survive."

"Oh, fuck you, Josh. Don't patronize me. I get it," she snapped angrily, pulling the straps of her bag over her shoulder as she slid out of the booth. Josh could see her composing herself. He was glad she was finally understanding and didn't want a scene in the crummy little hotel restaurant any more than she did. "See you around," she snarled, putting on her sunglasses and walking away.

"Yeah, see you."

He watched as she walked out of the restaurant, heads turning to watch her pass. He didn't expect to see her again; there was no reason to. If his leg didn't improve, he'd be off the circuit and off her radar. The thought made him both happy and sad. He'd dodged that bullet, but he'd put all of his eggs in one basket, and now that basket was broken, and he was losing all of his eggs. The only bright light, the saving grace, was Mia. Just thinking of her filled him with a sense of peace. They could be together no matter what. They would never have to worry about money. If he joined his father and brother in the family business, he'd have more money than he could spend in several lifetimes. Shaking off the creeping sense of melancholy, he flagged the server over and ordered a double Jack and Coke and a burger and fries.

CHAPTER
TWENTY-FIVE

Saturday, day two of the meet, dawned cool and overcast, but the waves, lined up one behind the other, were tall and powerful as the morning tide pushed them toward the shore.

The team was up early and pumped despite many of them not having gone to bed before the wee hours of the morning. When they arrived at the beach, a massive crowd, larger than the previous two days, had already assembled, packing the beach as far down as the waterline, and event security had their hands full, moving spectators back behind the cordoned-off areas for their safety.

The morning elimination heats were over well before noon. Josh had plenty of time before the afternoon sessions to meet with current and potential sponsors to talk about the team's success and plug his sponsors' products with trade journal reporters. He was on his way back to his team on the beach when the reporter from *Surf Rider Magazine* approached him for a quick, impromptu interview. Josh had given dozens of impromptu interviews all weekend, so he stopped to accommodate the reporter.

"So, how're you doing, Josh? How's the recuperation coming?" the reporter asked, sticking a mic in Josh's face while the cameraman kept the camera zoomed in on him. Josh couldn't place the reporter, considering he knew most of the crews from the bigger magazines, and as far as he knew, *Surf Rider* was a decent E-zine.

"Doing great, as you can see," he responded, flashing the cameraman a brilliant, engaging smile.

"What do you plan to do now that your surfing career is over?"

"What? Who told you my career is over?" Josh laughed, thinking the reporter was joking.

"From my sources, you're done on the circuit. Is that true?"

"Are you crazy? I'm still recuperating, but I wanted to come and support my team."

"How is your team doing now that you and Colin Mitchell are out? It's just Sean Hargrove left, right?"

Josh heard the rapid clicking of a camera as a photographer walked behind him, taking photos of his leg, the scar tissue still bright red from all the sun.

"I don't know who your sources are, but they're feeding you erroneous information. No more questions. This interview is over." Josh said, his face hardening as he blocked the camera lens with his hand. "No more pictures."

"Come on, Josh. You can talk to us. Your fans want to know what's happening with the great Josh Brenner. We heard you guys had a paddle-out last night for Colin. Did you explain how he died trying to save you, and you didn't even bother going to the memorial the family held for him?"

"What? Are you crazy or something? I was in the hospital on a fucking ventilator. Didn't you read the papers you supposedly work for or listen to the news? Get out of my face, man. I said this interview is over," Josh said harshly, turning away and dismissing the two men.

"What about Teagan Maddox?" The reporter screamed as Josh turned to walk away. "Lots of news going around about you and her. Ms. Maddox gave exclusives to several other outlets this morning, but we want to hear it from you, Josh. Is it true? Are you and Ms. Maddox engaged?"

"For the last time, get out of my business," Josh roared.

He was furious. The reporter wasn't interested in a real interview. He only wanted something sensational he could use to feed the rumor mills. Josh turned his back, only to face more reporters and plenty of familiar paparazzi. No doubt, they'd sensed a scoop.

Josh pushed away from them, trying to shield his face from the cameras that were now clicking pictures and recording him. It seemed the second-rate gossip rags were out for blood, more vicious than any shark in the water, and Josh had made the mistake of engaging one of them. He turned, and Sam was there, pushing through the crowd. Soon, everyone was pushing and shoving. Men who had been standing around, minding their own business and watching the competition, got caught up in the pushing and shoving, and scuffles began to break out.

His team rushed up from the beach to make a barrier around Josh and Sam just as a full-scale brawl erupted. Event Security rushed across the beach to stop the altercations and marched Josh, with several of his crew surrounding him, off the beach toward the Security Pavilion. Detained in a large tent that sheltered them from the sun but retained the oppressive heat, Josh's temper was simmering, ready to explode. He resented being questioned over and over about his part in the incident. When they were all released, in time for the afternoon events, Josh and his detained team members headed back to where the rest of their team waited. Maybe the look on his face or the fierce anger that radiated off him, no one—reporters or otherwise—approached him for the rest of the day.

As expected, Sean finished first in the line-up over Glenn Davies, a top competitor out of Florida, and Joey Maldonado edged past Will Meyers for third place, just shy of a fraction of a minute behind Davies' second-place finish. The team was in a mood to celebrate that evening, and they wasted no time returning to the hotel to party.

The younger members joined a pub crawl, anticipating a fun night at some of the trendiest night spots frequented by residents and tourists alike. Josh, however, felt older than his years and sent them off with a wave, preferring to spend the evening in his room. He'd sent Sam away, telling him to get some sleep, then fell across his bed. He opened his phone, looking for any new pictures and stories posted online, and found plenty of mash-up reports of him and Teagan and the brawl that had allegedly started between him and the two Surf Rider journalists. Josh snorted. One had to be immensely generous to call either of those hacks reporters, and he'd had nothing to do with the scuffle that broke out. It looked bad, as there were pictures of the magazine news crew bloodied and beaten, along with many pictures of Josh and his team members in the center of the melee and being led away by security. None showed Josh actually fighting because he hadn't thrown a single punch, but two of his team members were shown in the middle of the fight.

He scanned the article, which pretty much detailed the back-and-forth between him and the reporter and the eruption of the fight. He grunted. Fights were common when too many people were packed together, and emotions ran high; there was nothing specific about it that he needed to address.

Remembering the reporter's words that Teagan had given exclusives, Josh continued to scroll, checking many of the feature pages in women's magazines. True enough, a fairly long interview with pictures had been posted in an online magazine earlier that morning. There were at least a dozen pictures of him and Teagan. Some were individual shots of them on a sunny, white sand beach that he remembered were taken months before the accident.

And there were two grainy shots of them on the boulevard when Teagan had followed him to the hotel. He was glad he'd had the presence of mind not to take her to the hotel where he was staying. Apparently, she'd given the interview sometime before she'd caught up with him yesterday afternoon, and the story was coming out. And she'd obviously agreed to allow the magazine's photographers to follow her around, hoping to catch the two of them in a tender reunion. Josh felt like throwing his phone across the room. So stupid, he fumed. How could she spin a blatant lie about their relationship when the last time they'd talked, she'd been despondent that he was breaking up with her? He'd have to contact his lawyer in the morning and force the journalist to print a full retraction. No way could he allow people, especially Mia and those who knew her, to believe he was engaged to someone else. It would break her heart to believe he had played her and break his to see hurt her that way.

Josh got up and walked to the small bar in his room to fix himself a drink. It wasn't the first time Josh had been in a fight, but this time, the reporter and cameraman were accusing him of starting a fight, punching them in the face, breaking several bones, and smashing their equipment. They also threatened to sue for millions. It was ridiculous, a grandstand effort to sell more magazines. A year ago, maybe even six months ago, Josh would have laughed every bit of it off, including Teagan's claims. He would have denied it all and then made the rounds with another girl on his arm. He had intentionally cultivated his playboy image, never allowing a woman to get too close or too comfortable.

But now, things were different, and he wanted to protect Mia from his bad-boy image. He didn't want ugly gossip to touch her, and he didn't want her plastered on the covers of the gossip rags, which might happen if he didn't get on it right away. The paparazzi had camped outside the hospital for months, and when they'd gotten wind that he'd rented the Taylor-Reis house on the ocean, they'd tried to capture the two of them on the veranda with their long-range zoom lenses. They knew who she was. They just hadn't had a story to report before.

And Josh knew her well. She was still skittish, and any bit of scandal would make her run the opposite way. He didn't want her to doubt him or his feelings for her.

He rolled over onto his back, seeking to get comfortable, pulling one pillow under his achy leg and stuffing another under his head when someone knocked on his door. In his gut, he knew who it was and called out for them to enter. Sam wouldn't have come unless Josh needed him, so when Sean entered, Josh smiled weakly. Sean pulled up a chair and sat down, folding his arms over the chairback.

"What's up, Dude? You're looking a bit green around the gills, there. You okay?"

"I've been worse," Josh said, sipping his drink. "Congratulations on your heats. You're in a perfect spot to take it all tomorrow."

"Thanks. You're drinking that straight?"

"No, but there wasn't much Coke left after the first few drinks. If you've come to drink with me, call downstairs and get us another bottle and some sodas."

"I didn't come to drink with you. Where's Sam?"

"In his room, I imagine. Why? What's up?"

"I thought we could have a little talk, you know, face-to-face, brother-to-brother."

"Ummm," Josh hummed, relishing the slight burn of the liquor as it slid down his throat. It didn't sound good, but he nodded anyway. "What's on your mind?"

"I want to know what's going on with you."

"What makes you think anything is going on with me?"

"Oh, I don't know. Maybe the fact that you puked your guts out after the memorial service, that you stomp around with attitude, and that Teagan seems to be back in your life… any one of those things is cause for concern, I think."

"Don't worry about it, Bro. I've just got a lot of stuff on my mind. I'm working through it."

"Okay. But let's talk about it. We've always talked through problems."

"Not now."

"Then when?"

"I don't know, but not now."

Sean sat for a while, looking away from Josh, staring in the direction of the television. But Josh could tell from the set of his jaw and twist of his mouth that he wasn't watching the TV, and a storm was brewing inside him. Josh only hoped it wouldn't erupt tonight. He was tired, spent, and knew he was shutting Sean out. He and

Sean had never been unable to talk to one another, but Josh felt so screwed up and completely untethered from his life that he didn't know where to start or what to say. He hadn't been prepared for how strange and unnerving his old life felt compared to this new, abnormal state. Everything was rubbing him the wrong way, and he wasn't sure how to deal with it… or himself.

Noticing Josh's duffel sitting at the foot of the bed, Sean nodded at it. "You were planning to leave tonight?"

"I'd thought about it when I came up, but I've been laying here, hoping my leg would stop aching and maybe I'd fall asleep. So far, neither has happened."

Sean rocked back in the chair and hummed. "What about the meeting tomorrow with Elliot Enterprises?"

"I'll reschedule," Josh said, swinging his legs off the bed and sitting up. He put his face in his hands and looked at the carpeted floor. He absently massaged his bearded jaw. Sean leaned forward and stared at Josh.

"I'm looking at you, man. I've been watching you for a while, and things ain't right. First, it's the drinks. You've never drank this much before. You never drank much at all—the whole, my body is a temple thing. But, damn, you seem to have a drink in your hand all the time lately. You stopped training with Naghee after two weeks, and during the paddle out, you seemed terrified just sitting there on your board. I didn't really think about it, but when we all came in and I saw you puking your guts out, Bro, I knew something was seriously wrong. What's going on?"

"Drop it, Sean. I'm just trying to deal right now."

"Yeah? With what? What kind of shit are you trying to deal with?"

"Everything. Colin's death. The end of my career. The end of my life as I know it. And, if Mia catches wind of this shitshow with Teagan, it could be the end of us. My whole life blew up in the blink of an eye."

"Why would you think I couldn't understand that? You're deal-ing with so much right now, and I understand that. But you are not the only one having a hard time, Josh. Yeah, you lost a good friend when Colin died, but it seems like I lost both of my best friends. I was there with you, remember? I saw it all. I saw the shark cir-cling and called you, but you couldn't hear me. Then everything happened so fast. Colin went down. You were tossed like a ragdoll, and I couldn't do anything to save either of you."

Sean looked away, but not before Josh saw the pain in his eyes, in the stubborn twist of his mouth. He wanted to hug his friend, his blood brother. And at that moment, Josh realized how much of a toll the accident had taken on Sean.

"I'm sorry, man. I've been selfish."

"No. Not selfish," Sean whispered. "We've both been trying to cope. You needed to survive, physically and mentally, and I guess even emotionally. I just wanted to hold it together for you. I couldn't break."

Josh nodded. "You've been strong for me and for the team. I don't know what I would have done without you."

"The team needed me too. They all turned to me, confused and heartbroken. It's good that you came and that they got to see you, but they're all worried about you. I'm worried about you. I noticed back at the house how much you're drinking—like a fish, man, and downing pain meds with Jack and Coke. Swallowing sleep meds almost every night, but you hardly ever sleep. You walk around like some zombie, out of touch, and wonder why you've made fucked up decisions." Sean stopped and took a deep breath. "Why are you still here in the States?"

"I'm not ready to go home."

"Yeah? Well, it'll soon be out of your hands. Things at home are slipping through the cracks, and your visa expires in six days."

"Dammit. I didn't realize… I'll call Monica in the morning to see if she can get it extended."

"I've talked to her, and it's too late. It takes weeks to get approval, and if you stay here without one, even hoping to get approved, you'll officially be out of status and could be deported. You could be barred up to ten years from returning."

"You're joking, right?"

"No," Sean answered sadly, shaking his head. "If you leave before it expires, you can renew it in January. Then you'll have maybe six months or a year to visit."

"That's four months away."

"Yeah. Not long, right? But in the meantime, you have time to take care of business. Monica's been calling me daily, letting me know what needs caring for. She can't pay all the bills because revenue is drying up fast."

"I authorized a bank transfer the other day before we left San Diego."

"Your personal money?"

"Yeah. It's money."

"To pay team expenses?"

"And whatever else."

"I'm going back in a couple of days, Josh. Right after this meet. I'm also retiring from the team and both leagues."

"What? Why? You will win the top prize tomorrow. Why would you quit?"

"It was fun while it lasted. Now it's not."

"You're not having fun?" Josh teased.

"No. I'm not. And neither are you. You're a wreck. You need to clean yourself up, stop drinking, call that psych doctor, and get your head back on straight. You've got to settle this craziness with Teagan and *Surf Rider Magazine* and get new endorsements and sponsorships for the team. You can't stay here."

"Robb Cassidy, that psych doctor as you call him, says I have PTSD."

"Yeah, well, welcome to the fucking club, Mate. We probably all have PTSD right about now.”

“But I can’t go back in the water. You saw me. I can’t surf again.”

“And it’s not the end of the world. Is that why you’re still here in the States? Hiding out?”

“I’m not hiding out. I’m trying to figure things out.”

“Okay. Figure them out at home while you take care of the team’s business. Don’t you see what’s happening? You’re underwriting team expenses from your personal funds, which is crazy and not a solution. It’s a stopgap.”

“We underwrote team expenses when we started out. What’s so wrong now?”

“We were a two-man team. We didn’t spend thousands daily on travel, hotels, fees, food, and lodging. We made more money in prizes than we spent.”

“You think I might need to disband the team?”

“That depends. Do you want to be an owner-manager?”

“No.”

“Well, that settles it.”

“But I just can’t leave the guys hanging. That’s why I sent Monica the check.”

“Give them severance if that makes you feel better. Seriously, though, have you or that psych doctor considered you might get better if you left here? Staying here, where it all happened, could be the trigger for your nightmares, your PTSD. If you went home, it might help you put all this behind you.”

“I don’t want to put Mia behind me.”

“Listen to yourself, man. You can’t heal in the same place where you’ve been traumatized. You have to remove yourself from that situation. If you love her, you owe it to her—and yourself—to get your life together.”

“Yeah, yeah. Don’t you think I know all that? I’ve told myself a hundred times that she deserves better, but I don’t want to leave her. She wants me to get myself together. She’d expect no less, but it’s difficult. I can't leave her."

"Then take her back with you." Sean sighed, exhaling a long breath before standing. He couldn't tell if he was getting through to Josh or not. "Put the drink down, get some sleep. We'll talk tomorrow on the way back to San Diego. And when we get there, you should talk to Mia. If she doesn't want to come with you, explain that you must leave for a few months. She'll understand you don't have a choice."

Sean left. Josh got off the bed and walked into the ensuite. He ran water in the sink and splashed cold water on his face, head, and neck. Maybe Sean was right. Maybe staying here in the U.S. was a trigger for his problems. It made sense in a fucked up kind of way, and Sean was right. He needed to focus on the business. The brand was taking hit after hit, now with him and Colin out. Team expenses were at an all-time high, and once Sean announced his retirement and it became apparent that Josh wouldn't be able to return to pro surfing, it would be all over anyway. Best to stop the bleeding right away.

He poured the last of his drink into the sink and watched it circle down the drain. He ran water after it, rinsing the last bit of alcohol away. That was his last drink, he vowed. He would deal with his problems from now on with a clear head. Looking at himself in the bathroom mirror, he saw bloodshot eyes and a haggard appearance. He looked like a wreck, and he felt defeated. After a moment of self-pity, he unbuttoned his shirt and slipped out of his clothes. Tomorrow would be soon enough to start the wheels turning and restore some order to his life. Tonight, he'd take a hot shower to help clear his head, then try for a few hours of sleep. He needed a clear head to get through everything he needed to do.

CHAPTER
TWENTY-SIX

Mia

Rose followed Mia out the ER doors.

"Where are we going?" she asked. They'd picked up sub sandwiches, chips, and canned soda for lunch from the hospital cafeteria, and Mia wanted to lead the way to the back patio to eat. It was still warm outside; the temperature had been in the eighties during the day, and it hadn't cooled off much once the sun had set.

"It's dark out there," Rose complained, following Mia.

"The lights will come on. They're motion detecting."

"Oh. How often do you come out here?"

"Josh and I used to sit out here when he first started doing PT. An attendant or I would roll him down here in the wheelchair."

"I've been meaning to ask you about Josh. How is he? I mean… do you still keep in touch?"

"Yeah, and he's fine. Why?"

"Oh, I just thought… well, I wondered if he'd gone back to Australia."

"No, he's still here in California. He's in Huntington Beach, actually, with his team at a surf competition." Mia looked at her friend and could see something was bothering her. "Why? What's going on?"

"Well, I just remembered how much you used to worry about him when he was upstairs, but you don't mention him much anymore. I saw a picture of him and his new fiancée and—"

"New fiancée?" Mia swung around and looked at her.

"Yeah. She broke the news today, and it's all over the Internet."

"Really?" she ground out, her jaw clenched to keep it from dropping to the floor.

"She's a wealthy heiress and a model."

"When? Where'd you see that?" Mia set her food down on the table as Rose pulled out her phone and flipped through it. When she handed it to her, Mia was stunned. It was a picture of Josh with a girl wrapped around him, standing on the street, kissing as if their lives depended on it. "That was yesterday. There are a lot of pictures of them in Huntington Beach this weekend and before his accident."

"This can't be real," Mia said softly, barely loud enough for Rose to hear.

"It's him. You can see the scar on his leg." Mia tapped the phone to zoom in on the picture, targeting his leg; satisfied that it was indeed Josh, her Josh, she tapped to bring back the full article.

"That's odd. He never once mentioned a Teagan Maddox."

"Yeah, well, according to all the stories, they go way back."

"I see," Mia muttered, giving Rose back her phone.

"So you still talk to him?"

"Some. We text back and forth a little."

"I'm surprised you hadn't heard about it already. Look, here are some pictures of him in a big fight on the beach."

"A fight?" Mia shook her head. The things Rose said sounded crazier by the moment. This couldn't be Josh, her Josh, in the middle of this madness. He certainly wouldn't have gotten engaged to some model without saying something about it, about her. She needed to talk to him. It had to be a big misunderstanding.

"Look, can you excuse me for a moment? I… I need to make a call."

"Sure, of course. Take your time. I'll watch your food." Rose pulled Mia's lunch tray beside hers and covered it with a napkin while Mia walked away to make her call.

Mia paced the floor, back and forth, as she listened to Josh's phone ring on the other end, hanging up as soon as his voice mail kicked on. She redialed his number several times, hoping he'd pick up, but her calls went unanswered.

She turned to Rose, who was focused on her food and the game on her phone. Mia composed herself, returned to the table, and sat back down.

"Everything okay?" Rose asked, looking at Mia's face.

"I'm good. I was just surprised to hear he's engaged. It seems sudden."

"Well, Ms. Maddox wasn't sporting a rock on her finger, so it might not be a completely done deal."

"Maybe she's getting something special made. I'm excited for them," Mia fibbed. "Maybe they'll invite us to the wedding."

"I would think you'd get an invite. I can be your plus one." Rose stared out into space, a dreamy look on her face for a long moment. "Here," she finally said, pushing Mia's food toward her. "Eat."

"No, I'm not hungry anymore. Finish your lunch, and I'll sit with you. Don't rush on my account. I'm not ready to go back downstairs yet."

Back in the ER treatment rooms, Mia couldn't stay focused. The news had spread throughout the hospital, and many of the staff had come over to her to chat about it, wondering if Mia or any of the others would get an invite to the wedding. Mia gushed over the details as best she could while feeling livid and sick to her stomach over his betrayal. At every opportunity, she'd tried calling Josh's phone again, hoping to talk to him, but it started going straight to voice mail, and she hung up. Without the chance to talk to him, to hear what he had to say about the news reports, she could only accept the news at face value. He'd suddenly remembered he had an entirely different life and a girlfriend waiting in the wings.

Looking at them in the photos displayed on various social media channels, she hated to admit how perfect the two of them looked together. Teagan Maddox was beautiful and wealthy, having come from old money. She wasn't tied to a paycheck, two weeks' vacation every year, or an eight hundred square foot, one-bedroom apartment that cost more than a third of her salary for rent. Apparently, she was free to sashay around the globe, meeting up with Josh whenever and wherever the league took him.

And Josh seemed happy enough, a big smile lighting up his face in nearly every shot. Mia was aware she couldn't compete on any level with Teagan Maddox. She was everything Mia was not, and it made sense that if Josh was going to marry anyone, it would be someone like her. She'd always known in her heart that, at some point, Josh would realize they were from two different worlds and return to his… but she hadn't expected it to happen so soon.

Mia tried to accept the situation, yet she couldn't help feeling let down. *Who was she? Why would someone like her even bother to risk her professional reputation, not to mention her heart, on a silly fling? Why would she believe him when he'd asked her to give their relationship one hundred and ten percent? She'd been a fool to let her guard down.* Cringing inwardly, she let the memories flicker in her mind, every moment she'd spent with Josh spinning past like a movie reel, and not once had he mentioned Teagan Maddox. In hindsight, she should have considered she could have been a last fling before matrimony. Why wouldn't he have had a girlfriend, his future wife, tucked away? Beyond lip service, he'd kept their relationship on the down low as much as she had. She felt foolish. She'd had taken everything at face value and never questioned anything.

Unable to constrain her roiling emotions and self-recrimination, Mia found, maybe for the first time in her career, that she couldn't put her feelings aside and focus on work. She was barely paying attention to what she was doing, though most of it was rote, and she felt like everything was happening in slow motion. As soon as she was done with her patient, she sought out Dr. Reynolds and asked for leave to end her shift early. He nodded permission, and she only stopped to retrieve her belongings from the locker room before getting into her car.

The elevator chimed, the doors slid open on quiet rollers on her floor, and she exited. Walking up to Chelsea's door, she knocked, unaware it was two-thirty in the morning and that her friend would be asleep or could even have company. She waited, her arms wrapped around her body, for Chelsea to answer the door. She could hear her running to the door. As Chelsea swung it open, she was immediately alarmed by the tears that ran silently down her best friend's face.

"Mia. My God, what's the matter? Come in. Sit down," she said, gathering Mia in her arms and ushering her inside.

"It's Josh," was all Mia could get out before she started blubbering. "He has a fiancée."

"A what? A fiancée? You're kidding, right?"

"No. It's all over social media. Her name's Teagan Maddox." Mia's voice hitched as she tried to stop crying and mop up her face with the handful of tissues Chelsea handed her. She watched as Chelsea scrolled through her phone, likely finding the same news Mia had seen earlier. Chelsea spit out a string of curses in her native Mandarin, bringing a sad smile to Mia's lips.

"Have you talked to him?" Chelsea asked once her temper was under control.

Mia shook her head. "He's not answering his phone."

"No. I imagine he's pretty busy right now."

"Yeah, I imagine so. I feel so stupid, Cee."

"That's because you cared about him."

"I do. I did. I mean, I still do, but I wish I didn't. I wish he'd told me about her from the beginning."

"Did anything happen at work? Did anyone say anything to you, you know, about you and Josh?"

"No. Rose and I had lunch together, and she showed me the articles and pictures. She said everyone was so excited talking about it."

"Yeah, everyone always felt like Josh was a personal friend or something. News about a long-lost fiancée would naturally spread like wildfire. The only good thing is that it takes the spotlight off you."

"Yeah, I guess you're right. It could have blown up in my face, couldn't it?"

"And you know that. Just a whisper of an infraction could've brought the top brass down on you, and they'd try to destroy everything you've accomplished and terminate you on the spot. Me and Rose right along with you because they'd swear we covered for you, which was what Rose kinda did for you."

"You guys don't deserve any of that fallout, and they would've definitely killed their diversity numbers," Mia muttered. "In one fell swoop, they would've unchecked the boxes for having Black, Latina, and Asian female employees. But at least we won't have that hanging over our heads anymore."

"No, but I wish it hadn't happened, especially to you, Mia. You're a good person, and you deserve better."

"Thank you. I feel microscopically better. You're a good friend, and I'm going to go home and let you get some sleep. Thanks for talking me off the ledge. I'm sorry I woke you. I wasn't thinking."

"Nonsense. You can always wake me, especially when you're ready to jump off a ledge."

"I hate crying. Especially over a liar and a cheater."

"Then, let's not. Get some rest, and I'll check on you before I leave for work. I may even bring you some coffee."

"Okay." Mia hugged her, grateful to have a friend as wonderful and caring as Chelsea.

CHAPTER
TWENTY-SEVEN

Josh

Josh felt he'd been put through the wringer, emotionally drained, after the team meeting.

He'd come to a decision about the team's future. Disbanding the team was one of the hardest things he'd ever had to do, and it had made sense to break the news while they were all still in Huntington Beach. But it had caught most of the team off guard. He and Sean had promised to help those who needed help finding new teams or individual spots within the various leagues, and Josh gave each man a generous severance. Sean, Joey, and Will had been able to keep their weekend winnings. The money had gone a long way toward soothing sore feelings.

The meeting hadn't lasted long, and most of the team left the hotel afterward, scrambling to arrange flights and other transportation home. Only two lived permanently in the States and planned to leave the next morning. Josh, Sean, and Sam also remained behind to get a few hours of sleep before driving back to San Diego. Josh slept soundly for the first time since leaving Mia at the house and was excited and nervous to see her again. He hadn't been able to get a retraction of Teagan's interview out as fast as he'd liked, but the lawyers were working on that and the lawsuit with the reporter and photographer from *Surf Rider* magazine.

The sun was barely over the ridge of the Penasquitos Mountains when they arrived at the house in San Diego. Josh and Sean had multitasked as Sam drove, the time difference allowing them to talk with the account execs at the PR firm in Sydney and lawyers in New York. They'd had a productive morning by the time they turned onto the private road leading up to the beach house.

Virginia met them at the door, and Sean greeted her effusively, squeezing her in his usual one-armed bear hug, letting her hear his stomach growl. Sean was always hungry. He seemed to burn fuel at an amazingly high rate and remained slender no matter how much food he ate. Virginia shooed them off as she returned to the kitchen to fix them a hearty breakfast, and they headed for the main floor office.

As they ate, Josh's phone pinged persistently, notifying him the various files he'd requested had been sent to his email. They hurried through the meal, leaving them an hour to review the documents before dialing in on a conference call with the lawyers.

"Josh? Sean? Can you guys hear us?" A loud squawk resonated through the conference phone speakers, and Josh adjusted the volume.

"Yes, Tom. We're here. Can you hear us?" Josh said, lowering his voice intentionally. "Go ahead. We're listening." He sat across from Sean and flipped through some notes he'd written.

"You should have received the documents with the claims made by the reporter and photographer from *Surf Rider* of injuries, lost time from work, and lost and damaged equipment resulting from the fight you allegedly provoked on the beach. There is also a copy of the lawsuit."

"I have it."

"Good. We plan to meet with their lawyers to try and negotiate a settlement. Is there a figure that you're comfortable with?"

Josh looked at Sean, who shrugged and sat back in his chair. They had talked at length about what Josh wanted to do versus the *smart thing* he needed to do, and a predatory grin appeared on Josh's face.

"Tom, I want you and Nelson to handle a few things for me."

Josh stood, too amped up to sit. "First, no settlement. I want to countersue *Surf Rider* magazine. I'm not paying anyone a single coin. Nothing. I want you to file the countersuit immediately for perjury, harassment, etcetera, etcetera, everything we discussed. Secondly, I'm still waiting for the retraction from the *HER* magazine and Teagan's so-called exclusive. I want you to file a lawsuit against them immediately. I also want you to file lawsuits against the other magazines that ran the story and pictures. I also want a public apology. I don't care how they handle it. They can blame it on the over-zealousness of their reporter and photographer. I don't care, but I want every story retracted. I also want all the pictures the reporter and photographer took of me this weekend—with and without Teagan—delivered to your office along with any copies and destroyed."

"Wait, hold on, Josh. We can't do that..."

"Yes, we can, and we are. *Surf Rider*, Teagan, and *HER* magazine are exploiting me for their own benefit, and I will not roll over. I want my public apology placed prominently in the magazine, not squashed on the classifieds page. If they refuse, I'll buy up fifty-one percent of their stock and force a takeover. They're both shitty little gossip rags, Nelson. I will not pay them off. Or their staff off. I will bankrupt them first."

"Are you sure, Josh?"

"Very sure. And lastly, I want you to remind Teagan Maddox that she is playing with fire. Get an immediate injunction against her from making any public commentary linking me or my name with hers. I do not intend to pay her a dime to do it, either. She will, or I'll make things very uncomfortable for her. Tell her a little birdie told you about her little affair with Spiro Adolphus. They have been very, very friendly—maybe a little too friendly—for a man whose wife is battling a terrible cancer."

"Spiro Adolphus, the son of Leo Adolphus, the Corsican manufacturing tycoon?"

"The same. There are supposed to be pictures of them skinny

dipping off the family yacht, moored off the family's private Medi-terranean island. I heard his young children were supposed to be on board. You might have to dig a little, but a few pictures are suppos-edly circulating taken by friends on holiday with them."

"Hearsay, Josh?"

"It could all be hearsay, but I think the information's legit. Check it out."

"Hmmm, okay. I'll get right on this and check back with you as soon as I have something."

"Thanks, Tom. Nelson."

The lawyers clicked off the line, and Sean looked up at Josh. "A little birdie?"

"Yeah. Your boy, Devon Burke, thinks she's hot and was telling me all about her and Spiro. He said he saw a lot of pictures of her and Adolphus together."

"Our Devon?" Sean chuckled. "He's about ten, maybe fifteen years younger than her. But I guess that doesn't really matter, does it? You think he'll take a chance with Teagan?"

"I'm sure he'd *like* to have one."

"She's a gold-digger, and he's hardly rich enough to be on her radar, for which he ought to be grateful. She'd eat him alive if she ever got her claws in him. He should stick with the pretty young things and steer clear of Tea Maddox."

"I don't know, Bruh. I don't care one way or the other, but if she doesn't go away, I'll make sure he'd be the last person she'd turn down. You know what I think right now?" he asked, laughing. "I think she might have burned two boats with this big engagement lie. Think of how Adolphus is feeling right about now. He might be thinking he'd been played."

Sean looked at Josh, and soon, the two of them were doubled over with laughter, tears streaming down their cheeks, and neither could stop. Josh was the first to try to catch his breath, but seeing Sean still laughing as he lay on the floor, Josh started laughing all over again. Virginia peeked inside the office to see what all the commotion was about. Neither Josh nor Sean saw her or the smile that lit up her face. She was happy to see them in such a good mood and slipped away, heading back to the kitchen. She mentally flipped through the recipes as she went, thinking through all of her boys' favorite meals. She would cook them a fantastic dinner, as they seemed to be celebrating.

CHAPTER
TWENTY-EIGHT

Mia

Mia's phone rang off the hook most of the day and late into the evening.

Feeling numb and detached, she sat on her sofa and watched Josh's picture light up the screen. He'd called so many times, but she'd ignored each one, and he eventually stopped and started texting instead. She read each text, though nothing she wanted to hear came through the texts, so she declined to reply. He missed her. He wanted to see her. He loved her. The charade nearly made her sick. When she went to bed, she turned down the volume but noted each time the screen lit up. She wanted to call him, scream at him, and give him a chance to make it all go away, but she knew it would have been more foolish to believe any more lies, including lies of omission from him.

Sometime during the early morning hours, she fell asleep, her body and mind exhausted. When she woke up, she felt better and stronger. Josh had continued texting her throughout the night, concluding at some point that she had read the stories and seen the pictures. His texts were lengthy as he tried to explain, but Mia had hardened her heart, and his defenses could not move her.

That evening, she felt composed enough to meet him at the beach house. She wanted to see him again; it'd been over a week since she'd seen him. When she figured Chelsea was home from work, Mia knocked on her apartment door, hoping she'd be free for the evening. Chelsea opened the door, still in her scrubs, and stepped back to let Mia in.

"Hey, how are you feeling, Hon? Better?"

"Better. I'm still angry, but I'm willing to listen to what he has to say."

Chelsea looked at her as if she wanted to say something but thought better of it. Mia smiled. She could imagine what her best friend was thinking and was grateful that she wasn't going to say it.

"I came over to ask if you'd ride with me?"

"To Josh's?"

"Yes," Mia nodded, sitting down at Chelsea's kitchen island. Their apartments had the exact same layout as Mia's, but they seemed so different. Chelsea had stamped her personality all over every square foot. Two of her kitchen walls had been painted a bright lemon-yellow, and colorful prints hung on every wall. Jewel-toned pillows and throws ornamented every sitting space, and a bright orange rug covered the vanilla carpet. Mia liked Chelsea's colorful space, but she preferred the calm, all-white walls and muted colors of her apartment.

Refocusing on Chelsea, who hadn't answered yes or no, she continued, "We're going to have a long talk tonight. I am curious about what he has to say, but I need a legitimate out. I don't want to stay long. I don't want to be tempted to forgive and forget. With you as my wingwoman, there's no chance of that."

"What if you do end up wanting to stay the night?"

"I won't, and if you come with me, I can't. Please? I need your moral support."

"Why are you even going? Can't you talk to him over the phone?"

"Please? Just this once."

"Okay. But you're going to owe me big time for this."

"I know. I owe you big time for so much already. You can have my firstborn."

"You're right, you do, but no thanks, you can keep your kid.

When do you want to go?"

"Around seven, I guess."

"Okay. I'll be ready. We really can't stay long."

"I swear, no problem. You'll be home in your bed before ten, I promise."

Mia knew there would be a crowd at the house because of the lack of parking in the neighborhood. Chelsea had chosen to drive, and they passed cars parked along the private road on both sides. She thought he would've wanted to talk to her privately but was not surprised by the party atmosphere. Sean was likely still at the house, and they had to keep up their party-boy reputation. Besides, how long would it take to tell her about the engagement and break her heart?

Chelsea was right. She should have done this over the phone. However, she must be a glutton for punishment because she wanted to see him, to hear what he had to say.

They found space several streets over, and she and Chelsea walked to the house, taking the beachfront route. As they approached the house, Mia stopped and looked at the party in full swing. Shocked and disappointed, she could tell there were more people than there'd ever been at one time. People were everywhere, clinging to every bit of space on the veranda and spilling out onto the beach. They seemed to be having a great time, the heavy beat of the music pumping out over the water.

"They have to be celebrating something big tonight," Chelsea remarked as they trudged through the sand toward the house, completely lit up in the dark.

"Yeah, I guess so."

"Are we going in?" Chelsea asked, ready to turn around if Mia wanted to.

"I don't know. I can't imagine trying to find Josh in that crowd," Mia replied, hunching her shoulders. "He said we were going to talk. How can we talk about all that's going on? You can hear the music blasting from here."

She waved her hand toward a loud beach volleyball game in front of the steps of Josh's house. A roar would fill the night as the people watching cheered and slapped high-fives as their favorite side scored a point. Just as she spoke, her phone vibrated in her hand. He'd texted her.

Josh: How close are you? Are you still coming to the house?

Mia: I'm here. Where are you?

Josh: Down here on the beach.

Mia: Where? There's a crowd on the beach.

Josh: Past the volleyball game.

Mia: Okay, see you in a minute.

"Shit," Mia swore, looking around. "Don't get too comfortable, Cee. This isn't going to take long at all."

CHAPTER
TWENTY-NINE

Josh

Josh grabbed a bottle of water from the fridge, walked through the house, and descended to the sand.

He shook his head, looking at everyone who'd shown up to celebrate their wins in Huntington Beach and their return home. It was a massive crowd, and Mia would give him crap for it. He walked out onto the veranda and looked out to see where he might find an out-of-the-way place to sit on the beach. People were playing ring toss in the sand on one side and volleyball on the other. He walked to the far end of the property, sat down on a tuft of grass, and stared out at the horizon. The sun had set hours ago, but the moon cast enough light for him to see. He drank the water and listened to the music while waiting for Mia.

Josh felt good about many of the important decisions he'd made in the last twenty-four hours, and he could hardly wait to see Mia. He'd missed her, especially the past few days, and now that she was coming, they could talk about their future together. Sean believed she would understand everything he'd been dealing with and the stress it had caused, so he'd intended to lay all his cards out on the table. Unfortunately, a huge party was happening; people were everywhere, and it wasn't how he'd planned to talk to Mia. He hadn't invited any of these people; he'd been astonished when they started showing up. He'd asked Sean about it, and he had owned up to mentioning to a few people that they were having just a small get-together at the house. More than a little irritated, Josh had made it clear that both he and Sam were responsible for everything and everybody.

Mia was coming over so he could talk to her. Now, he just needed to find somewhere quiet where they could talk and not be disturbed. Where that might be, however, was going to be a challenge.

Josh thought about the bedroom, but he knew one thing would lead to another, and they probably wouldn't get around to doing much talking. Sean suggested he take her upstairs to the top floor. There was a nice little sitting area up there they hadn't seen since they'd taken a tour of the house on the first day, but some friends had come down from LA and Huntington Beach to celebrate, and Sean had given them those bedrooms for the night.

Josh scrubbed his hand through his hair and down his face, scratching at his neat, trimmed facial hair, then pulled his phone out to text her.

Josh: How close are you? Are you still coming to the house?

His phone pinged, and he read her response.

Mia: I'm here. Where are you?

Josh: Down here on the beach.

Mia: See you in a minute.

He'd find somewhere for them to sit and talk once she got there. Josh scanned the crowd for her and saw Sean waving to someone at the far end of the property. A moment later, he saw Mia, her friend Chelsea, and Sean slough through the deep sand on their way to where he sat.

"Mia, Chelsea, you guys want something to eat or drink? A beer? Water?" Sean asked, playing host.

"No thanks, Sean. I'm fine for now," Mia answered.

"I could go for a beer," Chelsea said, taking the opportunity to give Mia and Josh some space.

"Okay. Cool, Chelsea, come with me. I'll show you where you can get whatever you want to eat and drink," Sean said, turning to grin at Chelsea. She gave Mia a pointed look before following him up the stairs to the veranda.

"Hey you," Mia whispered, perching on a smaller tuft of grass in the sand and turning to Josh.

"Hey, Babe, I'm glad you made it."

"How come you're sitting out here in the dark?"

"It's peaceful here. I can think."

"Hmmm," she hummed.

"Come here." He pulled her so that she straddled him, her short shorts riding high on her thighs as she splayed her legs to sit face-to-face on his lap. She dug the toes of her tennis shoes in the sand to help her stay balanced, and Josh held her steady, one hand on her hip while the other trailed over her skin, exposed by the cropped tank top and short shorts. He brushed his lips against hers.

"I missed you, Dr. Mia Thomas," he growled.

He kissed her again before she could utter a word. She looped her arms around his neck, slipping one hand up the back of his head, fingering his soft hair.

"Are you staying the night?"

"No, I can't. Chelsea drove over with me, and she has work in the morning."

"I could call a car and have her dropped off. Or she can take your car, and Sam can drive you home tomorrow."

"No, it's okay, we'll be fine."

Josh kissed her rather than trying to persuade her further. He just wanted to hold and kiss her while she sat in his lap. Each day away from her had been hell. He'd even started having nightmares again. After several moments, he helped her stand up and got up himself, brushing the sand off them both.

"Come on, Babe, I know you're hungry. I'm willing to bet you haven't eaten much all day."

"You'd win that bet because I did not."

"Hey, I know my woman." He laughed, and Mia smiled, stomping the sand from her shoes.

"Where are we going? I think this might be the quietest spot on the entire property."

"We'll grab something to eat first and then find another quiet spot."

"Yeah? Good luck with that."

He took her hand and led her toward the aroma of meat cooking on the grill. As they passed through the crowd, loud laughter floated in the air. In the kitchen, a small cadre of cooks scrambled to prepare enough food for the guests. Virginia prepared plates two plates, one for each of them, while Josh grabbed two bottles of water from the fridge. Mia raised an eyebrow over his choice of drinks but refrained from commenting. Carrying her plate, she followed him out of the kitchen.

"I don't think there is a quiet place in this entire house," she scolded, looking around at people eating and talking, having a great time in every available space. A group had even commandeered the den, and people sat around watching two guys play a video game.

"I think it might be kinda quiet out front; come on, let's see." Josh led Mia out the front door and down the steps.

This side of the house faced east, at a meticulously manicured lawn and sculpted nature landscaping. Although they could still hear the music, talking, and laughter, the noise was more subdued. The steps ended at the edge of the circular driveway, packed bumper-to-bumper with expensive luxury cars and motorcycles, and Josh sat on the bottom step. Mia came down and sat beside him. He wasn't all that hungry, but he picked at the food anyway, hoping Mia would eat. He bit a chunk of meat from a barbequed sparerib and chewed, looking at her. She glanced up as if she felt him looking at her and smiled. Josh thought she was so beautiful, even without makeup, her hair pulled into a low ponytail, and a smile on her gorgeous face.

"So, is your fiancée here tonight?" she asked, knowing she was being snarky, but it was how she was feeling.

"Fiancée? So you heard."

"Of course, I heard, Josh. Why wouldn't I have heard?"

"I've been trying to do damage control all week. I was hoping to get it all under control so that you wouldn't have to deal with it."

"You've been trying to sweep everything under the rug?"

"No, Teagan is not my fiancée, and she never was. It was something she made up."

"You never mentioned her once. You had plenty of opportunities to tell me about her but didn't."

"There was never anything to tell you. I'm not in love with her. I was never going to marry her."

"So, why would she say you were? Was there some marriage of convenience thing going on? Were your parents forcing you two to marry? Wait, is that still a thing? You wouldn't think so in this day and age, but the ultra-wealthy have to protect their billions, and this might still be a thing with y'all."

"*Y'all?* I've never heard you use that term before."

"You took me back to my roots, Brenner."

"Yeah, okay, well, stop it, please. I don't know if it's a thing or not, but it has nothing to do with me, so stop. I want to explain, okay?"

"Okay," she responded, watching him warily.

"I'd hazard to guess that maybe ninety-nine percent of everything you read or heard was a lie, depending on the sources. Teagan initiated the lies about our engagement for some reason known only to her, which makes no sense to anyone else. The reporter and photographer are lying and are attempting to sue me for millions of dollars. The magazines and social media outlets are exploiting the stories to make millions of dollars, selling more copies and garnering more followers, but none of it—not one single word of any of it—is true. My lawyers are on it, and I'm expecting a public apology from the magazines any day now. I want that apology for you. I wanted you to know that they lied, and my lawyers are making them own up to their lies."

"I see," Mia murmured, still wary.

"Teagan's gone, at least out of my life for good, either back to London or wherever she lives now. There won't be any more lies coming from her."

"How can they publish those kinds of stories if they're lies, with impunity, no less?"

"I don't know. I ran into Teagan on the beach in Huntington, and she wanted to pick up where we left off. We were never more than casual friends, off-and-on lovers, but she knew it wasn't going anywhere. I told her about you and how I felt about you, and she was angry and jealous. Maybe this was her way of getting back at me. She wanted to break us up, so she started the lies. Always looking for a good scoop, the paparazzi ran with it. It's backfired on all of them."

"And it's over?"

"Completely."

"Mmm," Mia hummed. "And the big fight on the beach?"

"That is kinda true, and it's taking a little longer to sort out, but I never punched those guys. Another thing happened, but thankfully, none of the news sources carried it. Sean and I disbanded the team. Colin's gone, I… I'm done, and Sean is quitting. We had to let the rest of the guys go. It was a difficult decision, but it was the right one. We were losing money all around. Our sponsors were abandoning us like rats on a sinking ship."

"I'm so sorry."

"No, it's okay. It would've gotten worse trying to hold on with our top talent gone. It was a sound business decision."

"I'm still very sorry. I know that meant a lot to you."

"It did in the beginning, but things were going downhill."

"So, what will you do now that you've dismantled everything?"

"Well, that's kinda what I wanted to talk to you about. We both know I probably can't surf anymore, and we both know I have PTSD. I have to go home. My visa is expiring in… hmmm, I think

I have about forty-eight hours before I'm kicked out of the country. So, we're leaving in the morning."

"For how long? A week, a month, a year?"

"I can't come back until after the new year. But I still want us to be together."

"You want me to *wait* for you?"

"I mean, it's not like I'm going away to fight in a war for a couple of years or something, Just four months. I'll have to apply for a different visa, not the athletic P-1 that I have, and that takes months. But I'll be able to stay longer, maybe a year. Who knows. By then, you'll be able to come to Australia and see my home."

"So, you'll be back in the New Year?"

"Your Immigration people are bogged down in red tape and bureaucracy, so I don't know how long it will take, but Monica will get started on it as soon as I get home."

"I've never even applied for a passport, so I know nothing about the process."

"Do it. Apply as soon as you can so you'll have it. Sometimes it takes a couple of months to get it."

"You're leaving in the morning," Mia repeated to herself.

"That's why I had to see you tonight. You're sure you can't stay?"

"No, I'm sorry, but I can't stay."

"I understand. While I'm home, I plan to get my head straight, straighten out my life, and think about my future. I wish you had a passport; you could come with me."

"I couldn't. I have a commitment to the hospital. Will you still see Dr. Cassidy? He was helping you, wasn't he?"

"Not much. I don't think I was progressing much at all with him. But he did suggest I go back home if I wanted to get better. I guess maybe he was right. I can't eat or sleep. I can't breathe here, Mia. It's the PTSD that makes me feel like I'm gasping for air. When I try to sleep, my nightmares take me down into a black hole that closes in over my head. I have to fight every night to get out. I have to fight for every breath, and sometimes, I feel like I might die if I don't wake up. I'm so tired of it. I think I might be going crazy. It might be a long shot, but Cassidy, Sean, and my family all think going home will help me. I have no choice now. If I stay beyond the expiration date, I could be deported and barred for years from ever returning."

"You're right, of course. And you know what they say. Doing the same thing every time and expecting different results is a sign of insanity." Josh smiled sadly, and she looked away. "Why did you have me come here with all these people?" she asked, changing the subject.

"I didn't invite them. Sean did. They're celebrating his championship win in Huntington Beach. And they're also here to see us off."

"Oh yes. I'd forgotten. I'll have to congratulate Sean. I'll find him before I leave."

"I will. But that sounds like goodbye, Mia," he said, turning to look at her. Shafts of moonlight fell across her features, and Josh thought she was the most beautiful woman he'd ever seen. "You could come with me, Mia, if you wanted to. You could finish your training in Sydney."

"No. That would put me behind two years. I'd have to sit out until the next semester starts and then redo this entire year. I have another semester left before I'm finished here. I can't even think of leaving now." She looked at him and then down at her plate. "Here," she said, handing it to him and standing. "I have to go." She turned around and started to climb up the stairs without looking back.

"Why? Where are you going?" he called after her.

She faced him. "Home, Josh. I can't breathe here either."

"You won't stay a little longer?"

"No. I can't. I have to get back. Goodbye, Josh. I wish you the best."

"Damn it, Mia," he swore. "This is not goodbye."

She didn't flinch. She didn't answer. Instead, she turned and climbed up the rest of the steps, her back ramrod straight, her head held high, and never once looking back.

Josh wanted to get up and go to her, keep her from leaving, tell her he'd changed his mind, and make them both forget what he'd said. He would give anything to make it all go away. He'd even stay and let his passport expire. He'd do anything not to leave her. But Josh could only stand there and watch her leave. He knew it was the right thing for him to do—like going home was the right thing to do. It was a step in the right direction to getting his life in order. He sat down heavily on the steps, folded his arms across his knees, laid his forehead on his arms and let the hot tears run freely from his eyes. They soaked the front of his t-shirt. He'd lost her and broken both of their hearts. She never said she'd wait for him.

He wiped his face with the hem of his shirt and stood., Taking the steps two and three at a time, he hurried through the house. He hoped to catch up with her and swear to her that he would be back, and when he did, he'd be whole and capable—the man she deserved.

But she'd had plenty of time to make her escape. When he reached the veranda, he saw her standing on the sand, searching the crowd before walking over to where Sean and Sam stood. They'd been talking with a group of people, but as she approached, they both swung around, smiled at her, and glanced up at Josh. Josh knew what those looks meant and shook his head. Mia's friend also came over and joined them. They stood talking for a moment before they gave Mia big hugs, and the two women walked away. He ached to hug her. It pained him, a sharp slashing pain all the way to his core, and he went back inside.

PART III

CHAPTER
THIRTY

Sydney, New South Wales, Australia

Josh

Josh was the first to climb aboard the private Bombardier jet at San Diego's Lindbergh Field, followed by Virginia, Sean, and then Sam.

The long-range jet belonged to his family; his brother Ian had put it at their disposal. As they settled in the comfortable club seats in the main cabin, Virginia sat down beside Josh, patting his hand. He clasped her hand in his, holding it reassuringly but still too wound up to want to talk about what was clearly on his mind.

"I must say, Joshua," she started, giving his hand a fierce squeeze. "This has been a most interesting few months. Who knew I would come to California? I think I like it there. Maybe we can come back again someday."

"Of course, Ginny. I intend to return, maybe in a few months, once I've taken care of some things. You are welcome to come with me, though you won't have to take care of me. You deserve a long vacation after this."

"I wouldn't know what to do on a long vacation." She laughed. "A short trip might be nice, but I'd rather spend a few weeks working in the garden. And I missed the grandchildren. It'll be good to be back at home."

"I'm sorry I took you away from your routine. I should have pushed back when Pop decided to send you."

"Nonsense. I wanted to come. Someone needed to see after you. Deidre would have come. She would have gotten on a plane to come see after you herself, but knowing her fear of flying, I volunteered.

Deidre will be happy to have you back home again. She worried so much."

"Dee getting on a plane would have been nothing short of a miracle. I've never known Dee to fly. I'll be happy to see her too. I haven't been back home in nearly a year."

"I know. That was nasty business with the shark and Colin drowning. You'll be home for a while?"

"For a while. And you? You'll be going back to Dad and Ellie right away?"

"Soon. Your father's given me a couple of weeks off first. I imagine I'll relax, spend time with Olivia, John, and Clive, and play with the grandchildren."

"That'll be nice. How many do you have now?"

"Six total. Olivia and John have four, and Clive has two, though they stay mostly with Caroline. They're divorced, you know."

"I remember. Give everyone my regards and hugs for all of the grandkids."

"Do you think you'll be able to sleep? It's a long flight, and I know you didn't rest well last night."

"At some point, I imagine I'll doze off. You must not have gotten much sleep if you heard me bashing about."

"Old people don't need much sleep. That's what naps are for."

"Yes, I'm sure we'll do a lot of napping today."

Josh dozed off and on during the flight but didn't really rest. The last thing he wanted was to wake up screaming mid-flight, caught up in one of his nightmares. He'd spent most of the time reclined in his seat, reading on his phone and talking to Virginia. Sean and Sam had fully reclined their seats and slept most of the way.

The plane taxied to a stop in front of the private hangar at Sydney's International Airport just after noon, though they'd lost a day by crossing the International Date Line. In his ragged state and traveling at jet speed, Josh felt like he'd been pulled like a piece of taffy. He looked just as he felt, like hell. He was disheveled, his clothes were badly wrinkled, his eyes were bloodshot, and a pounding headache was in full flower behind his eyes. Sometime over the Pacific, jet lag had settled on him like a mantle. As he stepped off the plane down onto the tarmac, he added stiffness and body aches to his list of complaints. The others gathered behind him, looking relaxed and fresh, excited to be home.

It was a beautiful spring afternoon—the seasons flipped on this side of the equator, and much cooler after the extremely warm fall temperatures that were baking San Diegans. Josh grabbed the ibuprofen from his duffle bag and a lightweight leather jacket just as a long, black car pulled up in front of them. The driver hopped out to stow their luggage in the back, and after helping Virginia inside, Josh slid in beside her, his fingers running across the familiar B&I logo embossed on the back of the camel leather seats. A company car.

Sean had driven his car to the airport and parked it in the long-term lot. Sam climbed up front with the driver, giving Josh and Virginia plenty of room in the back. Josh let his head fall back on the headrest and closed his eyes, waiting for the three pain relievers he'd swallowed to take effect.

"Excuse me, Sam," Virginia said, reaching past Sean to tap Sam on the shoulder. "Would you direct the driver to my house, please?"

"Sure thing, Miss Virginia."

Even stopping to drop Virginia off in Haberfield, one of Sydney's oldest and most established neighborhoods, they came to a stop in front of Josh's home thirty minutes later. Josh was grateful, desperate for a hot shower and whatever Dee had ready to eat. The headache had worsened into a migraine, and the ibuprofen had done nothing to lessen it. He'd seen lights spinning on the back of his eyelids since leaving the airport, but now his stomach added to his discomfort, protesting loudly with nasty animal-like noises. Now that he was in the back by himself, he stretched out on the seat and put his hand over his eyes.

The car finally came to a smooth stop in front of Josh's three-story building. It had been zoned for commercial use on the first floor and apartments on the top two, but Josh hadn't done much more than renovate the top floor, which he occupied. Three large storefront windows spanned the front of the first floor, painted over with black reflective paint, obscuring the gutted interior of the storefront. *J. A. B. Enterprises* was etched in gold calligraphic letters inside a silver, mirrored horizontal band across the top third of the center pane. Josh thought it added a bit of mystery and style to the storefront that passersby remarked upon while putting his mark on the otherwise nondescript building. Even as it currently stood, the building would sell for a tidy sum, as properties on the strip and this close to the beach were prime and highly sought after.

Josh exited the car without glancing at his reflection in the window and inhaled deeply through his nose. The ocean was one block over, and he could smell the briny, fishy odors and hear the scavenging birds as they circled overhead, screeching and cawing loudly. On the sidewalk in front of the door to his building, he saw a man in motorcycle leathers sitting on the curb. The car had pulled up inches from him, yet he appeared unconcerned, unmoved. His motorcycle, a lipstick-red and black Ducati *Superleggera,* was parked at an angle to the sidewalk, and he sat hunched over, his elbows on his knees. At first glance, he looked to be resting after a long ride, but Josh quickly recognized him as security and gave him a slight, almost imperceptible nod, which the man returned.

Hurrying inside the building, Josh took the stairs rather than the elevator to the top floor. Winded, he stopped on the landing at the top of the stairs to catch his breath and rub his leg. The three flights told him all he needed to know about how much he was out of shape. He'd run up and down those same stairs a year ago like Rocky Balboa, not even breathing hard. Now, he thought he might have to crawl to the top with respites in between before making it inside.

Late afternoon sun filled the stairwell with a golden glow, flooding through a large window that looked over the buildings between him and the ocean, giving him a grand view of the street below and the horizon beyond. He suddenly realized how good it felt to be home. He entered the apartment, his breathing almost normal again, and called out for Dee. He could hear her in the kitchen and smell delicious aromas floating throughout the huge, open space, with its high ceilings and bank of windows along the far wall that let in natural light and cool ocean breezes. Many of the windows were opened, the drapes fluttering in the light breeze as it blew in.

"Oh my, oh my," she cried, coming around the corner, wiping her hands on a dishtowel. "Joshua, is that you?"

"It's me. I finally made it back." He hugged her, and she returned it with a ferocious one of her own, much stronger than one would think for a woman her age.

"Oh, let me look at you," she said, releasing him and stepping back. Deidre Gibbs had been his nanny after his mother had died, and when the boys had grown up, especially with Josh, the youngest, no longer needing a nanny, Dee had become a housekeeper in his father's house, then in Josh's small-ish apartment.

"Oh, Joshua. I'm so happy to see you and glad you're back home. Are you okay?"

"I'm okay. Just tired… and hungry. What is that I smell?"

"I made your favorite dinner. It's in the oven."

"Ohmigod. Is it firecracker shrimp and salmon? It is, isn't it?"

"Yes, it is. But I also took out steaks for later. I know how much Sean and Ian love beef. Ian called and said he'd be over this evening. I imagine Sean is coming too?"

"Yeah, he'll be by later. I'm glad you fixed seafood, though. I don't think I'll want anything off the grill for a long, long time. Ginny had the grills going day and night."

"Really? Why's that? Didn't she feed you healthy food when you got out of the hospital?"

"She tried, but when I've got a choice between a salad and a broiled chicken breast or some real meat, like a brat or burger, a rib, or a steak right off the grill… well, that's not a hard call to make. The salad didn't have a chance. Besides, we had people over all the time, and it was just easier to keep the grill going."

"Your boys followed you?"

"Yeah, some of the team, a few new guys."

"You know you can't save every runaway."

"I know, but I can help a few at a time. They don't stay long. Sometimes one night, sometimes a few nights. They know it's safer than sleeping on the beach or in old cars."

"Yes, well, I'm glad you're back home now. Did Ginny tell you how worried I was? I almost got on that plane with your father and Ian. I almost did it," she said, smiling, her head bobbing up and down as she stirred several pots. "But Ian, bless his heart, told me he'd let me know how you were doing and kept his word."

"You're terrified of flying, Dee. I can't imagine you making such a long trip for the first time. It's a fifteen-hour flight. I wouldn't have wanted you to go through that. And as you can see, I'm fine. Now, stop worrying. How long before I can eat? It smells so good in here; my stomach is knocking on my spine."

"Take a seat. I'll fix you a plate now."

"Okay, give me a few minutes first. I desperately need a shower and fresh clothes. Then we'll eat together."

"Go, go. It'll be ready when you are."

CHAPTER
THIRTY-ONE

Josh felt relieved to be home.

He'd left ten months ago, and yet it looked and felt as if he'd only been away a few days, maybe only a few weeks. He set his duffle bags inside the closet, took fresh clothes out of the drawer, and carried them into his ensuite. He stripped and got into the shower, letting the water, just shy of scalding, stream down over him from the rainfall shower head. He flexed to help ease the tension in his body.

The withdrawals from going sober cold turkey were tapering off. He no longer felt like he'd been hit by a train as he had during those first few days, but the aching muscles and joints and the pounding headaches behind his eyes frequently reoccurred, so debilitating at times he wished he hadn't tossed the last few painkillers he'd had left. His leg constantly ached, from his hip to his foot, and all he had to dull the throbbing was tablets of ibuprofen, which he washed down with water or fresh juice instead of the heavy prescription painkillers chased with beer or Jack and Coke. Ibuprofen took longer to work and only blunted his miseries, but at least he was functional, clear-headed, and aware of his body and mind most of the time.

He slid down the shower wall and sat on the tile floor, elbows on his knees, hands in his hair, and eyes closed. He raised his face to let the water run into his mouth and back out, wondering what Mia was doing.

He wondered if she missed him as she went about her established routine of work, home to eat, sleep, and back to work again. He was proud of her. She had her life together. She had mapped out her life a long time ago, and in a few months, she'd accomplish her life-long dream. She didn't need messy distractions in her neat and orderly life. He smiled. Too neat, too orderly, in her opinion. Too boring. Josh, however, thought she was the most amazing woman he'd ever met, and he respected her even more for her generous heart, steadfastness, and determination.

He grimaced. Things between them been good, really good, and then he'd gone to Huntington Beach. After that, everything between them had nosedived so quickly that he hadn't begun to comprehend the sheer unraveling of his life. When she walked away from him, leaving him sitting on the stairs of the beach house, it felt like she'd taken his world with her. He'd been stunned—stupefied. He should have stopped her. He should have taken her in his arms and kissed her, getting her to talk to him until she understood and forgave him. But he hadn't, and now, she refused to talk to him or respond to his emails and texts.

He understood her reaction, her feelings, and why she'd shut him out. He might have felt the same if their roles had been reversed. In fact, she might have even empathized with him, and his screwed-up situation had she not been poleaxed by everything all at once. Yet, her absence, her silence, made him feel lost, untethered. He could no more deny he loved her than stop his next breath, his next heartbeat. He had never cared about anyone like he cared about her, cherished her. He should have told her, though he thought he'd shown her. He was a believer that actions spoke louder than words, but he could see now that words were necessary. The right words could have made all the difference. All he could do now was take a step back, give her time to let her emotions settle and think things through, to parse it all out objectively. But Josh didn't know how long that might take and was afraid he'd lose her if too much time passed. He didn't want her to forget him.

He stood and shook his head, flinging back the wet hair plastered to his face, and began to wash. There was light at the end of the tunnel. Some good things were starting to happen in his life, which, considering how badly he'd messed things up, amazed him. First, he was probably fully detoxed after more than a week without a single drink or prescription pill, which was probably the reason why he felt like crap. He'd never been much of a drinker, nor had he taken drugs of any kind before, and truthfully, the combination hadn't helped much. They hadn't helped keep away the nightmares. They hadn't cured his insomnia, and they'd only marginally kept the demons from twisting and tearing at his thoughts and emotions.

He'd received the public apology and retraction he'd demanded from *HER* magazine, as well as from several other magazines and news outlets, and Teagan Maddox had quietly disappeared from the media and his life. He'd texted the news links to Mia, but she never replied. He hoped she had read them, as they should have cleared him of any duplicity still lingering in her mind. The counter lawsuit against *Surf Rider* magazine and its two employees had stirred interest in the surfing community, and public support had swung in Josh's favor. His lawyers had rightly cast him as the victim, and the reporter and photographer as avaricious con artists, and the magazine's execs had lost no time terminating their relationship with the two men, leaving them hanging in the wind. They'd also recused the magazine from the legal proceedings, which immediately sent a message to other journalists, both staff and freelancers working for big corporate publications. Josh's lawyers felt confident the entire matter would be dropped in a matter of days.

The hemorrhaging of money had stopped with the disbanding of the nine-man team, but then so had the influx of cash. It occurred to Josh he now needed a new revenue stream and a challenge, as in the back of his mind, he felt lucrative championship prize checks could be a thing of the past. And though he was in good standing with the U.S. Immigration Department, having left with one unexpired day left on his visa, he no longer had the U.S. or International Surf Federation vouching for and expediting a P-1 visa. This meant he'd have to wait the usual eight to twelve weeks or more for a regular tourist visa to return to the States.

He wrapped his arms around his legs and laid his head on his knees, the hot water streaming down, keeping him warm inside the massive, glass-enclosed space. He hadn't had much choice in leaving San Diego. He hadn't paid attention to how much more time he had left in the U.S. He'd have to make the most of his time at home and come back when he could.

In the meantime, he'd use the time wisely, like getting his head screwed on straight and buttoning up stray loose ends. The implosion of his surf enterprises might have been a blessing in disguise. In a few years, he would have had to retire anyway. Forty was considered old in the sport.

Now, he had the opportunity to take on a new challenge. He knew many retired surfers who'd turned to environmental issues like saving the ocean and global climate change. During his years at the university, he'd been interested in understanding the erosion and damage done to the Great Barrier Reef and efforts to save and restore it. He'd even supported various organizations that spearheaded such work. But in reality, they needed more than a few dollars here and there. They needed public awareness. More opportunities to educate more people, helping them understand the link between the quality of human life and the oceans. They needed more hands to pitch in and stronger government intervention and policies. Maybe, Josh thought, *there might be something he could do besides writing a check.*

Feeling more settled but also more jet-lagged, he got off the tile floor and finished his shower. He'd been in there for a while, and Dee was probably trying to keep his food warm. Stepping out of the shower, he knotted a bath sheet around his waist and dried his hair with another. He decided to call Mia later after he'd taken a long nap. By then, she should be getting home from work, and just maybe, she missed him enough to answer her phone.

San Diego, California, USA

Mia

Mia lay curled up in bed, her eyes red and scratchy but finally dry.

She didn't believe she had a single tear left in her, but the deep ache inside that made her short of breath was just as prevalent and painful as it was the moment Josh told her he was leaving. She'd tried to forget and forgive Josh, but it had proven too difficult. How could she forget someone who felt like an essential part of her, like a heart or lung? But how could she forgive him? He had abused her trust. He'd returned to his old life, to the people that had been important to him, and tossed her aside in the blink of an eye. She should have prepared herself when he first talked about going to Huntington Beach to support his team, schmooze his sponsors, and talk to the media, but she'd been too accepting, too naïve, to think about self-preservation.

The fact that she was heartsick was her fault. She'd set herself up. She'd fallen in love with him despite their differences. Her phone pinged beside her, and she reached for it, checking to see who'd sent a message this time. Both Chelsea and Rose frequently checked on her, seemingly every hour, making sure she was okay, that she'd eaten something, and that she'd rested. She sent them the same message each time. Yes, she had eaten, and yes, she was fine. But Josh texted her constantly since she'd walked away from him that night at the beach house, sometimes three or four long messages at a time. He also left her voice mail messages, letting her know he'd made it home safely, which she appreciated, but she refused to respond to any of them. What could she have said? *That's nice? Glad things are working out for you? Wish you were here?* It was another text from him. She read it and closed it, putting her phone down beside her.

She needed space and time and some distance from Josh to get control of her feelings. She was determined not to beg him to stay or run off with him to his home. She could never be so irresponsible to do something like that. From a logical perspective, she absolutely understood his situation with his visa. He couldn't remain in the States once it expired. She also understood that, at some point, he needed to return home. He was only supposed to be in San Diego for a day or so, the last leg of his vacation. If it hadn't been for the shark attack, he would have gone about his business, flying to South Africa the next day and doing the promotional tour. Life uninterrupted. They would never have met. If things had been reversed, she would never have been able to spend time in a hospital in a foreign country after an accident and remain there for months to recuperate. She would have been bankrupt in a matter of weeks and no doubt lost her job. She wouldn't have had the luxury of falling for someone, and she would never have been caught up in a little bubble that existed outside of her normal life.

So, the pain she was dealing with came from his absence, but also the possibility he might be seeing *her* again. She'd learned that Teagan Maddox had been staying in L.A. with friends and had left the country a few days before Josh. The coincidence and possibility of their reunion had shattered Mia's heart into a million pieces. But it also came from the overwhelming sense of shame and embarrassment over her impulsiveness, her sheer foolishness. Yes, he had betrayed her trust, but *she* had betrayed *herself*, her values, her promise to her grandma. She'd dropped her guard and put herself in an untenable position. She could have lost everything she'd worked so hard to achieve. Drunk off the feelings he aroused, she'd let things get out of hand. She had fallen in love with him.

Mia rolled onto her back and stared at the ceiling. She could see him clearly in her mind's eye. Dark blue eyes that sparkled with humor. A wide, mischievous smile that melted her heart. She felt as if she could reach out and take a lock of his honey-gold hair and wrap the loose curls around her fingers or cup his face and feel the soft scruff of his beard against her palm. Josh was a beautiful human being, inside and out, and she'd become enthralled by the silkiness of his skin stretched over taut muscles. She'd come to crave his touch, his kisses, and how he knew her body, playing it like a fine instrument. She had been lost from the first moment she'd seen him.

However, she should have been aware of the changes in his behavior after he was discharged from the hospital. She should have noticed that he drank every day and far too much and brooded as if the weight of the world was on his shoulders. She should have noticed that his PTSD was not improving, that he slept less and less, sometimes staying awake for several consecutive nights, and that he still had terrible nightmares. She should have seen him sliding into the abyss of depression, abusing prescription drugs and alcohol. She should have insisted, made it a condition, that he continued to meet with Dr. Cassidy. She believed he would have been able to help Josh. But she had seen none of it until it was too late. In fact, she hadn't put any of it together until things had almost spiraled out of control for him in Huntington Beach.

She pulled the brief note he'd written from beneath her pillow. He'd stuck it inside the overnight bag with her clothes and toiletries that she'd left behind at the beach house. It had made her cry for days. She opened it and read it again.

Darling Mia,

I understand that you're hurt and more than a little disappointed in me right now. But maybe in time, you'll realize I would never intentionally hurt you. Nor let anyone else hurt you. I can not help but give you the time you want and need to think things through; this is out of my hands. But know that I will never, ever give up on us. Please, don't you give up on us either.

He hadn't signed it, but there was no need. She sniffed as she refolded the note. One tear slid past a closed eye, catching on her thick lashes and dripping to her cheek, then rolled down and fell into her lap. Soon, others followed, fat and hot, rolling down her cheek and dripping off her jaw as she sat in the middle of her bed and cried—again.

CHAPTER
THIRTY-TWO

Bondi Beach, Sydney, Australia

Josh

Josh prowled his apartment like a disgruntled cat in a cage.

Despite the volume of space inside the thirty-three hundred square feet on each floor of the three-story building, it felt like the walls were closing in. He was restless, unable to settle down, and nothing seemed to hold his attention. He'd been away from home for nearly a year, but the novelty of being back had quickly dissipated. His family had welcomed him home, having him over for visits and throwing lavish dinner parties in his honor. Most of the extended family had celebrated his return that first weekend. Ellie and his father had hosted a big family dinner, and the number of people who'd shown up had taken him aback. Besides his father, Ellie, and Bekka, Ian, his wife Abbi, daughter Claire, and son Justin, and Sean, there were at least a dozen people Josh hadn't seen in years—aunts and uncles, cousins and their significant others, and their young offspring, and several close friends of the family. Ellie set up another long dining table and several round-top tables in the formal dining room and threw open the massive carved doors at each end to accommodate the overflow. At least thirty older adults were seated at the dining table in the center of the room, while two and a half, maybe even triple, that number of the young people sat at the round-top tables on either side. Josh was seated to his father's left, across from Ian, who'd been seated to his right.

For years, Josh had avoided these kinds of family social functions. There was too much food, too little space, and too many people sucking up all the air in the room, aunts and uncles-in-law, first cousins, and second cousins. Much of the conversation at the center table centered around business, as most of the men worked in some capacity for Brenner Industrials and his father. Josh knew little and cared even less about the topics and avoided being drawn in.

James Brenner had been subtle since Josh's return, never mentioning the firm or Josh taking a position now that he could not go back to surfing any time soon, but others had no such compunction. His uncles asked if he was ready to settle down, get his head out of the clouds and come back to work. His cousins worried how his return would affect their roles or ones they may have coveted. Though they smiled and laughed affably, Josh saw them squirming in their seats whenever his name came up.

As much as he'd railed against returning to the company, it was an option—a long shot, but still viable. He would be given a corner office on the executive floor with a view, and for a while, he'd have to shuffle papers until he relearned the lay of the land. The thought of being tied to a desk left a distinctly bad taste in his mouth, but he could manage it, at least for a while.

After several weeks of making the circuit from his house to his father's, then Ian's, and around to Sean's house and back again, hanging around and doing much of nothing, Josh decided he needed to get away. He'd traded one city, one continent, for another, but nothing had changed in his life. After consideration, he decided a trip to Treachery Beach, or Yakon as the locals called it, was in order. He could check on Charlie and the house—two birds with one stone. Doing so could also give his overworked brain a rest. He decided to drive up the next morning and set to packing and stuffing everything in the boot of his car so that he could get an early start.

A little over three and a half hours away, Yakon was one of New South Wales's wildest undeveloped coastlines. It was also a designated sanctuary for many varieties of migrating sharks and other marine life. Ian had thought him crazy for buying a house built on a deserted, windswept promontory that jutted above the craggy beach and then turning it over to Charlie Mitchell and his rescue boys. The property had called to Josh, and he knew Charlie and his boys would have a solid roof over their heads and be safe, protected from the elements.

With the ocean on one side of the freeway and the national park bordering the other, it was an easy, straightforward drive. Feeling a million miles from civilization, Josh couldn't wait to walk on packed sand along the ocean and hike through the dense undergrowth along the forest's border. There were beautiful beaches in Yakon, perfect for swimming and sunbathing, and they drew plenty of tourists in the summer and early fall seasons. But the house was situated farther up the headland, past the famous lighthouse and Lighthouse Beach. The Crag, as Josh had named it, was a natural beauty. The house was the only structure for miles. Built on a high outcropping and exposed to the winds and salt water, it could be seen for miles down the beach.

But it was a fair hike away from any tourist attraction and not meant for the casual beachgoer. The terrain grew rockier and scraggier with overgrowth the closer you got to the house; the sandy beach became coarser, more like grit in your shoes, and the waves crashed against jagged rocks hidden under the roiling water churned by the push and pull of the tide. It wasn't an ideal spot for wading or playing in the surf at any given time, especially not at high tide. When the tides thundered onshore, they forced a heavy spray to shoot up, arching overhead and falling back down like sheets of rain. If you were unlucky—or lucky, depending on your perception—you'd also have to deal with being swept off your feet by the rush of the receding water and the roaring or wailing winds that tried to snatch away anything not battened down. This would all occur as a laser-bright sun beamed in a cloudless, azure sky.

This wildness stretched at least two-hundred yards and deterred all but the most determined beachcombers. Tourists mainly stayed on the other side of the lighthouse, along the gently lapping water and fine sand beaches. But while The Crag was not a tourist destination, it was a siren's call to surfers. Josh had enjoyed some of the best times of his life surfing the raging water there.

Stowing the hampers of food, drinks, and Charlie's supplies in the back seat of the Audi, Josh set out to enjoy the relaxing and familiar drive. Parking the car on the asphalt-covered space beside the house, Josh saw Charlie sitting in the back of his dilapidated van, parked on the side of the house and propped up on concrete blocks. He was strumming an old, well-worn guitar, dressed in board shorts faded to a pale pink, a green plaid lumberjack shirt, sleeves rolled up over his thin forearms, and cheap rubber flip-flops on his feet. He looked like the quintessential beach bum. His long, thin hair, a silvery-gray now, hung over his shoulders and down his back. Looking up as Josh approached him, his watery-brown eyes filled with delight, and a smile spread across his face.

"Josh? Boy, is that you? In the flesh?" He laughed, setting the guitar aside.

"It's me, old man. I came to check on you. How are you?"

Josh sat on the van's bumper, and Charlie slapped him on the back.

"Doing just fine, thank you very much. How about you?"

"Pretty good. You heard about the tangle I got into with a shark a few months ago, yeah?" Being Colin's uncle, he had little doubt Charlie wouldn't have heard.

"Did hear about it. Sean even called me. Got hurt real bad, didn't you?"

"Yeah. I was in the hospital for more than three months. It tore up my leg." Josh showed Charlie the scars that wrapped around his calf.

"How're you doing now?"

"Not too good. The whole thing, losing Colin and all, kinda messed with my head. And I probably will never surf again, at least professionally. Most of all, though, I'm so sorry about Colin. He was like a brother to me."

"I know, Josh. It was hard on his mother, my sister. A real tough pill to swallow. Nobody blames you, Josh. None of it was your fault."

"In my head, I understand that, but if he hadn't tried to save me, he might still be here."

"Maybe, maybe not. Only the Lord knows when it's our time. But we're glad you survived. His sacrifice was not in vain." Josh nodded, only marginally better. "So, what do you plan to do now? Come home to work with your family?"

"No, at least not right away. I haven't figured out much of any-thing."

"Hope you're staying for a bit. This ain't no day trip like last time, is it?"

"I didn't have any plans beyond getting up here."

"Good. Let's go inside. I can fix us some lunch, and we can catch up. Then you can get settled in your room. No one's been in your room since you left because I tell everybody it's off-limits."

"How many up here with you, Charlie?"

"Four. Two of them were staying in an old, broken-down car parked on the street over by the adventure resort. The other two were sleeping on the beach, and they kept getting hassled. They're all good boys, though. I don't imagine the oldest is even eighteen yet."

"Runaways?"

"Yeah, mostly."

"You're teaching them to surf?"

"They're picking it up. A couple of them remind me of you and Sean. And like you two, I suspect they'll be okay someday."

Josh laughed as he followed Charlie up to the house. Charlie had taught him and Sean everything they knew about surfing, and they both were elite champion surfers. If the boys staying with Charlie were anything like him and Sean, they would be more than just okay.

Entering the house through the large living room space, Josh noticed the place was neat, clean, and airy, a far cry from how he'd kept the rental in San Diego. Charlie, however, was an exacting taskmaster and tolerated zero clutter, sand, or water in the house. He didn't mind feeding and giving shelter to the many homeless teens who had stayed with him, but they had to pull their weight and clean up behind themselves.

"I forgot. Dee sent hampers of food and stuff. Maybe there's something in one of them to make sandwiches."

"Did she, now? Bless her. And did she send coffee? Can't get the gourmet stuff around here. Just the local stuff, which is pretty good, I guess."

"I don't know what she packed since I didn't tell her how long I was staying."

"Well, we'll see in a minute. Where is it?"

"I left everything in the car. I'll go get them."

Josh turned around and went out to the car. He brought the big hampers inside through the back door and set them down in front of Charlie, who sat at the kitchen table. They were big and heavy enough to hold food to last a month. Dee knew there were always extra mouths to feed up at The Crag. As Charlie fixed lunch, Josh put on a fresh pot of coffee. Dee had packed several canisters of the gourmet roast coffee Charlie loved. While answering Charlie's pointed questions, Josh remembered that was one thing about Charlie: he didn't beat around the bush.

"Talk to me, Josh. I'm looking at you, and I see there's something else lying heavy on your mind."

"Jeez, Charlie. I don't even know where to start." Josh scrubbed his hand down his face and smoothed his jaw and chin hair.

"Let's eat outside, and you can tell me everything. Start at the beginning."

Josh followed Charlie outside, carrying their lunch to the heavy wooden table and chairs on the back lanai. They talked about every-thing except what was bothering Josh while they ate, and when he finished, Josh leaned his elbows on the table and stared at the last gulp of coffee in his cup, cradled in his hands. Charlie sipped his and waited for Josh to speak. Josh felt sixteen again as he recounted ev-erything that happened after he awakened in the hospital. Hot, angry tears seeped from his eyes and ran unheeded down his face. Charlie listened, nodding every so often to show he understood Josh's feel-ings of anger and hopelessness.

"You see someone afterward? A shrink while you were in the hospital?"

"A few times."

"And?"

"And I stopped. But now, the nightmares have gotten worse. They're like a horror movie on a loop in my head. They don't stop. I thought I could deal with it myself, but… well, obviously not."

"I've seen this too many times, Josh. It's hard to process death and trauma. Lots of guys come back from war and can't fit back into their regular lives because of what they've seen and done. Others can't process the trauma done to them through no fault of their own. The mind is a delicate thing. PTSD is a terrible thing, and it can hap-pen to anyone. You don't have to be ashamed of having it."

"You're saying it's okay that I'm going crazy." Josh laughed aloud.

"Nope. Just saying you need help. I know you've heard it before, but that's the only way you'll get better up here," Charlie said, tap-ping his temple. "You don't have to suffer."

"You know, I'm terrified to go out on the water. I get panic at-tacks when I do. I'm always waiting for a shark to sneak up on me, looking for it to happen again."

"Yeah. I've heard that it can be that way for a lot of guys. I've seen two shark attacks in my sixty-something years out here on the water, but I've met quite a few men who were attacked in the ocean and lived to talk about it. Most have reactions like that. Some never went back in the water, but they still led good lives. They had families and success off the water."

"Yeah. I've tried to give that some thought, too. I met a woman… the doctor, who saved my life after Sean dragged me out of the water. She was on the beach."

"Where is she now?"

"In California. She couldn't come with me, and I couldn't stay. Time ran out on my visa, and I had to leave, but I told her I'd be back in a couple of months."

"So, you have more reason to get better. Did the doctors give you medicine to help you cope while you work through it?"

"The drugs make things worse. I feel like a zombie when I take them. Plus, I was drinking."

Charlie sighed and nodded. "Some people need one or the other. Not a good idea to take them both."

"No, but I did," Josh stated, his voice barely above a whisper. He and Charlie sat quietly for a long while, unmindful of the coffee that had gone cold in their cups. Their thoughts were a million miles apart, yet their emotions were in sync. Charlie eased his stiff body out of the chair and began gathering their dishes to take back inside. Josh got up to help.

"I'll put these in the dishwasher while you bring your things in out of the car and put them in your room. You can take the time you need to get through this, and I'm here for you. There's no shame in needing help from time to time. None of us can do this thing called life alone. Take the help people offer you."

"The medical doctors say I'll need reconstructive surgery on this leg."

"So why haven't you done it?"

"I was so damn tired of the hospital and the physical therapy… I just wanted to be left alone. All I wanted was to spend time with Mia."

"Then there's no rush for that surgery, is there?"

"Nah. But I might as well get it done while I'm here. My pant legs rub against the skin, making it red, sore, and irritated."

"Seems you've got a lot on your plate, son."

"Yeah, seems like it. Thanks, Charlie, for listening."

"Anytime, Josh. Anytime."

When they finished their tasks, Josh watched Charlie as he ambled down the back steps and disappeared around the side of the house toward his van. Josh stood in the doorway and stared through the screen door out at the raw, undeveloped land, the lowering sun backlighting the field of tall grasses. The view out the back was more wilderness, ancient boulders and untamed overgrowth, scraggly trees with new leaves sprouting on bare, twisty branches under the most perfect blue sky. He was glad he came. It was a perfect place to sit and think. The panoramic vista of the wild blue ocean on the other side of the house would have been too distracting. He would have watched the surfers, the birds, or the water, anything but work out his problems. The view from the front of the house was a totally different feast for the eyes.

Yet, thinking was not something Josh wanted to do. He'd come up to Yakon to *not* think. Pulling his phone out, he checked the time in San Diego. Three-thirty AM. Mia would be at work. He also texted Sean and Ian, letting them know where he was. He walked back to his room and tossed the phone on his bed. Flopping back across the mattress, he closed his eyes.

It had helped a little to talk to Charlie, though he hadn't intended to dump everything on him like he had. Charlie had a way of getting to the root of things, and Josh felt emotionally drained, but it also felt like a burden had been lifted off his shoulders. Maybe he would stay for a while, at least a few days. And perhaps he could call Cassidy. At least Cassidy knew everything about him, and Josh wouldn't have to start over with someone new. It would be great if he could feel better, more normal. Even a little better would be an improvement over where he'd been for the past few months—stuck in the middle of his worst nightmare.

CHAPTER
THIRTY-THREE

San Diego, California, USA

Mia

Chelsea reached across the table for the bottle of Riesling the waiter had left behind and refilled their glasses. Emptying it, she set it back on the table with a loud thud.

"Josh and Sean are asshats!" she exclaimed, sitting back in her seat, her lovely Asian features screwed into a fierce scowl.

"Why would you say that?" Mia asked calmly, taking a delicate bite of her California Club pizza, heaped with extra grilled chicken and sliced avocado.

"They are, and you know they are. I can't believe Josh just up and left like that."

"He didn't have a choice. His visa was about to expire."

"And you believed him?"

"Why wouldn't I? Besides, it didn't matter. None of it mattered. It was what it was, and I just needed space."

"Have you talked to him yet?"

"No. He calls and texts, but I haven't answered his calls. Sometimes I miss him so much. I want to see him, let him hold me, and tell me everything will be okay. Then, at other times, I feel strong and in control, and I tell myself that everything is *already* okay. You know, someone ought to invent an amnesia pill—one with no side effects. I'd take it if I could forget everything for a little while."

"Hmmm, wait. Let me see if I have any in this purse. Umm, nope. I must've left them at home. But drink your wine. That should help."

"It's not helping."

"Then let's order something stronger. They have the best blackberry margarita; we could get them with extra tequila shots. I'll bet you won't remember a thing after one or two of those."

"No thanks. I don't want to get drunk."

"Question," Chelsea blurted, staring into space, making Mia wonder if she wasn't already buzzed from the wine. "If Josh was, or is, as wealthy as it seems, why was he okay with a bunch of people, complete strangers, hanging around? The beach house was beautiful, and they turned it into a stupid frat house. He had to have paid a pretty penny to have it cleaned up and returned to the owners the way it was."

"Josh has so many quirks. Treating his home like a shelter for broke and homeless surfers, turning his back on his family's business and the wealth that comes with it, oh, and let's not forget the misplaced and forgotten fiancées he racks up."

"Hmmm. Red flags all over the place, right."

"Yeah, but he's the sweetest, kindest person I've ever met—besides you. He has a good and generous heart, and when he looks at me, I can't think. I don't want to think. I want to feel. Man, you don't know how much I loved him, Cee."

"Past tense? Loved?"

"Past tense. I'm trying to get over him right now. I need to get back on track. And I can't admit that I still love him. I'm going to schedule the USMLE for January. I might as well get started studying for that and filling out applications for a surgical fellowship. I picked out ten. I hope I get at least one."

"Where?"

"My top is the Mayo Clinic in Minnesota, then Mount Sinai in New York, and my third choice is Mass General in Boston. Who wouldn't want to work at any of those?"

"Nah, too cold in the winter for me. Why don't you apply to Cedars-Sinai, UCLA, UCSF, or Stanford? They're in the state, at least."

"I did," Mia answered less enthusiastically. "I did. They're number four, five, six, and seven on my list. But I kinda want to get away. I've lived my whole life in California. I should see some other parts of the country. I'm going to get a passport so I can travel."

"Australia is nice this time of year. It's spring and summer there when it's fall and winter here."

"There are more places I want to see than Australia."

"True. You and I should go to Singapore. My parents took me there when I was a little kid, but I don't remember much more about it than it was hot. But moving cross-country or out of the country won't stop Josh. If you're not here, he'll go looking for you."

"You're just a big ray of sunshine today, you know? Who says I'm running from Josh?"

"I dunno, it sort of sounds like it."

"Well, I'm not." Changing the subject, Mia asked, "Are you going to eat any more of that pizza? If not, we can have it wrapped up to go."

"Yeah, no. I'm done. You barely touched your pasta. You're taking it with you, aren't you?"

"Yeah. Maybe I'll have the rest for dinner."

Chelsea nodded and waved to get their waiter's attention. Mia chugged half her glass of wine, then shrugged on her new designer cape-style coat. She couldn't resist it when she saw it in the boutique. It was cashmere, perfect for nice, late-season days like today, so she'd worn it out of the store. The weather had been glorious all afternoon for mid-November, and they'd been lucky enough to snag a table on the patio of Francesca's, their favorite Italian restaurant. It was always worth a ride to Little Italy for lunch or dinner, and they usually stopped at *Francesca's*.

Mia had given Chelsea grief when she'd suggested they go out, but she was feeling pretty good for the first time in months. Filling out pages and pages of applications had taken her mind off the breakup, and hoping to be accepted by one of her choices had kept it at bay. She did not need anyone to tell her how proud her grandmother would be of her, and she would have been the first to urge Mia to spread her wings and move cross-country in a heartbeat. It was things like that that made Mia miss her Granny the most. Fortunately, she had Chelsea to celebrate with, spend long afternoons with, and get in a little retail therapy.

She gathered up her bags from the seat next to her. She'd spent a small fortune tagging behind Chelsea, but she loved every purchase. Her favorites, beside her coat, were the leggings she'd purchased to go with a cream, tunic-length, cowl-necked sweater that came mid-thigh. It was the softest sweater she'd ever owned. She'd purchased it in brown, cream, black, and cheetah-print. She'd also purchased a pair of dove gray, over-the-knee boots—she loved over-the-knee boots—and another pair of short, slouchy boots in butter-soft brown suede to go with her coat. She was wearing the black pair today, the bottoms of her skinny jeans tucked down inside. The balayage hair treatment she'd let Chelsea talk her into for her first date with Josh several months back had grown out a lot, and the sun-kissed, gold and copper highlights in her sleek ponytail and the fly-away wisps and tendrils that framed her face shimmered in the afternoon sunlight.

Mia felt almost normal sitting on the outdoor patio in weak sunlight, the lenses of her oversized tortoiseshell glasses having transitioned to opaque chocolate and hiding her hazel eyes. She'd been smiling all afternoon and was blissfully unaware of the many passers-by who turned their heads to get a second, and sometimes a longer, look at her, wondering if they were celebrities. Those she caught looking, she presumed, were looking at Chelsea, very fetching in her red leather romper, brightly patterned silk blouse underneath, and ankle-high booties. She tossed a long, heavy cashmere wool shawl around her shoulders, looking like she'd just stepped away from a fashion magazine shoot. Her straight black hair hung in a shiny curtain almost to her tiny waist, and blocky, black-framed designer sunglasses were shoved on top of her head. Mia would never have been able to pull off that look, but Chelsea did it to perfection.

"So, you're really going to be okay now?" Chelsea asked as she paid the tab, leading Mia out of the restaurant.

"Yes, of course, I'm going to be okay. Josh and I were a summer fling; it was fun while it lasted. I shouldn't have lost sight of that. It was inevitable that he would go back to his real life, and I have to get on with my life, too, right?"

"Sure, sure. I was thinking about applying for a position at the hospital. My family wants me back home, and I won't have to join the family optometry-ophthalmology business, but this is close enough. I need a certain level of autonomy."

Mia nodded. "Going on vacation together would be so cool. That is until you can't go anymore. But I'll come and visit you and play with your tiny offspring as often as possible."

"Offspring. Who said anything about offspring?"

"Your mother will have you engaged, married, and expecting babies within a year. She probably has someone already picked out."

"In her dreams. I might marry Mark to spite her. He adores me," Chelsea said, and Mia snorted. Mark was Caucasian and probably Anglo-Saxon Protestant. Chelsea's mother would reject him on that basis alone. His only saving grace might be that he was also an entertainment lawyer who lived in Hollywood Hills, a wealthy enclave of LA. Still saying nothing, Mia raised her eyebrows, expressing her disbelief, and Chelsea refused to look at her. She knew Mia was right. Mrs. Zhao was one tough cookie, and what she wanted, she got... eventually.

~

Treachery Bay, New South Wales, Australia

Josh

Josh looked up as Charlie entered the kitchen the next morning, poured a second cup of coffee, and handed it to him.

"Bless Dee for sending the good stuff," he said, inhaling the rich aroma in the steam rising from his cup.

"She knows I can't drink that swill you make, Charlie. Root coffee? Is that what you call it?"

"It's an acquired taste, I agree, so you just keep drinking the good stuff and bring canisters of it for me whenever you drive up," Charlie said, taking a sip. "You think much about what we discussed these last few days?"

"Yeah, a little. I have an appointment today to talk to my doctor, my former therapist. I think he'll be able to get me a regular spot on his schedule."

"Good. That's a good first step. You young'uns don't know, but there ain't nothing wrong with talking with a shrink when you need to get some things off your mind."

"I also made an appointment with a plastic surgeon next week to see about getting this leg smoothed out. It's going to be major surgery."

"Yeah? Like how major?"

"From what I was told a few months ago, the surgeon will take skin from my backside and graft it with some mesh to the back of my leg. It's supposed to make it look less disfigured."

"Well, that's good. It will feel better inside your pant leg."

"Yeah, for sure. Can you see the bumps and indentations where I guess muscle and tissue are missing? It looks like a burrito, doesn't it? Like they wrapped the skin around whatever was left and stapled it down."

"Don't look all that bad right now, though," Charlie said, scrutinizing the back of Josh's leg exposed by his cargo shorts. "It is kinda puckered, though. Is your leg going to function better afterward?"

"I think this is as good as it gets. At least I don't need a cane all the time."

"And you don't need a prosthesis."

"Yeah, there is that."

"Well, take care of your business. I'm gonna go clean out the van. Did you hear what time the boys came in last night? I slept like a brick."

"Yeah, I did. They kinda snuck in. They must not have wanted to wake you, but I was awake. It wasn't too late."

Charlie nodded and continued on out the back door. As Josh watched him leave, his phone rang. He pulled out his phone. It was time to speak with Dr. Cassidy. He walked back to his bedroom and sat on the edge of his bed.

"Josh, how's the weather there?" Dr. Cassidy asked when Josh joined the meeting.

"Another day in paradise," Josh smiled. "And there?"

"The same. Any problems since we talked last time?"

"No. Only had a couple of dreams. Had one last night… well, this morning."

"You want to talk about it?" Cassidy said, more of a statement than a question.

"Yeah." Josh filled Cassidy in on the lucid dream he'd had that morning. Cassidy asked questions, prodding Josh along. It didn't take long to recount. "I thought it might be significant because I could see in the dream a lot more detail and remember it after I woke up."

"Maybe being in Yakon, around your friend Charlie, is doing you a lot of good."

"Yeah. Charlie's good people. Sean says he might be able to

drive up for a few days sometime next week. I'm looking forward to it. It'll be like old times, old, old, old times."

"You think you guys might get some surfing in?"

"No, not me. I don't want to surf."

"Are you nervous about going back on the water?"

"Let's just say I have some trepidation." Josh laughed.

"Hmmm. Seriously?"

"Yeah, seriously."

"We'll put a pin in that and tackle it at another time. But I'm glad you contacted me, Josh. We can conquer this, but you got to stick with me."

"I know. I will this time."

"We'll talk again next week. Schedule two sessions."

"Will do. Have a good weekend."

"You too."

CHAPTER
THIRTY-FOUR

Sean drove up early instead of waiting until the weekend, and like Josh, he brought hampers of goodies from Dee—cheeses, meats, fresh fruit, biscuits, and more tins of Charlie's favorite roasted coffee beans.

Charlie was as excited as a kid at Christmas. Lee, Bryan, Vic, and Adrien, the four young men Charlie let stay bunk at the house, were awe-struck having Josh around, but surfing with Sean was unimaginably awesome. Sean and Josh were icons for young surfers; having them to themselves, just hanging out with them, was beyond great. When they weren't surfing in the afternoons, the young men and their friends would sit around Charlie's van or on the front Lanai, talk surfing with Josh or Sean, and get tips and advice from them and Charlie.

In the evenings, after dark and the young people had drifted away, Charlie would hold court like a favorite uncle or grandfather as he and Josh and Sean sat out on the front Lanai, the fiery sunsets turning the sky and the water from a glimmering gold, then red, blue, and finally deep purple before it slipped below the horizon. Sometimes, one or two boys would sit with them and watch the sun as it set, but mostly, they partied down on the beach with people their own age, enjoying the nightly bonfires. Josh complained that watching them surf all day and party all night made him feel old. Sean and Charlie burst out laughing because that was exactly what Josh and Sean and dozens of young people had done almost every day and night when they were that age, and never once, Charlie said, had it made him feel old.

The evening before Sean had to leave, Josh, Sean, and Charlie sat outside on the front Lanai, watching the sun start its descent below the horizon. Sean and Charlie sipped cold beers while Josh drank sweetened iced tea.

"What are you boys going to do with your future?" Charlie asked. "Forty is kinda long in the tooth for Pro surfing," he said, looking at Sean.

"I'm off now," Josh remarked, holding his glass for the others to clink as if congratulations were due him. It made him moody to talk about the end of his surfing career and what came next.

"Don't look at me, old man. I'm done, too," Sean said, sitting back after clinking his glass with Josh's.

"Well, it wasn't supposed to be no lifetime gig, you know. Just something to do 'til you figured things out and make a little money in the meantime."

"Yeah. Well, we made some money, but we didn't have time to figure things out. Everything kinda slipped our minds."

"That's your excuse too, Josh?"

"Sounds like a good one."

"Whatever happened to the big ideas you used to have about saving the planet?"

"I was *enlightened*, you might say, before too much time and energy were invested."

"Enlightened, huh? Well, you don't need your Pop's permission now. I don't guess you'll need his money either."

"Oh, I'd need his money. Saving the planet can get pretty expensive," Josh admitted, his tone pretty snarky.

"It ain't for the meek either, huh?"

"What are you hinting at, Charlie?" Josh asked, watching the last bit of the sun burnish the sky with red, orange and gold where it met the horizon.

"I ain't hinting at nothing. Just wondering, is all. I remember how excited you boys were about starting something grand."

"Pipe dreams," Josh replied bitterly.

"If you say so. Sounds pretty sad, though."

"Honestly, Charlie. You know I've had a lot on my plate. Crap like that kinda focuses the mind."

"Did you see any extraordinary young surfers while you were out there on the circuit, Sean?"

"Yeah, a few. They'll be the ones to beat in a few years. Glad I won't be competing against them."

"Maybe you two can do something to support the next generation?"

"Maybe. It's an option," Sean agreed.

"What with all the sage advice tonight, old man?" Josh asked, a smirk on his handsome face.

"I dunno. Maybe I'm finally getting old. Maybe it's just the beer."

"If it's the beer, you're cut off."

"I was going to finish this one and go to bed anyway. Cheers!"

"To wise old men," Josh toasted.

"To wise-ass young men," Charlie retorted. Sean and Josh laughed, their guffaws carrying out across the quiet night air.

Charlie set his beer down on the porch railing, stood, and sauntered toward the front door.

"See you in the morning, Charlie," said Sean, draining the last of his beer.

"Have a good night, old man," Josh said, watching him, making sure he was steady on his feet.

"The same to you both." Charlie closed the screen door softly behind him. They were his first boys, not quite runaways, but neither one had any business hanging around the beach all day at their age. But they'd turned out to be good men. Smart men. He had faith they'd figure things out sooner rather than later.

Josh left The Crag a week after Sean. He'd stayed much longer than anticipated but felt better and more in control. He gathered his belongings and stuffed them in the oversized duffle bag, and carried it out to the car, stowing it in the trunk. The air was cool, the wind whipping his hair in every direction, and he looked up at the dark sky. In the east, he could see fingers of golden sunlight encroaching on the night sky. It was going to be another hot day, but he thought if he left early, he would beat the morning traffic into Sydney and chill under the air conditioner.

He strode back inside, stopping in the kitchen to put on a pot of coffee and fix himself a couple of sandwiches. He smiled wryly. He'd drunk a ton more coffee since swearing off alcohol, and keeping up with Charlie had it practically coming out of his ears. Luckily, caffeine didn't make him jittery, and before the accident, he could drink an espresso and take a nap. Josh heard light footsteps and smiled, turning around to see Charlie shuffling into the kitchen. Charlie had always been a light sleeper and woke up to the aroma of the strong, fresh brew.

Josh took two mugs from the cabinet and filled them, setting one in front of Charlie, who'd taken a seat at the island.

"So you're all packed and ready to go," Charlie said, blowing across the top of his drink before taking a sip. It was more of a statement than a question, and Josh nodded.

"Yeah. I didn't have very much." Josh sat down next to him, bringing his coffee, sandwiches, and waxed paper to wrap them in. "Why are you up so early?"

"Smelled this and figured you were up for a reason. Got up to see you off." Charlie took another gulp before setting the cup down on the countertop, cradling it between his large, bony hands. "It was good to see you. I enjoyed your company. Don't stay away so long next time."

"I won't. I'm glad I came up here, glad that we could talk. It's helped a lot."

"Good. You can beat this thing, Josh. It doesn't have to take over your life."

"God, I hope so. I have another call with Cassidy tomorrow. I talk to him twice a week."

"And you're going to see that other doctor, right? The one for your leg."

"Yeah. I've already set the appointment."

"Keep me in the loop, then. I got my new cell phone, and I keep it charged. I don't always hear it ring, though, but when I see it, I'll call you back. I want to know how things are going."

"I will. Maybe I'll come back here to recuperate."

"Come on, then. But you better bring Dee to cook for you and be your nursemaid. I'm not good at being a nursemaid, and you ain't all that good at cooking."

"I think we got along great. I made sandwiches, and you've hovered over me and the boys every day, the whole time I was here. I think we make a good team."

"Yeah, well, I ain't been hovering. I've been a proper host; seeing to the needs of my guests is what I've been doing. And if Dee comes, she can cook us up some good grub. I was about tired of your sandwiches."

"Yeah, me too. I'll give her your invitation when I get home. She might surprise us both." Josh grinned, meticulously folding the waxed paper so that it didn't tear and kept his sandwiches fresh. He was a stickler for soft bread. "Thank you for your kind and generous hospitality."

Charlie snorted. "What about your girl in the States? Maybe she'll come and take care of you."

"No, she can't come. Besides, I can take care of myself."

"Hmmph," Charlie snorted. "Well, I wouldn't make her wait too long if I was you. I know you've got a crap ton of stuff to take care of before you can go back, but she could grow old waiting until you took care of every little thing."

"Hah-hah, you're funny. I'm going back as soon as I get a new visa, and after I take care of a few things. She'll wait… I hope."

"You love her?"

"Yeah, I do."

"She loves you?"

"I think so. I hope so."

"That's good. Better keep her, then. She's done seen all your warts by now."

Josh rolled his empty coffee cup to the sink and rinsed it, setting it in the sink. He refilled Charlie's cup and clasped him on his thin shoulder. Charlie put his hand on top of Josh's and gave it a squeeze.

"I left a little something over on the table for you. I wasn't sure you were going to get up before I left."

"You know you don't have to give me anything. You do enough already."

"Use it to keep the boys fed and out of trouble."

"That, I will, then. They're good boys, and they'll be okay."

"I'll try to see you in a few weeks. Take care of yourself, old man."

"You take care too, Josh."

Josh walked out of the kitchen through the back door, with Charlie following him. Josh opened the car door and slid behind the wheel, backing the car smoothly out of the single paved space beside the house. With a final wave, he turned the car and headed home.

CHAPTER
THIRTY-FIVE

Sydney, Australia

Josh had an idea, and it bloomed large in his mind.

He'd come across it while flipping through a magazine in his doctor's office. He read the article but didn't think much about it, as he was nervous about what Dr. Campbell would have to say about his leg. This was their second consultation, and they were going to discuss what to expect before, during, and after reconstructive surgery.

However, a week later, it resurfaced in his mind and wouldn't go away. Josh researched it and became intrigued. *Adaptive Reuse Technology.* It was a new, emerging field of environmentalism and eco-sustainability, and the more he learned about it, the more interested he became. Transforming resource-depleted mines and quarries into public and private spaces, like research and educational and recreational campuses, housing, and commercial spaces. There were thousands of old, abandoned mines and quarries around the world. Brenner Industrials even had a few shoved like skeletons in a closet that no one thought about once the land had been depleted. As he let the idea stew, the more it took hold, and he'd called his father and invited him to dinner so he could talk it over with him.

Josh dressed to impress his father: a tailored charcoal suit, white shirt, patterned tie and hand-made Italian leather shoes. He had reservations at McAlister's Bar and Restaurant, a favorite of the Brenner clan and a ten-minute walk from the Brenner Tower in the heart of the central business district. His father would come over after his meetings, while Josh would drive thirty minutes if traffic was good, park, and walk over.

They weren't far from Sean's house, a ten-minute walk in the opposite direction. Much of the downtown district had been rezoned for mixed-use. Small stores and office buildings stood next to residential walk-ups, mid-rise and high-rise buildings, and cultural, institutional, and entertainment establishments. The mix brought life and vibrancy back to the district, drawing professionals and young families who preferred to live in the city rather than the suburbs. Over the past decade, property values, which had always been lofty, soared with the rezoning and the high demand.

Arriving early, he parked in the Tower garage and walked a short distance to the restaurant. Entering, he waved to Donovan "Donny" McAllister, a long-time family friend and cousin by marriage.

"Joshua Brenner, where the heck have you been?" Donny yelled across the bar. Josh walked over and gave Donny a hug, receiving an enthusiastic rib-crushing hug in return.

"All over, my friend. How are you?"

"Great. We're doing great. When did you get home?"

"About a month ago, but I went up to Yakon and hung out there for a while."

"Still chasing the waves, huh?"

"Not so much anymore. Thinking of doing something else. Maybe I can get a job here. Seems you might need a little help tending the bar, or better yet, I can do the big boss stuff, like sit in the back office and act like I'm doing paperwork."

"When you're the big boss around here, you've got to do some of everything. I even fill in sometimes on the grill for Mags. But Jake will be here in a couple of hours. I'm just holding it down until then. So, sit, sit. What do you want to drink? You hungry? Maggie's in the back. She'll be glad to see you and fix you something to eat."

"I'm meeting Pop here for dinner. He's walking over; should be here in a few minutes."

"Yeah? I think that's your Pops coming in the door now," Donny said, looking over Josh's shoulder. "Now, this is a right special occasion. Let me get you a booth in the restaurant, and I'll let Maggie know you're here."

After seating them, Donny left to tell Maggie they were out front. Josh grinned at his father across the table, and James sat back comfortably and looked around. Everything looked very much the same as it had in his day, back when Mac Senior had run it. The two rooms, comprising the bar and the restaurant, were spacious with lots of paneling, pendant and wall lights, not the recessed or fluorescent kind, the wide plank floors varnished to a deep, dark shine, and lots of generous seating. "How are you doing, Pop?"

"Pretty good. No complaints. How about you?" James Brenner replied, sitting back and relaxing in the booth. "You look good, son. The Crag did you some good?"

"Thanks, and yeah, I think it did. It's beautiful up there."

"I'm glad you wanted to come here. I don't think I've been here in years. Still looks good. A good place to eat and talk."

"Yeah, I wanted to run a few things past you. First, I met someone. Actually, it's the doctor who saved my life in San Diego. I think she's the one."

"A nice lady. So you're planning to settle down now? In America?"

"I don't know where. Maybe part of the time in America, part of the time here for a while."

"That's good, son. I'm glad you met a nice lady and want to settle down."

"Mia put up with a lot in the short time we were together, and she wanted to help me, but I needed to help myself first."

"Have you thought about what you might do now?"

"Well, that's the second thing. I've talked with a few doctors specializing in reconstructive surgery for my leg, and I'll be checking into the hospital Thursday."

"That soon?"

"Yeah. No use putting it off any longer."

"Okay. Makes sense."

"And I've been seeing a therapist, a shrink. I was diagnosed with PTSD after the shark attack, Colin dying, and all that…"

"A shame about Colin. Ian and I attended the memorial service."

"I didn't know that. Thank you." James nodded and spread his large hands on the table as Josh continued. "Anyway, I'm okay physically, but it's taken a toll on me mentally. They say I have acute PTSD, and I admit I'm a little screwed up. For a while, I couldn't eat, sleep, or go back on the water. I started drinking, mixing in the medications, and if it weren't for Sean, I guess I'd be out of control."

"What? Why didn't you tell us? Why didn't he tell us? Do you need special care? We can have some of the best doctors in the world…"

"No, no. I'm seeing a doctor, Robb Cassidy, who specializes in treating PTSD among military vets. He's helping me work through it."

"What about surfing?

"Yeah, well, that part of my life is over. So that's the fourth thing. I've been looking at starting my own business, and I think it might work out so that you and I can work together."

"You're almost thirty-four, and you talk like an old man. It worries me. Are you sure you're okay?"

"Yeah, I'm getting there. There are things I could do with the leagues. Announcing and stuff, but I'm not feeling that."

"You always have a place in the company, Josh. We've grown, expanded, and diversified a lot since you left. We're into mining, minerals, energy, technology… maybe you can find something that appeals to you."

"Well, that's another thing I wanted to run by you. I'm thinking of starting my own business. I've only figured out a few things, but you would be my first—and pretty much my only—client for a while. I'm not looking for a handout. I'll have a legitimate business proposal for you and the Board to consider."

"Good, good. I like the sound of that. When will you be ready?"

"I need a little more time, but it feels right."

"Perfect. We can talk about it while we eat. I'm a little hungry. What do you want to eat?" James picked up the menu that Donny left behind and scanned it. "Everything looks good."

"Everything is good, Uncle James," said a woman's voice. "I made everything with a touch of love."

"Maggie Girl. How have you been?" he asked, standing to give her a hug and a peck on the cheek. "That big lug taking good care of my favorite niece?"

"Indeed, he is, Uncle James. Josh, it's good to see you."

"Mags. It's been too long. Look at you. You haven't aged a day. I'd swear you were still eighteen."

Maggie squeezed in beside Josh and gave him a hug. "Go on with you, Josh. I'm staring down the barrel at forty."

"That's got to be a long barrel; you've got a few years yet. We're the same age."

"You flatterer. I'm a year older. I heard about the accident. How're you doing? Improving?"

"Good, Mags. Getting better every day."

"How's my brother? And your mother, Vivian?" James asked, referring to her parents.

"They're doing well, Uncle James. Retirement suits them, I think. They might've even been bitten by the travel bug. They went on a trip to Malaysia a few weeks back, and Mom's planning another trip this summer. She wants to spend a couple of weeks in Agios Nikolaos."

"It's beautiful there."

"I'm going to hold you to that! Dinner is on the house tonight. I'm going to fix something special for you. Okay?"

"Don't go through any trouble for us. We can have the beef pie."

"I'll send a couple with you then, but I'm cooking for you."

"Well, how can we say no?"

"I'll have Don bring a couple of beers. A shot for you, Josh?"

"Nah. I'm teetotalling. I'll have water now and an iced sweet tea with dinner."

"Me too, Maggie. I'll have the same."

They ate Maggie's delicious meal of stout-braised short ribs and vegetables with roasted fingerling potatoes, and when Maggie offered dessert, both men politely but adamantly declined. Josh talked, filling his father in on his time in the hospital, training with Naghee, and the fiasco in Huntington Beach. When Josh brought up his business idea, James listened intently, letting Josh work through his thoughts.

CHAPTER
THIRTY-SIX

Another thing to cross off my list, Josh thought, pulling a pillow under his head as he laid back on the bed.

He folded one arm underneath the pillow and curled onto his side. It didn't matter if he was in the U.S. or Australia; it seemed all hospitals had the same bland décor and citrusy, antiseptic smell. This was the second time he'd been admitted to a hospital in eight months, and Josh knew he was an ungrateful ass for wanting it over and done with. He knew he needed to take this step. Cassidy had him approach the changes in his life like a twelve-step program. This was another step in the process. Josh would stay in the hospital this time for a couple of days, just long enough to make sure he healed well. His leg had healed into a ropy mass of scar tissue, a horrifying reminder of his traumatic experience. Although this was primarily a cosmetic procedure, the surgery would help resolve much of the pain, irritation, as well as the repulsion Josh felt whenever he looked at it.

His surgeon, Dr. Campbell, a renowned expert in his field, planned to operate on Josh first thing in the morning but wanted Josh admitted the evening before so they could run some last-minute tests. He'd been in his room after the battery of tests and x-rays for almost an hour, staring at a spot on the ceiling and unsuccessful at taking a nap when someone rapped their knuckles on the door. As he sat up, Ian strode through the door, a big smile on his face.

"Seems I made it in time, huh?" he asked, reaching out to his brother as Josh slid off the bed. They grabbed one another in a bear hug.

"In time for what? What are you doing here?" Josh asked, confused.

"I couldn't let you go into surgery without being here for you. What kind of brother do you think I am?"

"How did you know about the surgery?" Josh laughed. He should have known Ian would find out.

"Are you kidding me, Dude? I have a personal interest in knowing everything about you."

"Deidre's your spy, isn't she? That makes her a double agent, you know, and you can't trust her."

"I can trust her with your life. Her information is always spot-on. I'm glad to see you."

"I'm glad you're here, too. I was feeling sorry for myself."

"So, explain this surgery you're having on your arse. I thought it was your leg."

"Your source filled you in?"

"Of course she did. I want to hear it from you."

Ian took a seat, and Josh climbed back onto his bed. He listened as Josh recounted what he'd been told, including that it wouldn't be a very challenging operation but would take several hours, and he'd need to stay in the hospital to ensure the graft took hold. Ian stayed for a while, and when visiting hours ended, Josh was sad to see him go. It'd been a long time since the brothers had spent as much quality time together as they had in the past few months. Coming home had given him the gift of time with family, including Sean, Lizzie and her boys, and Charlie. He'd been Mr. Bigshot, taking everyone for granted, and had missed out on a huge part of what made life worth living. He also couldn't wait to make up for his bad behavior with Mia.

Early the following morning, Josh was prepped for surgery. Ian had returned to be by his side. Ian would wait in his room until he came out of recovery. The procedure would take several hours. Dr. Campbell reassured them both that Josh would be pleased with the results. He promised Josh would have much less scar tissue and a smoother, more normal look and shape of his leg overall. Ian squeezed his shoulder when Josh was settled on the gurney, ready to go down to the O.R. "I'll be here when you come back."

Josh nodded and waved goodbye.

~

San Diego, California, USA

Mia

The holidays slipped away like the miles beneath the wheels of a speeding train.

Mia was busier than ever. The E.R. was packed every day, around the clock, giving the residents ample opportunity to act as primary on incoming cases. Mia also had the chance to assist in the OR during surgery. Her opportunity came when a man fell off the roof of his house while putting up Christmas lights and decorations. He suffered a broken left hip and leg and other serious injuries.

While the E.R. had been exciting, she looked forward to her next rotation. She had a chance to end her residency working in OB-GYN, which many residents said was a cakewalk compared to the E.R. If nothing else, she would be in the clinic from eight to six most days and would only have to be on-call a few times a month.

A week before Christmas, the staff doctors and nurses decorated the breakroom and held an impromptu celebration to send the residents off to their next assignment. They had food and cake, bottles of water and soda set out on the breakroom counters, and Dr. Reynolds gave a short but moving speech to the residents. A few other doctors and nurses followed suit, congratulating the residents and

expressing their sincere hopes that they would come to work permanently in the E.R. when they graduated at the end of May. Everyone
hugged one another—doctors, nurses, staff, and residents—wishing
one another the best of luck. Mia and fellow resident Jonathon Davis
were congratulated for planning to go on to complete a Fellowship
and wished extra luck on snagging their first choices.

It had been a good night. A lull in patient traffic in the E.R. had
allowed the staff to enjoy the holiday and end-of-rotation celebration. Mia was helping the nurses clean up when Dr. Reynolds called
her over. Together, they walked towards the chief physician's office,
and Mia took a seat in front of the ancient and badly scarred desk. It
was so laden with a giant computer monitor, tons of files in manila
folders, and so many books that there appeared to be little space left
to work.

"Dr. Thomas, I want to congratulate you on the outstanding job
you've done this semester, and I wish you all the best on your next
assignment and on your choice of Fellowships," he started, searching on top and in the drawers of the desk for something he apparently urgently needed.

"Thank you so much, Doctor. It was an honor and a pleasure to
work here."

"Have you sent off all of your applications yet?" he asked, shifting stacks of file folders from one place to another, as well as moving a few onto a stack on the floor.

"No, I haven't totally made up my mind yet. I have a few places
in mind, but I'd planned to start filling them out over the Christmas
break."

"Good. The sooner, the better." Finding what he'd been looking for, he breathed a sigh of relief, then came around the desk and
perched on a chair beside Mia.

"Think I'd prefer a two-year program," she said, "but there are a
couple of three-year programs I'm looking at."

"Well, here is a copy of your Performance Assessment to include in your application packet, and several letters of recommendation. There are copies for your files and a few with my wet-ink signature. Those you include in your application envelope. It may have a little cache, depending on where you apply. Some programs may want a copy of your performance eval, which I've included. If you decide, for one reason or another, that you want to work before going directly into a Fellowship, I'm sure we can find room for you with us."

He handed Mia a large manila envelope with her name on it, and she could barely keep her jaw from dropping. She was so utterly surprised and grateful that tears immediately filled her eyes and spilled out past her lashes. Dr. Reynolds smiled.

"Thank you so much, Doctor. I don't know what to say." Mia stood and gave him a hug. "You know, I thought you didn't like me."

"Why would you think that?"

"You didn't seem to. And I felt you picked on me. You made me extremely nervous."

"Liking you had nothing to do with it. You seemed to know more than many of your colleagues and care more than most. I didn't want you slacking off."

"Well, that's good to know. Thank you, Dr. Reynolds. Can I put this in my locker? I'll come right back."

"No need. I'm sending you guys home early tonight. Get some sleep, rest up, and complete your applications over the break. You're to report to your next assignment in two weeks. Enjoy the time off." Mia nodded and extended her hand. He gave it a firm shake. "Keep in touch. Stop in and see us every now and then."

"Oh, I will. I absolutely will." As she left, she gave everyone hugs and handshakes before hurrying to empty her locker and head home. She intended to hibernate until it was time to go back to work.

CHAPTER
THIRTY-SEVEN

Sydney, Australia

Josh

It was a beautiful summer afternoon, unseasonably warm for mid-January, and Josh pulled on a pair of khaki cargo shorts, a t-shirt that had seen better days, slip-on shoes, and a ball cap.

The surgery had gone well, and while he wore bandages, he assumed they would come off with his next doctor's visit. His leg looked and felt much better than it had even days after. He grabbed his keys, went down to the garage, and started up his Audi. He loved driving the car. Sean was back from his hiatus in a little town somewhere on the coast, and Josh was excited to run his ideas for the new business. He'd sent the proposal to Sean, along with reams of research, but they'd planned to sit and talk about it today. He slid behind the wheel and turned the music up. Rolling the windows down, he pulled out onto the street.

It felt like summer in San Diego, although in reality, it was winter there. He missed Mia and California. Everything made him think about her: the holiday, the summer weather, everything. Though he hadn't planned it, he'd had a full year of summer. He'd spent summer below the equator while it was cold and wintery in the northern hemisphere and vice versa. Every day, for an entire year, it had been summer in his world. It was crazy how things happened.

He drove out to Paddington, where Lizzie lived with her mother, three boys, and several dogs and cats. He parked the car and walked up to the front door. He rang the doorbell but received no answer. Texting Sean, he was told to come around the back. He opened the gate to the backyard and heard the happy laughter of George, Sean's young nephew, and Sean. Sitting on the back steps, Sean waved him over. Josh took a seat on the top step, making sure he was more or less out of the line of fire, and after watching Sean keep George pinned behind a tree with a barrage of foam darts, Josh commented.

"I don't think you're being fair to the nephew, Bro."

"Fair? Dude, this is war. He doesn't get fair," Sean said, laughing, then sent more rapid fire at the tree, bouncing foam darts off its bark. George giggled from his position behind the giant, ancient oak tree, and Sean pulled the priming slide back on his blaster to load more foam darts. It seemed he had an endless supply. Josh picked up a larger blaster, one that seemed to use bigger, fatter foam missiles and aimed it at Sean, hitting him in the neck and back. Sean jumped off the steps and ran into the middle of the yard as Josh continued pulling the trigger, the missiles bouncing off Sean, giving George a chance to run.

"He got you, Uncle Sean. You're dead. Uncle Josh got you!" George squealed, running over to hide behind Josh.

"Alright, buddy, he got me, but I'm not dead yet," Sean yelled, bringing up his blaster and sending darts at George and Josh. Josh returned fire, hitting Sean repeatedly, while George took the opportunity to gather some darts and load his blaster.

"Dude, you're really dead now. You've gotta give up," Josh yelled.

"You got him, Uncle Josh. I ran out of ammunition, but you got him." Red in the face, hot and sweaty, George sat on a lower step between Josh's feet, waiting for Sean to join them on the steps. After passing George and Josh a bottle of water and taking one for himself from the cooler at the bottom of the stairs, Sean flopped down and gave his friend a pointed look.

"I was winning until you came."

"You were taking advantage of the nephew," Josh said, slinging an arm around the sweaty little boy and giving him a manly, one-armed hug. George grinned at his two favorite uncles.

"Anyway, I came by—from my sickbed, no less—to run an idea by you."

"Your sickbed, you say? Then it should be a pretty important idea."

"Yeah, I think so. I've been thinking..." Josh started.

"Oh, no. Haven't you learned your lesson? No more thinking, Josh. It gets us both in trouble."

"Will you hush? This is primo."

"Okay, okay. It sounds serious. But hold on." Turning to the little boy, Sean rubbed the top of George's damp hair until it stood on end. "Hey, buddy, go on in the house and get some lunch. You gotta keep up your strength if you want to beat me."

"Can we play again when I'm done, Uncle Sean?" George turned to ask, the sun glinting off his Harry Potter-style glasses. In the direct sunlight, Josh could see the strong family resemblance between the two, right down to their style of eyewear.

"Absolutely."

Once George had gone inside, the two men got comfortable, and Josh explained his idea of land reclamation. Sean was impressed.

"Since we'll be saving the world, I presume you've bought a cape and some tights already?"

"Nah, but we will need a few new business suits. At least initially, they might be a little more effective in the boardroom than board shorts and wetsuits. Later, once we're up and running, we can wear what we want since you'll be out surveying old mines and quarries."

"Me, huh? Okay, I can get behind that. So what are we going to do?

When Josh finished explaining, he noticed that Sean looked dazed. "This kind of environmental remediation is a thing now, huh?" he asked.

"Yeah, a big thing. Dozens of American cities are investing in turning their old mines and quarries into all kinds of public and private spaces."

"Like building on a landfill?"

"There's some of that, too, depending on the project, but it's not just filling the void with rocks and gravel like before. It's about making the land fertile and safe again. Removing all the toxins so it can be turned back into farmland. No toxins. No dangerous materials."

"Hmmm. Sounds like quite an undertaking," Sean said thoughtfully. "And expensive."

"Yeah, it takes a lot of money. Some companies I researched are looking for investors, and governments and public use organizations are looking for someone to do the work."

"Are you thinking of becoming an investor?"

"That's one idea. But I really think we should do our own thing. We could buy a company out, keep the employees, take over their projects and contracts." Josh looked up, a gleam in his eye.

"What about the money? You finally got access to that trust fund?"

"Pop says he can fund us to get started. You in?"

"Hell yeah, of course, I want in. What do you need me to do?"

"We'll have to draw up a proper business plan and a proposal. We have to present it to the Brenner Board."

"Brenner Board? Wow, I'm really impressed. But I thought your Pop is going to bankroll us."

"We aren't asking him for a handout. He'll be our first client. We'll have to do a fair cost analysis, present our proposal, and draw up contracts like we would for any other client. The money he gives us will be an advance on the work. Then, we can shop our services around once we have a track record. The Australian government and a few other mining companies might want in. We wouldn't even have to stay in Australia, either. I mean, China's following in America's footsteps on this."

"You really have been thinking hard about this, haven't you?"

"Yeah. And Ian's been helping me with the research. He pulled a team together to help me with a feasibility study, and I still have a ton of information to go through. We're meeting at the house tomorrow night to review some of the bureaucracy we'll have to deal with. I need you there, too."

"Yeah, of course. Wouldn't miss it."

A smile spread across Josh's face as he watched his friend sink into deep thought. He could imagine the wheels turning in Sean's mind.

"We'll also create our timeline. Here, I brought this. You can start reviewing this. It'll help you catch up on everything. Ian thinks we might be able to get in front of the board in a couple of weeks, right after Boxing Day."

"You're moving fast. Is Ian going in with us?"

"Nope. Just you and me. He's helping me finesse this so there won't be any hiccups. What do you think so far?"

"You're shitting me? I don't know what to think, but I'm in, all the way in. Where do I sign?" Sean laughed and shoved Josh, and Josh pushed him back, practically sending him off the steps. Sean turned and blasted Josh in the chest with several foam darts, and Josh raised his foam rocket blaster and sent fat foam missiles at his friend, hitting him as he sprinted down the steps and out into the yard. He laughed so hard and screamed so loudly George peeked out the door.

"Are you okay, Uncle Sean?"

"Yeah, Buddy, I'm fine." Sean wheezed, splayed out in the grass.

"You're a lunatic," Josh declared.

"You are a genius. Walk me through everything again. I want to hear every single detail again."

"Now?"

"Right now."

Josh grinned. He knew Sean would've joined him no matter what, but it felt good to see him excited at the prospect.

"Hey, Uncle Sean," George yelled, standing at the screened

back door. "Wait for me. Mom says I have to eat my lunch before I can come back out."

"Take your time, buddy. I'm just going to pick up all of these darts."

"Okay," George said, disappearing back inside, leaving the two men grinning like kids.

Sean got up and came and sat back down on the steps. Josh laid a thick manilla folder on the stairs and watched as Sean picked it up and scanned the stacks of paper clipped together.

"You didn't come up with a name for our new company, huh?" Sean cocked his head, looked at Josh with eyebrows raised, and laughed.

"I had to leave something for you to do."

"Good thing, too. You'd probably name it after Mia."

"I wasn't going to go that far, but… since you mentioned it, it could work."

"We'll think of something. Don't worry about it."

"In the meantime, look at this," Josh said, digging into his pocket. "I picked it up from the jeweler's last night."

He pulled a tiny, navy-blue velvet box lined with pale blue satin from a navy-blue drawstring bag. The logo of a custom jewelry house in stark white graced the front of the little bag. Josh flipped it open to reveal a flawless two-and-a-half-carat marquise-shaped diamond set in the center of a cluster of blue sapphires on a platinum band. The stones flashed and burned in the light, and Sean jokingly shielded his eyes.

"Aww, man, That's beautiful."

"Yeah, I think so, too. They did an exceptional job on it. Do you think she'll like it?"

"Without a doubt. That diamond has to be worth a fortune."

"Yeah. Even the dude in the back, the designer, was stunned when he saw it. You know where this came from, right?"

"No,…" Sean said hesitantly.

"Remember the first time Pop took us to South Africa, to that mining company he'd just bought?"

"Yeah. We were what, fifteen, sixteen years old? He let us pick out a bunch of rocks for souvenirs. I still have mine in my underwear drawer."

"Really?"

"Yeah. What's wrong with that? I stuffed them in a sock, put them in a drawer and forgot about them. No, I take that back… I used to take them out and look at them, but I haven't done that in a long time. Why are you looking at me like that?"

"You're crazy, man. This diamond was one of the rocks that I picked out."

"What? That diamond? How…" Sean's mouth dropped open, and Josh nodded. "Those ugly, crusty rocks we got when we were kids are diamonds? Real diamonds?"

"Raw, uncut, unpolished diamonds. Dad told us to put them in a safe deposit box."

"No one goes in my underwear drawer. It's better than a safe deposit box. Holy shit, Josh. I had no idea your dad let us pick out a bunch of diamonds. I thought they were just ugly crusty rocks. If I had known, I would've picked up a boulder or two."

"We were at a diamond mine, Sherlock. Sometimes, you have to put two and two together. Anyway, keep this ring under your hat, okay? I plan to fly out right after the meeting with the board and fix things between me and Mia. We talk when I call her, but she tries to act so cool and unemotional and refuses to talk about us. I plan to surprise her."

"She still loves you, man. She was hurt, but she answers her phone when you call, doesn't she? If she hated you, she would have blocked you or changed her number."

"Are you going to get married, Uncle Josh?" George asked, back at the screen door, his forehead pressed against the wire mesh.

"Yeah, I hope so, squirt."

"Do I know her?"

Josh and Sean laughed. "I don't think so, little Dude. Her name is Mia. She's a doctor, and she lives in California. If I ask her, do you think she'll say yes?"

"Yeah, I think she'll say yes, Uncle Josh," George said very matter-of-factly. "Will you have to live in California if you marry her?"

"I'll be back and forth. You can come to America sometimes with me or your Uncle Sean."

"That's right, bud," Sean said, picking up his blaster again and loading it. "Go, finish your lunch so we can play some more. I'll have to leave soon. Uncle Josh brought me all of this homework."

CHAPTER
THIRTY-EIGHT

San Diego, California, USA

Mia

Mia parked in the employee lot behind the Emily Madison-Phlegar Pavilion for Women's Reproductive Health, or as most people called it, the 'Phlegar Pavilion.'

She had lucked out; her schedule was Mondays through Fridays, from seven AM to six PM, and half days every other Saturday. It felt like she'd entered an entirely new world of medicine from overnights in the emergency room, and she'd had no difficulty readjusting her sleeping habits.

Her office was on the same floor as the prenatal clinic, and she ran up the four flights of stairs every day. She stuffed her purse inside her desk drawer and locked it before pulling on her lab coat and heading for the clinic area. She passed a few mothers seated in the waiting area for the clinic to open on her way to clock in and join the morning meeting. Since starting the assignment three weeks before, she'd shadowed Dr. Jose Moreno in the clinic, and she was becoming familiar with a few of the late-term mothers. She was looking forward to helping deliver their babies. As the meeting began, and after much shuffling to absorb more people into the semi-circle around the nurse's desk, Mia found herself front and center of the group, facing Dr. Priya Thakur, the clinic director. When she saw Mia, she smiled and nodded, then leaned forward.

"Good morning, Dear," she said, pronouncing it Deah, "Please suit up and report to the delivery room. Dr. Emory is waiting for you there."

Surprised, she frowned, a questioning look on her face. "Dr. Emory? In labor and delivery?"

"Yes, yes. Hurry."

Mia turned and hurried to the supply room and grabbed fresh scrubs and a blue gown. She hurriedly changed, pushed her hair under a surgical cap, and ran toward the delivery room. A nurse at the station pointed at the room she needed to enter and pushed open the door.

"Dr. Thomas?"

"Yes, Doctor."

"Good. Scrub in. I think we're just about ready here."

Mia scrubbed her hands and arms and slid her hands inside a pair of gloves. A young African American woman was on the table, her feet in stirrups. She'd come up directly from the emergency room and rushed into labor and delivery. Mia came over to stand by Dr. Emory and saw the baby crowning. On cue, the mother began moaning and then crying. Dr. Emory and the nurses worked together to prep the mother, getting her to push, and when he was sure the baby was coming, he had Mia move into position to take over.

Mia swallowed her nervousness and reached to guide the baby as it turned once and then again before sliding into her hands. It was a girl. Hearing the first ferocious wail from that tiny body and seeing her tiny face all wet and red and screwed up as she screamed made Mia grin so hard under her mask that her cheeks hurt.

"Good work, Doctor. You can hand her to Michelle. She's the neonatal nurse and will care for the baby while we finish with the mother."

While it seemed a quick birth, when Mia looked up at the clock, she realized she'd been in the delivery room for nearly three hours. Dr. Emory had congratulated the mother and Mia before dashing down the hall to deliver another baby. Mia was grateful he hadn't taken her with him; she was sweating buckets under her scrubs, causing them to stick to her body, and her hair was soaked under her cap. But she wouldn't have traded the experience for anything.

Stepping out into the corridor between labor rooms, she stretched, executing several techniques from yoga classes she'd taken over the years. Her back, neck, and shoulders were stiff and achy, and they snapped, crackled, and popped as she flowed from one stretch to another.

The rest of the day sped by. She saw patients in the clinic, went to lunch, and came back to more patients. At the end of the day, she plopped down in her office chair and put her feet up on her desk. This was her first office during her entire time as a resident. Most times, she was lucky to get a locker in the women's locker room to herself. Once, she'd had to share a small locker with two other residents. Mia quickly learned to carry only the essentials to work.

She had no idea why she would need a whole office to herself, but it was nice to be able to put her feet up and relax at the end of the day behind closed doors. She could also bring her clean lab coats and extra scrubs and hang them in the tiny closet. Plus, it had a nice window that let in a bit of natural light and offered a minuscule view of the ocean if she squinted while looking between the Children's Hospital and the Cancer Center buildings. Leaning back in her chair, her feet crossed and hands behind her head, Mis thought she could very easily get used to having an office, even if it was the size of a closet. Offering perks like these must be how the Gyn department recruited and kept their staff, a matter of outright spoiling them. Looking around, she could feel it working on her.

She unlocked the desk drawer and took out her purse. Slinging it on her shoulder, she turned out the lights and walked towards the escalators. At the last minute, just before she took the step that would take her down, she turned around and headed toward the neonatal nursery. The second shift nurses smiled at her as she peeked at Baby Girl Jackson, her tiny brown face in cherubic repose, sleeping peacefully swaddled in a pink and white blanket, a pink knit hat on her head. The placard on her little bed said she'd been born that morning at 10:18 and weighed seven pounds, seven ounces.

"Good job, Ms. Jackson," Mia whispered against the glass. "Ni-night."

CHAPTER
THIRTY-NINE

Spring was in the air, and Mia could feel and smell it.

The drenching rains over the past few weeks had seemingly invigorated every living thing. It was only the middle of February, with temperatures already hovering in the mid-seventies, and the fragrance of growing things hung heavy in the air. Fruit trees, flowering trees, berry bushes, and potted plants gracing every front and backyard were waking up after a long dry season. January through March was the rainy season, and short, heavy bursts of rain went a long way toward alleviating the drought that had gripped the state.

This morning, the air was washed clean and crisp. The bright sun and cloudless sky promised another warm day, and Mia felt the need to go outside and enjoy it. Dressed in a t-shirt, jeans, and sneakers, she packed two bottles of water, a baggie of fresh-cut fruit, a small container of yogurt, and several slices of buttered French bread inside her tote, along with a thin blanket to sit on and a paperback to read.

Sundays were a day of rest. The maternity clinics and offices were closed, and rarely was she put on the on-call schedule for the labor and delivery rooms, the emergency and operating rooms, or the nursey and maternity wards. For good reason, those never closed. She liked this rotation, which moved along much faster than her five months in the E.R., and wondered if she should apply for a fellowship in maternal-fetal medicine. It would take another three years, which she was preparing to do anyway, but one devoted mostly to research. She could apply to the University Hospital, stay where she was, and work under Dr. Thakur and Dr. Emory. The idea appealed, but she was loathe to make a decision too quickly. She'd always wanted to work in the ER.

Tired of her own company, she walked to the park near her apartment and sat beneath a thick maple leaf near the playground to watch the children play, nibble at her food, and read her book. It wasn't long before other people came out to enjoy the weather, and the playground filled up. A man with a small dog sat a little distance from her and smiled. He'd come with a young boy who'd quickly run off to join the children on the playground. He smiled when he caught Mia's eye; she'd only glanced up for a moment, aware that someone was settling close by, and smiled at the dog. She loved dogs and cats, but she couldn't keep one. She had little enough time for herself.

"Hello. You're new in the neighborhood?" he asked, looking over at her.

"No, not really."

"Ah, you don't come very often then, right?"

"Right."

"My name is Garret. My son, Daniel, abandoned Jake and me before we even found a place to sit."

"Jake is your dog?"

"Yep. Jake's a good dog, aren't you, buddy? A good boy, yeah," Garret said, giving the dog a good scratch and pet. "He's a rescue Danny and I picked out, some sort of terrier mix."

"I see. He's very cute. Mannerly, too."

"We take him to obedience training twice a week. It helps Danny, too."

Mia grinned. The thought of a little boy leading a well-behaved dog around made her smile. Her only concept of dog training came from the Westminster Dog Shows she sometimes watched on television. Garret seemed keen to carry on a conversation, and Mia listened for a while but began to gather her belongings, stashing them in her tote, and got up.

"It was nice meeting you, Garret. And you too, Jake," she gave the dog a scratch behind his ears.

"Nice meeting you, Mia. We come out here all the time. Maybe we can meet up sometime."

"I work a lot and don't get a chance to visit the park much…"

Garret looked up at her, a flash of disappointment on his face, but got off the ground and extended a hand. He was taller than her, slender, and had a nice, friendly face. Not drop-dead gorgeous like Josh, but nice. Too bad she wasn't interested in getting involved with anyone. Only under duress would she admit that she was still in love with Josh.

"Enjoy your day, then," he said, a hopeful smile on his face.

"Yeah, you too." Mia waved and hiked across the grass.

Arriving back at her apartment complex, Mia decided to stop and get her mail. She was expecting responses to her Fellowship applications. Some residents had received theirs and were excited. Mia usually stopped to check the mail when she got in from work, but yesterday, she'd had her hands full of groceries and had gone right upstairs. She'd been both excited and anxious over which programs might accept her, having flipped-flopped over moving to Minnesota or Boston, should either accept her into their program. She felt less and less inclined to pack up and move halfway across the country and spend the next three winters in a deep freeze.

Born and raised in Oakland, it seemed almost inconceivable that a California girl could survive, much less thrive, in such an inhospitable climate. And she sincerely wondered how much more could the Mayo Clinic teach her than what she could learn right where she was, especially now that she was considering applying for the fellowship in women and infants health. She loved working at Phlegar and had helped deliver nine babies. It was hard to imagine anything more wonderful.

Unlocking the mailbox, she saw several envelopes tucked in among the sales papers. She gingerly pulled them out, knowing they held the key to her future. One was a square manila envelope with an official government seal and address for the California State Department. Her passport. She opened it to find the blue book with her picture inside. It wasn't a great picture, just a headshot taken at the post office, but she was excited to have it in hand. She flipped through the names printed on the handful of white envelopes. They were from six of the nine Fellowship programs she'd applied to. She hurried up to her apartment, unwilling to read them in the lobby, just in case the news wasn't something she wanted to share with her neighbors. Her heart was racing, and her hands were shaking so hard it took several tries to get her key in the lock and open the door.

She dropped her bag on the sofa, entered the tiny kitchen, and took a butter knife from the silverware drawer. Sliding it under the flap of the first envelope, she sliced it open. She pulled out a single sheet of stationery from the Mayo Clinic. She'd been the most anxious about this one. She unfolded it and read it.

Dear Dr. Mia Thomas,

Having given considerable deliberation to your application, education, and practical experience, we are pleased to extend this invitation to you. We would be honored to have you join our Surgical Fellowship program, specializing in trauma and critical care. The program will begin on August 25th...

Mia jumped around the tiny kitchen, waving the letter in the air. *It's official! I've been accepted at the Mayo Clinic!* Her hands turned cold and trembled, and she felt like crying. The letter fluttered to the floor as she bent to press her face to the cool granite slab of the island, gasping for air. Suddenly, she straightened up, screamed at the top of her lungs, and did another happy dance. She then snatched up all the letters and took them into the living room, where she could sit on the sofa and lay them out beside her.

The second letter was from Dr. Landyn Samuels, the Fellowship

Program Director for University Hospitals. She hadn't considered U.H. initially but applied because Chelsea had, and they could continue living next door to each other. The words *We are pleased to extend this invitation to join our Fellowship program...* practically jumped off the page. She set it aside and flopped back on the sofa, kicking her feet in the air. *Oh. My. God! I can't believe this is happening.*

She ripped the remaining three letters open and read them. Only one had turned her down, Los Angeles' Good Samaritan Hospital. Not even the tiniest pang of disappointment marred her happiness. She'd been accepted to five of six programs, all of which were her top choices, and she expected to hear from three—possibly four more over the next few weeks.

I've been accepted to the Mayo Clinic, or I can stay right where I am! I can go back to the Bay Area, work in San Francisco or Stanford, my alma mater. Taking her phone from her tote, she dialed Chelsea.

CHAPTER
FORTY

Central Business District, Sydney, Australia

Josh

At eight AM sharp, a sleek, black town car rolled up and stopped in front of Brenner Industrials International.

Josh climbed out the back, followed by Sean, both dressed in dark, bespoke suits and hand-made Italian leather loafers. They looked as different as anyone could've imagined when putting on a suit months ago meant zipping up in neoprene. They strode through the glass and steel doors of the striking office tower designed by Stanley J. Vonwebern, a testament to his genius as much as to the status and affluence of the Brenner family and their wide-ranging interests. The ultra-modern sculptural building sat on two-thirds of a block, fronting King Street at the intersection of Pitt in the heart of Sydney's central business district.

Ian had secured a meeting with the Brenner board for their presentation, though they were just a figurehead in many ways. James Brenner ruled with an iron fist sheathed in a velvet glove. He'd taken the middling-sized mining company his father, Josh's grandfather, had started and built it into the conglomerate it was today, ranking number two in the country and number four globally. With his track record of success, no one on the Board would think of going against his Midas touch.

Josh and Sean entered the lobby, nodded to security sitting behind the long, black granite reception and security desk, and walked to the bank of elevators that only serviced the top five floors. The private elevator doors opened, and Josh and Sean stepped inside.

They closed and sped to the top floor, opening outside the Brenner family's suite of offices. Josh and Sean stepped into the reception area. Filtered sunlight bounced off polished brown and cream marble floors from the wall of floor-to-ceiling windows. A panoramic view of the city and the ocean beyond could be seen through the almost transparent blue tint on the windows. Dark, low-slung, modern minimalist furniture with glossy and reflective surfaces; an oversized, stylized, and colorful painting of the city's skyline on the far wall filled the spacious interior. They walked past the vacant reception area and closed offices, stopping in front of the private conference room door. Josh put his ear close to the door but could hear nothing from the other side. He knocked once and took a deep breath before turning the knob and entering.

Josh felt a pang of nostalgia as he strode inside the room. It was as familiar to him as any room in the family home. Josh's eyes were drawn to the massive and exquisite twenty-foot conference table made of rare, polished cocobolo redwood in the center of the room. The extreme grain patterns as various hues converged, twisting and bleeding, blending then diverging, creating more color—streaks of yellow and orange, red, purple, chocolate, and black. He ran his fingers across the polished surface, following roads and rivers of lava, the dense jungle, and swirling oceans in his mind, just as he had as a child.

Josh had never seen the rare wood anywhere else, and he knew the table had to be priceless, yet he and his brothers had sat around it after school, doing homework, eating snacks, and playing board and card games while his father held meetings or worked in his office. Josh even played with his tiny cars on the table, the vibrant streaks of color determining the game's topography.

Ian entered the room and cleared his throat, interrupting Josh's musings. He smiled, gave his brother a one-armed hug, and clapped Sean on the back. It was Go Time, and he knew they were ready. The three of them had spent long nights planning and strategizing, sewing up as many details as possible in preparation for this meeting. James Brenner came in behind Ian, followed by Ryan McKinney. Uncle Ryan, as Josh still called him, was James Brenner's closest friend and business counsel.

"Josh? My God, boy, you gave us a big scare. Glad to see you. You doing okay?" Ryan asked, pulling Josh into a bear hug.

"Good to see you too, Uncle Ryan. I'm doing good."

"Good, good. We were worried about you. Sean," he boomed across the room. "Still thick as thieves, I see. How're you doing, my boy?"

"Hello, Uncle Ryan. I'm good. How are you?" Sean answered, matching Ryan's firm handshake.

"Pop." Josh went to his father and touched his shoulder. "You okay, Pop? You look tired."

"A little tired. We're having a little trouble with a few South African government officials. Nothing to worry about. How are you?"

"Better since the surgery."

"That's good, son. Glad to hear it."

"I'm good."

"Hello, Mr. Brenner," Sean said, extending his hand.

"Sean. Good to see you. How's the family?" James asked, shaking his hand.

"Everybody's good, sir. Thanks for asking."

"Say hello to them for me. I haven't seen them in a while. We'll have to get together for dinner sometime soon."

"They'd like that, sir."

"As would I. I'll ask Ellie to give them a call."

When greetings were over, Josh's father led them inside his office. "Come on. Let's sit down. Harlan will be here in a moment. He's updating the final numbers and should be right in."

Josh looked around as they walked inside the gigantic space. Some things had changed since he'd last been in his father's office, but it still felt comfortable and familiar. The floor-to-ceiling windows faced the western horizon, but the drapes were a new addition. The same teak furniture and dark brown leather sofas and club chairs sat on new thick rugs, embossed dove gray paper covered the walls, several new paintings hung around the room, and large potted plants sat inconspicuously in corners. It was apparent Ellie had tried to soften many of the room's harsh angles and edges, and Josh could imagine his father not allowing too much change. The office was his kingdom; he would not have given her as much sway in redecorating it as she had in furnishing their home.

Josh noticed the sprinkling of silver-framed family photos around the room, some tucked in with books and ornaments on the bookcase shelves, and others sat on the various surfaces around the room. Pictures of Josh and his brothers as kids mixed in with recent snapshots.

Josh walked over to the credenza and picked up a photo of Warren in his dress military uniform. At first glance, everyone had said he and Josh looked alike, favoring their mother. They had inherited her dark blue eyes, light brown hair, and deep dimples. Ian took more after their father with his crystal blue eyes and darker hair. There was also a picture of Bekah on her last birthday and one of Ian, Abigail, Claire and Justin taken on a recent trip.

A large, framed photo on the end of a long credenza caught Josh's eye, and he picked it up. It was a shot of him holding the championship trophy in Biarritz, taken two weeks before the shark attack. It was a clear shot of him on the platform. The photographer had zoomed in to catch every detail. He was holding up the big, heavy trophy and grinning after the pronouncement. He must have remained standing with it in his hand, lost in thought, that it startled him when his father called to him. Everyone was seated at the table. He set the picture back in its place and took a deep breath. He took his seat and looked at Sean, who nodded. It was time to get down to business.

San Diego, California, USA

At 10:45 a.m. Josh slid in and settled onto the back seat of the long, black town car as it pulled smoothly from the curb and into traffic.

The meeting with his father and the board of directors had run longer than he'd anticipated, pushing his itinerary back, but it seemed successful. Sean had stayed behind to button up a few loose ends, and with Ian's help, Josh felt comfortable catching his flight. The ride was short, and when they pulled around to the private hangers, the private Brenner Industrials jet waited on the tarmac, engines purring.

Josh grabbed his duffle, ran up the steps into the plane's cabin, and handed the heavy bag to the steward. Taking his seat and clipping his seat belt, he felt the plane roll, then turn, then roll some more. Soon, they were on the runway, and the pilot gunned the engines, and the plane soared into the heavens. He checked his watch. He'd be touching down at Lindbergh Field in San Diego in fourteen and a half hours.

It was evening when Josh stepped off the plane, the sun low over the horizon. He'd lost a day in the long flight, but it felt good to be back. There was a warm breeze filled with the scent of the ocean and rain and something beneath that, just beyond identification—both sweet and citrusy. It was the combination of odors, in his mind, that was quintessentially San Diego. There were traces of the light rain that had come through earlier, leaving dozens of rainbows shimmering in small, oily puddles trapped inside cracks and crevices of the uneven ground. A car pulled in front of the private hangar, and he tossed his bag inside, then slid in beside it. The interior of the car was cool, the air conditioner battling the unseasonably warm temperatures, and Josh relaxed against the cool leather of the back seat. He was still in his suit but had long since removed his tie and jacket and unbuttoned the top buttons of his shirt. He stretched his long legs out in front of him, folded his hands across his chest, and closed his eyes. The adrenaline of the busy day slowly seeped away, allowing his body, nerves, and mind to calm. It was a short ride north on the I-5 freeway.

When the car pulled into the beach parking lot, Josh got out, leaving his duffle in the car, and walked down to the wet, coarse, hard-packed sand. He approached the edge of the water, unmindful of ruining his expensive leather loafers or the rolling surf splashing his pants legs and heaved a long and heavy sigh. This was where it all happened. Not even when he'd been in the water with Naghee Nomura had they ventured this far south to this particular stretch of beach. It had loomed large in his nightmares for the past eleven months—the water, the shark, Colin, and sitting on his board. But looking around, he had to admit it was simply a beautiful sweep of white sand and serpentine coastline, expensive custom-built homes clinging to high crumbling bluffs. Immense palms, at least seventy feet tall with thick hula skirts, swayed in the light wind, sweeping the briny odor of the ocean inland, and gulls wheeled about over-head, screeching to one another.

He backed away from the waterline, the foamy whitewash creep-ing further up as it rolled in and back out. Josh watched, fascinated, as it scoured the sand, clearing away footprints and leaving twisted clumps of seaweed in the backwash. There were also clusters of peo-ple encamped on the beach, their umbrellas cocked against the sun blocking the glare; small children and dogs splashing in the water; and surfers further out, drenched in the late afternoon sunlight, were distinct against the horizon. The ocean rose and fell, undulating like a living thing, the waves lining up tall, powerful, and perfect. Still, a cold shudder ran through his body as he watched.

Three young surfers, probably no older than sixteen, ran past him, dripping water, carrying their boards, laughing and talking among themselves, flushed and exhilarated from their afternoon workout. They passed Josh without a backward glance, though he turned to watch them race over the hot sand toward the parking lot. We used to be like that, he mused. Him. Sean. Colin. Hot tears burned his eyes, and he turned to face the ocean again and blinked until the tears subsided.

As he jammed his hands in his pockets, his fingers touched upon the token he'd brought with him. He pulled it out and looked at it. He'd bought it from the same jeweler who'd made Mia's ring, and Josh had had him inscribe Colin's name, birth date, and the date of his death on the front and a bit of the Surfer's Prayer on the back.

St. Christopher, the Big Kahuna and Patron Saint of Surfers, dated back to the nineteen-sixties when surfers began invoking his intercession and protection. Josh rubbed his thumb across the relief of the surfing Saint standing on a longboard, the large medallion cool against his fingers. He recited the Surfer's Prayer from memory, and this time, he let the tears roll freely down his cheeks. With a heave of his body and a flick of his wrist, Josh chucked the medal across the ocean surface, sending it far out, past the shelf, to settle on the ocean floor. With a symbol of faith and a prayer for divine protection for all surfers, he marked the place where he'd last seen his friend, where he'd lost everything.

No, not everything. One chapter of his life had ended, but another had begun, and he'd gained something else—something and someone very important and exceedingly precious.

His phone vibrated in his pocket, and he pulled it out to see Mia's text. He scrubbed his face, erasing the salty tracks of his tears, and turned to see her coming toward him. His heart stuttered in his chest as he watched her. She was a vision out of time. She looked much like he imagined she had the day Sean had carried him out of the ocean and laid him at her feet. She was dressed in running shorts, a cropped shirt that bared her midriff, the arms of a thin windbreaker tied around her hips, and a pair of comfortable running shoes. Her hair was pulled back into a high ponytail, and the lenses of her glasses darkened against the glare of the sun. She waved, a gorgeous smile on her face, and he waved back.

"Hullo, Love," he said, reaching for her.

"Fancy meeting you here," she replied, stepping into his arms, and he pulled her tight to him, embracing her tightly.

"God, I've missed you. I couldn't have imagined how much until this very moment." He kissed her, and she clung to him, kissing him back just as fiercely. Then, taking a step back, she looked at him, placing her hand against his chest. His hair was darker than she remembered, more honey than blonde, and longer, pulled back into a thick tail that coiled on the nape of his neck. The dark suit and white shirt opened at the throat set off his deep tan beautifully, and he looked healthy—his chest and arms seemed thicker and stronger, and his body appeared bigger than before.

Smiling, his eyes shining, he took her hand and lifted it, placing a kiss on her palm, then pulled her into a one-arm embrace.

"Have you come back here at all since the attack?" he asked, turning her so they could look out on the ocean. She squeezed him around his waist, her arm beneath his jacket.

"A few times. After you left."

"I remember Sean, Colin, and I were right out there," he said, pointing to a spot that only he could see. "Sean was a little further out," he moved his finger, "and Colin was there," he moved it back, "and I must've been right there. He wasn't that far from me," Josh said, still staring out at the ocean as if he could see the three of them exactly where they were before the shark struck.

"You remember everything?"

"I do. Before. During. And after. All of it."

"And you're okay?" she asked, voicing her concern.

Josh looked at her worried, upturned face, then squeezed her against his side. "I am now."

She nodded and squeezed him back. "Let's take a walk."

She nodded, and they removed their socks and shoes. Josh rolled his pants legs halfway up his calves to avoid most of the sand and water, and with their shoes hooked on two fingers and their arms around each other's waists, they strolled northward. The sun was disappearing below the horizon, and the fading light blurred hard edges and sharp angles and cast a golden glow around the surfers on the water. The high tide scrabbled further up on the sand, reaching for their feet, filling the deep footprints left behind with water and loose, shifting sand, and leaving behind an offering of bulbous kelpy seaweed.

Exclusive Preview

Dear Reader,

Thank you for joining me on this remarkable journey through Shifting Tides. As the waves of our story continue to roll, I am thrilled to offer you an exclusive glimpse into the next chapter of the Summer Adrift Series, Wild Tides.

In Wild Tides, we reunite with Sean Hargrove, whose story takes an even more compelling turn. Haunted by echoes of the past, Sean finds himself in Carmichael, a coastal haven where new challenges and unexpected friendships await. Here, amid the high stakes of a surfing tournament and the fury of an approaching cyclone, Sean discovers not just a purpose but a community that changes him forever.

As we prepare for the late March 2024 release of Wild Tides, I invite you to dive into the first three chapters presented here. May they leave you eagerly anticipating the full tale of resilience, renewal, and the relentless power of the ocean.

Wild Tides will be available digitally and in print on Amazon, Rakuten Kobo, Apple Books, Barnes and Noble, and other fine outlets. Follow me on Facebook, Instagram and Pinterest and visit www.evmcmillan.com for the latest updates and more.

Thank you for your continued support, and I hope you enjoy this sneak peek.

Sincerely,

E V McMillan

Wild Tides
Summer Adrift

E V McMillan

Color Your World Press, 2024

I write not to add years to my life, but life to my years.
In every character, a part of me is born anew,
~E V McMillan

To my family and friends, whose strength and spirit
mirror the resilience of the waves—ever inspiring
and endlessly renewing.

Also By E V McMillan

The Summer Adrift Series:

Shifting Tides

Wild Tides

Inherit the Tides

PROLOGUE

San Diego, California, USA

The ocean was an endless sheet of glass, reflecting the late morning sun like a mirror.

Sitting on my surfboard, leaning forward, gripping the rails, and dangling my feet in the water, I took in the horizon and the sheer beauty of the Southern California coastline. Today was the last day of our vacation. Josh was flying to Johannesburg out of LAX to meet with execs at Walter Industries, one of our major sponsors, for some promo work tomorrow evening. Colin was going back home to Australia to check on family, and I had a few days before surfing the Pipeline in Hawaii. We'd free-surfed some of the most iconic spots along the Southern California coast from Ventura to San Diego, hitting seven beaches in ten days of pure relaxation, staying pretty much off the grid.

As I enjoyed the view and warm ocean water, I noticed Josh pointing at a drone that flew overhead. He seemed upset and gave Colin and me a thumbs-up, signaling he was heading back to shore. Always eager for a little friendly competition, Colin paddled toward him. Maybe I blinked or looked away for a second, I don't know, but seconds later, the ocean shattered into chaos. With an explosion of water, Josh was tossed high into the air, and his surfboard, still attached to the leash around his ankle, was broken into two pieces. My mouth dropped open, and my breath caught in my throat as I saw a dark gray horror rising from the depths—a great white shark, mouth gaping open like a baseball catcher's mitt, ready to catch Josh as he came back down.

Josh hit the water surface hard, his board smashing into his face, and the shark lunged repeatedly, hitting him and knocking him around like a ragdoll. It was a scene torn from nightmares.

Gut-wrenching panic clawed at me; my mind was racing, but my body was a statue of frozen terror. "Josh! Josh!" I screamed over and over, finally snapping out of my paralysis. I paddled furiously toward him as he flailed in the crimson-streaked water. Some other surfers had closed in behind me, their board slaps and shouts an ineffectual deterrent to the predator circling Josh.

With each stroke, my heart pounded a frantic drumbeat, and my focus narrowed solely on my friend, who had begun to pound on the shark's snout in a desperate bid for life. Then, suddenly, he was yanked downward into the ocean's dark abyss, and I screamed his name over and over.

When we reached him— me, several other surfers, and a few paddle-boarders—we converged in a protective ring around the blood-soaked patch of ocean where Josh had disappeared. As if he had been spit out, he resurfaced, clinging to the tattered remnants of his board, and I grabbed him and held on to him. Adrenaline gave way to a brief, shaky relief. "I got you, buddy," I told him, lifting his head above the surface.

The ring of rescuers protected us as I towed Josh back to shore, but as we got close, a chilling realization settled in—Colin. Where was he? I looked behind me. The ocean had settled back into a smooth, flat surface, except for the chunks of broken surfboards floating away. I didn't see him. I called his name over and over, still holding onto Josh, but he never answered. The unthinkable had happened, and our lives would never be the same again.

CHAPTER ONE

Sydney, Australia
Six Months Later

The sun had just dipped below the horizon, and long shadows stretched across the floor of my condo.

I sat slumped on the sofa, an untouched bottle of single malt whisky in front of me, my only company in a room too quiet for comfort. Six months felt like a lifetime and a fleeting moment all at once since that day in San Diego. The ocean, once a haven, had turned into a nightmare stage. Josh's screams, the blood, and Colin-well, Colin just vanished beneath the waves.

I was finally home, in the middle of Sydney's business district, at the top of a beautifully remodeled 1920s Art Deco mid-rise. However, it felt like the walls were closing in on me. Maybe I'd been naive to think returning home was all I needed to figure out my future. I wasn't sure of anything anymore. Perhaps I had hoped it would be like going back in time when opportunities abounded. But, of course, that was only wishful thinking. Despite being far from San Diego, where the attack happened and where we lost Colin, nothing had really changed. The echoes of that day were a constant, haunting presence, a painful reckoning that pain and memories were not bound by geography; they cling to one's soul like a persistent shadow.

I glanced out at the Sydney skyline, its lights twinkling like distant stars, but kept returning to that endless, dark ocean. The TV chattered in the background, some late-night host laughing at his own jokes. It was noise, nothing more, lost against the backdrop of crashing waves in my head. Surfing, my life's passion, now felt like a betrayal, and I had resigned from the pro circuits. How could I not when my heart was no longer in the game?

I looked around the open-concept space with stark walls filled with original and very expensive modernist paintings and minimalist furniture arranged in conversation areas, colorful, handwoven rugs scattered across marble floors and sheaths of heavy drapery framing the view through floor-to-ceiling windows. I'd been extremely proud to own such luxury, considering my family's meager beginnings. Once I'd started making money, I bought this condo and hired an interior designer to create a timeless design that reflected my success and status as a champion pro surfer. Yet, I hadn't hosted more than a handful of gatherings in the last two, maybe three years. Now, looking around with jaded eyes, it felt more like a museum, the luxurious trappings of a gilded cage. Cold and lifeless and frozen in time, tethered to a life that no longer existed.

I stood up and immediately began pacing. The den opened off the large living room, opposite the kitchen and dining room, and was filled with souvenirs of my career and my travels. But they felt distant now. I approached one of my surfboards, its surface smooth and familiar under my fingers. This board had been with me through triumphs and challenges, but now it was just another piece of a life I no longer felt connected to. My gaze fell upon a photograph set on a shelf filled with at least a half-dozen other photos and souvenirs from my years abroad, and I picked it up. It was of me, Josh, and Colin, arms around each other, laughing and hugging Josh after his big win in Bali. He'd just won his first World Surf Championship, beating Chris Cartier, the three-time and reigning champ from France. We stood shoulder to shoulder, our wet suits partially unzipped, saltwater dripping from our hair. Colin's bright green eyes and mop of ginger hair practically sparkled in the sunlight as he stood with an arm thrown across Josh's shoulder, grinning like he'd just pulled off the biggest prank. Josh was sandwiched in between Colin and me, his brown hair sun-bleached nearly platinum, a carefree smile on his lips, and his deep blue eyes staring directly into the camera. And there I was, next to him, trying to look cool and collected, a goofy smirk on my face. My skin was darker, burnished to deep gold, and my dark hair was much shorter, hanging free just past my shoulder. The photo had been taken five years ago, but we looked so young, so very carefree, and looking at it made me feel weary.

We were more than friends; we were a unit, a perfectly balanced trio. Colin was light-hearted and free-spirited like water. Josh was fiery, competitive, and passionate. My nature was grounding, analytical, and steady. Together, we were invincible in our brand and against the waves, our bond forged in our long friendship and tempered by saltwater and adrenaline. We were kings of the ocean then, and everything seemed possible. Fearless and free. The memory of that day, the sound of the waves, the laughter, and the unspoken understanding between us forced a sad smile from me. It all seemed like a dream now, a dream from which I had rudely awakened. Colin was gone, claimed by the very ocean we all loved. Josh, forever altered, was fighting his own demons. And me, the untouched survivor, fractured on the inside.

I rubbed the thick, titanium frame, tracing its edges with my fingertips as if I could somehow connect the gap between then and now. Once masters of the ocean, the unpredictable tides of fate had scattered us. A pang of guilt and grief twisted in my chest. I should have been able to save both Josh and Colin. We were all out on the water together. I should have been able to save at least one of them from the devastation, but that long moment that I'd sat frozen upon my board, watching in horror, the shark had come and gone, leaving excruciating damage in its wake.

I sighed, long and deeply, as I stared at our smiling, youthful faces, frozen in time. I was sorely reminded of what was gone. Reluctantly, I placed the photograph back on the shelf, feeling the weight of the past as I withdrew my hand and let my gaze rove over the many trophies and awards displayed in a glass case. The trophies glinted mockingly in the fading light, each a bitter reminder of victories and a life I had walked away from. The dozen or more trophies were a stark reminder of my past. The glass enclosure housed a collection of gleaming trophies and medals, each a testament to victories and triumphs on the international pro surfing circuit. I opened the case, the sound of the glass door creaking softly, breaking the heaviness of the room.

I opened the glass door, reached in, and examined the trophies one by one. I let my fingers linger over one particularly impressive trophy, a reminder of a championship that had once meant the world to me. For a brief moment, I allowed myself to be transported back to those days of glory —the adrenaline rush of competition, the exuberant cheers of the crowd, the sheer ecstasy of riding the perfect wave. Its surface is cool and smooth to the touch. First Place. It was the first, but not the last, time that I'd beaten Josh for first place in a major championship challenge. It was also the first time—tangible proof that I had what it took to be a champion, and I think that win marked my stepping out of Josh's shadow. I touched a few more, marring their cool, mirrored plate with my fingerprints. As I touched them, the floodgate of memories opened, and I briefly relived the thrill of competition and camaraderie. Such were the moments that had once defined my existence. The structured routine of training and competing had always given me a clear direction, but now my future stretched out like an empty road, vague, uncharted, and filled with an unsettling stillness.

Quitting the pro surfing circuit had felt like the only viable option in the aftermath of the tragedy. The ocean, which had been my sanctuary, now whispered ghostly reminders of loss and what could have been. In leaving the sport behind, it felt as though I had abandoned a part of myself, and I sometimes questioned whether I'd been too rash and whether or not I had done the right thing. I closed the door of the case and quickly turned away, striding back into the living room.

The Sydney skyline outside the windows glittered, indifferent to the turmoil within me, as real as the crashing waves in my tormented memories. I sighed deeply, the sound seeming to echo from the depths of my soul. A restless energy surged through me, and an idea began to take shape, unformed but as real as the memories that haunted me. Perhaps what I needed was a challenge to my mind and body, possibly one of the simpler pleasures of life that I had enjoyed before my world had become all about surfing.

Years ago, I used to take time off and relax by doing some camping and fishing. Josh and I'd met when we were ten years old while I was fishing in the Amblin' River as it crossed his father's land. He'd startled me as I was trying to unhook the biggest fish I'd caught that day, causing me to lose my grip and watch it flip and flop back into the river. I probably wouldn't have caught it again if he hadn't jumped in the river after it. I smiled. An unspoken decision began to form, and the idea had strong appeal. I couldn't remember the last time I'd been camping or fishing. Suddenly, my spirits began to lift, and I felt a surge of energy that I hadn't felt in all the weeks I'd been home. It seemed that getting out of the condo and into the wilderness and fresh air and leaving behind the ghosts that lingered in every corner of this place was a wonderful idea. No destination. No plans. Just me and the vast Australian landscape. Maybe out in the wild, I could find pieces of the man I used to be, or maybe I'd carve out a new path.

With a newfound resolve, I headed toward my bedroom and grabbed my duffel bag. I tossed in clothes and essentials without much thought. As I carried my bag to the living room, set beside the front door, I saw my surfboard. I reached out and let my hand hover over it for a moment. I had no real intention of doing any surfing. This journey wasn't about the waves, but old habits die hard. I picked it up and carried it with my duffle. At sunrise, I'll hit those less traveled roads and reclaim the parts of me I was afraid I'd left behind.

CHAPTER TWO

I pulled up on the driveway of my sister's house in Paddington.

My truck loaded for the long trip, and I was eager to get started, but I couldn't leave without stopping to see Mom and Lizzie, the two most important people in my life. Though I was thirty-six years old, I felt like a kid caught sneaking back in the house after sneaking out, a feeling I'd been very familiar with while growing up. I'd come over early to catch Lizzie before she left for work, and the three of us sat at the kitchen table, a dish of warm scones that Mum had baked sitting in front of us and nursing mugs of strong coffee. They listened as I explained why I was suddenly taking this trip.

My mother sat to my right, and Lizzie, my sister, sat across from me, watching me as I dusted off the crumbs of my second blueberry scone.

"If you want, I can pack you some food for your trip, son," my mum said, ready to hop out of her chair and start baking.

"No need, Mum. Thank you. They're very good, but I'll be fine. I'll only be gone a few days." I reached over to pat her hand. My mother was still youthful, in her mid-fifties. Her beautiful brown face and long-fingered hands were still smooth, and her long, dark hair had fewer visible strands of silver than my own. Her dark eyes reminded me of a hawk as she fastened them on me. Lizzie, however, appeared resigned. She was an old soul, and a lot of it was probably my fault. Growing up, Mum had worked long hours, sometimes weeks at a time, without a single day off, and Lizzie had been charged with taking care of me. It was not her fault she couldn't do a great job of keeping up with me. I could be as slippery as the fish I loved to catch.

Looking at my sister and me, you might find it hard to believe we were full siblings. In appearance, we are as different as night and day. I favored my mother as strongly as Lizzie favored our father, except for a few differences. She was short, five-two, maybe five-three, which she'd inherited from our mother, while I had inherited my father's height, standing head and shoulders above them both, at six-two.

Our father was a white British citizen, and Lizzie's sandy brown hair with reddish-blonde highlights was similar in color to his, but her's was wild, soft, and curly. She was also very fair, with a sprinkling of freckles and hazel-green eyes. My slender and athletic build is a testament to my love for physical activity, and my skin is a warm brown, lighter than Mum's but darker than my father's. My hair is like Mum's, nearly black and thick and straight, and it has grown so long that I wear it in a braid that hangs down my back, almost to my waist. Over the years, it has become a tactile connection for me to my Mum and our heritage. My nose and lips are thin, and my cheekbones and jaw are sharp and angular, reminiscent of my father's Anglo-Saxon heritage. But the feature that stands out the most is my eyes, which are a stormy gray, a color that neither of my parents has. And as it is not a feature of Torre Straight Islanders, maybe that and the color of my skin make them so striking, catching most people off guard.

I glanced up to see Lizzie's eyes narrowed on me, and she didn't seem very happy with my plans. I loved these two women deeply. They were the pillars of my life, having seen me through thick and thin and ups and downs, but they had no conception of how broken I felt. I hoped they wouldn't give me a hard time. I needed to embark on this journey to find myself again.

"Are you running away from something, Son?" My mother asked me, her voice sounding exceptionally sad, her islander accent thickly coating her words, though she'd left Torres Strait decades ago. Surprised, I quickly looked up at her.

"No, of course not. I'm just taking some time for myself. The only time I've had to myself in the past three years was wrecked…, well, by the shark attack. I need some time to decompress."

"You believe you're all healed from that ordeal?"

Taking a deep breath, I spoke from the heart, "No, not completely, but that will probably take a lot more time. And I don't want to go into it again right now."

"Can't you stay here with us and clear your head?" Lizzie asked, taking a sip of her coffee. "Can't we help you do what you need to do? I worry about you."

"I know you do. But I'll be fine."

"But you've only just come home after almost a year away."

"You should be used to me being away all the time by now. Don't worry. I plan to drive up the coast, spend time at the ocean, and maybe do some off-shore fishing. I was thinking of maybe stopping up at Palmer Station. It's been a long time since I've been up there."

"Why would you want to go there?" Mum asked sharply. "Nothing in Palmer Station for any of us."

Lizzie covered her hand with her own, and Mom looked somewhat abashed. We'd lived in Palmer Station in north New South Wales when we were small children, and Mum had had a difficult time there, trying to raise us, two obviously half-white children, with no husband. Everyone who lived in that tiny, rural community knew everyone else. They worked on the surrounding large estates, farms and ranches, as that was the only employment in the area. I was too young to realize how few residents had been kind to her, shunning us because they knew my white father hadn't married my mother. In fact, he'd been married to someone else for years, a British lady with whom he had two older boys. My affinity to Palmer Station was the idyllic childhood I'd had because of Josh and his family. Meeting and befriending Josh the summer when we turned ten years old had given me opportunities and freedoms I never would have had otherwise.

"You're probably right," I conceded. "It was just a thought. This trip is about the journey, not the destination," I grinned at Mom and then Lizzie, parroting one of my sister's favorite axioms. Neither of them seemed amused by my cleverness this time. I shrugged. They had always been a hard audience for my brand of witticism.

"We've seen how much you've been struggling, Sean. We want you to be happy." Lizzie reached across the table to squeeze my hand. It was the closest they'd come to talking about the crux of their concern. I could see the concern in her eyes.

"Seriously, now. How long do you plan to be away?"

I met her gaze with reassurance, "A few days, maybe a week, I dunno, but I promise to keep in touch. I'm sure I'll have mobile service most of the time, but when I don't, I'll find a landline some-where."

Mom stood, and her gentle hands found my shoulders. She hugged me tightly, then pulled away slightly, looking deep into my eyes. "You take care of yourself, Okay?"

"Yes, of course," I nodded. Mom hugged me again, and Lizzie came over and did the same.

"Don't make me come looking for you, little brother."

"I wouldn't dream of dragging you out into the wilds," I said, laughing. Lizzie screwed her face up at me, slapped me on the shoul-der, and walked away, while Mum continued to hover.

"I love you both. I'll be fine and come back with a clear head, I promise. I may even bring you enough fish to fill up the freezer."

"No thanks. We'll pass on the fish," Lizzie said from across the room.

I kissed them on the cheek, and after one last hug, I left the house. Climbing up on the driver's seat of my truck, I closed my eyes and allowed a sensation I hadn't felt in a long while to wash over me. It was like a jolt of electricity, an exhilarating feeling of happiness and freedom. I savored the feeling and intended to make the most of this good fortune. I pulled out of the driveway and headed northeast, straight for M1, the Pacific Highway.

CHAPTER
THREE

As I drove north, the Australian countryside spread out ahead of me, a breathtaking tapestry of natural beauty.

The road meandered through a landscape that seemed right off a postcard. The eucalyptus trees stood tall and proud, their silver-green leaves shimmering in the sunlight, perfuming the air with their distinctive scent, a blend of earthiness and the unmistakable aroma of the Australian bush. Gum trees lined the roadside, their twisted trunks and branches casting intriguing shadows on the ground, and among the leaves, colorful parrots and cockatoos flitted about, their vibrant plumage a stark contrast against the green backdrop.

The highway occasionally led me through charming coastal towns with quaint cottages painted in pastel colors. I saw fishing boats on the clear blue waters, the men casting their lines and nets, hoping for a bountiful catch. In the evenings, I would stop in whatever town I was near for dinner, the scent of fried fish and other delicacies on the salty sea breeze churning up a ravenous hunger in my belly.

The coastline of New South Wales, as it wound up towards Queensland, was a wonder to behold, with rugged cliffs and golden beaches that stretched for miles. Crystal clear waves crashed against the shore, inviting surfers to ride their crests, while the deep blue depths of the Pacific Ocean extended to the horizon, a vast expanse of endless possibilities. Occasionally, I would spot kangaroos grazing in open fields, their powerful legs ready to propel them into motion at a moment's notice. These iconic marsupials were far from the cuddly bedtime plushies tucked in with children at night. They were wild and often ferocious when approached in the wilderness, and I made certain to avoid them along the roads.

Once the landscape transitioned from coastal to inland, vast expanses of rolling hills and farmland were revealed. Cattle and sheep grazed lazily in green pastures, and the earthy scent of freshly tilled and fertilized soil filled the air. South of the border of Queensland, a hot shower and soft bed started calling my name, and I decided to find a nice enough hotel or B&B to spend at least one night in. Hoping to find something in the town of Carmichael, the next town six miles down the road. I followed the two-lane State Road that split off from the interstate. It seemed as if it had been cut right along the bottom of the rocky cliffs, weathered by time and the relentless ocean. At times, I could see the ocean from the road. The rhythmic rolling of the waves, one after the other, towards the shore and the foamy white spray into the air was hypnotic and soothing. The azure blue water curled and crashed against wind-carved stacks, some twice as tall as a man. It was also a beautiful, mesmerizing spectacle.

I soon saw a sign announcing I was entering the township of Carmichael, population 8,222. Thankful, because I was hungry and needed a pit stop, I took the road that turned away from the edge of the ocean. I rolled down the window, hoping for a fresh, cool breeze. Continuing down High Street towards the town square, I could see it was a busy little community, with people bustling in and out of the quaint little shops and knots of pedestrian traffic heading off in the direction I presumed was toward the beach.

It also looked like Christmas had thrown up over town. Twinkling fairy lights twisted in tinsel and garland had been draped around store windows and entwined in planters and baskets of blooming bougainvillea and fragrant Star Jasmine hanging from the lampposts. I shook my head. There hadn't been this much Christmas merriment across the entire city of Sydney.

Santa Claus, his sleigh pulled by Rudolph and the other happy reindeer, big plastic candy canes, big, colorful holiday ornaments, and twinkling multicolored lights were everywhere.

"Jeez, you've gotta be kidding me," I muttered.

A life-sized plastic Santa hanging ten on a surfboard stood outside a pub, his sunglasses perched jauntily on his jolly red nose, his white cottony beard fluttering in the warm breeze like it was about to take flight. I almost laughed. Almost.

Across the street, there was a display of kangaroos pulling an ancient, rusty Subaru Ute with rear-facing, plastic jump seats decked out like Santa's sleigh, complete with tinsel and a sack of gift-wrapped boxes. The bloody kangaroos had red and green bandanas around their necks, and the life-sized Santa had on a vivid Hawaiian shirt. I squinted and rubbed my temples.

On the corner, in front of a bakery with its windows steamed up, ruining the fake snow and lettering sprayed on them, stood a three-foot Santa with an umbrella drink in one hand, sunglasses, board shorts, and rubber thongs on his feet, welcoming patrons inside. He was grinning like he was on vacation in bloody Bali or something.

When I saw a parking space big enough for my truck, I swerved into it, cut the engine and got out, taking a second to look around. It was late afternoon but still sunny and bright. A large, neat sign announcing Lily's Cafe and Inn hanging over the door of a Victorian building in the middle of the block of shops caught my eye, and I strode towards it. Before I'd walked more than halfway there, however, I was sweating balls. My shirt was clinging to my skin, soaking up the sweat trickling down my back and abdomen and from my armpits down my sides. My jeans began to feel like a second skin. It was so damned hot it had to be in the triple digits, and I felt like I'd entered another dimension, one where there were only fake, vacationing Santas relaxing in this unseasonable, unreasonable heat and smiling away like there was no such thing as global warming.

Thank God, I thought as I pushed open the door of Lily's Café and Inn and stepped into the frigid air conditioning and the delicious aromas of roasting meat, baked fruit pies, and freshly brewed coffee. Also, thankfully, there were no plastic, kitschy Santas or twinkling lights. I felt like I'd been delivered to heaven. Lily, the grandmotherly proprietor, greeted me with a friendly smile. Her silver hair framed a handsome face that radiated warmth and good cheer.

"Good afternoon, dear," she said, smiling. "How can I help you?"

I returned her smile, luxuriating in the cool air. "Good afternoon. Do you have any rooms available, maybe for a night or two? And whatever you're serving for dinner tonight smells delicious."

Lily nodded, her smile never wavering. "I think I might have a nice, cozy suite available. And if you're ready to eat, you can go right through to the dining room, rest your bones and feed your belly while I get it ready for you. Where's your car? I suppose you drove into town."

"The next block down. I left it in a parking spot in front of the stores."

"Well, you can park it when you're ready in the lot behind us. It's for my guests."

That sounded wonderful, and I gave her my information and credit card. She told me to stop back by for my key when I finished dining.

"Good evening, Jack. How're you doing?" she asked an elderly gentleman who'd come in behind me.

"Doing better than ever, Lily. Still hot as blazes out there. I thought I'd come here to get something to eat, but mostly to cool off. And good afternoon to you too, young man."

"Hello, Sir," I responded. We walked into the dining room more or less at the same time, and I moved aside, taking a moment to decide where to sit. He tipped his head at me and pointed to a table next to a front window looking out on the street. Tinted, reflective shades were drawn to block the bright afternoon sunlight.

"Would you care to share a table?"

"I don't want to impose on your dinner," I said, looking around at the many empty tables in the room.

"Nonsense. But if you'd rather eat alone, no offense."

"No, no. It's fine. We can share."

"Emmie, Bring…what's your name again?" he asked, leaning toward me to hear.

"Sean, Sir. Sean Hargrove."

"Emmie, hand my new friend, Mr. Hargrove, a menu. I'll have the special." We walked to the table he'd pointed out, him leading and me following, and as we settled in our seats, he asked, "You come for the Big Wave competition that's coming up in a couple of months?"

"No. I haven't heard about it."

"Lots of young folk coming in from all around to surf the big waves on the north end. There's a natural, exposed point break out there that gives nice, big, consistent waves, and at the end of summer, they get even bigger and more powerful. Some promoters came here sometime back and signed with the town council to hold this competition. You might want to come back through for it if you can. It's supposed to be interesting.

"Yessir, it sounds interesting," I answered, perusing the menu.

"None of this Sir nonsense. Call me Jack. Do you know about surfing?"

"A little, but not about putting on a surfing event."

"Other towns a little further up and down the coast have held this contest, but this will be our first year. Makes a lot of money for the town, from what I hear."

"Yeah, maybe I will stop back through. This is a really nice town, and from what I saw coming from the highway, you have a beautiful spot on the ocean. But besides surfing, what else can I look forward to seeing here? Any good fishing?"

Jack's eyes lit up as he began regaling me with stories about places around town and some of their history. He spoke of hidden waterfalls deep in the nearby forest, a picturesque lighthouse perched on a cliff, and a secret beach known only to the locals. Emmie came over for my order and asked if I wanted something to drink while I waited. Jack ordered a pitcher of summer ale for both of us.

I enjoyed listening to Jack's stories and had a nice buzz going from the three pitchers of ale we'd downed with our delicious meal. I paid for our meals and left Jack downstairs a couple of hours later. I retrieved my truck and parked it in the lot behind the Inn. I then found my room, which was very spacious, clean, and nicely decorated. After a refreshing shower, I hit the sack and was out for the rest of the evening.

Acknowledgments

Thank you for reading *Shifting Tides*, the first book in the series *Summer Adrift,* and I hope you enjoyed the exclusive preview of *Wild Tides*. Writing these stories have been a labor of love and a dream come true. But none of this would have been possible without the help and support of the people who have stood with me as I struggled to bring it to fruition, and I want to thank them for their faith in me and this book.

First, I want to thank my family for their patience and understanding of the long days and nights I spent getting the story down. I especially want to thank my Erika—my greatest, most steadfast supporter and cheerleader, reader, editor, backer, and shoulder to rant, rave, and cry on. Without her support, this book would likely still be a file stored in the recesses of my computer.

I want to thank my beta readers for their valuable feedback, especially Victoria, Allyssa, and Barbara. They questioned me at every turn, kept the middle from sagging, and kept me on track when I tended to digress. I cannot thank them enough.

I also want to thank my editorial, production and marketing team. It takes a village to produce a good story, and they were my rock and my pillar throughout the entire process.

www.ingramcontent.com/pod-product-compliance
Lightning Source LLC
Chambersburg PA
CBHW071402200726
48294CB00002B/272